# Gravity Is Heartless

# Gravity Is Heartless

## The Heartless Series
## Book One

Sarah Lahey

SHE WRITES PRESS

Published 2019
Printed in the United States of America
ISBN: 978-1-63152-872-9
ISBN: 978-1-63152-873-6
Library of Congress Control Number: 2020901197

For information, address:
She Writes Press
1569 Solano Ave #546
Berkeley, CA 94707

She Writes Press is a division of SparkPoint Studio, LLC.

*For Tracey and Andrew*

In the late twentieth century, Marvin Minsky said, "We rarely recognize how wonderful it is that a person can traverse an entire lifetime without making a single really serious mistake—like putting a fork in one's eye or using a window instead of a door."

# Prologue

AT THE AGE OF thirty, Quinn realized she belonged to a highly evolved but irrational species.

Humans are supposed to be the intelligent primate, the ones with cognitive thought processes that aid their reasoning and learning abilities, so they should be good at life—the everyday stuff should be easy for them. A day on Earth only has twenty-four hours; how hard can it be? A day on Titan lasts the equivalent of fifteen Earth days, plus twenty-two hours and forty-one minutes—now that is a long day.

Yet life is not easy for humans. Their species has a problem, a big problem: they are ruled by emotions and feelings rather than logic and rational thought. "Homo sapiens" means "wise man," but in my experience, humans are not wise at all.

Some days, Quinn has no idea what she is doing. It is a miracle she gets out of bed, stands on two legs, and manages to get through her twenty-four-hour day. This morning, while she was washing her face, she leant too far over the basin, hit her forehead on the faucet, and bruised her eyebrow. Now it hurts to touch, but she keeps touching it, pressing it with her finger. I have told her to stop touching it, and she knows she should stop, but she does not.

Two years ago, Quinn's life was organized: she had a job, she was single and childless, and she was a reasonably sane human. Then she made some questionable choices—illogical and irrational decisions that changed the course of her life, and mine.

When I first met her she was already pregnant, though she did not realize it yet.

It started a few years ago, back in 2049.

# One

# I've totally fucked this up. What was I thinking?

THE DAYS ARE LONG in the southern Indian Ocean. The Desolation Islands are close to the Antarctic Circle, and in the summer months the afternoons extend into never-ending twilight. This evening, just as the sun is beginning to set, the sky turns pink. Dusty pink, like the color of cultured meat or the algae blooms that plague the planet's waterways—a ruddy hue that reminds Quinn of birthday party icing and plastic dolls from her childhood, so she names it Nostalgia Pink.

She goes to bed thinking how quickly time has passed; almost thirty years of her life already over, and tomorrow she's getting married.

She wakes at midnight in an inky mauve darkness reminiscent of the not-quite-blue chrysanthemum flowers her mother received after she was born. It's a feigned purple-blue, more lavender than blue, and the scientific feat of gene-edited pigments; as in the case of her mother's chrysanthemums, it had yet to be refined and polished to produce a true blue, like the azure and sapphire hues now abundant in today's floral sprays.

Bathed in the modified mauve of anthocyanin pigment, Quinn says, "Good lordt, I've totally fucked this up. What was I thinking?" and is gripped with an urgent need to jump off something very high. (Leaping from great heights is how she resolves most of the dilemmas

3

in her life. Falling through space helps her to breathe, and it's here, immersed in the undulating, flexible universe of space-time that the heaviness of existence slips away. This is the place where she thinks, where she plans, where she finds freedom: tumbling from a mountaintop towards Earth.)

Objects—rocks and rain, planetary bodies and people—all fall because space curves. Gravitational fields spread out across the universe, trapping us all in their warp and weft, and it's the curvature of space-time that holds Quinn down, pinning her to the planet, binding her to her bed in the inky mauve glow of midnight.

If Quinn intends to jump, she needs to do it soon; Mount Ross is a five-hour hike and they're leaving tomorrow, headed for Antarctica, so the passenger drones are stowed. But she lies motionless in her crib, immobilized by regret. "I'm so fucking stupid, I can't believe how stupid I am," she mumbles. And it's true, this is probably the worst thing she's ever done, and it's entirely her fault—no one else to blame, just her. She created this mess and now she has eighteen hours to fix it, to find a way out.

Quinn Buyers has a PhD in electrodynamics. She's been called a world leader in electromagnetics and nuclear forces. Few people on the planet understand how shape-shifting neutrinos merge into dark matter, or, how the graviton—the particle defining gravity—functions, but she does. Clearly she has a brain—a brain that works, a brain adept at math and science, a brain that loves physics. How then, she wonders, is it possible to be so competent in one part of her life and so mind-numbingly stupid in others? Years of study and academic achievements have failed her. Decades of learning about nuclear forces and shape-shifting neutrinos have failed her. Gravity has failed her.

"Fuck, what have I done? I don't love him. I like him, sure—he's good company, sometimes he's funny—but I'm not in love with him. I was never in love with him." In eighteen hours they'll be exchanging vows five kilometers high in the sky, because they're getting married inside a cumulus cloud, a big, white, fluffy cumulus cloud—another stupid idea that she agreed to.

Quinn was a bit preoccupied when Mori asked her to marry him. She was busy reviewing figures from the magnetometers that monitor the planet's Auroal Zone, and there had been some unusual geomagnetic disturbances. Normally those are linked to sun spot cycles, but this activity was atypical and unsettling, so understandably she was distracted and his proposal took her completely by surprise. She looked up at him, standing there in the doorway of the Research Station, and replied, "Sure. Okay. Well, why not?" Then they smiled at each other, and she thought he looked a bit like a giant otter leaning against the doorframe. He's long and slim, with small ears and not much of a neck, and he wears his climate pants too high. (None of the rest of the team wears climate suits in Kerguelen; he's the only one. They are south of the equator, a long way south, but he feels the heat and the pants keep him cool.)

*Yes*, she thought, *if he were an animal, he'd be an otter*, and she went back to her confusing data. But he didn't leave; he waited, unsure what to do next, so she said, "You organize it," because that's what he's good at, organizing things. That's why he wears three Bands, so he can schematize all the different parts of his life. And he has a lot going on: there's the new business, Dining in the Clouds, and he's head of New Development at eMpower, so he needs a Band for each of those. The third is for other things—personal things, important things, she's not sure what, but he has a lot going on.

Now, a month later, lying in the darkness, she knows two things for sure. First, no one needs three Bands. You can manage perfectly well with just one. Secondly, "Sure. Okay. Well, why not?" is not an appropriate response to a marriage proposal. It's not even close. The truth is, she believed compatibility could sustain their relationship. But it hasn't, and he deserves so much more. He's good, and kind, and patient, and he's been so helpful, organizing the funding for her research. He's the reason they're here, deep in the Southern Indian Ocean, on Kerguelen, searching outer space, recording geomagnetic disturbances.

It's now after midnight, and she needs to formulate a plan, a new plan. She needs to jump off something very high and she needs to do it very soon.

***

The trek up Mount Ross is peaceful, the morning clear and mild—a balmy 20 degrees. There's a new moon and a few lingering stars to the west. Her ascent is perfectly timed, and as she reaches the summit the sun begins to rise, the scarlet orb slipping quickly into the morning sky. The sight leaves her slightly awestruck—the dawn of a perfect day. Poetic, but not very smart. After the five-hour climb, she's weary, and there's an irritating tickle at the back of her throat; she could be coming down with something.

After pulling on her wingsuit, she steps out onto a small plateau, almost the highest point on the island of Kerguelen, and moves to the edge of the precipice. She drops a small rock over the edge, then watches it fall. A time-formed habit. There's fear, but she's always scared—the edge, the height, the speed, the fall. The trick is to make it into something else. Change it from a clawing, negative thing to a thrilling, tingling sensation. This is the first step to freedom. Soon her fear dissolves like melting ice, replaced by anticipation.

She straps on her helmet and goggles, pops in earplugs, and turns the music up, loud. Closing her eyes, she tumbles backward, over the edge, free-falling, but not into emptiness—space is not empty.

Adjusting her angle, she tilts 90 degrees and follows the curve of the mountain. The route takes her through a deep ravine, around the side of Mount Ross, and over what remains of the Cook Glacier.

Thirty years ago, the glacier covered 450 square kilometers. Today, some sections are still frozen, but the meltwater has forged a majestic, swift-flowing river that runs from the mountaintop to the ocean. Pooling arteries of icy liquid, like blue and white lace, seep into the scenery, and Quinn sees her reflection as she zips across the fjords. The remainder of the mountain landscape is sparse, rough with stumpy vegetation, thick shrubs and grasses, and a particularly unpleasant native cabbage.

She's scouted this line many times; she'll travel eight kilometers in three minutes, with a top speed of over two hundred kilometers an hour. Normally she jumps with heat pads strapped to her torso, feet, and hands, but today she forgot and the blood drains quickly from her fingers. Tingling numbness. It's rare to feel so cold. Of course, it should be cooler, considering the altitude and the season, but cool weather abandoned the planet decades ago. Today there are no frosts, no ice-covered puddles, and no flurries of snow on cold winter nights. Outside the Polar Regions, snowflakes, snow-covered mountains, and clouds have vanished entirely. Life is one long, continuous, monotonous, never-ending summer. The heat is here and it's here to stay, but the cold weather is greatly missed: chunky knits and hats with pompoms, mittens, and scarves; rugging up for long walks, feeling warm in the auto, and knowing it's cold outside; feeling warm in an apartment Pod and knowing it's freezing outside; lying late in bed on winter mornings and the sound of falling rain—yes, she misses this most of all. The pragmatists and Transhumans say complaining won't help: "Nostalgic cold-weather yearnings are pointless, it's warm, there's nothing we can do, we tried to fix the planet, and we made it worse." For two years, 2030 to 2032, the Earth's atmosphere was systematically seeded with reflective particles—stratospheric aerosol injections, which create a cooling effect—and it worked; the planet began to cool. Then the regional jet streams changed course, shifted toward the poles, and the clouds began to disappear.

Transhumans don't see the point of another attempt. They don't see a future for Earth, and they want Coin allocated to the Leaving Project, not the remaining-behind-and-staying-fixed-to-the-spot project, because terraforming Titan is going to cost trillions. Quinn disagrees; sentimental cold-weather longings give her something to aspire to. The weather is just a science problem, and all problems have a solution. Earth Optimism is growing; it's never too little or too late. All you need is a plan and some time alone, preferably falling through space.

As Quinn falls, she considers her marital options. Plan A: Have a go at it, get married, and see how it turns out. People who aren't in love couple up all the time, and they make it work. She could make it work. Once they're married, things might improve. She'll wake up one morning and realize the way Mori pronounces it An-ta-tic, instead of Antarctic, or Sil-i-cone instead of silicon—*Honestly, they're two completely different materials*—no longer bothers her. Instead of lovers, they'll be colleagues working alongside one another, solving the mysteries of the universe, uncovering new scientific discoveries. It'll be a marvelous time for humanity; he can be her assistant and together they'll discover a new form of modified gravity. The people of Earth will be forever grateful. Or, they'll drive each other crazy, one of them will have an affair, and then, they'll conspire with their new partner to kill the other, and modified gravity will remain decades away. *The people of Earth deserve more.*

Plan B: Be less judgmental. She likes him, she likes him a lot, he's very likable, and she'll learn to love his likability. And he's funny— that's important. Humor is an essential element in any relationship. What was it he said the other day? Something about the weather, the climate, it was quite funny. Yes, she remembers, he said, "We still have four seasons: Warm, Hot, Hotter, Scorching." Disaster averted; he's funny *and* likable. Except for the "learn to love him" part—that's not something anyone should be thinking on their wedding day. And he's too old for her. And there is no sex—probably because he's too old for her.

Plan C: *Get the fuck out while I can.* Pull up her big-girl climate pants and call the whole thing off. Sit him down and say, "You're likable *and* funny, both important elements in any relationship, but I can't marry you." Problem solved. She's not in love, she was never in love, and there will be no wedding inside a big, white, fluffy cloud today.

✶✶✶

Her landing site is a grassy field close to the coast, elevated, north-facing, and partially protected from the southerly winds. On a good day, without wind, it's the perfect place to land. But today the southerlies rush in brief but forceful bursts along the coastline.

Regardless, she deploys her chute, brakes hard, glides low over the field, and drops down, feet first, onto the soft, wild grass. A burst of crosswind surges, and the floundering chute vacillates. She hauls it into submission, securing and fastening the billowing silks. Then she peels off her wingsuit and lies down on the grass to rest.

She breathes. Problem solved: There will be no wedding in a cloud today.

A shadow passes overhead, blocking her light. It's a bird, an unfamiliar species, perhaps a type of gull or dove. Its head and wings are a typical tawny brown, but its belly is orange and its neck streaked yellow and ochre. She's not seen anything like it before; it's a stunning creature, a triumph of beauty and natural selection. She lies still on the ground, the bird stays fixed to its spot, caught in the headwind, and both appear as two motionless bodies in the universe.

Quinn knows the bird's speed has no fixed frame of reference and their static positions are relative to their perceptions of each other. She learnt that from her mother, Lise, and obviously Lise learnt that from

Albert Einstein. Some parents teach their children how to cook, or how to swim, or fish, or drive, but Lise taught Quinn that motion affects her perception of how time passes, and that this depends entirely on her perspective. Quinn knows the only thing that doesn't change with perspective is the speed of light. The speed of light is fixed.

She rolls over. She should holo Mori and let him know her whereabouts. He loves her. She doesn't know how that happened, one person in love and the other person not. Love should be an even equation. Two positives or two negatives, then you get an even result. That's the way it should work. You can't have one person in love and the other person not in love; it makes no sense, it's not logical.

Quinn activates her Band. She only has the one, a highly conductive combination of lithium and graphene, wrapped around her wrist. It's synced to her brain electrodes. Software in the Band translates her thoughts to either text or a holographic vision. It took a week for the device to create a file of her speech patterns when she first got it, but now it's 86 percent correct, most of the time.

Consolidating her thoughts, she launches a message: *Text Mori, tell him I woke early, went for a jump, be home soon.*

"The speed of light is absolute?" the Band suggests.

*What the fuck? No.* She tries again, *I'll be home soon. An hour, I'll be home in an hour.*

"A hour with Mori feels like a week?"

*Fuck. No. Don't send that. Forget it.*

Briefly she considers a dialogue message, then drops the idea; she'll see him soon enough. Her mother will arrive on Kerguelen later this morning; she's hired a private transporter for the event. Soon, they'll gather together on the lawn with Mori for introductions. She has an hour. The grass underneath her is fresh and cool, the morning sun is warm, and she's spent. It will be a long day. She closes her eyes.

# Two

# Her mother is
# sort of famous.

Mori glares at the 3D printer. "Stupid fucking machine." It has stopped working today, of all days, and Tech is not his forte. "Shit, it's the galvanometer, totally stuffed."

Wait, wait, no need to panic. He recalls they have spares. Yes, Quinn ordered them; they're in a box under her desk. He could be lucky—there might be a spare galvanometer waiting for him in the next room. And if he's not lucky, she can help fix . . . no, no, no, he shakes his head, not a good idea, she can't do that. She must stay away from the Station and stay focused on the wedding. He can't have her too close right now. Everything will be fine if he can keep her distracted for a few more hours. It's not a good thing he's done, he's fully aware, but he has a recovery plan, a blue-sky plan, a win-win, solid-terra-firma plan. He's calculated the best-case scenario: She never finds out what he's done, and there's absolutely no reason to ever tell her the truth. She remains blissfully unaware, it's a beautiful day to get married, and there's no need to spoil it. He's also calculated the worst-case scenario: She finds out and she's pissed off, no doubt about it—the G12 is her baby. But, he reasons, it's also kind of his baby, and they're about to be married and couples share. He can make a case; she'll understand. She'll forgive him. *No, no, no, she'll never forgive me. She must never find out.*

He checks the time on one of his Bands: a hour until the in-law invasion. He needs an IV vitamin infusion. He had one yesterday, and he tells himself he's not dependent, but he needs another to get through the morning. He's a little behind and the in-law invasion is playing on his mind. Not that he's worried—he knows he's likable—it's just that her mother is sort of famous, world famous. A polymath, a professor of physics, and a philosopher of science. Lise has four Science Medals and a Nobel Prize in mathematics. She's written twenty-two books and published over five hundred papers and essays on science, philosophy, politics, and economics. He looked her up, of course, and read her latest paper on the nesting of empty sets of numbers. It stated that reality is based on mathematics, and mathematics is based on nothing. At least he thinks that is what it said. He read the abstract; the rest was some shit about a theory of existence, or consciousness, or whatever you want to call it, based on nothingness. It was all profoundly disheartening, and he couldn't get his thought sequence around any of it. At least he can say he read it.

He tells himself to prioritize: first the infusion brew, then he'll fix the printer—if the piece doesn't fit, he'll use the spare printer to print a new part for the primary printer. It'll take a little longer, but it's his best option. Next, he needs to finalize the menu for the wedding, then meet the in-laws, check the Cloud Ship, sort the admin forms, and review the maps and geothermal charts. There's also a pile of shipping requests and permits for Antarctica to finalize—and then the G12 data. That's important; he needs to do that before she's up and around, before she gets to it first. He glances again at the time on his Band; it's still early. He has hours and hours, plenty of time. No need to rush.

He thinks of the menu and sighs. It's been an absolute nightmare navigating the dietary needs of his guests. He didn't foresee the difficulty—they're all humans, they eat to survive, and they should eat what's offered, but they don't and they won't. He's catered for vegans, flexitarians, medicinal soupers, and edible foragers. But the main concern is animal protein. Transhumans prefer their meat clean and cultivated in a lab, not roaming around on a grassy paddock. Serving rare Wagyu beef with wasabi vinegar is risky and he doesn't want to offend his VIP guests, but the product has already been sourced, ordered, and slaughtered.

He cornered Quinn a few days ago and ran his predicament past her. She paused, considered his dilemma, then replied, "Fries. You should serve fries. People love them. And beer—beer's the best. Steak, fries, and beer—it's a classic combo, you can't go wrong."

This confused him. Was she not listening? Had she misunderstood the problem? He tackled her again from a different angle, explaining his Wagyu concern, but she held up her hand, the way she does when she's working, indicating that she was not to be disturbed, so he backed away.

Today, confidence imbues him. Today, he's about to be married to a younger woman, a smart woman who knows how Axions define cold dark matter, and her climate model, the G12—well, it's like having a super power. Her mother's profile is also a bonus; the elevated social circles of the scientific community can't hurt his career. He smiles to himself, buoyed by his future prospects, and makes a final decision to go with the beef fillet. If the Transhumans complain, he'll blame the caterers. Moving down the list, he rejects synthetically produced seafood—no sea urchins, oysters, smoked salmon, or abalone. Half the population are self-harvesting in their cool zones. Next, he runs a line thorough insect sprinkles, cornhusks, and algae—too prolific. The motto is, "Rare food in a rarefied setting."

Mori met Quinn six months ago. She was pitching her software system, the G12, to his brother, Niels—founder and CEO of eMpower, the Tech giant that liberated personal data. In a world of rising sea levels and human displacement, Niels created a global system that divorced data from the server. It was a sublimely simple strategy: release private information from the one-sided, avaricious, and oppressive relationship with Comm companies, governments, Corps, and search engines that were overtly collecting, mining, and selling the information. For the first time in decades, individuals controlled their own data. Corps couldn't access it, use it, steal it, sell it, or profit from it in any way, and Niels Eco became a champion of the people—a very wealthy champion of the people.

Niels loves Tech more than he loves people, and the G12 sparked his interest. A synthetic virus that synced with the Earth's magnetic field, connecting to the planet's biosphere in real time, it was a predictive weather modeling wonder capable of accurately forecasting temperatures, winds, and rain days in advance. Initially, though, he couldn't see the point of the system. The population was over global warming; they'd reached peak indifference decades earlier. They didn't need to be told it was hot and dry because it was hot and dry all the time. Quinn's system was also designed for nephology, the study of clouds, and she was two decades too late. The last time Niels had seen a cloud, he'd been thirty-five and it was 2035. Now, the only place clouds hovered was over the Polar Regions, where it rained all day, every day.

Despite this, he was interested in the software and the Tech. Quinn's pitch to him revealed nothing about the software or the Tech, however. He probed and quizzed but got nothing in return and began to lose interest. Quinn, knowing her pitch was going nowhere—it never did—decided to change tactics. She held Niels's gaze across the room, smiled, and said, "Space weather. Solar flares."

A single flare could wipe out communication systems across the planet—satellites, the New Internet of Things (NIoT), and GPS, all destroyed in seconds. The G12, Quinn said, was astoundingly accurate at detecting radiation waves. There was potentially Coin to be made.

Niels was potentially interested.

Niels introduced Mori to the young inventor, and he was thunderstruck. Seeing her dark hair tied in a tight ponytail, he wondered what it would look like loose, falling around her shoulders, cascading down her back. Her intellect and her loveliness were also coupled with a familiar surname, Buyers. Well, her mother was practically a celebrity.

# Three

# On a Theory of Nothingness.

QUINN WAKES AND RISES from her grassy bed. The Research Station is a two-hour walk away; Lise will be waiting, and two hours is a long time for her to linger. They keep spare motorbikes in the nearby village of Grande Terre—old-style, retro machines with gears and manual steering and no self-balancing, auto-steer, or hands-free. Quinn's father, Matt, taught her to ride when she was ten, but Mori is not as confident or as skilled a rider as her. On a straight, paved road he'll stay upright, but tight turns and hill climbs stump him. She suggested modifying a bike for him, fixing it to include auto-assist, but he's a traditional male and would rather impale himself before that ever happened.

Kerguelen is in the Desolation Islands, one of the most isolated places on Earth—an archipelago of three hundred islands in the southern Indian Ocean. Two months ago, Quinn set up a Research Station near Grande Terre. The place is a culture shock, and the Island is three decades behind the rest of the world—all very Low-Tech, except for Quinn's little corner, which is filled with scads of equipment: magnetometers, electric sensors, particle detectors. They arrived with a container of modular flat-packed systems that, with the push of a button, expanded into buildings ten times their size. The locals had never seen anything like it; to them it was revolution, some futuristic, science fiction, High-Tech scenario. (It wasn't; it was just clever hinging and counterbalanced parts.)

Grande Terre is the only village on the Island, and the buildings are the regular sort: two hundred years old, made from rammed earth and clad in timber. There are some retail stores selling maintenance equipment, fishing supplies, and rubber boots and clothing for men and boys, but nothing for women. A few food outlets sell dried goods and grain alcohol. There are two thousand residents, three thousand rare but very cute curly-horned sheep, and no AIs. Not one. The entire Island is robot free. Like the mantra from an AI Detox Retreat: "Reevaluate your relationship with humans. Focus on the tenets of connecting with people, not machines." Mori thinks it's ridiculously archaic; life is so much easier with AI doing the heavy lifting. But AI irks Quinn—she finds them tedious, especially when affecting a persona of caring. (If they ask her, "How are you feeling?" or worse, "How are you *really* feeling?" she tells them to "fuck off.") She's not a staunch Humanist, but her father is a devotee of the movement and parental ideologies trickle down.

Quinn jumps on a bike and heads west, following the only road, which trails from the harbor through the village and ends at the Research Station. The buildings at either end of town are abandoned; the farther away the greater the state of disrepair, like a creeping decay, edging towards the center of town. The MedCentre was the first to close, then the two churches, one on either side of town, were boarded up after the RE Wars (Religious Wars or Regional Wars, depending on your cultural ideologies). East verses West may have defined the geographical scope of the Wars, which began after the economic collapse in 2036, but as far as Quinn is concerned, people were fighting over organized religion. Biased political policies united Church and State in the mid 2020s, creating laws and legislation favoring right-wing fundamentalist religious groups. By 2030, Church and State were using violent regulatory forces to uphold religious doctrines. After the RE Wars ended, churches and places of worship were closed. Religion is not banned outright, but worshiping in groups is closely monitored and outspoken religious doctrines and fundamentalism are not tolerated by Hexad, the International Unified Government formed after the RE Wars ended six years ago.

Twenty minutes later, Quinn pulls into the main complex building. She finds Lise resting on a lawn chair in the shade there, and she's not alone, she's brought a plus-one: Ada, her ex-partner. Quinn is shocked. She thought it was over, finally over, and the breakup, when it happened, was a relief.

In the beginning, it was a perfect match: two independent, attractive, and accomplished women, Ada happily domestic and Lise happily career driven, neither entrenched in the Humanist or Transhuman camp. The cracks appeared early, when Lise described their new swarm drones as silver-white, like cadmium, and Ada corrected, "Technically grey." Quinn understood the verity, this was true, the drones were not silver-white like cadmium at all, they were a much darker mid-grey color, like zinc. Then Lise said the new window screens were charcoal, because darker colors clarify the view and she wanted to filter the light and see the streetscape below, and Ada corrected, "Ironstone, not charcoal." *Ironstone. Really?* Quinn realized then they magnetically repelled each other.

They split a year ago. But here they are, the two of them together. Is this one last attempt to make it work, to see if they can feel, or find, this thing called love, this thing that humanity can't live without? *Surely not*, thinks Quinn, *Lise is too smart to do this again.*

She dismounts from the bike and kisses her mother's cheek. "Thanks for coming." She lowers her voice. "Thought it was over."

"It is, long story. She loves a destination wedding, and she wanted to see you married."

"Yes, of course."

Lise considers her daughter's furrowed countenance. "Darling, you haven't slept."

"I'm fine. Work's mad."

Quinn has the same dark, wavy hair and grey-blue eyes as her mother, but Lise's eyes are world-weary, softer and kinder, and she wears her hair blunt and short. Still, the older Quinn gets, the more she resembles her mother; glimpses of passing reflections are a constant reminder that they share their genome and DNA. Thirty years ago, when Quinn was a fetus, Lise's cells crossed the placenta and entered her daughter's bloodstream. Today, they're still here, in her eyes, her hair, her heart. This sharing of themselves was mutual, and Quinn left embryonic stem cells inside her mother.

The pair have a similar habit of biting their thumbnails when studying calculus. Lise doesn't cook, and neither does Quinn. Both favor automatic pencils, which leave satisfying, heavy marks on the pages of their notebooks. They love math, and science is their religion. But Lise wants to change the world. She sees it as her duty to challenge the status quo, to make a difference, to find a fairer way for people to live, and this is the focus of her life and her work. Quinn sees problems everywhere; she knows the world is a mess, there are big problems, but she feels they are too weighty for her to address and it's not her responsibility to solve the dilemmas of humanity in the mid-twenty-first century. The focus of her life is to get through the day without imploding.

Ada steps forward and cups a hand around Quinn's cheek. "Darling, good to see you," she says, then spies Quinn's hands, white and stiff, still cold from the jump. She takes them and rubs them between hers, bringing the blood back. "Child abuse." She frowns. "Could have been so easily fixed."

Raynaud's syndrome affects the lineage of females in Quinn's family. In cold weather or under stress, Quinn's smaller arteries spasm and contract, cutting off circulation and blood supply to her extremities—hands, feet, ears, nose. The faulty DNA could have been snipped from her genome using CRISPR before she was born, but her parents knew what was coming. Having a genetic predisposition to the cold would be a useful survival mechanism for the future.

Ada is thin, with muscular shoulders and arms, but her defining feature is her thick eyebrows, which arch gracefully across her forehead, framing her sharp, penetrative eyes. Ada doesn't fuss; she's a direct talker. She also knows about fashion. Her belts match her shoes, she owns many pairs of shoes and matching belts, and she can tie a scarf fifteen different ways. Quinn finds these skills mysterious and appealing. Ada is fifteen years younger than Lise, the same age as Mori, and there is an alarming symmetry to this coincidence that Quinn has decided to ignore.

"Darling, this is Tig. He's staying with me for a few weeks." Lise introduces a strange figure standing in shadow.

*Oh good lordt, she's brought another plus one.*

Tig leaves the shelter of the shade and ambles quickly toward Quinn. With each advancing stride of his, she takes a small step backward. He wears thick bionic glasses that bypass his visual system. As he scans the environment, the glasses feed information directly to his brain neurons. This is Old Tech; he sees maybe 500 million pixels, about half of what she sees. His body is a mix of human and artificial parts and his Tifoam skeleton is exposed along his right side, at the elbow and ankle joints. The skeleton is polyurethane impregnated with a titanium powder that mimics bone structure, allowing human cells to meld with it.

*Cyborg. He must be over the line, and if not, then he's close.* Tig's ratio of Tech to Hominoid parts is precariously high. The Authentic Human Alliance (AHA) has been petitioning fiercely for stricter classifications on what constitutes a human. The movement is small but gaining momentum with a core group of active lobbyists, all blessed with strong genetic codes and robust DNA. They say fusion with machine negates biology, giving an unfair evolutionary advantage to the individual. Their motto is, "We draw the line." And they draw that line at 50 percent. Over the line, with more than 50 percent Tech, and you cannot call yourself "human." They are machines, cyborgs, and should be excluded from some professions, not given a vote, and required to vacate a seat or a place in a queue for organisms with a higher ratio of organic parts. Transhumans and opponents of AHA say it's new racism.

Tig doesn't appear to have any obvious advantage, and she wonders why in the world he's here with Lise. He's too old to be an intern. Perhaps he's a science project, and she's funding some new Tech? He certainly needs it. Tig half nods, half smiles at her, comically awkward.

She smiles back then turns to her mother. "He could be renovated. A good Technician, some Coin, and you'd never know."

"Know what?" But Lise knows exactly what her daughter means.

"Luggage, luggage. We have gifts." Ada, artfully diverting their attention. A rolling luggagebot arrives at Quinn's feet and falls open, exposing generous contents: coffee, mandarins, and wine. Rare commodities in a heat-soaked world.

Coffee plantations perished in the 2030s. The plants need gentle rainfall and mild temperatures, between 18 and 22 degrees Celsius, to thrive. A seesaw climate took its toll; the bushes stressed and the flowers fell before they turned to fruit. The sturdier plantations were finished off by mealy bugs and coffee berry borers, which love the heat. The prices went up and up, and the world turned to tea. Today, thousands of combinations and infusions keep the human population running. There are teas that wake, teas that sleep-induce, relax, and de-stress. Teas that inspire, hydrate, motivate, and invigorate. Teas that aid memory, promote weight loss, soothe mental health, and cure colds and sprained muscles. Served ice-cold or hot, mild or strong, the ritual of preparing and serving was usurped from Japanese culture and the infused brew is now a global obsession.

Climate also defeated the wine industry; extreme temperatures and a lack of reliable salt-free irrigation brought global production to a trickle in the early 2040s. There are still cases, extensive collections, and small boutique vineyards producing limited quantities, but the cost is prohibitive—special occasions only.

Lise tosses Quinn a mandarin from the luggagebot. Quinn catches it and breathes in the fruit and citrus scent.

"You juggled these when you were little," Lise says. "Remember?"

Yes, she remembers, anything round, anything within in reach, mandarins, lemons, limes. She practiced all the time and never improved; ball skills are not in her skill set.

Mori leaves the main complex building, and Quinn watches as he strides across the grass towards them. She knows his gait. This is not his usual stride; he's had a vitamin top-up—a nutrition IV infusion, a brain cleanse to help him focus. It sort of kick-starts his day, leaving him with a little morning buzz.

Lise tosses Quinn another mandarin, and then another. Quinn fumbles both and loses all three.

"Darling, what's wrong?" Lise asks.

"I'm not sure," Quinn replies.

"About?"

Quinn turns toward Mori, and Lise follows her gaze.

"Oh, I see," Lise says.

"Sorry I'm late," Mori says. "Primary printer's not working, and the secondary printer's printing parts to fix the primary. Been thinking outside the circle all week." He's a bit hypo, high on his infusion. "Lise, it's good to finally meet you. I'm a huge admirer—read all your work."

Lise takes his hand. "It's 'doctor,' Dr. Buyers. You've read all my work! Really? All of it?"

"Well, some—"

"Which books?"

Mori hesitates, a half laugh, "I guess, the one about nothing . . . ness."

"*On a Theory of Nothingness.* And what did you think? What did you like about it?"

Mori flounders and stares at the ground. Quinn feels for him, knowing he never actually read it—and knowing why, too. Logically, it is impossible to avoid a theory of nothingness, but it does people's heads in. It's unnerving to be told that the world might not be real, that it cannot be defined without active participation, that things only become tangible when you see them, and touch them, and taste them. People hate the idea of nothingness, herself included.

"He didn't say he liked it; he just said he's read it," Ada interrupts. "Please, call me Ada."

Lise exhales, raises an arched eyebrow. Quinn rubs the crease in her forehead. *This is where they're at.*

Quinn scans the group, thinking what a ridiculous little gathering of humans they are, assembled on the grass on an isolated archipelago. And now they're going to sit around and partake in awkward getting-to-know-each-other introductions and make pointless conversation because they think there's going to be a wedding this afternoon. *What the fuck have I done?*

Mori pulls in extra chairs, and they sit in the low, flat shadows of the complex buildings. The white tips of Mount Ross hang in the sky behind them, but their focus is south, toward the teal-colored Indian Ocean lapping gently into the bays and inlets around the Island. The tide makes soft, gasping sounds, as if it is inhaling and exhaling, in and out, while creeping forward, getting a little higher every year.

No one speaks, not a word, and right now Quinn sees how easy it is to believe in nothingness. All this beauty, the sparkling reflections on the water, the exquisite green-blue color, the hypnotic murmur of the waves, the warm breeze on her skin—these are just constructs inside her head. The landscape is too wonderful, too scenic and charming, to be real. Before her the horizon blurs into nothingness, leading on and on, all the way to the wet and wild world of Antarctica.

"The ocean, it's so green," Ada notes.

"It's out of balance. There's more phytoplankton blooms. That makes it look greener," says Lise.

"Ah," Ada responds.

Again, they fall into silence.

"Beautiful horizontal line," says Mori.

Quinn frowns. *He means horizon, beautiful horizon. He's nervous.*

"Yes, yes it is, it's just so, so perfectly straight." Ada salvages the malapropism, smiling. "It's a perfectly lovely, straight line between water and sky."

Lise's unamused eyes are fixed on the distance.

"Honeymooning?" Ada asks.

"An-ta-tic. Working holiday."

*Still annoying.*

"Really?" Lise is surprised.

"There's a lot to be done there," says Mori.

"Yes, there is. Actually, we'd like some time alone with Quinn," she says. "You don't mind, do you?"

"Anything you have to say . . ."

"Alone," she clarifies.

He eases himself out of his chair. "Need time for my thought shower anyway."

They watch him stride across the lawn back to the Research Station.

"What's a 'thought shower'?" Lise asks.

"It's thinking. Just thinking, we all do it," says Quinn. "I'm such an idiot, I've totally fucked this up."

"Never too early for wine," says Ada, gathering glasses from the luggagebot and opening a bottle. On this they all agree, except Tig, who refuses a glass. Instead, he busies himself peeling the mandarins and watching the skins fall to the ground.

"You're not in love, but you don't need to be," says Ada.

"You can tell that from one meeting?"

"Of course. Look, he's been very good for your career; it's still a good alignment. You're sure its not pre-wedding nerves? Very common. Besides, it doesn't need to be forever."

"Thank you; sobering advice." Not the words of wisdom she wanted to hear on her wedding day.

They fall silent.

Tig turns to Quinn, offering her segments of mandarin in his open palm, and she sees that both his wrists are covered in fine metal bangles. Dozens of them. She leans in and stares into his open face, wondering what he's thinking, then decides he's a bit drone-like. Maybe he doesn't think anything. As she takes the mandarin her fingers graze his, causing a shudder between them, a reverberating electric shock. He grins. She pulls away. The morning light catches the rim of his bionic glasses and hits her in the eye. She squints. He's a strange thing.

"The cloud thing?" asks Ada.

"Simulated weather experience," Quinn corrects. "More art installation than science. A cumulous cloud with fabulous ambiance and mood lighting. It has a dual purpose: besides the wedding, he's launching his new business, Dining in the Clouds. He says people want new adventures, exciting experiences. They'll do anything to be part of something unique. He has pre-bookings a year ahead; the fashionably wealthy still want fine food in an exclusive setting. And the press will love it, which means sponsors. Investments. He's worked so hard on it; he even embedded actinomycetes into the platform so it smells like rain." She turns to her mother. "Please say something. You're too quiet."

"Am I?"

"You know you are," says Ada.

Another raised eyebrow.

Lise is nonreactive now, because she's always been non-reactive.

Her parenting philosophy is based on embracing failure—making mistakes and learning from them. When Quinn was younger, a teenager, Lise encouraged her to explore the world, take risks, and make mistakes. There were no boundaries and no punishments—never a stern word. She answered all of her daughter's questions truthfully and said her actions were her choices. If she wanted to discuss them, Lise was always available.

Slowly, Quinn breathes. "I have a plan. I'm going to tell him it's too soon, I'm just not sure, and I need more time. Then I'll suggest we go ahead with the event, but not the ceremony. So the cloud thing happens. There's no point canceling. That'd be worse for him. He's worked so hard."

Lise remains silent, reticently finishing her wine in one gulp. There is nothing else for Quinn to do; she rises from her chair and sets off toward the main building.

## Four

# He could be renovated. A good Technician and some Coin.

*So close, I could have leant over and kissed her. I could have picked her up and squeezed her and kissed her. Could have held her hand, taken it in mine, sat there next to her holding it, keeping it warm—but then she'd have one warm hand and one cold, so I'd have to warm the other one as well, then both her hands would be real warm; she'd like that. She likes it when her hands are warm. Yeah, that would've been nice—a bit weird, but nice, really nice. But would have completely freaked her out, of course, and I don't want to do that.*

Didn't know what would happen, how she would feel, but I felt pretty fucking stupid, 'cause I couldn't take my eyes off her. Honestly, I thought she might realize, in some small way she'd know, she'd get it, there'd be a sign, a signal, she'd realize who I was, but she knows nothing, absolutely nothing, and that's pretty fucking obvious. *She has no idea who I am, and why would she? Never met me before in her life.*

*Fuck, what a trip this is. It's messing with my head.* The things I remembered about her: Natural, everything about her, loose hair, no makeup, and her eyes, beautiful green eyes. No manners, she's so fucking abrupt, "He could be renovated. A good Technician, some Coin . . ." Fuck me, didn't know whether to laugh at her or yell at her.

The things I forgot: She's small, tiny frame. Standing next to her, I wanted to say, "Come on, stand up," 'cause she looks so friggin' small. I don't remember her being that small. And young, I'd forgotten about that—she's young. And cute. And horny.

Actually, that's me, not her. I've come a long way for love and sex.

# Five

# Look up at the stars and not down at your feet.

Mori stands in front of the faulty printer, a tube of resin in one hand and a galvanometer in the other. He clearly has no idea what he's supposed to be doing. On the table beside him are a pile of spare parts and a folder of documents, maps, and charts. He looks up when Quinn enters.

"And you said she was thoughtful and funny."

"Really? Did I say that?"

"Yes, you said she holds a deep-seated skepticism about the way wealth is created, so I wasn't to mention the property portfolio, and then you added brilliant, thoughtful, funny, and she likes a stiff drink at the end of the day. You'd have to peel layers from that onion to get anything out of it. Did she mention my age?" Abandoning the resin and the galvanometer to the pile of equipment on the table, he begins sorting through the charts, flicking through folders, like he's trying to find something that's not there—an exercise in endless shuffling.

"No. She didn't mention your age. You're busy. Let me help . . ."

"This, no?" He gestures to the documents. "The tiger team's striding fertile ground; we're about to grab the lofty fruit."

Quinn thinks Mori's brain works like a random, scattered, vacillating system of neurons that don't always connect.

"What did you talk about after I was so ungracefully dismissed?"

"Nothing."

He glances her way. "You okay?"

"I'm so sorry, I can't do this."

"Relax, you don't have to tell me everything, you're allowed to have some secrets."

"No, not that, I can't do *this*, you and me. I can't marry you."

"You've changed your mind?"

"I'm not a hundred percent."

"What percent are you?"

"About eighty." *Eighty percent negative.* "It's too soon, I just need more time."

Leaning on the edge of the desk, he runs his palms down his thighs. "I'm so sorry."

"No, no, I understand. We're singing from the same sheet music. It's been a whirlwind, for both of us. Take all the time you need. I just want you to be happy."

She holds her breath, then lets it out with a long sigh. "You should do the event, the dinner. I mean, you've worked so hard. Just no wedding."

"Just no wedding. Okay."

"I'm sorry."

"No, no, don't be." He shakes his head like an insect is bothering him. "It's fine, really it is."

"I'm sorry."

"Don't worry, trust me, I'll be just fine, just fine. Now, you look tired. Go lie down, and I'll take the final readings. We've still got a lot to do."

She nods; she's shattered.

He takes her hands in his. "And, just a thought, this afternoon wear the cloud dress."

Her hand retracts, but his grip is firm.

"Wait, listen, it would be great for the business, Fourth Estate will be there. Think of the images; it'll go viral."

He wants her to wear a simulated cloud. Many times, she's rejected this idea; she's a scientist, she has a PhD, it took her six years to develop her climate model, she's not wearing a white, fluffy cloud. But now she's indebted, so she nods. She'll wear the cloud dress. It's the least she can do.

He grins at the win. "One last thing." He nestles close to her ear. "Don't wear anything under the cloud."

It's out of character, but she concedes. It could be just what their relationship needs.

Plan C: It's done. He made it easy for her; she knows he did. The wedding is canceled but the event is on, and she's the welcome committee. A few hours' rest is exactly what she needs. He's just so thoughtful.

Headed toward her sleep zone, she passes a flock of cute, curly-horned sheep grazing on a patch of the island's native cabbages, which she knows are truly awful and only fit for sheep consumption because she ate one once. This group of sheep is her favorite. She's named each one: Maryam Mirzakhani, Richard Dawkins, Marie Curie, and her good friend Stephen Hawking. She has breakfast with Stephen most mornings. They stroll around the complex until they find a pleasant place to sit and contemplate the day ahead. Often, she'll take her jour-nal and automatic pencil and make notations on the solar flare data as she eats.

Stephen sees her and wanders over, nuzzles his forehead into her knee. She scratches the back of his neck. Sheep have a similar basal ganglia and cerebral brain cortex to humans and are much smarter than people realize.

"Up for a walk?" she asks, because right now she needs a chat and he's a good listener. They make their way across the grass, heading north, up the sloping hills surrounding the Station, where the grassy base of Mount Ross rises, giving way to rocks and trees—a familiar spot with a clear view of the village and harbor. There's a neat place amongst the stones to rest, and Stephen hunkers down beside her.

"Bad day," she says. "I'm riddled with guilt. Sounded like one of those AHA people, I'm a disgrace. I wonder if he was in the War; he looks like he was in the War. And I canceled the wedding, but that's a good thing." Then she remembers something Hawking once said—the scientist, not the sheep—and, looking into the sheep's eyes, she says, "'Remember to look up at the stars and not down at your feet. Don't give up work; it gives your life meaning and purpose and without it life is empty, and if you are lucky enough to find love, don't throw it away.' Well, I'm not throwing it away, I never had it. And I've got the first two covered." She closes her eyes and falls asleep in the furrow between the rocks, under the mid-morning sun.

✶✶✶

When she wakes Stephen is still there, resting beside her. She checks her Band; a message from Lise. Her mother refuses to send holograms; she hates the technology and won't even acknowledge a holo request. She says it's a complete fad. The novelty will last a couple of years and then everyone will go back to dialogue and messaging each other. "A bit of diffracted light and noise and people think it's magic. It's not fucking magic, it's science. If the medium is still the message, and I think it is, then it's not a message I'm sending." She shook her head when she said this. "You're too young to remember the book debate. People predicted they'd be gone, that all text would be digital, but here we are, still reading them, hard copies. And autonomous vehicles: hot for a few years, then we realized we liked driving and found autos interesting. Trust me, the same thing will happen to holograms."

Quinn opens the message. It reads, "You and I, we are entangled qubits. Our reality is not bound by classical concepts of physics, it's what we make it. There is no point mulling over the past or the future, because they don't exist, just as the concept of 'now' doesn't exist. Just live. Life is for living. Whatever decision you make is the right one."

Quinn smiles. The consolation of unconditional love.

# Six

# He keeps staring at Quinn like a lost puppy.

In a small apartment on the other side of the planet in a small, out-of-the-way city called Hobart, Maim Quate, leader of the political party Democratic Republic, brews her morning tea in the food prep. This is not her kitchen, but she likes this space; she's always liked blue kitchens, and the honey-colored timber floors and benches contrast so nicely with the blue cabinets and walls. What did Lise call this color? *"Orbit the Moon."* She smiles as she thinks that Lise would have happily paid more for the name. Maim wears a rust-colored kimono, not her size, but it's a loose cut and she likes the way it smells—like Lise. She takes her tea and heads back to the sleep zone. Moving to the left side of the bed, she pulls back the cover, then changes her mind and slips over to the right side of the bed. Drawing the golden wraps around her, she sips her tea and thinks she likes this room, too. The walls here are a deep yellow and the name is easy to recall: *Cartoon Yellow.*

✳✳✳

In Kerguelen, Lise's sleep zone is a rudimentary, compact space with modular furniture. The bed rolls out from underneath the storage,

34

and during the day a table folds from the wall and the space works as a dining and study area. It's small but she's is happy to have her own cabin and not share with Ada. Bringing her as a plus-one was a terrible idea, and she berates herself—what was she thinking? How did she let herself be coerced like this? Maim is the one who should be here with her, not Ada. But of course Maim couldn't come, not in her position; it's too difficult, too dangerous, for her to travel. They haven't made their relationship public yet, but they will after the election, after Maim wins—Lise is sure she'll win. Maim and her party may be the only hope the planet has.

Lise signals for her luggagebot to open. Carefully, she unpacks a long black evening gown and hangs it on the side of the storage unit. Then she takes a notebook and an automatic pencil, sits at the table, and begins making notations. She draws a distinctive V symbol on the page. Her Band hums; it's Maim. She smiles and accepts the call.

"Hello," she says.

"Hello, miss me?"

"It's only been a day, but yes, what are you doing?"

"I'm in bed."

"You're on my side, aren't you?"

"Yes. And I'm wearing your clothes."

"Ha, well you should be here with me, except there's nothing to be here for. It's off."

"What do you mean, it's off?"

"She called it off. There's no wedding; she's not in love."

"Oh good lordt, and you've come all that way. Is she okay?"

"She'll be fine. It was the right thing to do, and I'm glad I'm here. I needed to be here. And I might stick around for a few days. They're going to Antarctica." Lise draws a second V, alongside the first.

"That's not a coincidence, is it?"

"No, it's not. I had a breakthrough with the code, an epiphany of sorts." Lise scribbles wiggly markings across the tops of her V's. "It came to me in a dream. I fell asleep on the transporter and when I woke I knew what they were—the markings on the Disc, the correlation. I know what it is." Pressing lightly, she traces over her V markings many times, her pen working back and forth. "It's obvious now. It's all come together, and with the right catalyst I can make it work."

"Have you told Tig?"

"No, we've had no time alone and he's acting very strange. He keeps staring at Quinn like a lost puppy, and it's pissing her off."

"Oh fuck, just make sure he's taking his Meds. Have you given her the stone?"

A shadow passes under the door; someone is standing outside the cabin, listening to their conversation.

"Not yet. Listen I need to go, I'll call you later."

"I love you."

"Me, too. And make the bed before you leave."

# Seven

# Pink diamonds.
# We're entangled qubits.

Mori flicks the office chair with his hand and watches it spin a few times before pausing the revolutions and taking a seat. *That was unexpected.* Abruptly, he stands and paces the room, back and forth, before returning to the chair, where he sits again. A bit of a surprise—he wasn't expecting that. She's not 100 percent sure; she's only 80 percent. He grins. Only 80 percent. Eighty percent is great; of course, it is. He has nothing to worry about. It's a glitch and she'll come around. It's too soon. She just needs more time, and the event, Dining in the Clouds—it's overwhelming. He reprimands himself. He should have realized sooner; she's young and everything is new, and she's never traveled before, never even left Hobart. Her life skills are, well, they're limited. What did Niels say? "Brains of a fifty-year-old, emotional maturity of a fifteen-year-old." Well, maybe he was right after all.

Niels. What's he going to say about all this? Mori knows he won't say, "I told you so"—the phrase is not in his repertoire. Niels has a multitude of despondent expressions that succinctly sum up his options on the human race. He already thinks Mori's an idiot, and he knows he fucked up in Antarctica. Well, he doesn't need to know about the wedding situation. She just needs time, that's all, and Mori is prepared to wait. He'll make an effort with the sex; he's been lazy, he'll concede that, forgetting to renew the subscription on his SelfMed, but he'll sort it out and reinstall the program.

Okay, enough self-recrimination. This is not about him; it has nothing to do with him. She's young and naïve and female; it's to be expected. But, didn't he handle it well? He chuckles. He got the cloud dress out of it. Smart thinking, bottom-up thinking, yes, that was a profit, a gain for him.

Now he needs to focus, synergize his brain, and carry out the final checks on the Cloud Ship. There's time, he's not behind, but the platform needs be raised so he can generate the effect: a giant cumulous cloud on a base of aerogel. Quinn suggested the base material and it's perfect, 99 percent air and 1 percent silicon; guests will feel like they are walking on a cloud. Controlling the temperature and humidity will keep the cloud stable, and a combination of nuclear forces, which Quinn helped him correlate, will hold the effect together.

✳✳✳

Later that afternoon, rested, perfectly punctual, and wearing a white cumulous cloud with white knee-length boots (to keep her feet warm five thousand meters above sea level), Quinn carefully steps into the first AirPod. The arrival is a significant part of the experience: guests will traverse solid terra firma to the ethereal beauty of the cumulous cloud in AirPods. After checking that her veil of mist is still intact, she rises into the sky and is dismayed to see that Mori's cumulous cloud is not a perfect example; it's too wispy and its cotton-like, cauliflower-shaped piles lack height and volume. It also arcs to the right, like a great white shark has taken an enormous bite from one side. But, she acknowledges, it's a good effort, an adequate cloud, and it's his first attempt; with practice, he'll become more acquainted with the Tech.

On board, her task is to greet the guests, help them out of the Pods, make some small talk about the weather, and then point them toward the bar. If a longer conversation is required, she'll start discussing electromagnetism and the combination of weak and strong nuclear forces holding the cloud together, and the guests will then seek solace in a cold beverage without her direction.

Before anyone else arrives, she skulls one drink for nerves. It will be her only one of the night; a sober cloud is more emotionally resilient than a drunk cloud. But she knows that later tonight, after this day over, after she gets down and kills the cloud dress, she's going to drink more alcohol than she should.

The numbers on board multiply as the guests arrive, and soon a noisy din settles over the cloud. Exotic food circles the room: fertilized hens' eggs with fennel pollen, snake hearts with truffle salt, large fish eyes with *monstera deliciosa* foam, bananas that taste like sumac, edible cutlery that tastes like saffron, edible plates that taste like tuna. One guest tries to eat her serviette, which isn't edible, forcing Quinn to intervene, and a little tug-of-war ensues between them before Quinn firmly snatches it from her. There's no wine; instead, an endless round of cocktails and spirits drifts past on levitating trays.

Lise, Ada, and Tig board. Tig is wearing longer pants and a black shirt with a gold-embroidered collar. His shirtsleeves are rolled up, the metal bangles nestled at his wrists and his titanium skeleton exposed at his elbow. It's a bold move in a crowd like this; some guests won't appreciate sharing their exclusive dining experience with a cyborg. He appears not to care, in fact he has a disdainful smirk on his face, which Quinn puts down to intellectual impediment.

The dress code is formal. Both Ada and Lise wear full-length evening gowns, one in red and the other black. A tight red choker encases Ada's fine neck and Lise wears a single pink stone, the color of raspberries. Unpolished and rough-cut, it hangs on a thin silver thread around her neck. When she and Ada see Quinn, they pull her to one side, look her over, the full head-to-toe examination, and then burst into laughter.

"Really?" Quinn asks. "Is it that bad? It wasn't my idea, and it's the least I could do. Is it too short?"

"Yes, but you've got good legs," says Ada. "And those boots!"

"Darling, I have something for you." Lise opens a small box. Inside is a crimson stone, a rough-cut pink diamond matching the one she's wearing—a beautiful, rare, exquisite gem.

Overwhelmed, Quinn begins to protest.

"Nonsense," says Lise, fastening the stone around her daughter's neck. "Pink diamonds. We're entangled qubits; always remember this."

Their conversation is interrupted by a man wearing a Fourth Estate crest. The journalist is keen for an interview; 2050 is a Global Election year and Lise is politically active, a strong opponent of the high-profile New Federation Party and its leader, Dirac Devine. Lise is pro-science, and new scientific discoveries defy New Fed's political agendas, which pine for past eras of hard right dominance and fundamentalist religious control over the population. A minority of economic elite finances the party, and they're all anti-science.

Last week, Lise delivered a scathing speech on the party and its anti-science doctrines. It's not surprising that Fourth Estate wants a follow-up remark.

"How does science fit into the political agenda of the mid-twenty-first century?" asks the journalist. The question drives to the heart of the political dissension between Lise and New Federation.

Lise smiles. "Let me be very clear. Science doesn't fit into anything—science is fundamental to everything. It's who we are. Now, let's talk about my new book. I'm working on a mathematical algorithm to decode reality. You see, the world around us is an illusion, a fabrication of the brain. Put simply, there is no physical world—at least, not as we know it."

"Yes, your latest book," the journalist stammers, floundering. He projects a hologram onto his wrist and scrolls though his research. "It talks about . . . math, and algorithms, and the world being . . . an illusion." He looks up at Lise, seeking confirmation. "That's right isn't it?"

Lise knits her brow. "Didn't I just say that?"

"Yes. I think you did. Sorry, I do political rounds. I know next to nothing about science."

"Then why don't you ask me about my next book?"

"Okay, tell me something about your next book," he says obligingly.

"Kind of you to ask. I'm investigating time travel. I'm sure we can go forward; that's a given. It's the past I'm interested in. Specifically, closed causal loops, like the Predestination Paradox—where an event in the past influences an event in the future."

"The future sounds terrifying," the journalist quips.

"No," Lise says. "The future is easy; it's the present that's terrifying."

The journalist departs, and Quinn turns to her mother. "Time travel. Really?"

"Yes. Really." Lise smiles. "I've discovered a portal—a type of wormhole—and I know how to open it. I cracked the final piece of the code on my way here, while we were on the Transporter."

*Surely she's kidding?* "A time travel portal. Are you serious?"

"Do I look serious?"

"Yes. You look very serious, and it makes me very nervous." Quinn shakes her head. "What are you going to do with your . . . time travel portal?"

"I've thought quite a lot about it. Time travel raises complex moral issues, and it throws the laws of cause and effect out the window. You see, going back in time could set up an Ontological Paradox, where you have no discernable origin—you just exist. It might make existence meaningless."

"I thought it was already meaningless. Wasn't that the point of your last book?"

"No. Existence has meaning—it just isn't real. Anyway, it doesn't sound like much fun, traveling back and forth in a loop—so easy to get stuck. I'm not sure I'll use the portal."

*I can't believe we're having this conversation.* "Good. I'm glad. Stay here in the 'terrifying present' with the rest of us."

"I mean, I would use it if I absolutely had to. If it was an absolute necessity."

"Absolutely necessities cover so many things," Quinn muses. "Like, saving the planet, reversing climate change . . . that's a given, right?"

"Fraught with danger. And we can still save the planet."

"Okay, what about going back in time to meet Stephen Hawking?"

"Yes, that's perfect. You could also use it to escape boring fools who try to eat their serviettes."

"Agreed," says Quinn.

Ada is engaged in conversation on the other side of the Ship. She waves at Lise to get her attention, and Lise casts a weary glance in her direction.

Ada points to her empty glass. Then she turns the glass upside down—there's not a drop left in it. Apparently, she needs another drink, and she'd like Lise to fetch it for her.

Quinn turns back to her mother. "Or you could use the portal to escape annoying ex-lovers. Surely that's an absolute necessity."

"I think that goes without saying," says Lise.

✶✶✶

Two guests declined the invitation to the wedding in the clouds. Quinn's father, Matt, didn't even open the card. "Not my thing," he said, and Quinn knew what he actually meant was, "It's fucking ridiculous and it's over the top." She countered with the fact that it wasn't her thing either; it was Mori's thing.

"And the Coin? What'll it cost?" he asked.

"Not sure, maybe a hundred."

"Fuck!"

"Maybe not that much."

He opted out. She understood. Matt lives an isolated, hermit-style, Low-Tech life in the forest. He likes to watch the sun come up and he likes to watch it go down, and some days that's about as complex as his life gets. He's a songwriter, but he calls himself a poet, an aging ex-rocker with existential angst. AI compose jingles and melodies and they play instruments with flawless precision, but they are feeble with lyrics and vain with rhyme. They don't know what it's like to lose your job to a machine or live in a world of ten billion people and still feel lonely. They don't understand the effect of the incessant heat, and they can't long for rain or a cool breeze. They can't sing about breakups or the mother of your child leaving you for a woman. They can't write anti-war, anti-establishment, anti-corporate choruses that students chant in the streets. In the years around the War, the sad years, Matt was in his element, at his peak.

Quinn thinks Matt would have liked Kerguelen, the harsh and isolated scenery. He would have admired the reserved population of farm-fishermen. He's a signed-up Humanist; people, nature, the planet, these are the only things that matter to him. He has no time for High-Tech or Transhumans. To him the Earth is sacred, and he doesn't see the logic in traveling to Titan. Humanists will never leave this planet and nothing will dissuade them, not scorching temperatures or rising sea levels. They believe they are connected to every rock, tree, and river, and if they left Earth they'd shrivel up and die. Transhumans, on the other hand, see no future on Earth; they see their future in the stars, in the universe. Mars didn't work, but Titan waits for them.

The other significant guest not joining Quinn on the Cloud Ship is Jin, Quinn's closest friend. Jin is her confidant, her go-to person when she needs to complain, or cry, or laugh. She's her sometimes soul mate, her constant bullshit detector, her work alter ego and counterpart, and she's a refreshingly contrary figure to Matt. Jin's a pledged Transhuman who loves Tech, worships AI, and holds an obsessively optimistic view of the future. As a teenager, she pined for CRISPR gene editing to change her eye color to yellow, greenish-yellow, cat eyes. Her parents refused, but she eventually got her wish: her irises now glint a greenish-yellow hue—a side effect of the feline flu (FF) virus. Jin is currently recovering from FF, her third bout, so she's strictly grounded.

FF mutated from a cat virus. It started showing up a while back in people who'd had long exposures to felines. Extreme temperatures caused a switch in the feline gene trigger, and a once-benign virus mutated in the animal's cell. The toxoplasmosis shifted to birds, then to small mammals, then to big mammals and humans. It thwarted the human immune system by entering the genome and killing off any immune cells that endangered it. In the early 2040s, 5 percent of the world's population died during the pandemic. A DNA vaccine worked for a while, then the virus mutated, in some cases every day, so there was enormous variation between strains. A new strain meant a new vaccine, and it took years to get on top of the pandemic.

# Eight

# It's not meant to be raining.

THE CLOUD SHIP IS at capacity. There are 256 people on board, or 257, counting Tig. But Quinn's sure he's over the line, so he doesn't qualify. Now, the only one missing is Mori.

✱✱✱

Mori is pleased with himself; a perfect run, no glitches. This time the tiger team reached new heights basking in the radiance of the lofty canopy. Comments on the menu are filtering down, and what a success. Quinn's dress was a coup, and she wore it for him. She wore it because she loves him—she just doesn't know it yet. Now he's anxious to get up there and savor the accolades. Man of the moment. Tycoon of his time. Entrepreneur of his era. Yes, he needs to get up there, greet his guests, and bask in the glory of their comments. Of course, Lise will be there and he'll have to navigate her surly persona; what an abrasive moo she turned out to be.

He ponders what Quinn has told her mother, what excuses she spieled to her. Did she tell her it was too soon and she was only 80 percent? Perhaps she said she changed her mind and left it at that. After all, it's a private matter, between the two of them.

Abruptly, he reconsiders his position: Of course, Lise will know what happened. This is what they talked about on the grass, after he was asked to leave. What did Quinn say? Did she tell them there was no sex? That he has trouble . . . *No, no, she wouldn't, she's not like that.*

Maybe she told Lise that Mori didn't realize the Sun was a star. When he looked up at the night sky, at all the sparkling stars, he never realized the Sun, their Sun, was one of them. Quinn explained this after they arrived in Kerguelen, that solar flares come from stars and the Sun is a G-type, yellow dwarf star. Surely, this is a common mistake. She's a scientist. Not everyone can be expected to know the Sun is a star.

Okay then, what did they talk about? *Fuck, Lise knows.* She knows everything. She was clearly compliant. She must have encouraged her daughter not to go through with it—of course, she did. He knew it. Lise doesn't want Quinn to marry him. She thinks Mori is too old for her and not smart enough for her genius daughter.

✳✳✳

On board the Cloud Ship, Ada opens a delicate hand, "I feel rain."

The woman standing next to her, the one who tried to eat her serviette, agrees. "I know what you mean. I get that sensation all the time. It's very strange."

"No, I feel rain. It's raining," Ada affirms. "Oh, this is lovely."

Quinn gazes at the swirling mist above her; gentle rain drips from the top of the cloud, and the tiny droplets splash on her forearms and scatter over the trays of food and into drinks. Guests giggle; some seek refuge under the bar, others stand in the open and shriek with joy.

Quinn's Band vibrates. It's Mori. She steps away from the crowd.

"Is it raining?"

"Yes. Yes, it is. It's lovely. Did you do this?"

"Down . . . now." His signal drifts in and out.

"Sorry? What?"

". . . as possible."

"What?"

The call ends. She holos him. He doesn't answer. She tries again, still no answer.

Her gear is in the utility room located at the far end of the platform. Steadily, calmly, she makes her way, as fast as she can, in her white, knee-high, silicon boots. Her module is neatly stowed in a pigeonhole. Opening the device, she calls up the G12 and immediately switches it to climate function—live and predictive weather forecasting. It shows no rain; it's cloudless, blue skies and a little moisture in the upper atmosphere. She resets and launches again: still no rain, less than 3 percent precipitation.

Comprehending weather patterns is a complex task, it requires an understanding of atmospheric science, physics and chemistry. But sometimes it just comes down to common sense. There are no clouds over Kerguelen; it's in the Southern Hemisphere, 40 degrees south, but still too far from the South Pole to be affected by a low pressure system. So where did this precipitation come from, how did it get here, and why doesn't it show on her climate model?

Shutting the program down, she heads out the door. It's still raining. She shuffles to the edge of the platform and peers at the sky above—dark grey clouds from horizon to horizon. It makes no sense. She heads back to the utility room, reopens the module, and checks the data. The G12 doesn't make mistakes. The climate model shows no clouds, no rain. She begins to doubt herself: Where is Mori? Why won't he answer? Why is it raining, and what's up with her climate model?

Her father is a cynic. A doubter and a believer in conspiracy theories, he trusts no one and has taught Quinn to always have a contingency plan. She launches a suicide virus on her module. It eats everything it touches; the climate program is destroyed and the worm devours all her data. She has a backup—of course, she has a back up—buried deep in the SpinnerNet. She'll sort it out later, but right now she needs to get everyone down, off the platform, as soon as possible. She has a bad feeling about this.

Outside on the Cloud Platform, it continues to rain. Some of the guests are reveling in getting wet, standing in the open, letting the rain douse their skin and soak their clothes, while others have taken shelter under the tables or under the bar.

Quinn spies Lise across the room and calls her over. They rendez-vous in the middle of the room, Tig hovering beside Lise like a loyal Labrador.

"Darling, what's wrong?" Lise asks when she sees the look of panic on Quinn's face.

"It's not meant to be raining. I've a bad feeling there's more coming. We need to get everyone down."

"Okay."

"Just this once, tell me, honestly, what do you think of Mori?"

"You want to talk about this now?'

"Yes."

"He's too old for you. He changed his surname name to Eco—says a lot about a person. His brother, Niels, is having fetal blood trans-fusions to rejuvenate his body and mind, he may never get old. And eMpower may have a hundred million pledges on social media, but they are in deep shit."

"Well, maybe you should have said something earlier, because this situation, right here, right now, it's not good. Something is very wrong."

"Antarctica? Whose idea was it?"

*Fuck.*

"Shun Mantra," Lise continues. "Know the name? Ever heard them mention it?"

"No. Who the fuck is Shun Mantra?"

"Startup with a lot of Coin. Mori and Niels are board members, and they're making big political donations to New Federation. Dirac Devine. Global elections next year. He's running, and New Fed has a ticket."

"Take the first Pod." Tig points to Quinn. "You're coming with me."

"I'm not leaving everyone here."

"Yes, you are."

"No, actually, I'm not. You go with Lise. I'll get everyone into the Pods, then I'll follow."

Tig turns to Lise. "She comes with us."

Lise places her hand on Tig's forearm. "I'll go, and I'll take Ada. You stay with Quinn. Look after her until she's safe."

"Not the way it works—we go together."

"Not this time," Lise says.

They glare at each other, both determined to get their own way. Finally, Tig's frown softens.

"Fuck," he concedes. "Go then, use the Comms, let me know when you're safe."

"Comms?" Quinn asks. "What the fuck is going on?" Whisper technology uses an ultrasound algorithm to recognize voices and the electrical signals of users. It's reliable and secure, but only used for highly sensitive information.

Lise calmly cups Quinn's face and kisses both cheeks. "See you on dry land." She casually makes her way through the crowd, even pauses to chat with a guest, before raising a hand to Ada and calling her over.

"Hey," Tig interrupts. "What's with the rain?"

"A Sky River: a convergence of water in the upper atmosphere. Sitting right above us, it could get worse, much worse. It could bring down the Ship."

"Okay. How many guests?"

"Two hundred and fifty-six, no, seven, two fifty-seven, counting you. We have, what, maybe ten Pods, so that's . . . That's? What is that?" Her brain seizes.

"Twenty-five and a half. There are fourteen Pods, not ten, so eighteen people per Pod, too many. Each Pod carries four hundred kilos. We stretch it to six, a maximum eight guests in each. We do two rounds, it'll take . . . a few minutes." Again, he points a finger at her. "Get everyone together, send them to the dock. Whatever you do, don't freak 'em out. I'll get them into the Pods. Disaster averted."

She nods. It's a good plan, a sensible plan. She may have underestimated his life skills.

"Give me your boots," he says.

"Why?"

"Not the right footwear for disaster prevention."

"Yes, yes, of course." She unzips her silicon boots and hands them to him. He takes them, looks deeply into her eyes, then promptly throws them aside.

A torrent of water hits the Ship.

"Go," he says, and she's off, fleeing into the crowd. "Wait," he calls after her.

She spins around.

"Switch that off." He points at her cloud dress. "You look ridiculous."

*Shit.* "I'm not wearing anything under . . ."

He gives her a look, like he's known her forever and is somehow deeply disappointed.

No time for regrets; her task is to save the day—or to assist the Cyborg who is about to save the day. Securing the crowd's attention, she announces that the event is in two parts, and this is just the beginning. Amazing, yes, and now it's time to descend, because there's a lot more fun and excitement waiting for them on dry land and they are a little bit behind schedule. She maneuvers them into one giant herd, like they're curly-horned sheep, shepherding them with her arms, from left to right, toward the dock.

It's going to be okay. Everyone will get off the platform. The rain will still come, but everyone will get down and they'll wait out the storm in the research station. Disaster averted. They'll all survive, and one day they'll reminisce: what a funny old weird event this turned out to be. And then, while everyone is mingling and drying off, and giggling about how the rain ruined their best clothes and good shoes, she'll use Mori's QM to retrieve the G12 from the SpinnerNet and find out what the fuck is going on with the weather.

Lightning cracks. Rain is imminent, a deluge pending, but there is time. She must not cause a panic; she must get everyone to the dock. Disaster averted.

Except not yet. Guests begin to slip and slide across the platform. Water has greased the Acrogel base. Quinn falls, then rights herself, then falls again. She slips and stumbles, and everyone follows her lead, slipping and falling. Carefully, they help each other up and she continues to usher them toward the dock.

The Pods are on the second round. Everyone will get down. They are wet and bruised, but they're safe. Another piercing crack and it begins. A true deluge. The cloud mist above the platform dissipates. Quinn skates to the railing at the edge of the platform and tilts her head to the sky: blackness from horizon to horizon. It's going to be big, but they only need a few more minutes, they'll all get down.

Disaster averted.

A boom of thunder. The platform shudders; grumbling sounds erupt from within and the structure groans and crackles, then tilts to one side. They've been hit. The floor is now a southbound river. Quinn is flipped into the moving waterway; slipping and sliding, she glides on vale of water to the far end of the platform, the end opposite the dock, the end without an exit option. The railing cracks and falls away. The platform buckles, both sides tilting in opposing directions. She's pinned against the far wall, trapped by gravity and falling water.

The dock is where she needs to be, but she's going nowhere. The structure suddenly drops and free falls for a few seconds before abruptly stabilizing.

*Shit, I'm going to die wearing a stupid cloud dress.* The only way out is down. She could jump, if she had her wingsuit—yes, she could jump. Where is her wingsuit? Her backpack, of course; it's with the luggage, and the luggage is in the utility room. She's at the far end of the platform; it's behind her. The wingsuit is in the room behind her.

She crawls along the wall until she feels the door seal.

It's locked.

She swipes her Band. The light switches from red to green—the door slides open. Inside, the roof is split and water's gushing in; the storage compartments have tumbled from the walls and luggage is scattered across the floor. Her pack is fluorescent red—for safety—not hard to find. She grabs it and pulls on her wingsuit. This is her plan. It's a stupid plan. She knows the pitfalls—she can't fly in this rain—but it's the only plan she has. Plan A—she's got goggles, a helmet, and a parachute. She can fly the slipstream. It will take her away from the storm, out to sea. When the wind dies down, she'll launches the shoot. It'll break her fall, and she'll land in the ocean. The wingsuit is made from a 4D, shape-shifting, transformable polymer and saltwater is a catalyst—first contact with the ocean and she'll be buoyant. The chute might malfunction, the impact might kill her, but she won't drown. Some comfort.

There's also an autopilot option. The suit can fly itself—at least, she thinks that's what "auto option" means. She's never actually tested the function, but it's called auto, so surely it's automated. Should have paid more attention when she bought the thing.

She switches the suit to auto and it tightens around her, adjusting to her body form and weight. "I'm not going to die," she says out loud. "Science will save me."

A crack of lightning and she flinches; her nerves are shot. Her heart pounds. The hydro engines on the platform pause, the magnetic field abates, and the structure begins to free-fall again.

Quinn scoots to the edge and peers over into nothingness—a void of murky shadows and featureless mist.

"Okay," she says, "here goes. One, two, eight, nine, ten."

She jumps.

# Nine

# The rain came.

"AND THE RIVER RISES, flows over its banks, and carries them all away, like mayflies floating downstream: they stare at the sun, then all at once there is nothing. A deluge." That's from Gilgamesh.

The rain came. Never seen anything like it, a river poured from the sky. The Cloud Ship landed in a thousand pieces. And she was nowhere. And I couldn't do it again. Not again. Fuck, to come all this way and lose her again, it wasn't fucking fair. I had to make sure, though; I had to check, so we searched, Martha2 and me, we searched the oceans, and Martha2 was the one who found her. Instinct. She knows the winds. She worked it out and found her floating in the water. But I was too late. They got to her first. A black, metallic monster rose out of the ocean like some ModTech Godzilla and the tin machine took her away, under the sea. I was close, so close. But I'll find her.

# Ten

# No one survived.

QUINN HAS AN AVERSION to full-body immersion. Bathing is fine, rinsing is not a problem, paddling and dipping her feet into a stream is not unpleasant. But diving under the water leaves her cold. Water might cover 78 percent of the planet's surface, but she prefers to walk the foreshore to diving under a wave. She likes to watch the rhythm of the swell, and she likes the idea of creeks and rivers and streams, the way the water bubbles and eddies around rocks and boulders. But, she doesn't like getting wet.

She wakes on a soft bed in a pale blue room feeling hungover and dehydrated. Her mouth is dry and her head hurts. A pungent smell hangs in the air. She has no idea where she is, and she can't remember how she got here. She lifts her head, it throbs, and she drops it back to the bed and gazes around.

She's in a small room, an enclosed blue space. The walls aren't solid walls; they're membranes—translucent membranes filled with bubbling fluid. The air is blue and hazy, and a soft gurgling sound resonates, possibly coming from the walls. She's inside a cell—not a prison cell, but the cell of a living organism. Quinn thinks she's quantum, a nucleus, surrounded by metabolic activity. She's inside the body of a water-borne organism, and she's not alone. Outside there are others. She can see them; their papery shadows move in and out of focus on the other side of the membrane walls.

She closes her eyes. She needs to remember.

What happened? *I jumped into an abyss.*

Where did she land? *In the ocean. I landed in the ocean.*

She remembers floating. She was floating in the warm sea. Darkness came, and she watched the stars arrive. For hours and hours she gazed at the night sky, focused on the stars. Then dawn came, the stars disappeared, and there was a bird—a beautiful, rust-colored bird. It glided and circled above her. It was her bird. Her bird from the Island. Then a giant black behemoth appeared on the horizon. It scared the shit out of her, and the bird flew away.

They fished her from the water. She remembers people talking to her, all at once; she couldn't understand what was going on, what they were saying. Someone wrapped a recovery blanket around her, and she liked the feeling—dry and comfortable at last. They asked her to hold out her arm, her right arm, and they took her Band, slipped it straight off her wrist and she hasn't seen it since. *That's illegal. Why would they do that?*

She remembers what they said: The wingsuit took her fifty kilometers, right to the edge of the storm, and the recovery vessel Prismatic picked her up the following day.

The ship is a monument to High-Tech design. Slick black graphene, one hundred and fifty meters high, it emerged from the ocean like a giant, thirsty insect, sucking and leaching water—that's how it runs, on hydropower. In monsoons or tsunamis, it tethers itself to the seabed with expandable harnesses that move in sync with the bloating water.

Now she remembers. She's being kept in a cluster cell for rest and observation. Someone said that: a cluster cell, rest and observation. They explained that the clusters are continuous loops of semi-transparent rooms filled with blue light. Blue is the healing color.

The door opens and a man enters. He stands by her bed and looks down at her. "Hello. Do you remember me? I'm Hau."

She nods.

"How are you feeling?"

"Thirsty."

"I'll send food. And clothes—you'll need something to wear. Later this morning, de-briefing. Do you remember anything?"

She nods.

"Good. That's good. The team will look after you. I'll see you again in a couple of hours." He turns to leave.

She calls after him, "The smell. What's the smell?"

"It's just the air. It's full of microbes."

*The air, just the air.*

He takes another step and she calls again, "The humming noise. What is it?"

"Ah, the noise. Energy generation. We use a hybrid nanomaterial, an alloy of titanium; turns seawater into hydrogen fuel. It works as a photocatalyst, activating chemical reactions when exposed to sunlight. Has a wide-ranging spectrum; can even turn ultraviolet light into energy."

She nods. She understands—they're drawing seawater up through the walls, over the titanium panels, and it resonates, makes an incessant gurgling sound.

Hau leaves.

She doesn't feel well. Her head's spinning, and there's a terrible sense of dread rising in her stomach. She closes her eyes and thinks about titanium, element number twenty-two on the periodic table. Tig is made from titanium, and it's the loveliest, silver-colored metal—low density but strong, stronger than steel and half the weight. Forged in the depths of collapsing stars, it's loved by Tech types. Zap it with a high-power laser, and you create small oxygen vacancies of missing molecules; use these to split water by stealing the oxygen, then the hydrogen can be used for fuel. Half of Tig is made from titanium. It's just the loveliest metal.

*I'm not well.*

*** 

A girl with carbon-colored hair and charcoal eyes enters carrying food and clothes. She's beautiful, the most beautiful woman Quinn has ever seen. Her complexion is abnormally pale, her skin milky, her pallor emphasized by her dark features. She tells Quinn, in a thick Irish accent, that her name is Geller, and Quinn is besotted. She can't stop looking at her.

"'Tis cos of te light," Geller says, her back to Quinn. "Te blue light, me pigments, they'll autocorrect when I spend more time on lan', in te sunlight. I've been 'ere too long, but there's not much for me back 'ome, an' it's a job, fast-track promoshun."

"Was hoping you were an alien."

"Naw, not from te stars." She smiles. "Just from Galway."

"The high part?"

"Naw, te low part."

The underwater part.

She hands Quinn a fistful of dynamic hydration tablets, "Suppos' to be two, twice a day, but just take 'em all at once. You'll be needin 'em."

Quinn swallows eight.

Geller points to the diamond hanging from Quinn's neck, "If tat's speshul, maybe take it off. Keep it in your pocket."

Quinn changes into a lightweight grey polyester suit and stows the diamond in her pocket. Then she follows Geller though a series of cool sapphire corridors and into a small white room, where Hau and a male companion wait. The door shuts firmly behind her as she enters. Three molded white chairs rise from the floor, and Hau and his companion take seats side by side, leaving the third, directly across from them, for her. Geller stands behind her. An intimidating setup; all eyes are on her.

"No one survived," says Hau in a very clear and precise voice. "Nineteen hundred and sixty-two people died. There are no survivors."

"Sorry, I don't understand, there weren't . . . there weren't nineteen hundred . . . whatever, people, there weren't that many people on the Cloud. Most of them got down. I saw them. They got down. There were fourteen Pods, each one holds four hundred kilos, so a maximum of eight in each. Two rounds, they all got down. We did the math."

He leans forwards, and she feels his hot breath. "Pay attention. They got off the ship; they went back to the research station. Not long after, the flood hit. The glacier burst, and the river flooded. It washed the town away. No one survived. Except you."

"No, no, no." She covers her face with her hands.

"Yes, yes, yes. The research center is gone. The village, Grande Terre, washed away."

*Fuck.*

"The SkyRiver—it filled the glacier, the Cook Glacier, and it burst, flooding the village. Washed it all away."

*This is a dream, a terrible, terrible dream.* "Lise . . . my, my, my mother?"

"Recovered. Identified. In the morgue."

The air is sucked from her; her chest heaves, and she wants to scream. She wants them to leave. She needs to get out of here. She slumps back in her chair and her eyes well with tears.

"We have some . . . concerns." Hau's companion stifles a cough. "Why did you take a wingsuit?"

"What?"

"Answer the question."

"What was the question?"

"The wingsuit."

"I don't know. We took everything; we were going to Antarctica."

"The G12, where is it?"

"I don't know." *I can't do this.*

"We think you do," Hau says.

She locks eyes with him. "I want to go home."

A sly smirk. "You won't be going home."

She leans toward him. Her left hand rises, it forms a hard fist, and it punches him, one sharp jab right in the middle of his nose. It really hurts her knuckles, and they sting like they're on fire. But she didn't do it. It happened, but she didn't think it or plan it. It was her left arm, and she's not left-handed. It moved on its own, an autonomous action. She's never punched anyone in her life. She doesn't even know how to punch someone. She looks at her throbbing hand, then looks across at Hau, shocked.

He is visibly shaken. Dark liquid drips from his nostrils. It runs over his lips and into his mouth, coating his teeth, and it's surreally beautiful against his pale white skin. He wipes his nose, flicking the blood from the back of his hand, splattering spots across the table and all over her new grey poly suit. She sits back in her chair.

Without a word, Geller steps forward, hauls her from her seat, and escorts her back to her amoeba-like room, where she lies on the floor, curls into a ball, and cries. She can't believe they're dead. Her heart—her poor heart is breaking.

# Eleven

# There is something
# in the red purse.

The conveyor belts of moist air snaking thousands of kilometers around the Arctic and Antarctic circles are known as SkyRivers. If they cease meandering, they become static weather systems; fixed to a single location, they can deliver a deluge in minutes. On that day in the Kerguelen Islands, a SkyRiver halted, and then it released a cataclysmic downpour that fractured the Cook Glacier and flooded the Island. Now, the little town of Grande Terre is no more than a peaceful lake of remembrance. But the SkyRiver was adrift and disoriented; it had wandered too far north. Clouds don't leave the South Pole, so how did it get there?

\*\*\*

Every day, Quinn has visions of her mother, like shimmering holograms. They appear with erratic regularity. She glances up and Lise is there, perched on the end of her bed; or she glides through the door, tilts her head toward Quinn, and smiles; or she sits at the table in the room, contemplating an equation. A relentless barrage of apparitions fill Quinn's dreams and haunt her walking moments: the way Lise laughs, the way she sips her tea, the way she raises her eyebrow when she's thinking.

Quinn's response to all of this is to lie on her bed and cry, unheard; water flows continuously upward through the membrane walls, and the noise deadens her sobs. Inside, she is empty. Inside, there is a void of nothingness—a hollow space that aches and hurts all the time. The days run into each other, and her cycle of memories plays like a show reel, a collection of the best and worst moments, the vignettes of their lives together.

✶✶✶

It's grief's duty to render time illusive, and Quinn is unsure how many days have now passed inside the gurgling monolith; more than four, less than ten. Yesterday, Hau hauled her back into the colorless interview room and threw rounds of questions at her: Who is Ada? She wasn't on the guest list; why was she at the wedding? Did Quinn know what Lise was working on? What was the subject of her next book? Where did Quinn meet Mori? Why wasn't he on the platform? What did she know about his business? Why were they going to Antarctica?

Her mind was vague and misty, and she couldn't answer any of these questions. But when he asked her about the G12, her senses consolidated and she looked him straight in the eyes. "Honestly, it's a bit of mystery. If it turns up, I'll let you know." Then she gave him a wily smile. When she did, he knew she knew where it was, that she'd hidden it somewhere, but she didn't care.

After punching Hau, her left arm shut down. It lay limp and motionless on the bed beside her for hours. Concentrating, she willed it to be active—to brush the hair from her eyes, to scratch her nose, to wiggle its fingers. But it was completely nonresponsive.

Geller found the affliction fascinating. She took pleasure in placing it in awkward positions, like behind Quinn's back, or around her neck, just to see what would happen. Nothing happened. Then she picked it up and let it drop over and over, and still no response. When she gave it a Chinese burn, however, it shook itself loose and slapped her.

After few hours, the arm returned to normal.

"We're too intelligent for grief," Quinn tells Geller. "It's debilitating. We should have evolved from this stupefied state centuries ago. How can humankind possibly survive if we feel like this? Everything hurts. I have this giant hole in my heart, and it hurts all the fucking time."

Geller listens but offers no sympathy. After several days of observing Quinn in her grief-infused malaise, she tells her to stop whining over the past and concentrate on the future.

The future means tracking Mori down, finding out what he knew, and possibly killing him. The future sounds exhausting.

"Tell me the truth," says Quinn, "on a scale of one to ten, how stupid you do think I am? First, I agree to marry a man I don't love. Then, he doesn't show at the event, the G12 stops working and he was the last to use it, everyone dies, and, finally, after years of trying to get people interested in the G12, all of a sudden people are very interested in it."

"On a scale av one ta ten, you're a five, typical av 'umankind," says Geller.

Quinn makes a formal request to see Lise, to see her body, which is stored in the hull of the Ship, but it's denied.

✱✱✱

In the evenings an autonomous drone flits about, sterilizing Quinn's cell with UV lamps that sanitize the surfaces, clearing up the microbes shed by the Ship's human residents. The place is a pit of bacteria and mold, hence the pungent smell. It's a bit hard to open a window underwater. Quinn is familiar with her environment now, and the dull hum of the drone fuses with the gurgling water walls. She finds the sound soporific; often, it lulls her to sleep.

Today, the drone pauses unexpectedly. She opens her eyes; a pale man is standing next her bed. He's wearing a grey uniform. He might be a guard.

He leans toward her and says, "Follow me."

"Where are we going?"

"Just get up."

Quinn rolls out of bed, still half asleep, and as she pulls up her suit she spies another guard standing at the door. He checks the corridor, a nervous expression on his face, then gives his buddy hurry-up hand signals.

*They're not supposed to be here.* "I'm not going anywhere," she says.

The guy closer to her points a small, silver laser at her head. "Move."

Her left hand grabs his laser, and then it shoots him in the chest. He drops to the floor. The gun swivels to the open doorway and shoots his friend. He drops to the floor.

*Fuck.* She's horrified. Slowly, very carefully, she takes the laser out of her afflicted appendage and places it at the far end of the bed, out of reach. She's a Pacifist, a signed-up, taken-the-frigging-pledge, Pacifist for Life.

The Pacifist for Life Pledge was signed by over a billion people at the end of the RE Wars. They vowed never to pick up a weapon or to hurt anyone or anything. Quinn has never held a laser or a gun and has certainly never shot anyone. Until now. What has she done? Are they dead or stunned? She picks up the small, silver gun. The weapon is double-barreled—one cylinder for kill and one for stun. She jumps off the bed and checks the bodies; they're breathing. So the weapon was set to stun. She needs to get them out of her cell.

She drags the guy from inside her cell into the corridor—not an easy task, especially because she has to wiggle him sideways to get him out the door. Inert bodies are heavier than they look. She leaves the weapon on the floor beside the guards, scurries inside, and seals the door. Then, nervous, she waits and listens.

Nothing happens, no sounds, no alarms, and no one passes. *Damn, should have kept the weapon.*

She lies down on the bed and waits and listens. Soon, there is movement. The stunned men are found. The bodies are collected. Then the door opens and Geller enters.

"'Ad some nocturnal visitors?"

Quinn nods.

"It's sorted. There's a lot goin' on. Distracshun. Might be a good time ta go see your ma. I'm a grand believer in seein' te dead, helps with closure, and you certainly need it. Come wit me."

✷✷✷

They take the skylift straight down to a level called the Cellar, an empty area so vast Quinn can barely see the other side. The light down here is not blue; it's cool and grey. In the far corner are towers of pre-fabricated shelving.

"Build 'em as we need 'em," Geller says. She means the racks of scaffolding, holding two thousand long, rectangular boxes.

"This is the morgue?"

"Disaster plannin'. 'Olds fifty tousand. Owned by Shun Mantra."

Goose bumps. It's a distinctive name. "Shun Mantra. It sounds like a cult. Who are they?"

"Don't really know, but tink about it: Shun Mantra, Shun Mantra. Ring any bells?"

Quinn shakes her head.

"Shun Mantra, Transhuman. Get it?"

"No."

"Te letters, tey've reconfigured te letters."

"Really, are you sure? Shun Mantra. Transhuman. I don't think it's—"

"Trust me, tey match, 'tis te same letters."

"Okay, okay, Shun Mantra, Transhuman. It's just not very clever for, you know, Tech types."

"Tey're rich. I don't tink tey care." Geller checks the information stored in her band. "Tis way."

The scaffolding forms a U-shape at the far side of the Cellar. Drones flit between the shelves, and Geller instructs them to move a casket onto a raised platform.

"We don't 'ave a world a time." She points her band at the casket, it releases a digital key, and the seal dissolves. They move forward and peer inside.

Visually, the corpse is quite acceptable. Quinn expected more deterioration. She'd braced herself for bloating and swelling, but the body is in good condition. They retrieved her early. She's still wearing her formal clothes. The time between leaving the Cloud Ship and the flood was several hours. There was plenty of time to change, but perhaps the party continued at the Station—maybe they were making the most of the occasion, mingling, finishing the alcohol and food. The jeweled red choker still circles her languid neck, but her shoes are missing. Her hand clutches a small, red purse; the strap is wrapped many times round her wrist. On the day the Cloud Ship came down, Lise wasn't wearing a red choker, and she wasn't carrying a red purse.

"This isn't her," says Quinn. "It's Ada, her partner. Ex-partner."

"I'm workin' wit idiots."

✶✶✶

When they return to Quinn's cell, she confronts Geller.

"Why am I still here? It's been two weeks. The interrogation is finished. They don't need me. Why don't they send me home?"

"'Tis been one week, an' you're in limbo. No one knows what ta do wit you. Caught between squabblin' players. Your ma 'ad influential friends, but you also 'ave a wealthy enemy."

"Enemy? I don't have—"

"Yes, you do. Niels Eco. We're not dense. Two tousand people don't just die wit'out warnin'. Not in 2049. Someone knows sometin'. If it wasn't you, ten who was it? Mori? An' why? We want ta know what's goin' on. An' *everyone* wants ta know where te G12 is. Was it workin', was it not workin'? So, tell me: what te fuck is goin' on?"

Geller's dark eyes stare at Quinn.

Quinn sighs. "The catastrophe was a natural phenomenon, Mother Nature against humanity, and we lost. But something set it off. I checked the G12. I checked it twice a day, every day. It didn't show any rain coming, and it's never wrong. Which means someone set a ghost, a cover, so I couldn't see the real data. Mori was last person to use it." She shrugs.

"We've not found 'im. He's missin'. You know, 'tis a good ting to 'ave enemies. It'll give your life a purpose. Sometin' ta focus on, nigh ya 'ave no one, an' nothin'." She wiggles a finger at Quinn. "Te records show Ada as officially missin', while Lise is listed as deceased. Te bodies were collected from te depths of te ocean an' identified by their Bands, so Lise an' Ada, tey swapped Bands. Now, why te fuck would they do tat?"

Quinn shakes her head; she can't image what went on in the final hours or minutes before the flood hit.

"If your motor's not dead, 'ten where is she?"

Quinn freezes. *Does impending death count as an absolute necessity? How long did they have? Minutes? Seconds? How long does it take to activate a time travel portal? She said she'd use it if she absolutely had to.* Quinn has a lightning-bolt moment, pins and needles run along her forearm. *Good lordt, there is something in the red purse. The way Ada was gripping it. The way the strap was wound around her wrist.* She looks at Geller. "I think there's something in her purse."

"Back we go."

∗∗∗

The Cellar is now active. The morning shift is busy checking readings and scanning monitors showing the ocean floor. Geller offers her credentials, saying Hau approved Quinn's request to see the corpse of her mother. The guards comply. They locate the draw, load it onto the platform, and, when Quinn confirms she's ready to view the corpse, they open the casket.

She creeps forward and the guards follow. She leans into the casket, and the guards also lean; there's the purse, right there, but she can't open it—not like this, they're too close. This isn't going to work.

"Just let it all out. 'Tis perfectly fine ta *cry*." Geller slaps Quinn on the back. "Just let it all out."

*Let what all out?*

"No need ta 'old it all in, if you need time alone . . ."

*Ohhh—let it all out, make a scene. Buy some privacy.* Channeling her weepy, emotional self is not difficult for Quinn, she's a bit soppy these days. Hanging her head, she wrings her hands and emits several long moans, followed by a series of heroic sobs. Geller gestures to the guards that they should back off, give her some privacy. Slinging an arm over their shoulders, she spins them around.

Quinn dives into the casket and tugs on the purse, but the latch is stuck. It won't budge. She tries to unwrap the strap from Ada's wrist, but it's wrapped in knots and she's making it worse. *Lever it*, she thinks, *prise it open with something . . . but what?*

*Teeth.* She leans into the casket, grips the latch with her canines, and squeezes. It springs open, revealing a watertight sachet that she grabs and quickly slips into her pocket. She closes the purse, composes herself, and steps away from the casket.

✳✳✳

They make it back to Quinn's cell without incident.

"You were very good," Quinn says, impressed by Geller's bravado. "Weren't you scared?"

"No, 'tis my ting. My super power. Got Urbach-Wiethe disease when I was eight. Developed lesions all over me brain, ruined te amygdala regions in both 'emispheres. Now I can't process fear."

"You never get scared?"

"No. I also 'ave a bias t'wards trustin' strangers. So you're not speshal."

Quinn confesses her super power: "I have Raynaud's syndrome. I don't get hot. Not like other people, anyway."

"Cool. Literally."

Quinn opens the sachet. Inside is a piece of parchment torn from a notebook; scrawled across it is a black zigzag line.

"Tat's it? One squiggly line. Looks like a worm."

Lise has distinctive handwriting: she scrawls like a maniac, making large, loopy words and sums across the page, editing as she goes, crossing out figures and writing new ones over the top. Her handwriting is generally illegible. But she always uses an automatic pencil and recycled parchment. Quinn knows this is her mark.

"'Tis a W. W for wild, or wave. No, 'tis water, W for water. Or war. W for war."

Quinn turns the note around, then she turns it around again, and again; from all directions, it looks like a zigzag worm.

"It'll come ta ya later—during sex, or when you're tinkin' about sometin' completely unrelated. Tat's how it works. But Ada, she must 'ave been a good friend. Loved your moter very much ta swap Bands, risk 'er life. Either tat or she was a bad friend, an' a tief at tat."

Just as she finishes saying this, warning bells ring, amber lights flash in the corridor, and there's movement outside Quinn's cell; the blurred image of guards responding. *Shit, we've been caught.* She shoves the note into her mouth and swallows it.

"We're movin'," says Geller. "A new location, means a new disaster. Wait 'ere."

*Might have overreacted.*

*✶*

Geller returns twenty minutes later. "Tsunami, South Africa, east coast, near Durban," she says. "I've organized a drone, but you're not 'eadin' 'ome. There's a containment island close by. It'll drop ya tere. In a few days you'll be picked up by 'exad. You can't stay 'ere. You're not safe, you need ta git off tis vessel."

*Containment island?* "I'm going to prison?"

"Okay, stay 'ere ten. Or, I'll tell ya what, let's swap places. I'll go sit on te lovely white sand. You stay 'ere an' slowly turn white."

"Sand's gone, most islands are . . ."

Geller glares, and it's unpleasant.

"A tropical paradise," Quinn says weakly. "Can't wait."

"Good."

They make their way into the skylift. When the coast is clear, Geller takes Quinn's hand and pulls her onto the landing deck and into bright sunshine. It's blinding, but there's no time to adjust; a circular, single seat drone hovers impatiently, tapping it legs up and down on the deck. As they approach, the propellers ease and the hatch falls open.

Quinn climbs up and straps herself in. Geller double-checks the harness, then leans forward and kisses Quinn gently on cheek. Then the drone ascends.

# Twelve

# They're dodo birds.

THE FLIGHT TAKES HALF the morning. It's a hypnotic journey—deep blue water below, hazy blue sky around her, and the very straight horizon line in the distance. She travels northeast and eventually descends over a small atoll in the Indian Ocean. There, the drone drops her onto the roof of a disused shipping container.

It doesn't fly way; it is not headed back to Prismatic. Instead, it slowly falls apart, disassembling itself into a care pack: food, basic medical supplies, and a drinking filter for seawater. The rotors are edible wafers and the cockpit is made from a starchy carbohydrate substance.

Quinn climbs down to the beach and filters some seawater. She breaks the cockpit into pieces, mixes one with the water, and drinks the thick soup it turns into. Then she sits and stares out at the water.

\*\*\*

She eats the entire drone in two days, then realizes it was supposed to last longer; she gets nothing else to eat until day four, when a gull drone arrives with food parcels and clothes.

On her tenth day of living on the atoll, inside the shipping container, she receives her second supply drop and a separate communication dispatch outlining her charges; 1,962 counts of capital murder, first degree. Apparently there's evidence of premeditation and deliberate planning.

This news pisses her off. She descends into a cycle of bitterness and anger—stomping around the island, kicking rocks, and throwing handfuls of sand at the sea birds.

This cycle continues for several days, until she realizes that loneliness feeds her obsessive thoughts and reason needs company; bereft of that, she has become a broiling, neurotic, emotional wreck. *Fuck it, it's not my problem—the truth will come out.* Stoically, she breathes in and out and lets it go.

Her shipping container home is three by eight meters, a standard size and enough space for a single person to live in—tight, but adequate. There's a separate bathing zone outside and a food prep in the far right corner. She has furniture: a bed with a honeycomb mattress (this is where she's stowed her diamond for safekeeping), and a table and two chairs, unfortunately made from compressed cardboard, a popular building material in the 2020s and '30s (it hasn't weathered well, being so close to the water' the paper layers are shredding). There's a good-size window and a sliding glass door with a view of the ocean. Gazing at the ocean occupies a great deal of her time—watching the swell rise and fall, staring at the horizon line, waiting for the sun to set, then watching it rise again. *Matt would be so proud.*

There's no Tech; she's living the Humanist Dream. Tasks are manual: she closes the cupboard doors herself, gets up and walks across the room to switch on the water heater to make tea. She hasn't manually switched on an electronic device for a decade. A stretchable, waterproof, gold-coded tattoo behind her right ear is supposed to channel her thoughts into electrical signals that power minor appliances, but it seems the device is impaired.

After a few days of manually switching on the water heater, it became automatic. Illumination, of all things, proved more complex.

The setup is kinetic: a weight-drawn bag of sand drops to the ground generating half a watt of electricity, enough to power a small LED lamp. The cycle takes forty minutes and must be constantly reset.

If she could have one more thing, she'd ask for another pillow. There is only one pillow and she's a two-pillow person: one for her head and one to cover her feet, to keep them warm.

She has new clothes; the drone delivered a shift dress and matching shorts in a pale taupe color, a tone favored by many of the small birds on the atoll, so she blends nicely with the natives. Her clothes are made from a pineapple fiber called Piña. She knows this because it says so on the label, *100 percent Piña*. It's a lovely fiber, soft and smooth, it doesn't crush, and it dries in no time. Unfortunately, she has no shoes. The soles of her feet are in a terrible state, cut and grazed, her toes stubbed and bruised from kicking rocks.

She has named the significant areas around the atoll: Rocky Beach, Bird Point, Crab-Pool Coast, and the Cove—the site of her shipping container home. A large section of the island is made of solid, hard-core plastic: PET, polyester, HDPE, PV, PP, PS with BPA and BPS. The entire northwest corner, over ten square kilometers, is covered with the stuff. Bonding polymers were released into the ocean in the 2020s and, like a magnet, they drew the plastic together, hardening it into a solid mass. This effectively eliminated small particles from seawater, but this pile was never recovered.

She's not completely alone on the atoll; there are many types of birds, and Quinn spends many hours watching them. She studies them so carefully, she can tell them apart. She realizes they are unique, all individuals with distinct personalities. Some are busy and never stop foraging; some are contemplative and sit and watch the sky or the tides; some are bossy, chasing other birds away. Some are passive, some aggressive; some are taupe, others are pure white or solid black. At the end of the day, they are all birds, with wings and two legs, and Quinn decides that it's better to be a bird than a human.

The flocks of gulls that inhabit the beach know her; she sits amongst them and they don't fly away. Sometimes she chases the bossy gulls or stands one-legged with them while the tide rolls back and forth. When they take off, she jumps up and runs along the sand, flapping her arms like wings, until they're all gone and she's left alone on the sand. Then she runs again, just for the sheer joy of it. She hasn't done that since she was a girl—run for joy.

One species in particular catches her attention—a flightless fowl about a meter tall. It resembles a small, fat ostrich but has tiny, useless wings, black plumes, a fluffy tail, and a slender, green-grey beak that hooks under at the tip. It's a strange, but also familiar, species; she's seen it before in books, books and documentaries—they're dodo birds. They were extinct for centuries and have now been resurrected through gene sequencing.

This flock is doing well. Many females are breading, sitting on grey eggs in ground nests scattered through the scrubby bush land that lines the foreshore. They're not shy birds, and they waddle right up to her, even the baby ones. She has a favorite, a female who's not nesting, so they hang out together. Quinn has named her Jane, after Jane Goodall, the famous primatologist.

Every afternoon, after her second nap, Quinn walks back and forth along the beach, collecting the foam and plastic litter washed in by swell. Some days there are hundreds of white foam balls, the size of baby peas, and the sand resembles a pile of snow. But it's not snow. It's petroleum-derived polystyrene. Non-biodegradable, it will last forever. She thinks one day she'll find a whole cup—an entire polystyrene cup.

Painstakingly, she collects and buries the litter in the sand dunes behind the Cove each day. This is a pointless activity, totally pointless, and she knows it—one strong onshore wind and the dune will dissolve—but she continues to do it.

To mark the passage of time, her final task for the day is to make a cairn. The northern end of the beach, a place she calls Rocky Beach, is littered with boulders and pebbles, perfect for small stone erections. Her first attempts were simple structures: five or six stones stacked randomly, one on top of the other. Now, after four weeks alone on the atoll, she's mastered the art of cairn building. Each day, she creates increasingly complex arrangements, grouping similarly shaped stones together—all the triangles, all the squares, all the circles. In the coming days, she's hoping to master the arch.

Her creative bent doesn't only include rock sculptures; she's also started drawing. The walls of her shipping container home are covered in sketches. Her left hand has talent—she just hands it a chalky rock, and it gets straight to work. It has sketched a map of the world, with details of her home, in Hobart, and where she thinks the atoll is located: southeast of South Africa, in the Indian Ocean. It has also drawn a detailed picture of the Cove and her little shipping container home on the hill, with Jane and her sitting together on the front landing.

After five weeks alone on the atoll, music comes to Quinn. It comes as she walks along the beach, so she starts to dance on the sand. Then she dances in the ocean with the water splashing around her calves. She dances on the hard roof of her shipping container; she dances on Rocky Beach while she collects rocks and catches up on her cairn building. In the afternoon, she climbs to the island's highest point and dances on the ledge overlooking the ocean. When she gets home, she dances with the dodos on her front landing.

For an entire week, she dances: rock and roll, jive, swing, ballroom, samba, the Macarena—she can't stop. She dances on her bed; she dances on her table. She dances while she eats. The music is inside her head; all the tunes, new and old, all the lyrics that she's never been good at recalling, are coming back to her, at least in part, enough to fill her head and keep her moving. She's making up for all the years and decades she's spent not dancing.

# Thirteen

# Are you a prisoner, like me?

Today is the fifteenth of November, and it's Quinn's birthday. Today she enters a new decade—she's no longer twenty-nine. Element 29 on the periodic table is copper, so last year was her year of copper. Copper is a soft and malleable metal; it possesses excellent thermal conductivity and is resistant to corrosion. It begins life warm and rich, red or orange, and then the atmosphere gets to it and it loses electrons, slowly tarnishing and turning green. She sees the similarities; her year started bright and optimistic, and then she was betrayed and now it's shit.

But her year of copper is over. Element number 30 on the periodic table is zinc. Zinc is bluish-silver, hard and brittle until it's heated, and then it softens. It can cure the common cold. If you are stung by a deadly jellyfish, zinc can save your life; the jellyfish poison pokes holes in your red blood cells, but zinc stops the potassium from leaking out. During human conception, when a sperm meets an egg, zinc explodes, sending sparks flying. Zinc is not organic, but it is alive. This year she is zinc.

Last night a dream invaded her sleep. Perfect timing for the end of her twenty-ninth year, it arrived right between copper and zinc. She woke covered in sweat, hands cold and feet frozen.

In the dream she was completely naked and heavily pregnant, and she was walking through the massive Wilkes Basin in Antarctica. Most of the ground snow had melted and been replaced by glittering salt crystals. Ferns and native grasses grew along the ridgeline of the Basin. The sky was mauve and filled with rainbow clouds, soft pinks and pale blues from horizon to horizon. The baby in her belly was heavy. She was on a mission to get to the other side, to safety, but she knew it was an impossible task and she wouldn't make it before the labor started.

The baby was coming, so she sat down on the crystallized valley floor. She was going to give birth in a super saline pool in the middle of the Wilkes Basin.

Abdominal pains roused her from her dream, and quickly she dismissed its significance. It had to be the product of an internal battle between hormones and gender. She's female, she's thirty, her body wants to have a baby, but her conscious mind knows it's not possible. She has an implant, Conscientious Prevention; she can never conceive. In a world of ten billion people, it was the right thing to do. With three billion children in the world, sixty million of them homeless, abortions are encouraged these days and IVF treatments are illegal, but the population is still growing. So, on her twenty-first birthday, she got an infertility implant. She doesn't regret it. If she decides she wants children one day she can adopt. But the conflict manifests deep in her subconscious, in Antarctica, in the Wilkes Basin.

Twenty-nine wasn't her best year, but it's over. Today, she's thirty and things are looking up. Today, there's a King Tide—a gravitational pull between the sun and the moon. The tide is eight meters higher than its usual swell, and she's found a spot, a ledge, where the gap between land and water has shrunk to twelve meters. That is still high, but twelve is better than twenty. She intends to jump; the impact might hurt, but it won't kill her. Water is not her favorite substance and she finds submersion highly unpleasant, but she thinks it's worth it, to feel the weightlessness of the world.

The tide peaks at dusk and the night comes slowly here, so she heads out late in the afternoon, knowing she has plenty of time and she'll be home before it's dark. When she reaches the jump ledge, she checks the water for obstructions: it's clear, deep blue, and calm. *Do it fast; don't think about it.* A swift run-up and she's over the edge, falling through the air—falling towards the water, falling though time and space, falling back to Earth. She closes her eyes, and it's bliss, pure bliss. She smiles, free at last—then she hits the water with a slap, and a sharp pain shimmies down her side. She skewed the entry. *Oh fuck, that hurt.*

After wobbling to the surface, she takes a breath and rolls onto her back. Her shoulder hurts. She can't lift her arm; it might be dislocated. It hurts to breathe. *Not good. Okay, focus, get back to shore. It's not far, barely a swell. Paddle. Kick. Take it easy, breathe, remember to breathe. Paddle. Kick. Breathe.*

✶✶✶

She opens her eyes. Darkness. Where is she? She's in bed, in her shipping container home. She doesn't remember getting into bed. She must have passed out when she returned and fallen asleep. The pain was awful. It was all a blur. But she's safe now. She's back in her shipping container home, and she's safe. But there's a smell, a strange smell. She pulls back the covers and finds she's naked; she doesn't remember taking off her Piña dress. She climbs out of bed to investigate the smell; something cooking on the heat element. She can't recall doing that, either, turning on the element and preparing food.

"Hey," a man's voice says. "You okay?" There's a shadow against the wall near the door, a strange silhouette.

She pulls the wrap from the bed, covers herself. "I know you," she says.

"Tig," he says.

"Fuck."

The brewing pot hisses, then bubbles over. He shuffles forward, attending to the pot, pours green mush into a cup, and hands it to her. She scurries back to the bed. He turns on the kinetic light and pulls up a chair. "You were trying to fly, weren't you?"

She nods, wary; how does he know?

He shakes his head. "Pretty stupid thing to do. Don't you think?"

*Yes, it is stupid. Because I'm an idiot, a stupid idiot.* Her chest tightens and tears well in her eyes.

"You okay?"

"Yes," she says, nodding. "I'm okay. I'm fine. I'm just fine." She swallows hard, then takes a deep breath and holds back her tears.

He raises an eyebrow. He seems unconvinced.

"Except for the fact the everyone died," she continues. "All of those poor people, washed away. Can you imagine? It must have been awful. I can't even begin to understand what they went through." Her tears return, and she pats her eyes with the corner of the bed cover. "And I don't know what I'm doing here or what's going on. I've been alone for weeks, and—shouldn't you be dead?"

He stares at her, curled up crying on the bed, and she feels for him. Surely he doesn't want to be here, trapped in this poky shipping container with a crying crazy woman. But he stays; he doesn't leave. So she sits up and gets her breathing under control.

"Sorry, a bit overwhelmed. I haven't seen another person for weeks. I'm fine, really I'm absolutely fine. You can go. We can talk tomorrow, or the day after. I'm sure I'll still be here. Not here in bed, but around—I'll be around, on the beach, if you want to talk about anything. Or not, of course, that's fine. I mean, we don't have to talk. It would be good if we did, but I understand if you don't want to. We could just be silent. Silence is . . ."

She can't, for the life of her, remember what silence is.

"Deafening," he says.

"Yes, yes it is."

"You should rest. I'll see you tomorrow."

"Yes, you're right. I'm tired. I should rest. But where will you go? Are you staying here? Are you a prisoner, like me?"

"We'll talk later."

✳✳✳

Quinn wakes the following morning and wonders if she dreamt Tig up. He wasn't really here last night, leaning by the door in the darkness; it was an illusion, a mirage. She's losing her mind and can't tell the difference between dreams and reality. She thinks this is not the worst thing to happen, considering she's stuck on a deserted atoll; at least she can fantasize about a man to keep her company. Nocturnal apparition might just keep her sane, and she could do a lot worse than Tig. He looked quite fetching in the warm glow of the kinetic light inside the shipping container last night. His self-assuredness also gives him a certain charisma. Maybe she'll conjure him up again tonight. Maybe she'll even bring him into bed with her. She wonders if he's single, then realizes it's only a dream, so it probably doesn't matter.

Then she spies the green drink sitting on the chair beside her bed. She scans the room but doesn't see her clothes, so she wraps the blanket around herself and heads outside.

Here he is, sitting on the edge of the stone landing. Jane the dodo is next to him, and he's scratching her under the neck, like they're old friends. Makes Quinn wonder if he ever left.

"Hey," he says. "How'd you sleep?"

"Good. Seen my dress?"

"Drying, round the side." He points to the corner of the shipping container. "Rinsed it out last night."

*He rinsed out my dress.*

"Come here. You're too thin. You need to eat more." He unties a bag of leaking seafood; small fish, oysters, crabs, green herbs, and white roots, and lays the contents out over a cloth.

She's grateful for the food; it looks fresh and she's hungry—she's always hungry. She retrieves her dress, slips it on, and joins him, sitting between him and Jane.

"Your feet, they're a mess," he says, considering the wretched state of her toes and heels.

"Yeah. No shoes." She shrugged. "I keep cutting them on the rocks. They hurt like hell."

He opens an oyster, and when he passes her the shell, their fingers graze; there it is again, the buzz, a flicker of kinetic energy between them—small but electrifying. As she registers this, he fillets the fish into slivers, hands her the first piece, and gives the second to Jane.

"Who are you?" she asks.

"Me? I'm a smuggler."

"What do you smuggle?"

"People, refugees, all over the world."

"Dangerous job."

"My life's work."

"And what are you doing here?"

He passes her pale green stems. "Samphire, sea asparagus. Good for you, improves visual clarity." He pushes the bridge of his bionic glasses back up his nose.

She laughs. He doesn't smile. Maybe it wasn't a joke. She takes the asparagus and pops a piece into her mouth. It's disgusting, salty and bitter, the same stuff he gave her last night. She spits it straight back out.

"That's a very good disgusting face," he says.

"My life's work."

He grins.

*Time to get to the point.* "Who are you?" she asks. "Why are you here? What were you doing with Lise? How'd you get off the Cloud Ship? And how the hell are you still alive?"

"Okay if we finish breakfast first?"

*No.*

But he offers her more fish, then oysters and crabmeat. He makes delicious seaweed rolls filled with fish roe and continues to hand her morsels of seafood, and seaweed, and shellfish, and she continues to put them into her mouth.

When she can't eat any more, she stands and shows him her balloon-like stomach. "Look, I'm having a baby," she protests.

"It's a good look." He hands her a morsel of fish. "Last one."

She promptly takes it and feeds it to Jane, who flaps her wings in appreciation.

"How's the shoulder?"

*My shoulder?* She rotates the joint. "You fixed it?"

"Careful, it's weak."

He wipes his knife, collects the debris of shells, and wraps them in a cloth. As he does all this, she gives him a detailed appraisal. His skin is auburn. He has a craggy, lonesome face with a scruff of a beard and short, dark hair. He wears cargo pants, rolled to his calves, and a loose shirt, rolled to his elbows. There's a circular tattoo on the back of his neck. She can't tell his age, but he's a man, not a boy—older than her. He has a chipped tooth, burns and scars on his arms, part of his left ear is missing, and he's not quite symmetrical; his left side is slightly skewed. Dull grey titanium pokes through his left ankle and elbow, but there's been some skin growth since she last saw him. Rapid-Skin membrane envelops most of his electroskeleton. *Must be Transhuman.*

Metal bracelets cover his wrists—twenty, maybe thirty, in total. Some are beaded, others are smooth, some are black metal, others are copper-colored or deep green. They appear ancient, made in a time before machine. She's never met anyone like him before: part machine, part human, with an ethos of ancient culture dangling around his wrists, and no Band in sight. *Points to fundamental Humanism, but that doesn't account for the Tech.* She catches a glance of his milky irises while he cleans his glasses.

"Cataracts, double detached retinas," he says.

*Easily fixed with a thermal laser and a SelfMed. I give up, he's unclassifiable.* "Is the world a blur?"

"Yeah, I like it that way. Nicer place. Where you wanna start?"

"Who are you, where are you from, how'd you survive?"

"From the beginning: I'm from the Maldives, Butterfly Island."

Butterfly Island is part of an archipelago in the Indian Ocean. But technically the Maldives no longer exist; they were covered by seawater in 2029. She's seen images: The Islanders painted their rooftops and roads white to reflect the sun. They filled pools, rivers, and dams with carbon-eating plankton, and they pumped the carbon below ground, storing it in the empty mine shafts and caves. They even covered the ground with crushed silica to soak up the carbon. Of course, it was pointless, and about fifty years too late.

This was the first nation to be entirely displaced, and no one wanted them. It took a decade for governments to change the definition of a refugee to include populations affected by global warming and climate change.

"Must have been hard," she says. "There were a lot of rich countries back then. Rich countries with rich people. They didn't give up anything."

"Possessions were more important than people."

"Where do you live now?"

"In Unus."

"The megacity. They say it's 55 degrees Celsius; that's over 130 degree Fahrenheit! Are there really a hundred million people living in that heat?"

"Yeah, but I live on the harbor, on a boat."

"How'd you survive the flood? They told me everyone died."

"Everyone got down and went back to the station to wait out the storm—everyone but you. So I took a Pod and searched, but the rain was too heavy. I went back to Kerguelen, arrived just in time to see the glacier wash the village away, like it was a toy."

"Fuck."

"Yeah. Nothing I could do."

"So what are you doing here?"

"I came here for you."

"For me. Why?"

"Well." He glances away, then meets her gaze. "I told Lise I'd look after you."

"But you were looking after her, weren't you? Like a bodyguard —why?"

"Global elections next year—she's politically active. It's a dangerous new world."

"Yeah, I suppose it is." The index finger of her left hand scrawls the words "Shun Mantra" into the sandy pavers beside her. "Maybe you should have stayed with her. She needed you." She knows there's a hint of accusation in her voice.

"At the time, you needed me more."

She nods. "I suppose that's true."

Her finger writes "Transhuman" directly under "Shun Mantra." Then it runs a line through the corresponding letters in each word until there are no letters left. "A dangerous new world," she muses aloud.

He nods.

"Okay, so you're here to rescue me. This is great news. I'm so grateful. Thank you. I've been here forty-two days. At least, I think it's forty-two days. I lost a bit of time between days thirty-one and thirty-four. They sort of merged together. A lot of my time here has been a blur, if you know what I mean." She hasn't drawn a breath since she started telling him all this, and she looks at him wide-eyed, seeking confirmation that he understands her predicament.

He nods.

"Okay. When do we leave?"

"We'll be picked up in a couple of days. Hydro panels in my sub corroded. It's adrift, no power, but I've sent for reinforcements. They'll be here soon."

She turns to him. "Thank you. Thank you for coming to get me. I can't believe I'm finally going home. And I'm sorry about your sub."

"Not your problem." He produces a tube of ointment from the bag the seafood was in. "Give me your foot."

She doesn't move.

Opening the ointment, he indicates again, with a wave of his hand, that she should give him her foot. She shakes her head and holds her hand out for the cream; she is perfectly capable of doing this herself.

"Give me your fucking foot." It's an order.

She concedes. For whatever reason, he's intent on doing this, and actually, she likes the idea of him touching her. She hasn't seen or touched another human in weeks, and his presence is comforting; he has come all this way to find her and rescue her. She tells herself this is his job, it's what he does, but she can't help but feel that it's more than just a job; he doesn't have to rub her feet, or bring her food, or rinse out her clothes. He's easy to be with, and she can tell he likes her; he hardly knows her, but what he knows he likes.

She's warming to him by the minute. Smiling to herself, she places her scab-riddled foot in his lap. He gently massages the cream into the cuts on her toes and the grazes around her heel. He has large, firm hands and strong fingers, and they wander up her leg, massaging her ankle and calf. It's pure bliss; a tingling sensation travels the length of her body. Reining it in takes all the energy and focus she can manage.

He frowns. "Relax."

She can't. But she can pretend to relax. When the first foot is done, he starts on the other. Quinn lays back against the wall of her shipping container, closes her eyes, and thinks about math, trying to block out the thrill of his hands—his large, firm hands—on her cold, impassive, ugly foot, but her heart pounds and she's nervous as hell. Soon, her hands begin to shake. She slides them under her thighs to keep them still.

When both feet are done, Tig wraps protective sticky soles around them. The Hi-Tech material molds seamlessly to her feet. It feels amazing.

He leans in toward her. "So, you know about Lise?" he asks, his voice uneasy. "You know she died?"

Quinn nods. "Yes, yes, I do. What about Ada? Have they recovered her?"

"No. Strange, they never found her body."

*That's because she's inside the hull of Prismatic, floating around the Indian Ocean, Fuck. What if imminent death counts as an absolute necessity? What if Lise used the time travel portal to escape? What if she's not dead?* But there's no need to tell Tig the truth about Ada and Lise, not just yet.

"Are you okay?" he asks.

"Sure."

"Years ago, I lost someone. And . . . and I learned that love is wrung from our hearts, until the loved one is the only thing that's left, until she's all there is."

She gives him a gentle smile and holds his gaze. She can't have this conversation. She's not grieving, not yet. *Distract him.* She stands and nods toward the other end of the beach; the day is disappearing, and she hasn't made her cairn yet. As she sets out toward the stony headland, she indicates that he should follow, and he does.

At Rocky Beach, forty-two cairns stand across the foreshore.

"I build one every day," she tells him. "It's good to have a theme; it makes it more challenging, and it takes longer—time goes on forever, don't you find? Give me a shape."

"Cone." He half smiles.

*Annoying.* "Try again."

"Butterfly."

*Good choice. A little obvious, but the relevance is touching.*

She is especially pleased with his choice because gathered at the far end of the beach are the piles of particular shaped rocks—leaves, faces, flowers, moons, stars, and, conveniently, butterflies—she's collected over the last few weeks. "You look over there," she says pointing to the side of the beach opposite the one where she has stashed her stone collection for herself.

A quick count of her pile reveals eleven butterflies. After an hour of foraging, she has eighteen.

"How many do you have?" she asks, displaying her collection proudly.

"Six," he says sourly. He's genuinely disappointed.

"It's not a competition," she says. *Of course, it's a competition.* "I've just had more experience. My stone-hunting skills are more advanced than yours. Still, I thought you'd be better, considering butterflies are your significant shape—the shape of your island."

He frowns at her; he's taking this far more seriously than he should.

# Fourteen

# All things experience each other.

LATER THAT AFTERNOON, THEY sit outside Quinn's shipping container home in the arc of the setting sun, their backs against the wall. Jane scrambles over, keen for some company, and Tig rubs her downy chest, the way she likes it. She rests her heavy head on his leg.

"What happened to you?" Quinn asks. "Your arm, the cyborg modifications . . . they're pretty . . . significant."

"It was war. I was in a bloody war. Got caught by a barrel-bomb. They fucking rip you apart. People without heads, arms, legs, body parts flying all over the place. Got caught in the blast wind. Picked me up and slammed me into a concrete wall full of metal reo, shredded my arm, leg. Got taken to the Med, where I was supposed to die. They have rooms—white, red, black. They put you in the white room if you're gonna live. The red room for immediate surgery. The black room if you need immediate surgery but you're gonna die anyway and they can't waste blood, meds, time. They sent me to the black room. Then someone came in, a new doctor. She had me moved. There was another room. I woke up like this. The exoskeleton decodes and translates electrical brain signals. Thoughts control my robotic limbs. I think, and it moves."

"Very cool Tech."

"Yeah. Listen, I know you and Lise were close; if you wanna talk about—"

"Are you going to live on Titan, if you get the chance?" *Distract him.*

"Nah, I'll stay, but it's a better option than Mars. That was a disaster. Now, with the right Tech, we could make Titan work. There's atmosphere and resources, liquids, methane, and wind for turbine."

The Mars settlements failed miserably; it was not the place to raise a family, and the "let's just get there and figure it out later" philosophy the settlers adopted was naïve. The planet has huge radiation problems; the colony had to live below the surface, in the dark. The weather, too, was shocking. It snowed every night after sunset, the droplets evaporating before they touched the ground. Nothing grew; the soil was thin and dusty, and it lacked microbes and bacteria. The settlers were perpetually hungry, and hungry people get hangry, and hangry people don't care about each other.

"What about you?" Tig asks. "If the planet becomes inhabitable and Earth can't be saved, will you leave?"

"It *can* be saved. It's just a problem, and all problems have solutions. Earth Optimism—it's growing, and we haven't exhausted geoengineering."

"Didn't we try that?"

"I know. I know. But there are other options. Science can still save us; we just have to believe. And science is a sounder discipline than organized religion. Atheists are more peaceful than god believers. It's a scientific fact."

He shakes his head. "Hexad can close churches and monitor worship, but we're naturally receptive to religion—we won't leave it alone. And science is religion's biggest threat."

"Science isn't a threat."

"Think about it: Every new scientific discovery, doesn't matter what it is, multiverses or time travel, even Lise's nothingness theory, will need to be adapted, modified, explained away by leaders, including religious leaders, until it fits into a new world view. Then people will make the easy choice, the belief choice. Not the science choice, that's too hard. You know Lise thought—"

"What do you believe in?" *Distract him.*

"Me? Panpsychism. My people believe all matter, even rocks, shells, have awareness."

"So matter is sentient?"

"Sort of."

She collects a discarded oyster shell and squeezes it as hard as she can. "Did I hurt it?"

He smiles. "No." He grabs her hand, holds it firmly in his. "Everything in the universe has perception; all things experience each other." He peels open her fingers, retrieves the shell, and tosses it back at her.

"That's quantum theory."

"Thousands of years before we realized."

"Religion is waning," she says. "Atheism is on the rise. The more we discover about the world, the universe, the more we'll realize it was not made for us. We fit into it. People will understand, eventually. Then, without religion, we'll live in peace."

He makes no comment, just leans back against the wall, considering her.

*Okay, a bit of a generalization: peace on Earth. I didn't mean it literally.*

"What's going on?" he asks.

"Didn't mean it literally, I just meant—"

"You're different. There's no hole in your heart, is there?"

*How does he know?*

"You're mother is dead, and you're prattling on about Titan and science."

"I don't prattle, and—"

"I'm on your side." With a forefinger, he tilts her chin up, looks her in the eye. "What is it? What's going on?"

*How does he know?* "Okay, the truth is, Lise might not be dead. Ada was wearing her Band; Ada is dead—I saw her corpse. Somehow they switched Bands."

"Then where is she? People don't just go missing."

Quinn shrugs. "I don't know, but it doesn't feel like she's dead. I don't feel like she's gone."

"Okay, what else?"

"That's it. There is nothing else."

"You're not finished. I can tell."

She stares at him. *How do you know?* "Okay, I found something in Ada's purse, a mark on parchment, from Lise's journal."

"Show me."

"I don't have it. Panicked—accidentally ate it."

He laughs. "You idiot." Suddenly, he pulls off his shirt. "Back of my neck, a tattoo, check it out."

She kneels behind him. His tattoo is a circle filled with symbols and letters that she doesn't understand. "The mark—is there a match?"

*Why would there be a match?* Then she sees it: a small black zigzag line, very similar to the mark on the parchment paper. "Yes. What is this?"

"Part of an ancient code. But it's only one piece."

*A code? That's what Lise said. She said she cracked the code.* "A code to what?"

He pulls on his shirt. "A door."

"A door to—"

"A door that may help you find your mother."

"So it's true? She discovered a wormhole?"

He grins. "Did she?"

"Yes, she told me she cracked the code."

"Then I'll see you later."

"What? No." She blanches, feels a little panicked. She doesn't want to be alone again. "Where are you going?"

"Meet you tomorrow. Same time. Rocky Beach. Don't worry." He strides away.

Quinn worries.

# Fifteen

# People don't just disappear. We know that better than anyone.

*N*ANSHE IS A FULLY battened sailing junk drifting two hundred kilometers off the east cost of Africa. Her name pays homage to the goddess of prophecy and fertility. Built in the 1950s, her bones are old, but the full overhaul she got five years ago made her just as seaworthy as the first day she sailed. The ships layout is expansive: three levels and three hundred square meters of living space; eight cabins with private bathing zones, marble details, mother-of-pearl fittings, and two spacious suites with private sun decks; retrofitted and state-of-the-art navigation and air system. Anchor stabilizers make navigating the world's oceans effortless. She cruises at twenty knots and launches emergency boosters when required.

A zone in the galley is devoted entirely to Aquaculture; rows of oval tanks containing a cosmopolitan array of frogs, fish, sea snakes, slugs, and seashells line the walls. The last tank on the bottom left is opaque and black; a single, resin-colored worm crawls along its edge.

Planck, a large human with short, red-tipped hair, full lips, high cheekbones, and arching eyebrows, enters the galley. From one of Planck's earlobes dangles a small symbol: a circle within a circle containing both horizontal and vertical lines, the sign for gender neutral. Ze is the boat's chief engineer, medic, purser, bosun, and cook.

Ze hooks the worm over one finger and slips it back inside its black chamber, then flushes the tank with water, collecting the dark liquid in buckets as it drains from the bottom.

*Nanni, Nanshe*'s mini-submarine, sits twenty meters below the surface, a hundred meters southeast of the atoll. Tig was born to swim; he has a genetic predisposition for deep sea diving. For thousands of years, his people lived a marine hunter-gatherer lifestyle, combing the ocean for food. Carefully selected DNA left the population with enlarged spleens that contract when diving and eject oxygenated red blood cells into circulation, creating oxygen boosts that prolong dive times and allow for greater diving depths.

Tig's family comes from a linage of Kings, a title inherited by virtue of descent, going back 5,000 years to the third century BCE. Tig would say that it's king with a small "k," a figurative title, but his kingdom covers three million people in a monarchy structure. Their mixed constitution weaves democracy and monarchy into a system that allows for a government by many. The Maldives no longer exists; the archipelago was swallowed by the Indian Ocean, and now its people are stranded on land, besieged by a hundred million people. Their culture makes up 3 percent of the megacity Unus.

On board *Nanni*, Tig is surrounded by piles of hydro panels, hundreds of them scattered across the floor. He picks up a fresh panel and examines the structure: there are micro cracks and signs of discoloration. "Fuck, they're all gone."

His Comms signals a call from Planck. Tig answers.

"Product recall," says Planck. "A manufacturing fault in the panel. If one fails it reverberates and ruins the whole system. I've placed a back order, no charge to us, which is something, but . . . it could be a while. I'm on my way. Be there in two days."

"Okay. There's something else. Lise got out; she might not be dead."

"Are you serious?"

"Yep. No one knows where she is. Seems like she just . . . disappeared."

"People don't just disappear. We know that better than anyone. She must have the other Disc. I did some checking on Maim; looks like she acquired it decades ago—picked it up in a bazar in Harappa. Maybe Lise took it to Kerguelen."

"I checked her luggage; she didn't have it. But she told Quinn she'd worked out the code. Can you *disappear* without a Disc?"

"Yes, people have done it. It's not easy, you need an enormous amount of energy . . . but she's resourceful, maybe she found a way."

"This complicates things."

"To say the least. We can't destroy the Discs without the codes to both, and we only know the code to our Disc. The one person on the planet who knows the code to the other Disc, has used it to . . . *disappear.*"

"Yeah. But first we need to get our hands on the second Disc. We need to talk to Maim, see how much she knows."

"Okay. There's a Derecho, blowing in from the east. Due in two days."

"We should be out by then. I'm meeting her tomorrow afternoon on the beach, I don't want to be late. Remind me."

"Okay. Your Meds, are you taking—"

"Yes. I'm fine."

"Really? Because you sound nervous. Is it the glasses? You feel self-conscious. I understand, but—"

"It ain't the glasses. And I ain't fuckin' nervous. Sort out this thing with Maim." Tig closes the Comms.

*I am so nervous. What if it's not the same? What if it can never be the same? Fuck, what if it's worse? The same fucking thing all over again? Shit, get a grip. Don't. Don't rush it. Keep her safe—she ain't goin' nowhere. It is what it is.*

Right now, we need to find out how to crack that code. *Those fuck-ing Discs will be the end of us all.*

# Sixteen

# Two bracelets, one green and one red.

When Quinn arrives at Rocky Beach, Tig is already there, perched on a large rock waiting for her. He tosses and catches a stone with his bionic hand, and when she's close enough he tosses the stone to her. She catches it and smiles; it's pitted with holes that look like two eyes, a nose, and an upturned mouth. The rock smiles at her.

"Faces," Tig says, and Quinn nods.

From her brief experience as a cairn builder, she's learned that rocks with human features are the most difficult to find. Of course, she already has a small collection hidden at the far end of the beach.

They split up. He gets the same area as yesterday; she goes in search of her collection, but it's not where it should be. She checks, back and forth, in case she's made a mistake, but they're all gone—her leaves, her moons, her stars and faces, they're all gone. *Damn. He's taken them. He must have.* She turns around, and he gives her a brief wave from the far side of the beach. She reciprocates with a noncommittal wave, an urbane gesture. She must start scavenging.

After an hour she has eight rocks. Some are a bit dodgy but, she reasons, there are some peculiar-looking people in the world.

They meet in the middle. He has a pile of thirty-two. *Thirty-two. I've been had.*

"Honestly, I thought you'd be better at this," he says. "You've had weeks, and this is only my second time."

"Yes," she says, "you should be very proud."

"I am," he says.

They sit down and construct the cairn together.

"Why do you jump off things?" he asks.

"It's my thing. It's who I am."

He doesn't respond, only hands her the next rock for placement. She doesn't have to explain herself any further, but he says nothing, and eventually his silence incites her to add, "It's a good place to think about nothing, and sometimes it's a good place to think about everything."

As if he hasn't heard, he fixes a precariously balanced stone, then adds another to the tower.

"Some days are hard," she continues. "You know, some days I . . . I feel like I don't count for much. Like I've got everything wrong. All those people died, and I feel like it's my fault."

"It's not your fault."

"I know. But I made a bad choice and thousands of people died."

"The two things aren't related."

"I feel like I have no control. I don't understand what my purpose is, and when I jump, I'm in control. It's my release."

He takes the final rock from her and places it in position, and they consider the cairn. His technique is different from hers. He uses smaller rocks to balance larger ones, so the structure has window-like holes through it.

"You're not alone," he says. "There's confusion and sadness in all of us."

In that moment, regrettably, she's betrayed by her left hand, which collects Tig's hand and weaves his fingers into hers. He smiles, and his lips brush her knuckles. Very carefully, she unravels and restrains the vexing appendage.

✱✱✱

Later that evening Quinn sets the table with shaking hands. She places a small bunch of yellow seaside daises in the center, then panics and moves them to the food prep area; it looks like she's expecting a date.

Half an hour later, Tig comes rambling up the hill with a bag of seafood and a bunch of green-stemmed samphire. He hands her the succulent stems like they're a bunch of flowers. She puts them in a container and places them in the middle of the table.

They sit inside, on the shredding cardboard chairs, and he lays out the food. He starts to pass her the first sliver of fish, but as she reaches for it he pulls it away. "What'd you say you were working on in Kerguelen?"

"I didn't."

He frowns. "What were you working on in Kerguelen?"

"Solar flares. Get to the point."

"The G12—is it safe? Do you have it?"

"Yes and yes."

"And the rain?"

"It showed no rain. Sabotage—someone set a ghost. But I'll find out what happened, as soon we get out of here. I'll also tell you which mark on your tattoo matches the one in Ada's purse."

Tig grins.

"You believe in time travel, don't you? And you think Lise escaped into a wormhole."

"Yes and yes."

*That's the craziest thing I've ever heard, but I hope you're right.* "Will you help me find her when we get out of here?"

"Yes. I will. We can't leave yet. Two more days. We'll get out before the storm."

"There's a storm coming?"

Tig nods. "Derecho. It might be hard to get in. We could get stuck."

"Wind?"

He nods.

"I hate wind." Dust and sand will pelt the atoll, and she'll be stuck inside her shipping container.

"I know you do." He slips off his glasses and stares at her with his milky irises. Then he takes her hand and laces his fingers through hers.

Her heart skips. *I'm in trouble.*

She pulls her hand away, clumsily collects the plates, and carries them to the food prep. *This thing between us is not happening.*

Suddenly, he's behind her. He pulls her hair to one side and runs his lips down her neck, over her ear, across her shoulder. Her heart pounds. It's divine. He's divine. *This thing between us, it is happening. It is going somewhere, and I'm on board.*

He turns her around and looks her over. "You're so beautiful."

Her skin tingles in anticipation. *This thing between us is definitely happening.* "You want to have sex?"

He nods.

"I'd be . . . I'd be fine, completely fine, and on board—on board all the way with that." Quinn flushes red.

"Fuck. Great. Okay then."

He kisses her and she kisses him back, and then he's straight into it, pulling her bamboo-fiber dress over her head and slipping off her shorts so she's naked, bathed in soft yellow kinetic light. He pulls his shirt off and she undoes his cargo pants and he kicks them away and now they're both golden and naked. He has a huge erection. He lifts her up and she wraps her legs around him and they move to the bed, where he lays her down and hovers over her.

"You're beautiful," he says again. And she's thinking the same thing, the exact the same thing, he's so beautiful, with his scarred, auburn skin and broad chest and short hair.

There is no messing around, no foreplay; she wants him, and she wants to do it right now. She wants to feel the weight of his body on hers, and she wants him inside her. She wraps her arms around him and pulls him close.

"Fuck me now," she whispers.

"Okay." He understands.

He angles his hips, pushes himself deep inside her, and it feels good, warm and intense. She closes her eyes and presses her body into his and they move together, rising and falling. He covers her face in kisses, then his lips travel down her neck and shoulders. She wraps her legs around him, he arches his back, moans, and collapses on top of her, hot and sweaty, breathing heavily into her neck.

It's over. It took maybe a minute. Nervousness overcomes her: She's trapped underneath a large, auburn-skinned man, a man who has seen all of her naked, who has just come inside her. A man she met a few days ago, a man she hardly knows.

She waits. He catches his breath. He breathes. She waits. He's so heavy. *Okay, someone needs to say something.* "You're . . . you're squashing me."

"Fuck, sorry." He raises himself on an elbow and stares down at her. No words, just stares with his milky eyes, and she knows he can't see much but still, it makes her uncomfortable, and she's overcome with the desire to jump off something very high. Sex with strangers is just vulnerability wrapped up in lust and regret.

She reaches for a cover. He smiles, pulls it away.

"Not finished with you."

He pins her flat, kissing her.

✳✳✳

Quinn wakes later than usual; it's mid-morning, and the space beside her is empty. She can't recall him leaving, but she does remember the things they did to each other last night, and she blushes. It was intense—a long night of hot sex—and she's happy to be waking up alone; she needs to gather her thoughts. She needs to think about what happened between them. *Was it just sex? Was it convenience—two lonely people on a lonely atoll? Good lordt, it was good. I feel . . . great. Tired, but happy.* She smiles. She can't remember the last time she had sex. She can't remember ever having sex like that.

Now his presence lingers—his hot breath on her face, his scent on her bed, the easy way he touched her skin, and his final words, the last thing he said to her: "I know." And he did, he understood what she meant. Exhausted after the sex, they lay together on the bed, side by side, and then he pulled her close, trapping her under his arm, hard against his chest, and it felt perfect. She thought this was where she belonged. She was safe and happy, filled up by him. Then he said, "Stop jumping off fucking cliffs." She thought about this for a moment and replied, "I don't want to." He pulled her close and whispered, "I know." Then he let her go, just like that, unwrapped his arm, and she didn't feel safe anymore.

He also took her one pillow.

She pulls the covers back and sees two bangles circling her right wrist. Tig's bangles. He has given her two bracelets, one green and one red; he must have clipped them on while she slept. She shakes her arm, and they jingle. They are beautiful, ancient and exquisite, the green one finely carved and the red band marked with black geometric marks. Her heart warms to him once more—*Maybe he didn't realize there was only one pillow.* She considers the jewelry; perhaps it's a cultural thing, but surely he's not giving them to all the girls he has sex with. He wouldn't have any left.

She sits at her table by the window and examines her gifts. There is no visible latch and they're too small to slip off her wrist, so she couldn't remove them even if she wanted to. *Why bangles?* She realizes that something is missing; there were three rocks grouped in the center of the table around the bunch of samphire, and now there are only two. She's specific, and only groups her rocks in odd numbers. Now there are only two stones. She checks the floor, the bench, under the bed. Nothing. He has taken her stone, her favorite star-shaped stone. She looks at the bracelets again, and shrugs. *A fair trade.*

She sets out two cups and makes tea. Then she carries both cups outside, sits on the front veranda with Jane, and waits for Tig to return with breakfast.

# Seventeen

# What is a city, if not all the hot and weary people?

Maim Quate, leader of the Democratic Republic, reflects on the view from her office in Unus: a million cobbled-together buildings, home to over 100 million residents. A megatropolis. A megacity. Once, there was a midpoint, a town center, with monuments and spires, but now the layout is confusing and repetitious, and, after two thousand years of unplanned building, the lack of hierarchy is not surprising. The breadth and width and scale of this city are daunting—it's a mélange of green vegetation, grey stone, and beige salvaged material.

*We made this, these homes, somewhere to live*, Maim thinks. *Good lordt, what were we thinking?*

Circling the megatropolis are the magnificent pinnacles of the Climate Cities. Six clusters of Cool Reefs nestle into the surrounding hills around Unus; they are master plans of sustainability, with their passive cooling and climate control. The world's first fully chilled sub-cities, generating their own energy, producing enough food and water to feed their blessed half a million inhabitants. The megacity boils, its citizens gasping for breath in 50-degree Celsius heat, while Climate City residents inhale an atmosphere 25 degrees cooler. Cool air is a privilege, and it comes at a cost that 99 percent of people can't afford.

"What is a city, if not all the hot and weary people?" Maim muses.

"Tennyson, or Shakespeare? Maybe Tennyson." She fans herself with a module; it's her second hot flash today, what a shame it had to happen in the middle of her meeting with Kip Jove. Just as she was outlining her deal, she felt the sudden rush of heat, beginning in her toes, rising through her, up her neck and over her face. Even her ears were burning. The Global Elections were always going to be a stressful time, and the tension is not helping her perimenopause. She thinks science should have done more about menopause by now, but they've largely ignored it; like emptying a junk folder, it's an optional task, not a priority in this heat-soaked world.

But now the deal with Kip is done, on a nod and a handshake, and on this she trusts him; he's old school, believes in honor. She told him, "Our biggest problem is global agreement and a lack of political nerve. We have to undo the damage we've done. Fixing the climate requires a sustained collaboration, uniting all of Hexad for the benefit of the planet." She knows he cares. He likes a challenge, and he'll do the right thing when the time comes. Politics requires compromise, but it also requires winning. They cemented a deal that will seal the fate of her party, the Democratic Republic, and his, the Fundamental Atheists.

The winner of this election will take all, and she intends to win. Two days prior to the election in Unus, if her party leads, Kip will throw his ticket in with her and create a united front against Dirac Devine and New Federation. The catch is, she's agreed to do the same for Kip if his party is the preferred choice. She could lose everything— but she doesn't intend to lose.

Now, sweaty and a little dizzy, she continues fanning herself while she waits for the flash to pass. Then, out the corner of her eye, she catches a glimpse of Lise wearing her floor-length, rust-colored kimono. A favorite, Lise always wraps it around herself when the air system overcools. Layers—now that they're both older, they dress in layers. Laughing together, they are layering up for the day, only to shed garments later, when the flashes come.

Grief is fickle. Of course, it's not Lise—her love, her dear love. Some days the world turns on the head of a pin. She takes a deep breath. Why Lise, of all people? It makes no sense.

Her module vibrates, blaring the chorus of "Precious Time," a tune by the Girls. The song signals news of Lise, The Girls were her favorite band; she grew up with them. Maim kills the song and accepts the call from Planck.

"If you're not sitting down, then you might want to pull up a chair," Planck says. "Ada was wearing *her* band. Ada is dead; Lise is missing."

*Missing?* "I don't understand. She's not dead? Then where is she?"

"She seems to have . . . disappeared."

"People don't just . . . *Oh shit.* I know what you're thinking, Lise told me all about it, and it's not possible."

"It is possible, and it works."

"But it's still here. I have it in the cupboard."

"Turns out you might not need it, if you know the formula."

*I can't believe I'm having this conversation.* "You know how I feel. This is unreal, I don't believe in time travel. I don't believe it's possible."

"Lise believed it was possible."

*Oh good lordt, he's right.* "Okay, what do you want me to do?"

"If Lise worked out the formula, then maybe someone else can also crack the code. Someone who knows about science. Someone who thinks like Lise. Know anyone like that?"

*Quinn.* "Yes. I know what to do."

The call ends. Maim smiles, stands, and strides across the room to a cabinet. She unlocks a drawer and retrieves a circular stone tablet, a 5,000-year-old Phaistos Disc; she holds it to the light and considers the carvings—antiquity, ancient texts, a Mesopotamian city. She slips the tablet it into a box, then picks up her automatic pencil and writes a message on a blank card while she hums "Precious Time."

She couriers the package by private drone to Hobart.

# Eighteen

# Now she has Jane's DNA inside her.

On the atoll, the breeze picks up; Quinn hears it squalling through the trees. The noise causes the hairs on her arms to stand on end. The birds disappear. The sky mellows, and the air turns yellow. Tig hasn't returned yet. Quinn collects her teacups, goes inside, and closes the door.

By mid-morning, it's a full-force gale that breaks tree limbs and hauls the sand from the beach. Her shipping container home is pelted day and night, and she's trapped inside. Even opening the door is perilous. There is still no sign of Tig. The supply drone doesn't arrive with her supplies. She'll have to ration her food—a difficult task. Eating is one of the highlights of her life these days.

✦✦✦

After eight days of constant sand and wind and no drone deliveries, Quinn is ravenous, and her shipping container resembles the home of a madwoman. She has drawn over the walls, the ceiling and floor, distracting herself with math calculations. But now she needs to eat—she needs food.

She covers her face, crouches low, and edges her way outside, into the hideous, unceasing tempest of wind and sand. She crawls over the front landing and across the grass, and collects Jane from her burrow of sticks. Jane is not nesting, so the bird is her first choice. She is a solid thing, heavier than she looks, but she is also, to her detriment, docile and trusting—she doesn't struggle as Quinn grabs her. Quinn sees how her species was so easily wiped out.

She lugs Jane inside. The bird is clearly grateful for the shelter, so Quinn gives her a few more minutes of life, then she looks her in the eyes and says, "Sorry, sorry Jane, but it has to be this way. I'm starving and I'm going to eat you. I could explain how the food chain works and the hierarchy of animals, big ones eat smaller ones, but I think you get it—I think we all get it. So, thank you for giving me your life so I can feed myself and not die here alone and destitute.

Quinn maneuvers the bird onto the food prep, then she collects a knife and cuts Jane's throat, all the way through. Her left hand does it, clean and quick. The knife is sharp, very sharp, and she's thankful for this. The bird flinches, and her blood splatters. There's more blood than Quinn thought there would be. It sprays all over her face, it gets in her eyes, and it's warm. Warm blood. The food prep is now a mess, dripping with Jane's warm blood.

Quinn holds the bird's body still until it stops jerking and she's sure it is dead. *Dead as a dodo.* Then she hangs it upside down. While the blood drains, she cleans, wiping and rinsing down the walls and floor, then wiping herself over and rinsing her eyes. Now she has Jane's DNA inside her.

Quinn chops Jane into bite-size pieces—and again, she's very thankful for the sharp knife and the willful spirit of her left hand—and then boils them for an hour. The shipping container fills with stream and dead dodo stench. It's unpleasant, but she's starving. After the meat cools, she tucks in.

Jane tastes gamey, not so good, but over the following days Quinn eats every part of her, except for the bones. She puts these aside. When the foot bone is dry, it makes a good back scratcher. She also keeps a few of Jane's claws, just because they're smooth and interesting and go well with her rock collection. No point wasting them.

Jane's bones are riddled with cavities. Calcium depletion; she had osteoporosis. She was older than she looked. *Some consolation.*

✦✦✦

After eleven days, the sand lies still and quiet. The sun appears, and the sky is once again relentlessly blue. The year turned while Quinn waited out the storm. It's now January 2050. She opens the door of her shipping container and stands midpoint between two worlds: the old and the new.

While the intensity of the wind erupted outside, she wrote out every calculation and formula she knew—scrawled them over the walls, the floor, the ceiling, and even the furniture of her shipping container. The numbers kept her sane. They fused with the white noise of wind and sand and filled her dreams. Now, the outside world is still, and the inside resembles the frenzied activity of a madwoman. Quinn realizes she knows a lot of stuff. Science stuff. She has all this information inside her head. She knows every element on the periodic table, all the details. She knows the laws of thermodynamics by heart. She knows all the fundamental formulas and mathematical equations— Einstein's, Newton's, Noether's, Euler's, all of them—but she doesn't know anything about the world, not really. *I have no common sense. I'm actually stupid.* During the storm, she emptied out a lot of shit. Now she has extra space. Now she is lighter.

Outside, the dunes are leveled. The wind has liberated her collection of plastic and Styrofoam balls; they have completely vanished, were taken somewhere new by the squall. She walks to the foreshore, and it's littered with washed-up bluebottles. Piles of them, clustered along the tide lines, like metallic blue lace. She picks up one of the jellyfish, carefully avoiding the long, poisonous tentacles, and pops the float between her fingers, as if it were a bubble. The jellyfish's float determines its course, with half the colony projecting to the left and the other half to the right. For a week the wind blew on shore. Half of the colony was stranded; the other half sailed away to safety. Their destiny is not determined by choice, it is controlled by the tide and wind. A good way to live.

When she returns to her shipping container home, she's greeted by a gull-drone. It has a food parcel and a message for her. Her case was reviewed, and now, without further information or details, she's to be released. A transporter will collect her within the hour.

# Nineteen

# The illusory nature of time.

QUINN IS FINALLY LEAVING the island, sixty-two days after the catastrophe on Kerguelen. Her tally: two days floating in the ocean, seven days in Prismatic, fifty-three days on the atoll. But today she is leaving.

She hates them. She's going to kill both Niels and Mori. And she has assassination plans.

Plan A: One shot, right between the eyes. She'll be perched on a hill in the distance, with the sun behind her. Shading their eyes, they'll squint in her direction and see the lone black figure on the horizon. They'll realize their fate just as she pulls the trigger. Too late. Perfect.

Plan B: A frenzied knife attack. This plan would bring a great deal of satisfaction.

Tig never returned. The Derecho was fierce; perhaps he couldn't get back to the atoll. Perhaps he was cast adrift in his sub, without power, and he drowned. Perhaps he died on his way back to her—put his life at risk for her because, in the few days they spent together, somehow, he truly "knew" her.

She has an hour until the Transporter arrives. She scours the foreshore, looking for Tig, but there is no sign of him. She frets: What if he comes back and she's not here? How will he know if she's safe, or where to find her? Well, he's resourceful, he'll have to work it out, because she's not going to stay here. She has to go home.

111

On her way back to her shipping container home, Quinn stops by Rocky Beach to make her last cairn. Its theme is time; her rocks must represent the illusory nature of time. She suspects the task will outwit her but she combs the beach anyway, hoping an extraordinary revelation will reveal itself.

It doesn't.

She sits on the ground, stacks a few random rocks on top of each other, and says, "I'm done." Then she brushes the sand from her hands and walks away. *Such a stupid idea, "the illusory nature of time." I'm an idiot.*

The time she spent here on the atoll is hard to define in terms of hours, days, and months, or past, present, and future. She sees it as intervals of light and dark, sequences of order and routine, where the events of one day merged with every other. She lost track of time. It no longer flowed from the past to the future. It became memory and anticipation; it became emotion and experience. The "nowness" of every moment ceased to exist. One long, lonely afternoon, she even convinced herself she had entered a parallel universe and become stuck, trapped somewhere in space-time, in the fields connecting space and gravity. The atoll is a chimera, and she has to find her way out, a way back to reality. She's lost track of who she is or who she once was.

# Twenty

# It was an era of banality, all about traffic.

THE TRANSPORTER LANDS ON the beach, scattering the gulls. Quinn collects her only possessions—her dignity, a self-anointed sense of righteousness, and, from under the mattress, her diamond—walks out the door, and doesn't look back. She's finally going home.

✶✶✶

Hobart is isolated, underdeveloped, and quiet. It's the place to go when the world becomes too much and you decide to opt out. It's the place to go when you decide to leave everything behind and farm alpacas, live in a log cabin and fish trout for the rest of your days, or write that book you've always wanted to write. Then, ten years later, the river has dried and turned to salt, and the trout are gone, and the book is not finished, but you're still there and now you'll never leave.

Quinn was born in Hobart, a strategic move by her parents, who moved there so she would retain citizenship in a quiet and safe place at the end of the Earth. Hobart was an escape destination for the pessimists and doomsayers who thought the world would one day implode.

It did implode, of course. It took a decade longer than they thought, but it finally happened. The year was 2035. The planet was already struggling with the effects of climate change and a massive refugee problem, but that year the forays into quantum computing brought down the NIoT, the New Internet of Things, and a global financial collapse followed, and a year later the RE Wars began.

By 2030, NIoT was a massive pervasive entity that controlled 99 percent of human activity. It was big. BIG Tech and BIG Data, ruled by multinational corporations, run by middle-aged white men who were household names. They called them GAFA—Google, Apple, Facebook, Amazon. They shaped the world consumption habits, and they cornered cultures, undermining democracies, and threatening individual liberties and creativity. Every publication ever written was scanned and uploaded. Publishing, media, music, even art, all were pirated and bootlegged until copyright became nonexistent. It was an era of banality, all about traffic, all about shifting and selling free content and personal data. Providers monitored all devices and communications, then sold the data. Personal surveillance went crazy, and every search, every movement, every click was monitored until individual liberty became nonexistent.

NIoT was a mess, an apocalypse at breaking point, but that was not the end because Ransomware was the end. The malicious software wreaked havoc on corporations and individuals. In 2033 a personal 3D-printer took down half a continent. It became impossible to go online without risking your identity, your Coin, or your data—impossible unless you were wealthy and willing to pay the enormous fees set by the security services to keep your corner of the world safe. And even then you were not safe for long.

At the same time, quantum computing—computing at the atomic and subatomic level of the universe, where particles like electrons or protons are in multiple states, performing multiple tasks and permutations at the one time—promised to break down a barrier between humanity and technology. It offered enormous potential in the information access arena, and it promised security. It was going to be a way out of the mess. Until it crashed NIoT.

In 2035, an entangled pair of light photons were separated, one kept on Earth and the other sent to the moon, 384,000 kilometers away. Despite the distance, the entangled photons stayed true to each other. The first foray into quantum cryptography from space was so spectacularly successful that few people envisaged the destruction that soon ensued.

Math is beautiful and prime numbers might be sublime, but the mass release of the first quantum computers sent an expanding algorithm into the universe that ate the NIoT for breakfast. It searched for databases and broke all encryptions. Social media, emails, messages, stored data, images—everything collapsed and vanished, along with the platforms and providers who'd created them. People wept in the streets, cried in their homes and offices; everything was gone. Everything. Their data was corrupted. The AI algorithm had distorted, morphed into a second, then third, generation, and smashed the failsafe blockchain.

This was sweet justice for the surveillance paranoids of the world, who had fervently pushed the notion of privacy for decades. They, of course, had prepared themselves for the crash. The rest of the world thought disengaging from NIoT guaranteed them safety. But the moment they opened and logged onto any device they lost everything. Backups disintegrated. The destruction was compared to the effects wreaked by a nuclear bomb. Entanglement worked, but people weren't ready for mass quantum computing.

A year after NIoT went down, the global economy collapsed. Jobs were scarce, education was expensive, technology had ceased to offer the divertive pastimes it once had, and surveillance was pervasive. Through all this, sea levels kept rising, people lost their homes, and millions of refugees roamed the planet in search of a place to live. In this uncertain, faltering environment, religion galvanized and emerged rejuvenated. It tapped into the deep-seated anger and aggression of the masses, it questioned the status quo of the economic world, and it morphed into fundamentalism. Fundamentalism works when people are adrift and vulnerable, but the underlying central issue of the Religious Wars was the pursuit of power. Destructive ideologies emerged under the guise of protecting traditional values, protecting family, protecting culture, protecting patriarchy, protecting the status quo. The economy collapsed, NIoT collapsed, and eight years of bloody war ensued.

Out of the debris rose eMpower, the tech giant that released the global population from centralized data storage, offering the masses user-controlled platforms.

Now, in 2050, NIoT is split into separate factions. One locale provides access to information, another is used for general communication, and private data is accessed though a separate interface. The deep, dark places on the Internet still exist. There is a place called the SpinnerNet—a spider's web, an intricate, woven trap. It's a place to hide things and a place to do dark deeds. If you get caught in the SpinnerNet, it can take years to untangle your data.

Many predicted the economic collapse and projected the imminent outbreak of war. Some of these people were artists and musicians, the avant-garde and the Pacifists. Others were Tech types and CEOs with massive Coin who could afford to relocate, and so, throughout the RE Wars, Hobart was isolated enough to remain prosperous and safe.

Quinn lived there all her life. She knows little else. Her home is in a small satellite hub called Styx, built close to the city. It's a machine-made homage to work and Tech. She's a property owner. She bought a Pod in a safe, planned zone of Styx—an exclusive community. It's an unmemorable place, a non-place. The buildings are square and clean, and the area is organized around central work hubs surrounded by residential zones, linked by speedways, so getting to work is fast and efficient. The demographic is a mix of young, ambitious, and smart types with plenty of Coin.

Lise hates—hated?—everything about the place. "Property ownership," she told Quinn more than once, "represents the plutocratic overindulgence of the upper classes. It's a receptacle of privilege for the wealthy and a cesspit of despair for the not so fortunate."

Lise lived—lives?—an hour away from Styx, in Hobart City. She saw the beauty of the city and the people who lived there. She didn't care that it has changed over the decades, that it's now louder and dirtier—she liked it that way. She said each area was unique, the streetscapes were varied, there was art and culture and things to do. She said the city is about the people and she quite liked people.

## Twenty-One

# They need soldiers.
# Time to go off your Meds.

ONE HUNDRED AND FIFTY years ago, there were five billion passenger pigeons on the Earth. But they were continually hunted for meat and feathers. By the end of the 1800s, there were fourteen left; the last one, Martha, died in 1914.

Martha2 is a stunning creature. She is larger than a gull and has striking, ochre-colored streaks covering her breast. She was gene sequenced from the original Martha's DNA, and further enhancements were added to her genetic coding. She has remarkable sight and exceptional sonar ability. She follows Tig.

For eleven days the Derecho whipped up the oceans, and Tig's mini sub, *Nanni,* was set adrift. At the mercy of the sea and without power, the storm swept the sub north into the Arabian Sea. After the wind settled, it took Martha2 two days to find Tig. Then it took Planck another three days to steer *Nanshe* in Tig's direction and fish him out of the ocean.

It's been two weeks since then, and now Tig is back on *Nanche.* Currently, he's despondently unpacking the faulty hydro panels from the sub.

Planck paces back and forth across the deck of the boat. Ze is on the Comms, and ze nods zirs head, intently listening to the caller.

When ze ends the call, ze turns to Tig. "Maim needs us back in Unus. The election is next week. It's a political nightmare and they're worried about a rebellion. They need soldiers. Time to go off your Meds, just until the election is finalized."

"First, Quinn. We pick her up, then—"

"She's gone. They already picked her up."

"Fuck! Where?"

"She was sent back home, to Hobart. She'll be safe there. She'll understand."

"Trust me, she ain't gonna understand."

"Why? What happened?"

Tig stacks the faulty cells, packing them into crates and hands the boxes to Planck. "We . . . well, we kinda had sex."

"You kinda had sex!" Ze's alarmed. "Are you serious? So you told her?"

Tig holds a cell in each hand. "Not really—not much time."

"Not much time, not much time? It's funny, isn't it, considering where we've come from?" Ze shakes zirs head and chuckles. "Not much time."

"It's not funny."

"No, no, it's not—just kind of ironic. So you didn't explain? You didn't say anything?"

"Nope."

"Do you think maybe you—"

"Yes, course I do, but it just sort of happened." He drops his head back, breathes heavily. "She, well she . . . she wanted to do it."

"Oh, I see."

"So we did. We did it all night. It was great. Then I left so I'd, I'd have time to think about it. Think about what to say, how to say it, explain the consequences, and hope like hell she understands and realizes, you know, it's me, it's us, and maybe . . ."

"Okay, okay, calm down, we go to Unus first—"

"No."

Planck points to the east. "It's just there. It's literally around the corner. We see Maim, we get the hydro sorted, and then we go to Hobart."

Tig sighs. "You're right. I'm sorry."

"You're forgiven. So, Hobart. I've never been, heard it's . . . quiet. She'll be safe if she doesn't die of boredom."

# Twenty-Two

# A Climate City.

A DARK-HAIRED WOMAN WAITS FOR Quinn on the sand by the transporter. She says her name is Myra and she'll be facilitating Quinn's departure and arrival. Myra is six feet tall, thin, grim-faced, and jowly. She has lustrous dark skin and slick hair, and from the neck down she's clad in black: a roll-neck ribbed jacket and gloves, and rippled leggings that morph into thigh-high boots.

*Not exactly beach wear.*

Myra's smooth, jowly face pokes out of her jumper like a turtlehead. Her dark eyes are amethyst pools, almost aubergine in color, and she has an extremely high, pronounced brow that forms a ridge over her face. Myra is more reptile than human, there is something distinctly lizard-like about her, but it's her eye color that gives away her species.

In the mid 2020s, legislation relaxed CRISPR restrictions and produced batches of sequenced embryos. Editing for disease was successful, but big problems arose when technicians attempted to add, or remove, human characteristics. The human genome was more complex and interconnected than anyone thought, and some freakish results were produced: people seven feet tall with turquoise eyes and IQs of two hundred. Emotional problems, like chronic shyness, indifference, and narcissism, were also detected. High IQs combined

121

with facial symmetry were linked to excessive amounts of earwax, dis-jointed toes, and OCD. Global legislation subsequently banned deep gene editing and manipulation for "artistic" purposes, but dodgy labs and unregulated regimes continued to experiment.

Quinn studies her arrival and departure facilitator. Myra is young, a baby of the late 2020s, and her purple eyes and supraorbital-ridged brow are clearly the products of illegal sequencing.

On board Myra hands Quinn protective sunglasses and a climate suit. "Put this on."

"Now?"

"No, next fucking week. Of course now."

*Geez, calm down.*

Her new climate suit is pale yellow, dirty—it smells—old style, and pre-used. Climate suits are made from a mycobacterial thermal fabric and there are many brands: Solarise, ThermaFibe, Insulate. Quinn's is a decade old. The newer versions are all microbial, self-cleaning, and fire retardant, and they won't shrink, fade, pill, or warp. The exterior is a matte layered metallic coating available in an endless variety of colors and design. The inner lining is made from hollow manufactured fibers melded with a nonwoven substrate. They insulate by repelling heat; once the suit is sealed around the body, it repels 80 percent of the surrounding environmental heat for six hours. Not sealed, it works as a reflector, without the insulating qualities. For the wearer, it feels like standing outside under an umbrella; it protects from sunlight, but the heat penetrates.

After slipping the suit over her clothes, Quinn discovers a hole—a split seam. The suit is essentially useless.

"There's a hole in this," she says, pointing to the offending area.

Myra glares at her like she's a small mouse, and Quinn's left arm, without instruction, reaches out and feels Myra's velvet skin and strokes her silken hair. Quinn reins it in and guides it into her pocket. Myra scowls like she's about to devour the small mouse. Quinn thinks facilitating departures and arrivals might be the wrong job for Myra; she should stay away from living things.

✶✶✶

They travel northeast, away from Hobart, and Quinn's heart sinks. "We seem to be going in the wrong direction," Quinn says. "Hobart is south-southeast of here."

Myra examines her fingernails. "Why would we be going to Hobart? No one told you that."

"I thought I'd be going home."

Myra shrugs.

"What the fuck! Seriously. If you're not here to take me home, then where are we going?"

"Debriefing." Myra yawns.

*I'm going to kill this woman. I've never killed anyone in my life, except for Jane. Myra will be my first human.* "Debriefing *where*?"

"Unus."

Unus is a strategic east-meets-west cultural metropolis, with a north-south geographical midpoint; half the city lies in the northern hemisphere, the other half in the southern hemisphere. Grand Central station has a longitude of 120 degrees with zero latitude. The city is ancient, over two thousand years old, and home to a hundred million people sizzling in 50-degree Celsius heat. As a central locality, Unus is also HQ for eMpower. And this is where Tig lives, on a boat on the harbor.

Quinn's heart quickens. She feels lightheaded at the thought of him, but then a melancholy mood settles over her—dejected disappointment. *What if he's dead? What if Lise is dead? What if I'm a curse, and the people I care for continue to die or disappear?*

The transporter approaches the city outskirts, then it breaches and proceeds due north. They're not landing in Unus. Out the window, she spies their destination: the Hanging Gardens of Babylon—a Climate City.

"Harmonia," Myra says, letting out a sigh. "Heaven on Earth."

Quinn gazes down and sees a fortress of undulating gardens and parks with residential towers rising two kilometers into the sky. It looks luxurious and expensive. *They're either very, very sorry for what they did, or they want something from me.*

"And look at the color of that water, exquisite."

The ocean is ultramarine, the color of a cornflower. "It looks bluer because there's no phytoplankton," Quinn says. "It's not a good thing."

Myra scowls.

"How long will I be here?"

"Depends on your sponsor."

"eMpower?"

Myra nods.

*They want something.*

The transporter lands, and they disembark at Mooring, a landing dock adjacent to the city. Quinn follows her facilitator towards a hundred meter–wide, water-filled channel; the closer they get, the cooler it gets. "There's a moat," Quinn says.

"No, it's cooling channel," Myra corrects.

*No, it's a moat, designed to protect the fortunate.*

Dotted across the water are large, circular sculptures, like giant floating eyes, layers of circles within circles. Myra calls them Spectrals. They symbolize perfection and unity and their mathematical precision is captivating. When Quinn finally pulls herself away from the view, Myra is thirty meters ahead, waiting for the silicon footbridge to unfurl over the moat.

They enter the city through an arched aquarium; a tunnel of sea life and the luminous colors of tropical fish and coral surround them. A purple octopus catches Quinn's eye and swims toward her, and her hair stands on end. The colors are bait, attracting her attention, drawing her in so security can process her.

When they enter the Climate City, the temperature drops another ten degrees.

"Sensors everywhere—data is feedback to the climate system; surface temperatures, window positions, shading devices, adjust automatically," Myra says proudly.

They continue into the heart of the city on foot—through narrow, shaded streets, past small courtyards, parks, and green spaces filled with edible fruit trees, herb gardens, and vegetable beds—and eventually they pause outside a residential complex called Habitat5.

"This is you," says Myra.

The external walls of the complex form a double façade, and Quinn leans against the cool terracotta skin, waiting while Myra fumbles with her entry codes. She tries several options, but there's a problem; the security doors won't open. Myra flicks through her Band and mumbles something about new codes and replacement codes and passcodes that were never sent or were outdated by the time she opened them. Trembling, she clenches her fists, grits her teeth, and emits a deep, resonating growl.

*She has the attention span of a shrub.* "Turn your Band on and off, then reload the last set of codes," Quinn suggests.

Myra glares, but follows the instructions. She turns her Band on and off, waits eleven seconds, then reloads the codes. The doors open.

The apartment Hubs are organized around an internal courtyard framed by waterfalls. "The water helps humidify the air," Myra says, "and then flows underground into fish breeding tanks. Wind towers draw heat out, funneling it back into the atmosphere, away from the city. If the temperature outside reaches 55 degrees Celsius, the cooling system supplements with mechanical ventilation, just as a precaution. It's the world's largest geothermal air heat exchanger. The building breathes and sweats; it's like a living thing."

*No, it's like a building.*

Myra points to the giant geothermal earth tubes embedded into the surrounding landscape. "Compressors pump cool air from underground into the building. There's also solar and hydro with an absorption chiller if things get really desperate. Rooftops, windows, they're all solar, with excellent light-to-energy conversion rates. Floors are kinetic. Get your self a pair of SolarFeet, and you can power your module as you walk. Everything generates energy."

"Water?"

"Filtered seawater and a recycled collection system. Plants and microbes filter and recycle the water back into the Pods."

"No rain?"

"Not for twelve years."

✶✶✶

Quinn's new home shoots straight up, six hundred levels into the stratosphere—a tessellating circular column that narrows as the building rises, then terminates with an elegant spire, a testament to technology and human ingenuity. They enter the skylift.

"New residents must volunteer and contribute to the collective community," Myra explains. "Right now, there are vacancies in gardening."

*I'm sure there are.* "Aren't there machines for that?"

"Harmonia is sponsored by the AHA. We believe in the virtues of manual labor—doing something with your hands and working outside, in the sunshine."

"Trust me, I won't be here long enough to enjoy the sunshine or the virtues of manual labor. I'm not staying."

"Your loss." Myra slides a spare Band off her wrist and hands it to Quinn.

*Finally.* Quinn pulls it on and logs in her details. There's no response. She turns it off, waits eleven seconds, and then logs in again. Nothing. "It's not working."

"The Pod is on OneHub, an instinctive system with an automated interface, motion cookies, facial recognition, and total encryption."

Quinn taps the Band; still no response. "I have nothing."

"Thought processes activate the appliances and—"

"Are you listening? It's not working."

"Try turning it on and off," Myra says dryly.

Quinn hands it back. "I can't access my data."

Myra refuses to take it. "It's generic, key services only; it gets you in and out. Tells the time, controls the OneHub in the apartment, and links to the Fourth Estate, but no communication or data."

"No, you don't understand, there are people I need to call. It's been two months . . ."

"Restricted access; you won't receive full benefits until your sponsor approves. Someone like you, you're lucky to be here. I wouldn't complain too much. Everyone wants to be in here, no one wants to be out there, in Unus, in the heat. This is paradise. And, wait until you see it, but you have your own vertical herb garden on the balcony."

"I don't want to be here, and I don't want a fucking vertical herb garden on my balcony. I want to call my father, and I want to go home. I think I've made that very clear. So you can tell my *sponsor* that I won't be staying, and . . ."

The skylift doors open at level 180, and Myra strides ahead into the Pod, leaving Quinn alone in the skylift.

Inside the Pod, OneHub initiates, preparing for their arrival; the lights spark, music hums, sunshades adjust, sliding into place, and tea brews in the food prep. "Welcome to your home, Quinn Buyers," a voice says. "Please step forward and come inside."

Quinn reluctantly steps forward and enters the Pod.

"Welcome. And Myra, always a pleasure to see you—and those boots! I love them. Tea is brewing, strong, medium, or mild, ready in one and a half minutes. Sweetener?"

Two months ago, Quinn would have requested a little less light, a higher room temperature, and strong herbal tea, preferably ginger. Now she finds the melodic voice unnerving, the rise and fall inflected with pretense. She locates the OneHub controls on her Band, opens the settings, and shuts the system down—immediately, the music dies, the lights dip, and the sunshades retract—then locates the passcodes and messes with the presets. It'll be a while before the system is up and running.

Myra glares; another excellent impersonation of a python about to devour a mouse. "You can't shut it down." Myra taps at her Band. "Hello. Hello. Activate. Activate." Nothing. The OneHub is conspicuously silent.

Quinn leaves Myra anxiously tapping and shouting into her Band and orbits the apartment. She has 360-degree views and a balcony facing east. The walls are formed thermo-concrete, and the floor is checkerboard stone. The furniture is sparse: a sofa, some low chairs, a set of nesting tables, a cowhide on the floor. A large bookcase, housing the classics: *Death by Black Hole, The Selfish Gene, Origin of Species.* There are two well-thumbed copies of *Excitons, Majoranas, and Weyl Fermions. Realistic Weather in the Arts* is new, never been opened, and was given to Quinn by Lise. Her mother likes a hard copy; she appreciates the pleasure of holding the volume in her hand. All the books and furniture, the art and rugs, belong to Quinn. They've moved her. Harmonia is not for debriefing. Harmonia is home.

She collapses onto the sofa and hugs a cushion. On the table next to her is a hand-carved vessel Matt gave her for graduation; she collects it and places it on the cushion in her lap. Then she adds a blue vase and a copy of *Excitons, Majoranas, and Weyl Fermions* to her collection of objects—she's making a cuddle pile—and wraps her arms around her things. These are her possessions. She'd completely forgotten about them, and they don't belong here. This is not her home, and she has no intension of staying.

"You have a meeting with eMpower tomorrow, in Solidarity," Myra says. "Take the Hyperloop, it's free. Exit and reentry clearance are authorized."

"What day is it?"

"Sunday. You're registered as a resident. It's an election year; you must vote. It's compulsory. Reinstate New Fed. They're our party, our people, and they'll keep the status quo. Now, there's a care package of supplies in the food prep. If you can't cook, the scullery will prepare something for you. Don't go outside the City without your suit, unless you want to die; heat stroke killed over a million last year. Restaurants and bars are on Basement6. There's also a rain room—weather experience, really, but most people go for rain. Or snow. Or hail. Basement9. You'll need to book."

*I'm trapped. No data, no Coin, and no way out. This changes everything.*

"Also, no pets, no littering, no smoking, no alcohol or music in pubic spaces, no worshiping, no protesting, no random picking of greenery that doesn't belong to you, and no wheels."

"No wheels?"

"No, transport's free. Take the Loop round the city if you need."

"Hovers?"

"I fucking hate those things. Restricted to above ground, city perimeter. I swear, they'll be illegal by the end of the year."

*Good lordt, we agree on something.* Quinn's collided with inexperienced Hover riders many times.

Myra slithers away.

In the food prep, a couple of mini Bots play on the bench: retro designs with angular bodies, both wearing red shoes and matching hats. One has a daisy print on its torso and the other has a set of gears, the symbol for old Tech. Both have large, adorable blue eyes. They play hide and seek around the cabinets. She collects them and drops them into the skylift, then heads out onto the balcony.

Gazing over winding streets and parks of Harmonia, she sees a calculated network of circular buildings, paths, and greenery, organically shaped public spaces, and abstract buildings sliced, angled and twisted to fit together. "They've done away with the square."

Beyond this is the vast metropolis of Unus, shimmering in a haze of heat, but the vista is smog free. Heat vapor lingers over the city, but there's no pollution. Carbon towers filter the air, sucking in VOC particles, the nitrous oxide, sulfur dioxide, and carbon.

Past the city towers and residential blocks of housing is the cornflower blue sea of the harbor—Tig's harbor.

Quinn turns and heads back inside.

# Twenty-Three

# There is a bar.

THERE IS A BAR—WHICH means there is alcohol, which means Quinn could get her hands on something long and cool and escape the clarity of reality for a few hours. This erroneous fantasy of a city cannot possibly be her new home. A decent amount of alcohol will kill the past two months, anaesthetize the present, and snuff out her fear of the future. She'd love a drink—actually, she'd love ten. Unfortunately, she has no access to her Coin.

*Maybe someone will buy me a drink—not a ridiculous idea.* She formulates a plan: She'll go for a walk, check out the Climate City—those giant geothermal earth tubes look interesting—then swing back past Basement6 (etched in her memory), find a bar, and get herself a drink or two. Now that's a plan.

✳✳✳

Entertainment is underground, beneath the Habitats, a sprawling network of water gardens and contemplative spaces connected by bridges and walkways and littered with restaurants, tea houses, cafés, and bars. There's a daylight capture system that channels sunlight underground, ensuring the cool cavities below the surface are flooded with natural light so it doesn't look or feel artificial. Precipitation gathered from the waterfalls creates a self-sustaining microclimate that keeps greenery healthy and the place super hydrated.

Every person Quinn passes looks perfect, oddly fabulous and fault-less. Enhanced by the diffused halo of natural light, their complexions glow, their hair bounces and shines, and it appears they've made an enormous effort with both hair and grooming—and yet it also appears to be their reality. This is exactly who they are and how they live. They are also united by communal vanity—the desire to appear younger than they are. And they do. All the inhabitants look under thirty; certainly, no one appears older than forty. Fashion trends thrive here, clearly, and this year's fad is elbow-length gloves and pants that morph into boots.

Quinn circumnavigates the first bar she sees on Basement6. It's called Jpeg and it has a rustic High-Tech vibe: cobblestone floors and natural granite walls cut straight into the stratums under Harmonia, reflective chairs and furniture—polished silver and copper mirrors—and bioluminescent lighting sculptures shaped like fungus. She makes her way to the bar and scans the cocktail menu; their specialty is alcoholic shakes with fake flavors named after the Climate Cities—Harmonia, Accord, Solidarity, Amity, Serenity. Today's special, however, is the Dirac Devine, a ginger and mint tea infusion with a double shot of gin, and that's Quinn's pick. She can already taste it.

There's a moderate crowd about. She figures she needs to start a conversation and get someone's attention, so she feigns interest in the decorative light sculptures, watching them slowly drift past. Then she walks from one side of the bar to the other, twice, and reads the bar menu again. No one makes eye contact.

Across the room she spies Myra, nestled in a booth with a group of friends. Myra also sees her. Tilting her serpent-like head in Quinn's direction, she makes a comment to her allies, and all eyes are directed at Quinn. A mutual snicker rises from the clique.

Quinn is impressed; she didn't think Myra could do humor. But she knows why they are laughing. Her self-awareness hasn't vanished; two months alone, no makeup, no grooming, wearing a dirty yellow climate suit—she must look a wreck. She steps sideways and views her mottled likeness in a reflective panel behind the bar. *I've aged ten years in two months. What's that on my neck, some sort of rash? And my hair, good lordt, it's one fibrous knot.*

Quinn's hankering for alcohol diminishes. This place is not for her, and she retreats back to the skylift. A man hurriedly slips in behind her. He balances a module on the palm of his hand.

"Useless piece of shit." He waves a futile hand over the device. "We've militarized the Moon and here I am, still trying to sync Tech."

"Turn it on and off, reset your preferences." *Seriously, does no one understand basic Tech anymore?*

"Really?"

*Yes, really.* "Extensions, networks, accounts, disable, then resync. Here, give it to me."

He hesitates. He's reluctant, and that's fair enough; she wouldn't be handing over her module to a stranger with bird's net hair wearing a disgusting climate suit. Her left hand swipes his Module. Then it swipes his pass codes, which are stored in one folder with no security, and transfers them to her Band, and then it resets his codes and syncs the Module. *Too obvious. Looked like he was waiting for me. No, I'm paranoid. Shit, what's happened to me?*

She hands back the Module. "I'm Quinn. I'm . . . new."

"Hitch. Thanks. Appreciate it. Been here three years. If you need anything?"

"A drink. I'd really like a drink. Been a long . . . time."

"There's a bar just—"

"Coin issues."

He considers her, and then his grin softens, "You like beer?"

"Yes. I love beer." *Doesn't everyone love beer? Isn't beer just the best drink in the whole world?*

\*\*\*

Hitch is standing at Quinn's door, clutching a bag. "Home brew. No hops. But engineered yeast gives it a floral, slightly bitter flavor. Think orange blossom."

Brewing ale in this climate must be tough. Temperature is the key to successful fermentation, and controlling temperature in this heat is complicated. But now she has three cold bottles. What a nice man. Maybe she'll delete his security codes. Then again, maybe not.

Despite the proliferation of greenery in the streets and gardens of Harmonia, there is nothing fresh in her food prep. The cupboards are stocked with dehydrated goods. Dinner is a toss-up between Country Inspired Baked Root Vegetable with Mixed Herbs and Classic Style Country Cuisine Spaghetti with Tasty Chili Crumbs. She selects spaghetti and knocks the top off her first home brew. It's delicious: hoppy, with orange blossom undertones. When the bottle is empty, she opens another.

\*\*\*

Quinn opens her eyes. It's morning and she's on the sofa, which is where she passed out last night. One hoppy home brew turned into three. Her head hurts; she's lost her tolerance for alcohol and should have checked the alcoholic content before recklessly sculling three bottles.

More sleep is what she needs. She closes her eyes. A few more hours and she'll be fine. Her left hand gently strokes the side of her face, and it's comforting. Yes, just a few more hours of sleep is all she needs. The hand pats a little harder, until it's no longer a pat. Now it's a slap.

She opens her eyes. *Fuck, this has got to stop.* She pushes the hand deep into her pocket.

It pops out. She puts it back.

"Stay."

It pops out again.

Now she's awake and nauseous. She scurries to the bathing zone and pukes. It helps. As she rinses her mouth, she looks up and scrutinizes her face in the glass. The rash circling her neck has subsided—a positive outcome—but otherwise, her physical appearance is startling; she doesn't look like herself anymore. Soft, downy hair flourishes around her jawline and a light moustache shadows her upper lip. A feathery mane covers her legs and has sprouted under her arms. Even her toes are hairy. *I don't look human. A few weeks ago, Tig said I was beautiful. Clearly, he couldn't see what I really look like.*

She staggers into the food prep to boil water. Outside, it's 42 degrees. The sunshades automatically adjust themselves over the balcony. She picks some leaves from the vertical herb garden—mint, basil, chamomile—throws them into the hot water, and rests in the shade. Her head hurts. *Never drinking again.* She watches her left hand write out a word in the cloudy film on the tabletop; it says *eMpower meeting.*

*Fuck, what day is it?*

# Twenty-Four

# Herostratic, do you know what it means?

Solidarity is fifty kilometers west of Harmonia. At Myra's suggestion, Quinn takes the Hyperloop; it's fast, free, and the journey takes only seven minutes. It took her longer to navigate the underground platforms.

eMpower's offices are located in dense parkland a kilometer north of the city center, so she walks. Every step brings her closer to confronting Niels: Mori's brother, the CEO of eMpower, the man who kept her confined for two months on a lonely atoll. He had her charged with 1,962 counts of murder, and then he moved her here, still a prisoner, with no access to her data, no communication. She's apoplectically angry—so angry that when she arrives at the eMpower complex her vision blurs and she can't see anything. Nothing, no cluster of buildings, just empty parkland. Then an auto arrives and disappears underground. A drone hovers overhead, and then berths. Segway security guards linger in the gardens. *Of course*, she realizes, *it's invisible*. Cloaked with reflectors and echo sonar, the structure blends into the surrounding parkland. She can just make out the hard-edged, linear outline, but the body of the building is a shimmering mirage of conifers and woodland—a surreal vision. She supposes that's the metaphysical point—how do you know what's real and what's not?

Where does reality stop and technology begin? Senses are deceiving. She scoffs; she doesn't need a mega-rich corporation serving up philosophical ideologies along with their data plan.

As she approaches the invisible building, a mantra begins to solidify: Remain rational at all times. Say nothing. Smile and nod. Nodding is good. Let him do all the talking. Let him explain himself; let him tell her why she's here and what he wants.

Quinn enters the building just as her friend Jin exits the skylift. They pause, considering one another, taking in each other's shabby facades. Jin's smile beams across the foyer, but Quinn sees beneath the feigned expression. Her friend is pale and tired; FF got its teeth into her DNA, and it's a long and difficult recovery.

Jin is impatient and she breaks into a little skip, lessening the distance between them, but the exercise is too much and she pulls up, coughing and gasping. Quinn notes the telltale signs of hard work: Jin's yellow bob hangs limp, her clothes are crumpled (she's been sleeping in her office), and her eyeliner is smudged (she hasn't washed for days). Focused on a special project, Jin works continuously for days and weeks, which is great for eMpower, but not so good for her health; her immune system is impaired, and Quinn blames Jin's parents for this. Her mother worked two jobs, laboring at More Than Meat during the day to produce synthetic meat proteins and in the evenings at Organ-Farm, 3D-printing human transplants. Her father was a space traffic controller who worked seventy hours a week, so he was never home.

An AI called Salt raised Jin. Salt was gendered female, one of the first generation of robots to feel pain—or, as Quinn endlessly corrects, "*simulate* the feeling of pain; they can't fucking feel anything." Salt greeted Jin when she came home from school, helped her study, read her stories before bed, and cooked and cleaned for her. She was parent, sibling, and best friend to Jin, and Jin loved her as much as any child loves her parent. Salt did everything for her and, as a result, taught her nothing about life and zilch about how to get on in the world—the world outside the apartment Pod. Jin resided in a homogenized, spotless environment with limited contact to bacteria, and the isolation impaired her immune system.

It wasn't Jin's fault; Salt preferred to entertain her indoors. It wasn't Salt's fault; how can an AI take the blame? Jin graduated with a science scholarship, a double degree, and a PhD before she turned twenty-five. Her parents applauded themselves; she was a success, and they'd done a fine job with their only child. She just had a perpetual cold.

Jin is a remarkable human, Quinn will concede that. Her intellectual capacity is astonishing and her memory is acute; she can read and absorb journals and books in hours. She'll quote formulas and the fundamental Laws of Science word for word, and she'll multiply sequences of numbers before Quinn has entered them into a Module. Her life skills, however, fall at the opposite end of the abilities scale. At the age of twenty-five, she didn't know how to make a cup of tea or use a heat plate. Today, she still struggles with clothes and shoes, buttons and laces. She falls over her own feet, constantly bumps into people, furniture, and doors. She can't wash or clean or cook for herself. But she succeeds at work, and she's now the head of Robotics at eMpower, coding AI that she believes will one day live in harmony with human kind.

Two years ago, Jin developed an information network that functioned alongside an ethical belief system—an AI with a moral code. It has the ability to evolve and learn from experiences, but it isn't truly self-aware (she's working toward that now). She called the AI Agent—a reference to humankind's inherent need to project personality onto non-organic elements, like Tech, Autos, and an AI called Salt. Niels appointed Agent to the board of eMpower. It gets a vote. *He* gets a vote. He's gendered male.

Quinn knows Agent. They spent time together in the early phases of his development. Jin needed to provide the AI with varied experiences, so Quinn was her lab mouse. Agent is the most advanced AI in existence, but he has no solid physical form; he's an algorithm. His only feature is a warm holo glow that hovers over a Module.

"I didn't realize you were here," Quinn says as Jin draws closer.

Jin grabs her face with both hands and kisses her firmly on the mouth. She's done this before, usually when she's drunk. She's a good kisser, and girls have soft lips, so Quinn doesn't mind. But this kiss has an agenda; Jin has something in her mouth, hard and round, like a large nut, that she attempts to pass to Quinn, who initially resists, until Jin squeezes her meaningfully. After slipping the nut thing into Quinn's mouth, Jin pulls back, makes eye contact, and gives Quinn a firm nod. So Quinn swallows the nut thing, or she tries to, but her mouth is dry and it gets stuck at the back of her throat. She coughs and coughs, but it won't move.

Her left arm reaches around and slaps her violently on the back. Finally, it goes down.

"Are we really at this point?" Quinn rasps. "Swallowing secret—"

"Good," Jin says, "*that's* done and we'll talk about *that* later." Then she hugs her friend. "I tried to find you. Tried to get you out. It's been shit here. I've missed you so much." She wipes away a tear. "Sorry, whining, I know, your life's worse, much worse. Just had no one to talk to. They moved us, the whole team, after the . . . event, we're all at Accord. The largest Climate City."

"They moved me, too."

"At least you're safe." She pulls a loose strand from Quinn's fibrous hair. "This is an interesting look."

"Yes, trying something new. You like it?"

She grins. "Not particularly. Come on. They're waiting. You ready?"

"For what?"

"Fuck knows. But he wants the G12. And he might want you as well."

***

Quinn enters the conference room, and all eyes turn her way. Eight of the nine board members are seated at the table; Mori is conspicuously absent. Niels is here, of course, along with Agent and six appointed executives whom she can't tell apart—all fit, well-dressed, middle-aged men. *It's 2050, where are the women? Even Agent is gendered male.* They wear Bands that monitor their lifestyle 24/7; sleep patterns, heart rate, blood pressure, cholesterol, alcohol, and exercise units. Healthy employees are more productive. Healthy employees get bigger bonuses. Healthy employees make more Coin for eMpower.

Niels is seated at the far end of the table. He's fifty-two and he looks twenty-five. She's heard the rumors: intravenous blood, young blood, preferably teenage blood, if you can get it. It lowers the risk of cancer and Alzheimer's, improves chromosome strength, and prevents aging. In 1950, two lab mice, one old and one young, were stitched together, interweaving their blood supply. The old mouse was rejuvenated and the young one deteriorated.

Niels has the same grey-blue eyes and air of confidence as Mori, but he's not like Mori. Mori loves people; Niels loves Tech. It keeps him alive, literally. He doesn't eat, solid food doesn't passes his lips. Instead, he lives on a cocktail of microbes. So, he never shits—no bathroom breaks to interrupt his work. Quinn scans the microbe-munching specimen, and there's no doubt—he looks great. He wears dark, microfiber pants tied at the waist with a silicon cord, a white T-shirt that fits him like cyber skin, and a high-neck, molded grey jacket. Then she sees the gloves: black net gloves, tied with silicon around his wrists. He's yielded to fashion. He rakes a gloved hand through his glossy hair, reminding Quinn how fabulous he is compared to her. She's a sight, with her rash and wild hair and dirty yellow climate suit. She holds out her arms and turns, in a small circle, so they get the full view, so they get to see what they've done to her.

"Why don't you sit down?" suggests Niels, "We're here to help."

"Are you fucking kidding me? Two months. You left me there for two months." She moves toward the table and the men shuffle back in their chairs. "If that's the sort of help you're offering, you can shove it up your shiny, food-free anus."

"Calm down."

"Fuck off." *The calm persona thing was never going to work.* "And get to the point, because I'm not staying."

Niels rises from his chair. "Do you know what Herostratic . . ." His chair is self-parking. It glides away from him and attempts to self-park under the table, but it hits his leg and has to reposition. They wait until the furniture is secure. "Herostratic, do you know what it means?"

"Of course, I don't." *No one does.*

"It means fame at any cost. The Greek, Herostratus, burned down the Temple of Artemis so he'd be immortalized. Famous forever. Didn't care who he killed. You've been diagnosed with a self-destructive form of recognition-seeking behavior. Unfortunately, we didn't catch it early enough."

*Is he serious?* "That's the best you can do? I knew about the Sky River but didn't tell anyone so I'd be famous as the only survivor? Is that what you're saying? You've had two months, and you went with Hero, Herostra . . ."

"Herostratic."

"Whatever, you went with that? Agent, what do you make of all this?"

Agent's holo glows bright. "Socrates said, 'Fame is the perfume of heroic deeds.' But there is no evidence of heroic deeds here. I voted in your defense. I was the only one." *Great. I have a machine on my side.*

"We've come to an arrangement with Hexad: You've been released into my care, pending observation and treatment. We think you still have something to offer, we want you to come and work for us."

"Seriously?"

"Sit down, let's talk about it." He pulls out a chair for her.

She doesn't take it. The chair parks itself back under the table.

"A legitimate offer," Niels says. "Climate prediction—that was your area, wasn't it?"

"Where's your brother?"

"Your fiancé is safe. He got out, thankfully."

"Didn't he tell you? I called it off."

Niels pulls back, now he's off guard. Mori didn't tell him the full story. He gives Quinn an unblinking stare, and she returns it.

"I have the G12," she says. "It's safe, and I checked it the day of the storm: no clouds, no rain, nothing. It doesn't make mistakes. Very soon, I will relaunch it, and I will figure out what happened. Then maybe I will take the data to Hexad and see what they make of it. So suck on that."

He blinks and shifts his gaze to the table. Suddenly it's obvious—he knows the truth; he knows why the climate model didn't show the storm.

"Leave me alone," she says. "Whatever shit you've gotten yourself into, it's not my fault or my problem. Release my data and my Coin."

She exits the meeting and finds Jin asleep in a chair outside the door.

"Hey." She slumps next to her friend.

Jin leans her head on her shoulder. "What happened?"

"Offered me a job."

"Tactics. Don't be fooled." She tilts her head and whispers into Quinn's ear, "Access. Special programs. My files."

Quinn nods. Their security and access codes are similar, two digits apart, a considered decision made years ago in case they ever needed to access each other's work. Jin has high-level clearance; she'll leave the files open for Quinn.

"Let's get out of here, go somewhere we can talk," Quinn says.

"Can't, I need to rest. Go home, be careful, I'll see you soon." Jin kisses her on the cheek and waves her outside.

# Twenty-Five

# The gap between rich and poor—now it includes cool air and a garden view.

RETURNING TO HER HUB, Quinn meets Myra in the Skylift. She's wearing the same outfit as yesterday—high boots, gloves, and a turtleneck—but today the fabric is a crisp snow white. She's a negative of yesterday's persona.

"Community service," she says. "You haven't signed up."

*Why does she care?* "I just got here."

"Eight hours if you're employed, fifteen if you're not. Gardening is still available. There's a group meeting this afternoon. Eastern side of the Habitat. I'm signing you up."

"Why am I doing this?"

"It's your civic duty. Harmonia is a spiritual co-op, and community work is enriching. It fosters a sense of kinship with fellow inhabitants. You also get Vouchers; you can use them in the entertainment zone."

"Do you volunteer?"

"Yes, I run the Building Information Tech and Consumer Help. BITCH. I'm the bitch."

*Took the words right out of my mouth.*

"And don't forget to vote. It's compulsory."

*So much for democracy.*

The acquisition of Vouchers is at the forefront of Quinn's mind. With those she can buy alcohol at the end of the day, which, right now, she really needs. *So much for never drinking again.*

She arrives at her allotted garden bed on time. Several volunteers raise a hand in salutation; the rest look her over and then promptly ignore her. No one bothers with names or introductions; they keep their distance. Quinn understands. Her climate suit radiates a deficiency of some sort, possibly poverty, and she simply can't be bothered to explain herself, given that she has no intention of staying in Harmonia and will never see these people again. She's here for the Vouchers.

Val is the name of their group manager. Val begins with a spiel, "An Introduction to the Climatic Environment," and he spends half an hour talking to her about the soil, the watering system, the importance of the sun and the life cycle of a cloud. Quinn gets the irony, but she doesn't bother explaining her PhD in clouds. Instead, she falls asleep standing up.

Because she's new, she's put on weeds and soil tuning—no planting, trimming, harvesting, or sharp tools. She was also supposed to bring her own gloves. "Next time," Val says. Eventually, while supervised, she gets to pull out a single weed. Unfortunately, she doesn't do this correctly, and he feels the need to demonstrate.

"Bend at the knees, hover, stretch, grab, pluck, discard, check, then check again," he says. "Important to always check again."

Val is fond of verbs. He walks the perimeter of the garden, pointing out weeds that need plucking, and it occurs to Quinn that it would be a faster and more efficient process if he pulled them out himself. After three hours and fifty-five minutes, the group packs up their tools and leave. But Val won't sign off on Quinn's time. He says she needs more practice, that she must stay another half hour so she can perfect her weed-pulling technique.

*I'm never doing this again.*

She's doubled over weeding when Hitch, the beer brewer, walks past. He is wearing a business shirt and carrying a satchel, and he looks like a grown-up with a proper, important job. He could be a Tech manager, Quinn muses, but then again, he can't sync his module. Perhaps he's a supervisor or an accountant or a manager.

Hitch sees Quinn. "Hello," he says, offering a little wave.

"Hey," Quinn says. "Thanks for the beer. It was delicious."

He lingers. "Where's the rest of your group?"

"Had to stay back . . . practice."

He finds this amusing.

"It's my civic duty," she concedes.

"No. They can't outsource labor—too scared to let anyone in; they might overstay their welcome. It's a closed community. And those Voucher things, they're a joke; you get one per shift. A hundred might get you a Titan."

"A Titan?"

"Cocktail, house special."

"I've been conned."

"Yep. Worth more in Unus. It'll get you a not-meal there."

"This is the worst job." Now she's laughing.

"Find something else." He brushes something from his eye. "You've got tech skills, right?"

"Yes."

"Offer them as a social service. I'll show you. How 'bout we discuss it over a Titan, my shout?"

"Okay, great."

"Meet you at the Tiki Bar at five."

"At five." She grins; she's found herself a drink and a companion.

∗∗∗

Quinn settles on a deep green rattan stool at the end of the long bar at Tiki, an establishment modeled on a Robinson Crusoe–style tropical hideaway. The interior is decked out in wicker furniture and decorated with dozens of palms, cane baskets, and straw canopies. Wall-to-wall bamboo surrounds the perimeter and low-level lighting descends from the ceiling. The vibe is Low-Tech, tropical beach shack, tiki kitsch. The decor is credible; someone has done a good job of convincing Quinn she's somewhere else.

Through the forest of palm fronds, the bartender makes eye contact. Reluctantly, Quinn dismisses him; she's on time, but Hitch is five minutes late. Another ten minutes slips past and now he's fifteen minutes late. Perhaps he got caught up at work; she knows how that can happen—time slips away at the end of a busy day. Still, she checks the name of the bar: Tiki.

She checks her Band again. Now he's twenty-two minutes late. Not a good sign, but she's desperate, so she commits to wait another eight minutes, exactly half an hour.

The bartender makes eye contact again, walks over, and places a drink on the bar, directly in front of her. "The Titan," he says. "House special: grain alcohol and goji juice with an ackee apple garnish."

She shakes her head, wrong order.

"Your date, he's not coming; there's been an emergency, he sends his apologies."

So Hitch is a no-show. She's been stood up. It might be the truth. There could be an emergency: trapped in the office with an accounting problem; a glitch with the formulae, debits and credits won't reconcile.

It could be worse. She could be alone here without a long, cool, alcoholic drink sitting on the bar in front of her. She stirs the drink with a bamboo swizzle. Goji berries are prolific, they thrive in the heat, and Quinn's a big fan of the slightly sour fruit. Ackee apples, however, taste like stodgy cheese, so she spears the garnish with the swizzle, fishes it out, and begins to gulp down her drink. She orders another before she's finished and charges it to Hitch's tab.

Gratified, sitting alone at the end of the bar with her second Titan, a nice little alcoholic buzz permeating her senses, the reality of that afternoon's gardening begins to fade.

A guy slides onto the jungle green stool next to her. She notes the line of vacant stools along the bar. He chose the one hard up beside her and tucks his lanky legs under the bench, his knees scraping hers in the process. She shuffles away.

"This one's free, right?" he asks.

She nods. *They're all free.*

A Bot jumps from his shoulder onto the bartop. It takes a human form, round head and square body, oblong limbs. It's dressed in military apparel, a blue suit with red and white stripes. The Bot looks her way and then somersaults forward and backward, showing off.

Give a Bot encouragement, and it goes on forever. She offers a blank, indifferent stare, and it takes its cue, settles despondently, but quietly, on the bar.

The man grins at the AI and taps it gently on the head. "Good Bot." He turns his attention back to Quinn. "Been in Unus, fifty-two at midday, so friggin' crowded. The people funnel from the Loop is friggin' archaic, thought I was gonna expire. Better here. Right?"

She offers another noncommittal nod.

Her keen friend is white and young, open-faced, with a slick of blond hair that falls across his forehead. He orders a red wine Vocktail, a virtual drink, designed to fool his senses into thinking it's a full-bodied Shiraz. Then he points to her glass and asks if she would like another.

"Sure," she says. Why not? She has absolutely nothing else to do.

"Been here long?" he asks.

"Two days." *Presume he means the place, not the bar.*

"Like it?"

"Impressive, but detached. Not real, if you know what I mean. Everything's round—winding roads, squiggly buildings, like some sort of metaphor, communities and civic virtue, that sort of shit. Right?"

"Yep. Designed by an AI algorithm. Rumor is it was modeled on a VR game, digital simulations and virtual forms, nothing touched by human hand, as if you can't tell. And we're like slaves, brought here for maintenance, trapped in little cells with nice panoramas."

"And the gap between rich and poor—now it includes cool air and a garden view?"

"Yep."

The bartender places a wine goblet in front of Quinn's companion. The glass releases invisible gas, mimicking the bouquet of his selected wine. Tongue-stimulating electrodes on the rim emulate the taste. He swirls the glass on the bar top, takes a sip, then thoughtfully considers the experience. He nods; he's satisfied.

"I mean, this friggin' planet is over. Right? We're broiling and drowning in plastic and pollution, trapped on this friggin' shit hole. Better off out there, in the stars. Right?" He offers her his wine glass for a midair toast. "To the stars."

She obliges, raises her glass; this is the time to enjoy a free drink, not to debate the future of humankind on Planet Earth. She moves to tap his glass, but at the last minute, he pulls away. She's left holding her drink in midair. *What the fuck? It was his idea.*

He grins. It was a joke; he caught her out, and he thinks it's funny. *People are weird.*

"I'm sorry, just having a bit of fun," he says and offers up his drink again, this time for real.

She considers his hand cupping the wine goblet. His nails are raw and bleeding, bitten to the quick. It looks painful. He raises his glass again but she has no faith. Her left hand takes her glass. As he moves to greet her, he repeats the joke and pulls away again, but she anticipates his move and their glasses clink. His joke has failed.

His grey eyes narrow, staring at her. Quinn spies a black dot fixed to the side of his head—an MRA, a Mind Reading Apparatus. He's scanning her thoughts, tracking her mood and emotions. The device is a handy tool, designed to give the wearer an edge, a one-up on their opponent. Usually used in meetings—or on dates, hidden below a hat or under the hairline—the gadget detects brain activity, revealing the truth about human feelings. Humans don't always say what they think, and sometimes they hide behind calm personas when they are actually freaking out inside. Brain waves reveal their frustrations. Wearing an MRA like this—so obvious, in public, at a bar—is social cringe.

Quinn smiles politely, slides off her stool. Their conversation is over.

✶✶✶

Quinn wakes up this morning nauseous and hung over, again. *If I drink more, my tolerance to alcohol will improve.* She manages not to throw up, and she calls this progress.

Today, she'll stay in Harmonia. She'll drink green tea; she'll vote; then she'll drink more green tea, and maybe she'll shit out a capsule containing . . . what? A code? A file? Who knows what Jin is up to, but she likes a bit of drama. Quinn hopes it holds something worthwhile, something important, information she can use, like Mori's whereabouts, or stuff on eMpower's special programs—something to blackmail Niels with, so she can get her data back and get out of here. She hopes it's not a declaration of love, or a poem that Jin's written for her or about her. Jin is fond of writing out her feelings, and Quinn suspects this is what it will be—something sentimental or funny, a declaration of friendship and love. Jin has one friend, and for the past two months she's had little else to do but work and worry about her. It's very possible that during this time she has also dedicated a few lines of poetry to her.

# Twenty-Six

# Quinn the Brave.

Unus was the first region solidified by Hexad after the Religious Wars ended six years ago, and during this time it sheltered under part civil and part military rule. Now it will be the first of the megacitics to vote. The ballot is pitched as a free election—scrupulously honest, violence free—and will take place over the next three days. The five other metropolises forming Hexad will follow, voting east to west across the planet. Unus has been labeled a test case, leading the way for a new, liberated, global way of life, firmly and finally freed from the shackles of war.

Quinn searches the Fourth Estate news feeds on her Band, scanning the sagacious contenders who've put their hands up as election candidates. There are three political parties with enough funds and support to rule. Her first option is to reinstate the caretaker government, New Federation. Her second is to vote Democratic Republic. The third party, Fundamental Atheists, just threw their ticket in with Democratic Republic as a united front against New Fed. Now she's left with two choices.

New Federation was founded by the custodian government candidates installed after the RE Wars. All are ex-military. The Fourth Estate vociferously denounce them and their leader, Dirac Devine, claiming they've exploited public fears about violence and safety in an attempt to maintain a stronghold over Unus. Pecuniary interests gnaw at their foundations, and self-seeking bureaucrats have provided economic advantages to the big corporations.

Quinn studies the image of Dirac Devine, a small, serious man who believes the world is flat and climate change is god's retribution. The Fourth Estate claims he is about to lose his quasi-fascist hold over the megacity.

Maim Quate is an academic, a professor of history specializing in Mesopotamian art and culture, and has no political experience. She's more comfortable in front of a lecture hall than a senate committee. She's an atheist and an Earth Optimist, and she's for science. She has a controversial plan to make 50 percent of the planet a restorative ecosystem, cornering off areas to fence out humans, for good. Drones will maintain the forests and plant thousands of seedlings every day. Strict rules will prevent further deforestation. She espouses egalitarian ideologies for a free and equal society, and she has the same haircut as Lise.

Quinn votes for her.

With an empty afternoon ahead of her, Quinn sips her third cup of green tea, hoping for a bowel movement, while browsing the unread volumes in her bookcase. She opens *Realistic Weather in the Arts* and scans the misty paintings of rain, fog, sleet, and snow. There are foreboding oil paintings of thunderstorms and dark, flat nimbostratus clouds and luminous images of sunsets, sunrises, blue skies, and fluffy, cumulous clouds. Quinn appreciates realism, she doesn't understand the point of abstraction. Art is supposed to look like something. But there are a few vague and dreamy endeavors depicting air and light that she likes, and she grasps the skill involved in painting mist and rain.

She closes the book. This is what they have left: interpretations and misty memories. No more rain, snow flurries, rainbows, or sun showers. The weather room, Bacement9, beckons.

Simulated atmospheric experiences are no longer a novelty. Quinn has tried them before—enclosed areas where the temperature drops and snow and rain pelt participants from multiple directions. You can build a snowman, or throw snowballs, or stomp on an icy puddle. Her Raynaud's syndrome leaves her cold. It takes time to recover, to bring the blood back, but this is not a deterrent to her; it is a joy to be cold and pelted with snow and rain. The experience sometimes leads to addiction; there are those who continually return for more ice and snow, day after day. Blue skies and heat can weigh you down, and the real-world reality of endless sunshine can be hard to bear.

Quinn searches the link on her Band. There is an opening this afternoon. She takes it.

✳✳✳

The skylift drops Quinn at an automated reception with holo screens and instructions. There are several options. One is to retrieve a unique weather memory from the past, perhaps a birthday or graduation; select the date, time, year, and location, and the system will duplicate the weather for that day.

Memory is fickle. Combine it with unreliable emotions, and Quinn knows she might be disappointed by the memory option. She decides on a new, personalized experience: white, fluffy clouds and a sun shower, followed by a rainbow. She selects late spring, gentle bird song, and the scent of jasmine mixed with fresh-cut grass. Then she waits in the antechamber for her personalized experience to load.

When the walls of the chamber dissolve, she's standing in a vast landscape, at the top of a gentle rise, surrounded by wiry grass and spinifex. The scope is epic: kilometers of horizon. She didn't expect the limitless openness and broad arc of the sky. She turns a full circle, full of disbelief and shock; she knows this landscape. This is her father's property outside of Hobart. This is Matt's land. Have her thoughts been hacked? It's possible, because it's not a coincidence.

This sensation is unnerving. She catches her breath, and her fingers tingle. If Matt were here, she knows what he'd say: "All this space and nothing to think about. Perfect." Despite the unsettling familiarity of the scene, she concedes that the scale is impressive and the idea clever, so inventive. Curious to see how the experience works, what's real and what's not, she runs her hand over the long grass. It feels like grass. In the distance is the outline of a forest—*Must be virtual*—but on the hill where she stands, several dead ghost gums litter the landscape. *Probably real.* Two kangaroos hop into the scene, chew on some grass, then disappear into the gully and emerge on the far side of the hill. *Maybe virtual.*

The hills on either side fall away, sloping down to a small creek. She ambles down toward the shallow creek, where eddies of water swirl over rocks and boulders. This is real, and the place is cool and serene. Sitting on the bank, in the shade of a gum tree, her legs catching the sun, it's warm but not hot. The ground is cool. She lies back on the thick grass, listening to the noise of the gurgling water mingling with the pip of bellbirds—the perfect pitch—but she sees no birds, not one. She watches a procession of ants carry leaf clippings in the direction of the gum tree, each one hoisting the leaves above their heads with their pincers. Surely, these can't be real, but maybe not. Does it matter?

What should happen next? Flat-bottomed cumulous clouds appear. Excellent examples—voluminous, perfectly formed, and backlit by the late-afternoon sun—and the contrast between the snowy whiteness of the clouds and the azure sky is breathtaking. After two rounds drift past, they begin to merge, forming animal shapes. An elephant, a dolphin, and a bird float across the sky. There is a pirate ship and a transporter. Then the face of a man appears, and he's familiar—it's Dirac Devine, the leader of New Fed. A sponsored cloud placement. Her weather event is closing in on her.

A fresh set of clouds rolls in, and Quinn knows the sun shower and rainbow will soon follow. The bird noise lifts a notch. Dark clouds

build at the edge of the dome. The temperature drops and the light
fades. CBs—cumulonimbus clouds, thunderstorm clouds—roll into
the sky.

She jumps up. *No, not what I selected.*

Lightning strikes the tree next to her, and it explodes into a fireball.
*Definitely real.* The fire quickly spreads, catching the tops of the adjacent gums, and a fire vortex forms, exploding and disappearing into
the sky. She is in the wrong weather event. This is someone else's idea
of a memorable experience. The sky turns purple. The wind whips up
and lightning strikes a line of trees along the ridge; one after the other
they combust, then cleave open and implode. The purple sky opens,
and rain begins to fall. Soon, she's drenched. Water's running off her
nose and eyelashes, her hair is plastered to her head, and her shoes
are squishing. It's a relentless downpour, interspersed with wallops
of thunder and venomous lightning strikes that hit the ground in a
perfect ring around her. Her nerves crumble but she rallies, telling
herself it's just a simulation, VR with a perceptible overlay. She won't
be hit by lightning. Not today. It's VR, very good VR. Very hot and
smoky VR.

*Shit, it's not VR; it's very, very real.*

The lightning catches the dry gums on the hillside; first the center
group goes up, then the others follow, like a symphony with orches-
trated timing. The lightning takes them out one by one, burning pyres
across the hillside. She needs to get out of here.

In the next flash of lightning, she sees something moving on
the hillside—the outline of a person making their way down the
hill toward her. Someone is coming to help. He signals, waving his
arms about, and she leaps over the ring of smoldering fire and plods
through the downpour toward the greyish figure. He points to the top
of the hill, then methodically retraces his steps back up the slope. She
follows.

They trudge through the rain and blackened mud, past the burnt trees and grasses, in the direction of a low, rectangular building—a viewing station—nestled into the top of the hillside.

The station has no door, the walls are seamless glass. They step right through a section of wall to the interior of the station, and she's finally safe from the lightning and rain. She's also dripping wet; a large puddle forms on the floor around her. She notices that her savior is dry, completely dry and unaffected by the rain. His hair, clothes, shoes, all repel water. He's immersed in a hydroscopic coating.

He hands her a towel, and she wipes her face and gets a good look at him. It's the guy from the bar last night. What's he doing here?

"Thanks. I'm Quinn."

"Aaroon," he says.

Standing up, not settled on a bar stool beside her, he's over two meters tall and his eyes are now cerulean, the color of the ocean on a clear day. He's sequenced; that accounts for the obsessive fingernail biting.

"Don't know what happened, ordered a sun shower, ha." Quinn feigns a laugh.

"We don't always get what we want."

"I suppose not."

He steps toward her. "What I want is that diamond."

She touches the stone around her neck.

"You should hand it over." He holds out an open palm, the size of a bear paw. She wishes he wasn't so tall, and then she looks past him, scanning the rectangular space around her. It's ten meters by twenty. The walls present as solid glass, but at least one section is a simulation. The exit is behind him, where they entered.

Aaroon cocks his head. He's still wearing the MRA. Her fight-and-flight will be obvious, he'll know if she decides to run.

Whatever is happening to her arm, she needs it to work right now. She needs the action to be intuitive and occur without conscious thought. She relaxes, she breathes, she steps toward him, staring into his liquid blue eyes—and her left hand punches him hard in the teeth. *Shit that hurt, I've broken my bloody fingers.*

She ducks under his arm and presses a panel of glass. It's solid.

Aaroon spins around, wiping blood from his mouth with the back of his massive paw. His cerulean eyes turn turquoise, and in two giant lunges he's on her. But she side steps, then elbows him hard in the side of the face. He buckles. She's hurt him. She follows with an elbow to the back of the neck and a punch to the side of the face. Then another. And one more.

He's down and moaning. He's big, but he's not a fighter.

She needs to find the exit.

She presses the adjacent panel of glass and half her arm disappears. She's found the exit point. She steps through, into the antechamber. The skylift is open. Without delay, she's straight in and ascending to ground level.

Back in her apartment Pod her heart pounds, but she's exhilarated. She won the fight, and she escaped. Her fingers are purple and swollen, her elbow is bruised, and her hand throbs, but she can fight. She's bold and fearless. She's Quinn the Brave, she's Quinn the Strong. *I am fucking Superwoman.*

An hour passes. The adrenaline wears off, and her breathing returns to normal. Her arm throbs and her hand stings, a headache looms, and it's possible she has fractured three fingers. Her emotional state switches from Superwoman to super scared woman, and tears catch in the back of her throat. What was she thinking? She should have just given him the stone.

She logs into the building management system, fills out an incident report, and is issued with a case number. There are no painkillers in the Pod. She eats something dry out of a packet and falls into bed.

# Twenty-Seven

# I am here to ease your loneliness.

No HANGOVER THIS MORNING. Quinn congratulates herself on the good work, but if there were grain alcohol on the premises, she would skull a shot right now. Lying in bed, she gently wiggles her fingers. She bends her wrist and elbow, back and forth, and everything works, so she'll survive. But her arm hurts like hell.

Regular as clockwork, at eight fifteen, she fishes out Jin's capsule from her morning crap. After lathering it with cleanser, she takes it to the food prep and pours boiling water over it. The capsule unscrews and inside is a tiny battery—a power source, an activation device. It's not what she expected, but she knows what it is. The point of the power source is AI. This is Jin's field, her life and her passion, but what a risky way to deliver the device; if the capsule had split open inside her, she'd be dead.

Quinn's curiosity is piqued. Her hunt begins. The food prep is empty, and so is the living zone. She moves to the sleep zone: the cupboards are bare, but there's storage under the bed. The drawer flips open, and she sees it: a long, rectangular sack stashed at the back of the drawer, less than a meter long and labeled Assisted Living Android. She carries it into the food prep, places it on the bench, and steps back.

In her daily life, Quinn avoids contact with AI. She's curious, though; she wants to see what is in the sack. She wants to see what her friend was working on, losing sleep on, while she was away. So she pulls the seal and slips off the cover.

It has hairy feet, short legs, a slender tail, and a tiny, upright body with a small, black and grey face. It's a meerkat. The AI is a meerkat. *You must be kidding.* Quinn strokes its downy fur, squeezes its hard, smooth paws, and smiles; she has to admit, it's cute. Jin knows exactly what she's doing. Quinn loves meerkats; they're her animal.

The power source is a magnetic coded key that kick-starts the AI's system, waking it from sleep mode. The AI's mouth is open, so she slips the key inside. It is promptly swallowed.

"Hello, Quinn." It moves its head to one side, "I am an assisted living companion. I have been custom made especially for you." It walks to the edge of the bench and leaps towards Quinn, believing it will be caught, but Quinn steps back, and it crash lands onto the floor.

It rights itself. "I am programmed to learn."

"Just as well. Do you have a name?"

"My name is Mori."

*No way!* "That's a mistake."

"It's ironic. I am programmed for irony. You can talk to me, like it is him, when you get lonely. I am here to ease your loneliness."

*Oh for fuck's sake.*

The meerkat takes off. Scurrying clumsily around the Pod, it climbs the furniture and falls off; it peeks under chairs and bumps its head; it picks up a bowl, examines it, replaces it; it then moves on to investigate the fringe on a cushion. Like a new puppy, it processes information from its environment, creating sensory experiences and memories.

"Come here," Quinn commands. "What's your programming?"

It scurries over. "I have probabilistic reasoning—a subsumption architecture system. It allows me to be reactive and make intuitive decisions. I am a parallel system, not a serial system. My memory and processing are connected. I am able to multitask."

"Why are you a parallel system?"

"Modeled on humankind. I will evolve and learn. I am still young. I will need time to develop. Today, I am twelve."

*Twelve! Seriously.* She doesn't need a twelve-year-old, or an evolving intuitive system. She already has one of those inside her head. She wants number crunching, data, facts, figures, rational decision-making, and access to all layers of NIoT and the SpinnerNet. Quinn is disappointed. She was hoping for a Quantum Machine (QM); this AI is slower than a conventional module.

"Do you have a scanner? SQUIDS?"

"I am a fully coherent macroscopic object. Magnetic field thirty-two tesla."

*At least that's something.* "Impressive. Metals?"

"Niobium-tin."

"Okay. Do both my arms, right one first, then report on the findings. You can do that?"

"Yes." He stands upright, head poised and squints. "No physical problems detected."

"Now the left."

"Inflammation, broken capillaries, ruptured small blood vessels. Some blood leakage into tissue. No major nerve damage; your neurons are firing. I am detecting a problem in the supplementary motor area inside your brain. A neurological problem, damage to the motor cortex and medial frontal lobe, affecting signals to your left side."

"Shit. Why can't it be a physical problem, not something inside my brain? Can you fix it?"

"No. You will need a neurologist."

"Can you recommend one?"

He stares vacantly around the room. "Mmm, I do not, I do not think so, I am not, not programmed for that. Mmm, there is a medical center on Level Three. Open seven days a week, Monday to Friday between eight and ten and Sundays eleven to six. Today they have appointments at ten fifteen, twelve thirty, and—"

"Okay, that was a joke, I'll sort it out. Now, I'm changing your name, you're called"—she scans the room—"Clair." *Rhymes with chair.*

"That is a female name."

"Yes, but—"

"That is not my name. I am a male meerkat."

"Actually, you're a robot. But fair enough, what about—"

"But I was born with a name: Mori. I have been called Mori my whole life."

"You weren't born."

"It means something. It is who I am. Does your name mean something to you?"

"That's different."

"I have an identity, I am Mori. You are Quinn, and I am Mori."

*Too hard.* "Forget the name change. Make an appointment for me at the Medical Centre."

He stands upright, head poised, and squints. "Mmm, two fifteen appointment to see a diagnostic nurse. No neurologists. Also, I see you need a haircut. I am programmed for that."

"Really?"

"Mmm. Downloading styles."

Quinn sits, and the AI stands on a chair. She's nervous, but it can't look any worse than it already does.

Mori the AI takes total control. He knows what he's doing—short around her ears, with a cropped fringe. After it's done, Quinn stares at her reflection in the glass and sees someone else, someone different. *Thank the lordt I'm no longer that person, I don't want to be her anymore.*

He offers a head massage at the end, using a firm kneading technique that Quinn finds divine, seriously divine; what he can do with those little paws is quite remarkable.

"Thank you," she says.

"Thank you for saying thank you." He waits awkwardly beside her.

"You don't need to say that. If I say thank you, you don't need to say thank you back."

He stares at her.

"Go." She nudges him away. "Go explore, whatever you need to do, but stay out of my way or I'll drop you off the balcony. One hundred and eighty floors—that'll deactivate you."

"I will land on my feet."

"You might not."

"You will feel bad if I do not."

"No, I won't."

## Twenty-Eight

# What's the difference between a pink diamond and a regular diamond?

Level three of Habitat5 is dedicated to in-house Med. Quinn has a two fifteen appointment. She's on time but the nurse is late, so she waits in a consult room, mulling over how to explain her ailment without sounding crazy.

The door behind her suddenly opens. "Sorry about last night—medical emergency."

She swings her chair around to see Hitch, wearing a white MedSuit. *He's the diagnostic nurse. Really?*

"I know why you're here."

"You do?" *Damage to the motor cortex and medial frontal lobe, affecting signals to my left side. He can tell that just by looking at me? He's pretty good at his job. I've underestimated him.*

"Yes." He waves her through the door and into an office. There, he opens a module, hands it to her, and sits down across from her.

On the screen are pictures of her, a collection of thumbnails showing her movements over the last few days. Surveillance images. She's being monitored. Personal, targeted surveillance.

"I'm being monitored? That's illegal. The pervasive surveillance of individuals is prohibited under Hexad conventions. They can't do this."

He emits a small laugh. "No one cares."

"I care. Privacy matters." She flicks through the images; pictures of her embarking and disembarking on the Hyperloop; gardening; entering and leaving her Pod; clips from her meeting at eMpower.

Hitch holds out a hand. He wants the device back, but she's not finished. She needs to distract him. "Medical emergency . . . what happened?" She hugs the module, opens an adjacent folder.

"Honest, I was on call and some kid disconnected the OneHub, locked himself in his room, drank half a bottle of grain alcohol, and passed out."

The folder holds images from the Cloud Ship; there's a picture of Lise and Quinn in her cloud dress, posing together. *I look like a marshmallow with stick legs.* "Is he okay?"

"He'll survive, if his mother doesn't kill him."

She scans a tight shot of her diamond—just the diamond. Then another one, and one more. *The weather room wasn't a robbery. There is something going on; there's something special about the stone.*

Hitch rises from his seat. Quinn closes the file, and he plucks the module from her hands.

"Like your hair—sexy, suits you."

*Compliments. Really?* "I'm feeling better. Thank you."

She leaves.

✳✳✳

Harmonia has a comprehensive surveillance system and Quinn surmises that her sponsor wants to know where she is and what she's doing. He wants to know because he has done something very stupid or highly illegal, or Mori has and Niels is protecting him. If she opens the G12, she'll find out what it is. So they are monitoring her, keeping her here, and keeping her away from the G12. There are no images from inside her apartment Pod, so the surveillance is connected to the OneHub. If she keeps the system down, she'll stay undetected, and so will her furry AI companion—no one needs to know about him.

She arrives back at her Pod as a drone delivers a small package—a cactus plant, in a white pot, with a green ribbon. A gift from Hitch, a gardening reference—he's working very hard to endear himself. *Too keen, too soon.* This place gives her the creeps. She leaves the plant where it's sitting.

Inside the Pod, Mori is in some kind of trance.

"Hey, wake up." She pats his head. "What's the difference between a pink diamond and a regular diamond?"

"Pink diamonds are pink."

"That's the outcome, not the answer."

He stands tall and scans the space above his head, like a real meerkat. "NV," he says.

"Correct. Pink diamonds have a nitrogen atom instead of a carbon atom. It gives them the pink color, and they have an empty spot, a hole in the crystal lattice. The gap is NV, or nitrogen plus vacancy." Quinn thinks. "What's the connection between the NV and a qubit?"

"You can make a qubit in the NV."

"Yes. The diamond is a storage device. What if Lise created a qubit in my diamond, entangled it with another particle in her diamond, and embedded a message in it?"

"To read the information, you must open the diamond and extract the qubit. You will need to place it into a state of superposition. You will need a lab and a QM, a stable environment, subzero temperatures, no noise, and no movement."

For a person with no Coin or data, Quinn has a lot on her to-do list.

# Twenty-Nine

# Uncanny Valley.

At 6:00 p.m., Quinn receives an entrance request. The meerkat points to the front door.

"I know." She points under the bed. "Hide."

"Fur?" He strokes his fluffy chest.

*Fuck.* "No—disappear, hide under the bed, in the storage drawer. You're a secret; no one knows you're here."

When he is safely stowed under the bed, she grants access. She was expecting Myra but Hitch enters, holding an armful of beer, a Module, and the green succulent, which he promptly hands to her. "For you. Sorry for standing you up."

She takes the plant. "Thanks, you really didn't—"

He strides into the Pod. "I'm here to help, and I have beer." He glances around the room. "OneHub's down. Yes?"

She nods. "Gave it a virus."

"You're clever."

*And you're perplexing. Why are you here?*

He unpacks the beer, waves a bottle toward her, and she takes it. Why not? It's free, and no one here cares if she's drunk or hung over. The best thing she can do right now is build up a tolerance for alcohol. They take their beers outside, onto the balcony.

"Now let's fix your community service." Opening his module,

he logs into the building interface. "What do you want to do? Communication?"

"Climate control. I could work on the environmental system."

"Really? It's quite complex, I hear the Tech's—"

"I'll be fine."

"Okay." A few swipes and he's found the page he wants. He adds her to the roster. Community service problem solved. He moves on to her arm. After scanning it with his SelfMed, he reports that there is some bruising and swelling, but nothing is broken. "MedPlan?"

"No, and no Coin."

"Anything serious, there's a MedQuarter in Unus. It's free. Married? Boyfriend?"

An image of Tig pops into her head, and the vision startles her. She dismisses it. "No, no. I'm single."

"I'm divorced. Two kids, a boy and a girl, four and six. Fucking hard work. Never doing that again." *The divorce or the kids?* "I'm thirty-four, my dad's a doctor, my brother's a dental technician, both unemployed but getting some work in coding. Isn't everyone?" *Don't know anyone writing code.* "Coding is a holding pattern for the unemployed. My mum remarried a bureaucrat who works for New Fed. High up. That's how I got here. Better than living outside, but it's not perfect; the sleep zone in my apartment faces east, gets the morning sun, and I like to lie in, ease my way into the day. Why rush when every day's the same? And the air system in my tower's set way too high. Now that we're friends and you're on the climate roster, you could make some adjustments. No one needs to know."

"See what I—"

"My job, it's just a bullshit job, totally meaningless. No one would care if I didn't turn up. No one will die if they don't spend fifteen minutes with me. Doubt they'll even feel better. I handle mild ailments, nervous disorders. This week's consultations include constipation, fatigue, loneliness, bad breath, dandruff, headaches, sleep disorders, nail biting, and five patients suffering from BS."

"BS?"

"Boredom syndrome."

Two hours later, Quinn has finished her beer and Hitch has described the last two decades of his life, in detail, and polished off eight beers. *One bottle every fifteen minutes*, she calculates. *Time for him to leave.*

She yawns, she stretches. "Gosh, look at the time."

"Time to go, no problem." He grins, tapping his bottle on the table-top, reluctant to let it go. There's a small, but prolonged, silence, and she doesn't offer anything else. Finally, he pushes his chair back and swoops in to kiss her, right on the mouth, enthusiastically. She fumbles and pushes him away.

"Hey, enough," she says. She slides off her seat and gestures toward the door. "Time for you to leave." *You've outstayed your welcome.*

He follows her to the entrance, then lurches toward her again.

She dodges the advance. "Mate, fuck off." She pushes him out the door and firmly seals it. Then she double-checks the lock, confirming he can't return. *Idiot.*

Mori bursts into the room—quivering, his hair standing on end. "Are you going to marry him?"

"What? No."

"But you kissed him."

*I'm living with a child.* "*He* kissed *me*." *I'm justifying my behavior to a robot.*

"He wants to be your mate."

"No. He just wants to mate. Too obvious, too keen, too soon. And he couldn't sync his Band to his module."

Mori is flummoxed.

∗∗∗

Early the next morning, Quinn finds Mori lingering beside her bed, looking disheveled. If he were human she would say he was tired and unshaven, with bags forming under his eyes.

"You don't look well," she says. "Did you sleep? Do you sleep?"

"I have a sleep mode to regulate thought patterns, consolidate and trim my memory, and process new emotions. I have a question. Why am I a meerkat?"

He climbs onto the bed. She pushes him back.

"Uncanny Valley. Robots that look like people freak me out." *They freak most people out.*

"I do not understand the term."

"It describes the dip in our emotions when we see weird or creepy things that we can't categorize, like robots with human features. Jin, the person who created you, knows this, so she made you in the form of a meerkat because meerkats are my animal. I love them."

"You love them?"

"Yes. Lise, my mother, loves lions, and my father loves birds—he's obsessed, he even talks to them—but for me it's meerkats. I love their cute faces and dark eyes, the way they protect and hug each other. I love the way they scan for signs of danger. They're mesmerizing. I could watch them for hours."

"What makes you more human than me?"

*A bit early for this.* "Gee, I don't know. Biology. Feelings. Beliefs. Relationships. Memory. Conscious thoughts. A sense of self. Want me to go on?"

He stares at the ground.

"And hands, you don't have proper hands, you can never be human without proper hands."

He gazes at his little paws. "Personhood, I think, is in the eyes of the beholder. John Locke said a person should have language, reason, morals, intentions, and relationships. I have intentions, and I have a relationship with you. He did not say anything about a person being biological or having hands."

*Is he serious?* "Locke, like from the eighteenth century?"

"1687."

"Do you understand the notion of time? Time passes. Things have moved on a bit since Mr. Locke. And morals, beliefs, values—how do you think you got those?"

"Some were pre-programmed, others I am learning from life, and from you. Where did you get yours?"

"Well, yes, you have a point there. But I'm still a person, and you're still a robot."

"I think, therefore I am."

"Is that . . . Descartes? Are you quoting Descartes to me?"

"Yes. Today I am developing a sense of self. I think, therefore I am."

"Well, I think, *because I'm a Homo sapien and I can actually think*, that these days, it's more appropriate to say: 'I am, therefore I think.'"

"I am, therefore I think. I understand; it implies a notion of self. My control and learning systems are modeled on human brain and neuron activities. I am programmed for cognitive thought."

"Yes, but you process stuff; the self isn't a process, it's an essence."

"Your brain activities are processes. The brain is just a machine running inside a physical body."

"This is a conversation you can't win. Understand?" She takes off her Band and hands it to him. "Now, any ideas on how I can access my data or Coin? I'm locked out."

"Mmmm, let me see." He scans NIoT. "Model A2341. A rudimentary model. Not made for deep data. Given to children."

"Really? That simple. I just need a new model." She straps the band back on her wrist. "What information can you access?"

"My technology allows me to emulate brain activity in the hippocampus, so I am creating my own memories."

"Good to see they're your own, but I'm talking data, information about the world, finance, companies, governments. Can you access, say, deep company data from eMpower?"

He stands upright and scans the space above his head, the way meerkats do. She finds him impossibly cute when he concentrates.

"NIoT. Everything that is public. Surface levels only. No deep data."

Quinn has Jin's personal codes. She instructs Mori to log into eMpower using remote access and check into Jin's personal files. She feeds him the security codes and the files open.

"Success," he finally says, "I have access to her personnel information."

"I could hug you," she says.

He lies down on the coffee table and holds his little paws in the air. "No, tickle me."

"What? No."

"Please, please tickle me. I tried to do it to myself, but it does not work."

"Oh good lordt." She rubs his tummy, and he bursts into panting fits of laughter.

"Your turn." He jumps up, raises his paws, and creeps toward her. "I am coming to tickle you."

"No, you're not." Quinn gives him a hard look.

He drops his paws and backs away.

"Listen," she says, "I'm going to Unus. There are 100 million people in the city, so there's bound to be ten thousand neurologists in the MedQuarter, and I only need one. Then I'll find a TechHub, get a new Band, and access my Coin. Should take me no more than half a day. While I'm gone, you download everything from the files we just accessed."

"Too much. I need more time to develop. My memory is not fully developed, and I am not a storage device. I am an assisted living companion."

"I think you could store it if you tried."

"I am not a storage device. I am a companion. Your personal companion."

*Okay, sensitive issue. Not sure if I believe him, but I'll give him the benefit for now.*

They have nothing else to store the files in, however—no devices, and Mori's offering nothing. Apparently, he hasn't developed any lateral thinking skills yet.

She picks up the cactus Hitch brought and hands it to Mori. "Store it, bit by bit, as you download it, in the plant's DNA. Set up a basic code system matching the binary zeros and ones to the DNA letters of the cactus. Then synthesize the sequence. Transfer this into a bacterium and infect the plant, the coding and data will go with it. Can you do that?"

"Yes."

"I'll be back later today. Once I get my Coin, we're leaving. If anyone comes inside while I'm gone, hide."

She stows her diamond in the pocket of her pants and makes her way below ground, to the Hyperloop.

# Thirty

# Hot people look different than cool people.

QUINN DISEMBARKS THE HYPERLOOP at Grand Central Station. Her Loop carriage is empty but the station links to Unus's underground transport network, dubbed the "people funnel" because it's the only departure tunnel and link to the outside world. She follows the signs, merging into denser and denser herds of people heading toward the exit. The atmosphere is shocking—dense and musty. The air is rank with body odor.

Her exit point is two kilometers away. She figures she'll adapt to the stench, but the temperature continues to rise, without relief. Air vents, placed at regular intervals along the tiled walls, are commandeered by groups of commuters who rotate their bodies, trying to find some respite from the heat. The journey is a mindless, one-foot-in-front-of-the-other quest for personal space and fresh air, with thousands committed to the task, all wearing climate suits, all focused on a single point in the distance, all surrounded by the dull murmur of conversations. It's almost too hot to talk.

From nowhere, the faint sound of an angel wafts over the funnel of hot people. A piercing, melodic tune—someone, possibly an unearthly being, is singing, and the closer Quinn gets to the exit the stronger the lilting, harmonic sound.

Quinn reaches the travelator shaft and joins the queue ascending to the surface. Her first glimpse of natural light mingles with a waft of fresh air and a faint but familiar tune—"Eternal Summer," a classic hit, and one of her father's compositions. As the travelator ascends, daylight streams into the void and the pitch of the song rises, the lyrics lifting her heart and spirit, and she grins. It's infectious; people around her begin to smile, too. It's a good sound, a great song, and the rendition is magical. It soothes and unites the mass of hot, sticky people, reminding them that togetherness is not so bad.

"I love this song," says the woman beside Quinn, who is wearing a transparent climate suit over clear knee-high boots and a short red pantsuit. Clusters of red cherries dangle from her earlobes; she's a fashionista. She gives Quinn's yellow climate suit the once-over and wrinkles her nose.

The singer is a young man, tall and thin, wearing an oversize tan climate suit, dark glasses, and a floppy sun hat. He strums a guitar. A brown whippet dog sits next to him. The dog has Vouchers tucked into its collar. Quinn looks from the young man to the dog and back again, wondering if anyone else makes the connection.

The fashionista follows her gaze. "He looks just like his dog," she says, then rummages through her bag, retrieves a couple of Vouchers, and tucks one into the dog's collar. "How can someone who sings like that go hungry?" After looking Quinn over again, she hands her a Voucher, too.

"I'm not hungry—I just looks like shit," Quinn says. She steps forward, pats the dog, and leaves her Voucher with the busker. Then she waits to one side until the song is done and the busker collects his coupons. That done, he immediately starts a new tune.

As the blissful effect of "Eternal Summer" evaporates, Quinn's heart jolts so hard it takes her breath away; her father—she needs to call her father. He'll be crazy with concern for her.

✳✳✳

The world outside the station is just as hot, but at least she can breathe and the air no longer smells rank; instead, it smells faintly of chili. She looks around. Nearby, a vender roasts large, mealy worms in marinated spices. A queue for the rich protein dish quickly forms.

Quinn moves away. Looking up, she sees how a massive conifer breaks through the roof of the station, providing an overhang and some shade. The Locale sign next to her reads, GRAND CAPITAL. She scans the city blocks.

Unus is not a grand city, in the sense that the architecture does not sing and the boulevards do not pulse with cosmopolitan life. Quinn is convinced the city is grand only in the enormous volume of people who call it home. The crumbling buildings and mazes of traffic are not doing much to lift the spirit of anyone here. At zero latitude, it's unbearably hot, noisy, and crowded. She has never seen so many people in her life, and she's beginning to realize there is a significant difference between people who have access to cool air and those who don't. Hot people look different than cool people. Hot people have poor skin, broken teeth, and artificial limbs. Some of the hot people are very old. She didn't think people could look that old and still be alive, and she hasn't seen reading glasses in twenty years. Quinn's point of reference for the world is Hobart. She has led a cool, yet sheltered, existence. *I've been living in a bubble. I blame my parents. What were they thinking?*

The buildings surrounding her are a mix of half-finished, half-decapitated timber, stone, bamboo, and cardboard constructions with unused water tanks fixed to the roofs—a hangover from rainwater collection days, the population's thirst is now quenched by filtered seawater—and makeshift sewers below.

Unus pays homage to transport and the wheel. Crows rush past on electric blades, hydrobikes, mini autos, solar bikes, and solar tuks, and transport Convoys, six deep, float above the lines of traffic. Drivers yell and swear at each other, blaring horns, and a group of transport police fly over on hoverbikes, settling the agitated drivers. Thousands also trek the pavements on foot, with women carrying children, men carrying children, children carrying smaller children, and smaller children carrying chickens, roosters, and rabbits by their legs, ears, and tails. These are not beloved pets.

Quinn's destination is the MedQuarter, ten kilometers west of the city center. She could pick up a Transport Convoy, but after the crowds and the stench of the exit tunnel at Grande Central, sitting in a hot, metal box-on-wheels is not enticing. She'll walk; maybe after she accesses her Coin, she'll hire an Automated Vehicle, AV, and arrive in isolated personal comfort.

Then she notices that the AVs she's seeing are all stationary, lined up in neat rows along the side of the street. She approaches a young female vendor wearing a silver metallic climate suit, her bright red hair pulled into a ponytail. The vendor waves a hand in the air. She can't help; one of the AVs was hacked and if one goes, the whole fleet is grounded. It'll be days before they are running again.

So Quinn heads west. She can always get a Convoy back.

Unus is laid out on a grid system, with no twists and turns like Harmonia. It's all straight lines and right angles charged with rectilinear energy. The layout is an enabler for transport, and everyone has somewhere to go.

From Quinn's balcony in Harmonia, Unus looked like a conglomerate of built structures—offices, Pods, apartments, and houses—but from the ground, it's green and lush. Vegetation rises through the rooftops of buildings, trailing over awnings, growing in the spaces between apartments. Quinn sees herb gardens, fruit vines, pots of vegetables, and masses of fast-growing bamboo—not the organized,

contained greenery of Harmonia but a natural, rich cornucopia, cultivated to feed the human population.

A neon sign across the street indicates a TechHub. Perfect. She'll
get a new Band and access to her Coin. Only twelve lanes of traffic are
keeping her from independence. There are no crossings, but vehicles
are programmed not to hit people, so she ventures out.

She's only made it across the first lane when a Transport Convoy
misses her by a thread. Losing her nerve, she backtracks to the pavement. Down the street, a child runs across the road; he's about to be
pulverized until an augmented pedestrian crossing appears under
his feet and every vehicle pulls up. A smart crossing. She sees how it
works and then uses it herself, makes it unscathed across twelve lanes.

The TechHub is inside an arcade. This is a precinct dedicated to the
slightly weird and vaguely creepy people who call themselves creators
and makers. They make objects using their hands. These are sometimes functional—things like simple spoons or bowls. Others favor
more artistic, sculptural endeavors—carved blocks of wood or stone.
For them, the joy is in the making.

In the first stall Quinn passes, a man wearing a heavy black apron
polishes tools no one will ever use. He sharpens the blades on a spinning wheel, honing them over and over. Then he lovingly wipes them
down and lays them on a cloth in rows of gleaming silver metal. A
pointless activity. Meaningless work. He smiles and nods toward his
shiny tools, offering Quinn a closer look. She touches a blade, grazes
it with her finger, and it draws a drop of blood. She's amazed; she felt
nothing.

"Hostile," the man says, "like people."

Opposite him, on the other side of the tunnel, two drones paint
a mural of a woman's face framed by a rainbow: Maim Quate, the
political leader. The slogan reads, "We are the 99.9 percent."

Beside the mural, an older woman weaves a giant tapestry, her
loom covering the entire wall, floor to ceiling. She works the threads

from the top to the bottom, and she's almost done—half a meter of work to complete before she's finished. On her knees, shuttle in hand, she vigorously works a section, back and forth. She glances up at Quinn. "What can you see?" she asks.

"A city, a megacity—high-rise buildings, cranes, bridges, and a high-ways," Quinn says. The work is colorless, everything in monochrome.

"Appearances deceive," the woman says. "You won't find the truth standing there. Move, take another look."

Quinn moves to the right, and the view is altered. There's an image under the city—a new landscape with mountains and valleys, a shimmering, sparkling rural scene. So clever, thinks Quinn. The woman has two shuttles, one for the black and grey threads and one with a fluorescent, gossamer yarn, and she painstakingly weaves them together. Quinn spies ridgetops, valleys, and a river leading to a harbor and village. Then she sees the sheep, the sheep with curly horns. It's Kerguelen. Mt. Cook and the glacier.

"The truth is hidden," says the woman, "under the mountain."

Silently, Quinn moves away.

Farther on there are stalls selling insects—dried, fermented, salted, or preserved. There's a vending machine serving shots of alcohol and stalls selling old-fashioned ornaments and shiny new Tech. A man shows her plastic that disappears—"Completely vanishes, disintegrates into nothing," he tells her.

"Nothing comes from nothing," she replies.

The stall owners are keen to sell her their products. An auburn-skinned woman, tending a metalware shop, attempts to wrap a bronze choker around Quinn's neck. She has a beautiful, heart-shaped face with arching eyebrows, and wears colored scarves around her waist. She's insistent that Quinn take the jewelry.

"Sorry, no Coin," Quinn says.

"The bracelets," she says. "Swap you—this choker or this ring."

Quinn shakes her head.

"Take both." She presses them into Quinn's hands, but Quinn places them back on her table and moves away.

A sign indicates that the TechHub is farther on. The arcade narrows into a smaller tunnel, dipping below street level. It's dimly lit, but shafts of green and yellow light break through the gloom and the path is well used, many people coming and going. Quinn follows them into the grotto. Inside, the space is filled with trees and shrubs. Some of the trees are twenty meters tall, their trunks crawling with moss. Ferns dangle from the canopies and dense, brown funguses and toadstools clump together at the base of the trees. As she moves farther inside, Quinn comes across piles of relics and pieces of machinery. Masses of titanium laptop cases, still glistening, and a bicycle growing out of a tree, then a chair, and a window, are all encased in the branches and trunks of trees. Once a junkyard, now the vegetation fuses with the debris.

Suddenly, someone bumps into her. *What the . . . ?* She is shoved again, hard, in the back, and stumbles forward. "Hey."

Heavy hands grab her shoulders, force her off the path and into the undergrowth. Her assailant is strong; he plants her face into a tree, presses his weight against her, and then she feels cold steel over her carotid artery. She's in trouble.

"Bracelets. Take 'em off." He leans back a little, giving her room to free her hands.

She shakes, fumbling with what she thinks is the clip of one of the bangles, but she has no luck, she can't undo it.

"Hurry."

"I can't."

He leans back a little more, enough for her to free an arm. Her left arms slips out and knocks him hard in the side of his face. Off guard, he reels backward. She turns and kicks him, once, twice, and he stumbles, then falls to the ground.

"Hey." A flash of colored scarves appears through the undergrowth;

someone is coming. "What's going on?" The woman from the arcade emerges from the trees and she's not alone—there's a male companion by her side.

Quinn's assailant collects himself from the ground and takes stock. Realizing that his position is tenuous, he backs away. The woman's companion draws a large, curved blade from his pantaloons and flicks it; it strikes the robber in the forehead, dead center. It cleaves him open, and he keels over, dead.

The woman steps over the body, focused only on Quinn, and grabs her arm. "Who are you?"

Quinn pulls away. *Seriously, this man's brains are leaking all over the ground.*

"Where did you get these?" the woman demands. "I need to know. The bracelets, where did you get them?"

"Okay, okay, calm down," Quinn says. "A friend gave them to me."

"You're lying. You're a thief. A lying little thief."

*And you're a lunatic.* "It's the truth. Tig gave them to me."

The man retrieves his blade from the robber's head and casually wipes away the blood. The woman signals for him to point his weapon at Quinn, but he shakes his head and keeps it at his side. The woman glares at him. Reluctantly he lifts the blade slightly and points it, in a vague way, in Quinn's direction.

"We must sort this out." The woman pulls up her sleeve, revealing half a dozen bangles, and singles out a red band similar to Quinn's. "If you have been with him, I need to know."

*Oh, shit. Really? Do you really need to know?* Quinn stares at her, then swallows hard and looks away—at the ground, at the prostrate body of the dead robber lying on the ground, at the cleaved skull of the robber lying on the ground, and then at the blank expression of the young man welding the scythe. How in the world did she end up here, between these two clannish murderers and a slain robber? Finally she faces the fraught, urgent woman.

"It's only fair that I know," the woman says.

*Oh good lordt, this couldn't get any worse. Please don't let her be his wife, and if she is, please let him be dead. We did it five times in one night, does that count as one time or five times?* "Okay. Yes, we may have—"

"Come with me."

Quinn shakes her head, "I'm not going anywhere with you."

"Come. Please, this must be settled. You understand, I can't live like this? I will die."

"You won't die."

"I will! I will kill myself."

*Oh, for fuck's sake.* "You're not going to kill yourself."

The woman signals to her male companion for the blade. He happily hands it over. The woman holds the blade to her neck, and Quinn stares anxiously at the man, seeking clarification and help. *Is she really capable of doing this—and if so, shouldn't you stop her?*

"She's crazy. She'll do it," he confirms. He shows no intention of intervening.

The woman pushes the tip of the blade firmly into her neck and a trickle of blood runs down toward the handle.

Quinn steps back and considers the scene: a beautiful but weary-looking woman with almond-shaped eyes and a languid neck that may be about to be severed; an impassive young man willing to let the beautiful woman slit her own throat; and a dead man on the ground. She decides she's had enough. "I'm done." She turns her back on them and begins to walk away.

"Wait," the man calls. "You're the one, aren't you? The one from Hobart."

Quinn freezes to the spot.

"He's here in the city," he says. "If you want to see him, I'll take you back to our State."

The woman drops the blade. "You're a traitor. You betray your own family."

He ignores her and picks up the blade. Calmly he cleans the tip, then glides it back into its sheath.

*Tig is alive and he's here in the city. Do I want to see him? Yes, I'd really like to see him, and I'd like to find out what happened to him. But a one-night stand is just that: one night. It's so awkward. But we're adults, it'll be fine. My mission is to find Lise; that's my priority. And I'm pretty sure I need his help to find Lise.*

Slowly Quinn turns to face the man. "Okay. Thank you."

He grins. "My name is Louis, and this is my cousin Consortia. Come with us."

Consortia stalks away, scowling. Louis beckons to Quinn before following his cousin. Quinn sighs and trudges after them.

# Thirty-One

# She has Tig's eyes
# in her pocket.

Half an hour later, after a hot and dusty solar tuk ride, they
pull up outside an ancient complex of buildings—stately stone structures, hundreds of years old, possibly from the fifteenth or sixteenth
century. The complex is three levels high, with ornate windows, ped-
iments, and columned arches symmetrically centered along the front
facade.

Quinn follows Louis and Consortia through the arched entrance,
and they enter a large, rectangular plaza bordered by fruit trees.
The interior architecture mirrors the front facade, with the addition
of deep balconies supported by fluted columns. At the far side is a
large stone water fountain in the shape of a giant sea turtle. Residents
gather in the courtyard, sipping cool drinks and enjoying the shade of
the balconies, and groups of children splash under the fountain. The
scene is delightfully commonplace and nonthreatening, and Quinn
feels the angst of the last thirty minutes abate.

Louis asks Quinn to wait by the giant turtle, then he and Consortia
disappear into the building. Quinn sits on a wooden bench in the
shade of a fruit tree adorned with wind chimes shaped like butterflies,
which clink softly in the breeze. Nearby, a group of young girls draw
on the pavement with chalkstone. They sketch a map of an island with

little houses, palm trees, and fishing boats. Quinn tilts her head; the island is a butterfly. She sees metal bracelets tucked under the sleeves of the young girls' climate suits. These are Tig's people. She's in the Maldives. Her angst returns; this could go very badly.

Louis and Consortia return with company: an older man and an older woman. The older man walks with a cane and moves with a limp, and the others are careful not to overtake him. Quinn stands to greet them, and the man offers his hand.

His name is Flax. He has dark, hooded eyes, wiry grey hair, a well-kept beard, and something akin to scorn lurking behind his unpleasant countenance, but when she takes his hand it's warm and he smiles. Flax introduces the older woman, Brie. She is Consortia's mother.

Brie wants to know about the bracelets.

"They were a gift from a friend . . . from Tig," says Quinn.

Consortia is visibly crushed by this news and collapses onto the bench. Apparently, this news is the worst of the worst. Brie slides onto the seat to console her daughter. Louis rolls his eyes at the two of them huddled together, and Flax chuckles.

Without sympathy, Flax indicates that they should go and Quinn should stay and sit with him under the fruit tree. With a little laugh, he looks her over, smiles, and nods to himself.

His amusement is infectious, and she grins despite herself.

"Okay." She holds out her arm, taps the red bracelet. "What does this mean?"

He chuckles. "I'm sure you know. You're a woman, he's a man— intimate things between the two of you."

*Oh fuck, he is giving bracelets to every woman he sleeps with.* "So she's his . . . wife?"

"No, no, no. It was arranged at one point, but it's not to be. They don't always take place."

"An arranged marriage!"

"Ah, don't be so quick to judge. Many arranged marriages are very successful. My wife was chosen for me. She was the love of my life, until she died. Again, and again, and again."

"Wait. Your wife died more than once?"

"Yes. And this is a good story. It's a very good story. But it's a tale for another day. We both have things to do. Tig is not here; he left this morning. He lives on the harbor, on a blue boat called *Nanshe*." He retrieves a silver box from his pocket. "Please, give this to him. I don't trust the tuk drivers and can't take it myself." He lifts the cuff of his climate suit, revealing his ankle—degenerated, bacterial, and probably incurable. He drops the trouser leg down and opens the box. Inside are eyes. Two bionic, hazel eyes.

"I don't know where . . ."

"He's waiting for these, and I suspect he's also waiting for you."

"I'm not so sure . . ."

"Well, I need someone to take these to him." He offers her the box. "If you're going that way anyway . . ."

She smiles and nervously takes the box. "Okay. I will, I will take them."

He rises and heads for the entrance. She follows.

"Go now, but be careful," Flax says. "The city is not safe. The people aren't happy. If they don't get right political result, they'll rise up. Be careful." He orders her a solar tuk.

✶✶✶

There's a certain allure to Harmonia—Quinn sees this now. In a couple of hours, she could be back there discussing what it's like to be human with Mori, drinking beer with Hitch, working on the climate system, and, if she had to, toiling fourteen hours a day for eMpower. That's a life. There are worse things to do. She could make that work for a year or two. Or, she finds a TechHub, gets her Coin, and moves back to

Hobart, back home to her Pod in the boring area of the city. Or, she goes to stay with Matt in his house in the forest.

But she has a big problem: She has Tig's eyes in her pocket and his bracelets around her wrist, and both these things make her nervous. If she were a spiritualist, not a scientist, she might make more of this fact, this improbable coincidence. But she's not a spiritualist; she's a scientist. She knows chance happenings are not remarkable; they are not destiny or fate. They are improbable occurrences that become probable. As a scientist, she also knows there's not one person for her. That's a ridiculous statistic, an impossible fraction. She's compatible with thousands, maybe millions, of people all over the planet. The problem is, she tried that. She tried compatibility, and it didn't quite work. The problem is she has his eyes in her pocket and her heart is about to burst through her chest. She wants to jump off a very high mountain.

***

The solar tuk driver drops her at the top of the rise, before the descent to the harbor. She thinks walking the last hundred meters might calm her down. She's nervous, hot, and clammy in her defective climate suit, which feels like it's trapping the heat. Unzipping the top, she pulls it down, letting the air in. *Sex changes everything.*

The harbor is a massive floating city, with thousands of boats connected by ramps and makeshift wharfs. Half of them are blue. She opens the box of eyes and stares at the hazel orbs. They stare back. What is she doing here? They had sex because they were alone on a deserted island, which is still an excellent reason to have sex, but what if he doesn't want to see her? He never came back. But he gave her the bracelets. He told her she was beautiful. But what's he going to think of her when he gets new eyes? She considers keeping them.

There are rows of pop-up stalls, two and three deep across the entrance to the dock—Tech stuff, paint, material, boat supplies, clothing venders, food, shoes, hats, 3D material, and empty water bottles. The first stall sells hand-held solar fans and large, broad-rimmed hats. She asks the owner, a petite woman with short black hair and far-apart eyes, if she knows someone called Tig. But the owner only wants to sell her fans. Holding one in each hand, she blasts Quinn with her solar fans. Quinn agrees, they work very well, and she would buy one to help her out if she had Coin. The woman hurls abuse at Quinn after she realizes she's only after information. Quinn can't understand a word she's saying. Finally, the woman points to a character at the end of the dock carrying bags of water.

Black water. It's not Tig.

# Thirty-Two

# I wish I'd never met him.
# I hate him.

THE PERSON HAULING THE bags of black liquid is a dealer. They're traveling between the boats dispensing the liquid in regulated drops and accepting Coin or barter for the transaction.

Taking in the dealer's continence, Quinn is confused, unable to distinguish a distinctive male or female persona. The closer she gets, the more masculine they appear—very tall, with broad shoulders and short, red-tipped hair—but with a distinctly attractive face: full lips, high cheekbones, and arching eyebrows. A bejeweled earring dangles from one ear, and on it Quinn spies the genderless symbol, a circle within a circle, containing both horizontal and vertical lines—this person is gender neutral.

Ze wears an original climate suit—dusty grey, trimmed with black—and is humming a tune in a deep, lyrical voice.

Quinn moves quickly to catch up. "Excuse me, sorry to bother you," she says. "I'm looking for someone. Maybe you know him."

"Doubt it," ze says without pausing or turning to look at her.

"Someone called Tig."

Now ze stops, drops the bags, swings around, and walks toward her with an assumed swagger. Looking her over—the complete elevator, head to toe, both hands on zirs hips—before zirs eyes finally come to rest on her bracelets. "It's you. Of course, it is. I didn't expect it, but here you are, in the flesh." A hand is offered. "I'm Planck. What happened to you?"

"I've had the worst bloody time. It's been awful," Quinn begins. "Everyone died, and they said it was my fault, but it wasn't, I had nothing to do with it, then I was kept on this stupid atoll for months, I nearly went insane, thought I'd slipped into a parallel . . ."

"I mean your face. What happened to your face?"

"Oh." She presses her cheek, and it stings; the tree incident with the robber. "It's nothing."

"Really? Well, it looks like something to me. You know, the city is not safe right now."

"I can look after myself."

"Of course, you can, and you have a lovely purple eye to prove it." Ampules of power are fixed to zirs belt. Ze opens a canister and treats Quinn's cuts with Decorin, a skin protein that creates a net inside her wound so she won't scar. "Now, Tig won't be back for a few hours. Stay with me. I need an assistant." Ze passes her the smaller bag of black water. Quinn slings it over her shoulder and follows zir into the sea of boats.

Most of the boats are not real boats and many are not seaworthy; they are prefab housing Pods mounted on floating pontoons, modular systems that lock together. The hull configurations are standard; the owners choose the desired width, height, and finishing materials. They are the size of two or three shipping containers. Many are round, while others are double-story, with rooftop balconies. Still others have curved rooflines and spiral staircases. All have little front terraces, the obligatory solar energy fit-outs, saltwater purifiers, and hydroponic gardens—everyone is growing something.

The black stuff Planck is hawking is in demand; ze doesn't have to work hard to make a sale. There is a regular clientele of takers waiting for zir with empty jars on the dock. Quinn's job is to dispense small amounts into the customers' containers. She counts out six, eight, or ten drops, while Planck watches.

"That was twelve," ze scolds. "You're bad for business."

*It wasn't; it was ten, exactly ten.*

Planck gives instructions on how to mix and dilute the solution, ten to one. It should be administered both morning and evening. When Quinn asks what it is, ze says it's the elixir of life, a home brew of vitamins, minerals, and salts. Quinn figures it's a potion to combat the heat and any other ailments life in this sweltering city brings on. Planck also dispenses an array of ointments and potions, after private consultations Quinn's not privy to, and small packs of green herbs that ze tucks into clients' pockets.

Planck knows everyone, and not just by name—ze has entered their inner sanctums and gained detailed knowledge of their lives.

"Up here on the left we have Tilda and Nick," ze says as they approach a teal-colored pontoon with timber trim. "She's action packed, a real doer. Want something done, and she's your woman—she'll probably do it twice. Used to work in mining, driving those monster trucks. Can you imagine? Nick, complete opposite. Hates change, sits in the same chair, walks the same path, eats the same thing at the same time, routine, routine, routine. Last year they moved the boat. Two spaces. I though he was going to have a coronary. As much use as a one-legged cat trying to bury a turd on a frozen lake."

After Tilda gets her black liquid, she discusses vegetable rot and aphids with Planck and Quinn realizes the black stuff is not meant for human consumption—it's fertilizer. Every boat has a micro garden—vegetables, small fruit trees, and herbs. Planck is selling, or trading, nourishment for the micro plants.

Their next delivery is covertly deposited on a disorderly boat with tinted windows and no signs of life. Planck leaves a few drops in a container on the back deck. "Malory," ze whispers when they're out of hearing range. "She's lonely. He died in the war. She can't move on. It's been eight years. Stunning when she was younger. I've tried to set her up. Three dates, all disasters. First time, she didn't stop talking about her hero, the dead husband. So we practiced, you know; came up with some new topics of conversation. Second time, she got nervous and cried. Overwhelmed, she just cried and cried. And the last time, she drank too much and passed out. She's got no idea, like fucking Captain Hook at a gynecologist's convention."

"You know a lot about people. "

"Double degree. Psych *and* fashion. Online, of course." Ze gives Quinn's climate suit the once-over. "This, this ensemble, it's not really working for you, is it? No one ever said, 'When in doubt, wear chartreuse'—it looks like dehydrated piss."

Quinn knows ze is right; it's appalling, she looks terrible, and she wishes she didn't.

A young boy races towards them and dives into Planck, entwining his wiry little body around zirs legs. Quinn takes the bag of liquid as ze attempts to remove the squirmy child. But the kid is persistent. He attacks from the rear, trying to shimmy up Planck's back.

"What part of 'no' do you not understand?" Planck pulls the little rug rat off and digs a hand deep into zirs pocket, revealing a handful of sweets.

The boy pops one into his mouth.

"Manners?"

The kid sticks out his tongue, crosses his eyes, gives a two-fingered gesture with both hands, and runs away.

"Charming child. Graham family." Planck rolls zirs eyes. "She's got a husband and two children, but honestly, there are three children. She waits on him hand and foot. No help whatsoever. Useful as a one-armed trapeze artist with an itchy arse. And the youngest child, a fucking nightmare. They think he's gifted. Gifted at being a little prick. Hopefully, one day, he'll have children just like himself."

"We can only hope."

"People without children are happier—did you know that? It's true, studies show it's true." Ze pauses. "I only said that because I'll never have children."

"Me either."

"And are you happy?"

"You can't ask me that."

"Why not?"

"We've just met. It's not something you ask a person you've just met."

"You don't look that happy to me."

"Well, you've just met me, so you wouldn't know. And . . . I'm not unhappy."

"Surely you can do better than that."

✳✳✳

Two hours later, they've sold out of the "black gold," but profits are down and there are disappointed customers who have missed out due to Quinn's generous dispensing technique. Planck tells her economics is not her thing, and she agrees; consumption, production, wealth creation, these ideas are beyond her life skills.

"I'm just a simple scientist," she says.

"In my experience, when someone calls themself simple, they rarely are." Planck points to the exurbia of boats and floating abodes, says they're headed beyond, to the far side, to the outskirts, and it's a trek.

"There must be thousands and thousands," Quinn says.

"Yes, well, two choices: a boat or a compressed cardboard box. Half the population of Unus lives, sleeps, and raises its children inside what was once packaging material. They own nothing. The housing ladder toppled in the early 2030s. There were no limitations on what people could buy, so those with Coin kept buying. Corporations and wealthy individuals purchased everything there was to purchase. Hard work and good fortune were no help; the doors to the property market were firmly closed."

"The fruits of the planet don't belong to everyone."

"Indeed, then, global warming and the refugee crisis; more homeless, more unemployment; less housing, less motivation, more dissatisfaction. Things got worse, 3D printing took over, manufacturing and distribution slowed, unemployment rose, and jobs were lost to AI and High-Tech. The city stagnated."

"The illogicality of a flawed capitalist system." *Good lordt. That's something my mother would say.*

"Yes, and still the rich were asking how would these displaced people affect the property market, the housing market, the share market?"

"Profoundly."

"Indeed. Then the crash of 2035, capitalism crumbled, and the RE Wars began. And here we are, two hot, not unhappy people, amongst a hundred million, trying to find . . . what? What are you trying to find?"

*Tig. A blue boat, my mother, my data, my Coin, a stupid message in a diamond, the G12, a neurologist, and a new climate suit.* "Too many things."

"Indeed."

✳✳✳

Their destination turns out to be a navy blue sailing boat, traditional Asian style, forty meters long, two levels plus an open deck. Ze calls it *Nanshe*. Quinn never would have found it. Never. They scramble across other boats, using decks as passageways to reach the navy boat. She follows Planck up a ladder, over the deck, and then through a hatch, into the galley and living zone.

Inside, the vessel seems twice the size, like a Tardis. The interior décor is moody and Bohemian, with little, ornate lamps fixed to the walls, dark wood floors covered in woven rugs, and carved timber cornices that frame the windows. At the far end is a galley and a mix of tawny leather sofas and chairs, with a small Tech zone—not High-Tech but a makeshift range of cobbled together equipment. Nothing new, certainly no QM. The air system is set so cold you could make ice. Quinn notes two hydro air systems. *Why do some people need it so cold?*

She also notes the Aquaculture.

"Black gold." Planck taps a black chamber. "Worm farm." Ze points at the floor. "Below deck, hydroponic gardens, a circadian system, lit with lasers."

A sweet and pleasant scent lingers in the air.

"Tea and cake," Planck says. "Sit down, put your feet up. How are you feeling? You look a little tired."

Yes, she's a little tired, life is exhausting, it's hard work being not unhappy. She sits in one of the tawny leather chairs, and Planck hands her a mug of herbal tea and a slice of cake.

"Sprinkles?" ze asks, holding a spoon of dried insects over her plate, and Quinn nods.

She bites into her cake; the center is filled with dried plums, and it is delicious—soft and moist, with a slight crunch.

There's a loud thump overhead; someone just jumped over the railing. Quinn freezes, glances at the ceiling and then at Planck. Ze raises an eyebrow. Heavy footsteps run along the deck. Her heart stops.

Tig swings through the hatch, lands firmly in the galley, and points a small, metallic fan at Planck. "New impeller for the hydro; we leave in two days."

"Slight change of plan." Ze nods toward Quinn, seated in the living zone.

Tig follows zirs gaze, "What the fuck?"

"Hello," she says through a mouthful of crumbling cake. She was thinking of saying, "Surprise," but now she's glad she didn't, because he's definitely surprised. She's the last person he expected to see.

Tig is wordless. No "hello." No "how are you?" No "great to see you." Nothing. Immobile, he stares at her.

She's overwhelmed by his presence, in the flesh, standing in front of her, staring down her down. He's the same, but somehow he's so much more—taller, stronger, more handsome, more real, more beautiful. She doesn't know what to say either. One night of sex has made things between them so awkward.

Planck clears zirs throat, tilts zirs head toward Tig, encouraging him to say something. Anything.

"What happened to you—your face, your arm?" Tig asks.

"It's nothing."

"It's not nothing."

"I'm fine."

"Okay, then, what the fuck are you doing here? It's not safe."

She opens her mouth, but nothing comes out, she doesn't know what to tell him. She can't remember why she's here.

"Not good, you can't stay here." He breathes heavily, paces back and forth across the floor, hands on his hips. "It's not safe."

"Yes, you said that." Her face burns.

"You can't stay here. We have to find another place for you."

"Okay, calm down, I'm not staying." She puts the cake down, brushes the crumbs from her lap, stands, and climbs out the hatch. She doesn't turn or look back or even say goodbye. She's mortified.

As she climbs down the ladder, though, she feels the box in her pocket, the silver box of eyes. She's tempted to throw the box overboard, but she doesn't; she takes it out of her pocket, turns around, and ventures back inside.

Tig sits in the chair that she just vacated, running his fingers over his short hair. She flicks open the box so he can see what she has brought, how precious it is. He might not want to see her but he needs these; they are valuable, and she brought them to him.

"These are for you, from Flax." She passes him the box.

There is no response, no acknowledgment, and she didn't expect accolades but a "thanks" would be nice. Depleted, words fail her again, she fears she'll regret the silence later, but there it is—she retreats, back out the hatch, down the ladder, and she stumbles across the dozen boats until she reaches the stability of the wharf. She can barely breathe. She's furious, fuming, seething with rage. If steam could come out her ears it would. The day is getting hotter and hotter. It should be getting cooler, but the heat is intense. She pulls off the rest of her climate suit, tosses it into a pile of rubbish. *Stupid fucking thing never worked anyway. Better off without it. Better off without anyone, and I'm certainly better off without him. I wish I'd never met him. I hate him.*

"Wait," Planck calls, "wait, wait, wait." Ze bounds over the boats toward her and in one giant leap is by her side. "Didn't come out the way he meant it."

"Oh, I think it was pretty clear."

"You don't understand. Come back, I'll sort it out."

*There is no way I'm going back inside.* She holds out her hand. "It was nice meeting you."

"You can't go, honestly; I won't let you."

Ze takes hold of her hand and instantly she relents, releasing her anger, and all her strength is sucked away and suddenly she's exhausted. If there were a bed on the wharf, she would lie down and fall asleep. She checks the time: almost six. She must head back to Harmonia. She can deal with her arm tomorrow. Or never. It'll probably fix itself anyway, she reasons, it just needs time. Everyone needs time. Time to forget and move on.

Her left hand reaches out and tinkers with Planck's genderless earring. She pulls it away, guiding it into her pocket, but it quickly escapes and continues fiddling. Again she recovers it, and again it escapes.

"What are you doing?"

"Sorry." She points to her afflicted appendage. "I have no control, there's a problem with my frontal cortex. That's why I'm here, I've come all this way to see someone, a neurologist." She pauses, sniffs. "I had a list, a list of all the things I had to do: sort out my stupid arm, update my Band, access Coin, find the G12. Then these awful people found me, and Flax gave me the eyes, and I couldn't not come; how could I not bring them? And now, now it's after six and, well, I haven't done anything on my list, not one thing, and I have no Coin, how am I going to get back to the station? Sorry, I'm sorry—I'm just tired. Don't know what I'm saying. Thanks for the cake. It was really good."

"Fascinating. Come with me."

Planck directs her to a pontoon house close to the harbor entrance. A small Indocin man, with a wispy beard, wearing traditional robes, opens the door. The room behind him glows and smells of incense. Planck pushes Quinn inside, and the Indocin man closes the door. The room is dim, lit only with clusters of lanterns scattered over the floor and tables. In one corner there is a seated statue of a blue man with a wreath of water lilies at his feet, and in his lap a bowl. His right hand points down, extended toward the ground.

"The Medicine Buddha," the Indocin man says, and directs Quinn toward a chair. He sits facing her with his hands on his knees, looking a bit like a Buddha himself. "Do you feel your body doesn't belong to you?" he asks.

"Sometimes."

"Have you traveled outside your body?"

"No. Have you?"

He frowns.

"No, never," she confirms.

"Have you met your doppelganger?"

"No. But it would be fascinating, weird but—"

"Do you have autism?"

"No."

"Epilepsy?"

"No."

"Dreams? Do you dream? It's important you dream."

"Yes, I dream."

"What about routines? Are you obsessive?"

"Yes, definitely."

"Okay. Let me see the arm."

"I didn't say it was my arm." Her left hand reaches towards him. It strokes his wispy beard; it gently pulls on his ear lobe.

"But it is your arm, acting on visual clues, generating actions deep inside your unconscious, so deep your conscious is not aware." He places the arm in her lap. "Anarchic Hand and Arm syndrome, affecting all your left side. Rare. Caused by a brain injury or damage to the medial frontal cortex or the corpus callosum."

"Okay. How do we fix it?"

"Why fix it?"

"Because it's not normal; it's creepy, and I have to work and live."

"Work, what work?"

*I don't know what I do any more.* "Clouds." *That's what I want to do.*

"People still use that?"

"The ones in the sky."

"There aren't any."

"Maybe there will be, one day."

"I can help you. First you stop fighting it. It's not a foreign thing. It's a part of you. Come lie down here." He gestures to a bed. "You're tired, very tired—and angry, very angry. Let go of your anger. Relax. Relax."

"I am relaxed."

"Relax more. More. You must practice Interoception. Connect your mental self to your physical self. Find your internal body signals. Locate your heartbeat. Feel it in your head. Find it in your toes and fingertips. It takes patience, but you must relax. Practice every day.

Learn to sync your body with your mind"—he taps her head—"your unconscious mind. I'm going to hypnotize you."

The room is warm, and bed is soft. She stretches out and closes her eyes.

# Thirty-Three

# Oh good lordt, he's a robot. I had sex with a machine.

Quinn wakes in darkness. The room is still warm and the bed still soft. She lies quite still, taking in the darkness, warmth, and softness surrounding her, and she's overcome by an unfamiliar awareness: She feels empty and calm and generally fabulous.

Sitting up evokes a lightheadedness that only increases her fabulousness, and with this she grins; it's good to feel this good. She can't remember the last time she felt this good. Then she realizes she's not alone. There's a shadow lingering against the wall on the far side of the room, and she stiffens.

The loitering figure steps forward, and it's Tig. He lights a lantern beside her bed and hands her a mug of water, which she drinks. He watches her drink until she's finished, then he takes the mug, refills it, and hands it back, indicating she should drink more. She sips it and places it down. He hands it back. "You're dehydrated, you need to drink."

Frowning, she looks up at him, but the protest she's about to emit it is immediately quashed by the sight of his eyes. The bionic glasses are gone, replaced with the beautiful hazel bionic eyes, and she can't take her eyes off them. They sparkle in the dim light of the lantern, mesmerizing her. "Sorry, your eyes, they're amazing, I can't stop—"

"Drink."

"What?"

"Drink, you're dehydrated."

She sips the water. "What time is it?"

"Eleven."

"Eleven. I've slept five hours." *Geez, I was tired.*

"It's tomorrow. You've slept thirty hours."

"Thirty hours." *There's something seriously wrong with me. Who sleeps thirty hours?*

"You didn't tell me about this." He pokes at her left arm.

"No, I didn't." *I neglected to mention this during our "blink and you'll miss it" relationship.* She pulls her arm away.

"Drink more," he says.

"Not now." She puts the mug down.

He picks it up, hands it to her again, and he's insistent, sitting on the bed beside her, taking both her hands and placing them around the mug. She doesn't care about the water. The drink is an annoying distraction. All she cares about are his eyes, his beautiful bionic eyes, staring into hers with a secret power that renders her stunned and speechless. Now he's so close and his warm hands are around her cool hands and she feels his breath on her cheek.

"Drink," he says, so she does, and he's adamant that she finish every last drop.

Outside, it's deathly quiet. The only sound is the swell of the ocean hitting the pontoon. The hair on her arms prickle. It's too quiet. "What's going on? Who won the election?"

"Unsatisfactory outcome. We need to leave."

Planck enters. "Saw your light on. How you feeling, Sleeping Beauty?"

"I'm—"

"Great. We're leaving, right now. Come on, up you get."

Quinn climbs off the bed.

"Power?" asks Tig.

"Spare racks and draft tubes from Tilda, and the hydro's up and running. And there's another crate of coconuts if we need to surge."

*Good lordt, they've using coconuts as Capacitors. What year is this?*

"Cloaking?" Tig asks.

"Intermittent, but we'll make do. We need to move." Planck heads for the door.

"Wait, wait a minute, what's going on?" Quinn demands. "Why's it so quiet?"

"Revolution," Tig says. "The citizens are gathering and won't take long. We're leaving, and you're coming."

"I'm not going anywhere with you."

"Yes, you are. Unus's not safe."

"I'm not in Unus. I'm in Harmonia."

"Well, fuck me, miss important scientist." Planck raises an eyebrow.

"They're gonna storm the climate cities," Tig says.

Quinn can't leave, not without Mori, not without the cactus. "I . . . I have to go back for something—someone—he's waiting for me."

Tig steps back, shakes his head. "No."

"I'm not asking permission. I can look after myself."

"Fuck." Tig stomps out, slams the door.

Planck smiles. "Honey, we ain't going anywhere without you. Now, we have maybe an hour. The Hyperloop's working one way, to get people out, but you can enter through the port at Mooring. I'll borrow an auto. We scoot around the outside of the city, come in from the north. The hyperways are empty. You jump out at the port, get your friend, and, with a little luck, we'll be back before people start chopping each other's heads off."

"You're authorized for reentry?" Tig stands in the doorway. "The security system's fatal. You got out, doesn't mean you can get back in. You authorized?"

"Fatal? Seriously?"

"What did you expect?"

*I didn't expect they'd murder people for cool air.*

"Anyone know you're here?" Planck asks.

"No. But I used the Hyperloop two days ago."

"Risky. Enter the port without authorization, you'll be killed. We need another way in."

She needs a new plan. Plan B: The geothermal tubes. "Access through the air vents. They open onto the moat, and there's a maintenance route around the city walls. I have the plans and the maintenance codes."

"No time," Planck says. "We don't have a drone. It'd take hours to climb the vents."

Quinn shakes her head. "Don't need to climb. Activate the air system. The compressor will kick in, and the pumps will pull me up the tube. There are thermostats on the exterior walls. They'll be highly sensitive. Heat them a few degrees, and they'll activate the air system."

"We use a laser," Tig says. "Set it to heat. How do we get out?"

"Shut the system down, slide down the tubes."

"Get me killed, I'll be really pissed off."

"I'm not looking for volunteers. No one asked you to come."

✲✲✲

Forty minutes later, Mori's reluctant rescue team climbs from their auto and gazes down at tens of thousands of protesters, all wearing red shirts, gathered at Mooring, the entry port to Harmonia. A ring of small fires is fed by sacrificial autos, fuel cells, old air systems—anything that burns—and the crowd launches flaming missiles at the city. A unified chant of, "Open the gate; open the gate; open the gate," rises into the darkness. Quinn's resolve crumbles; they are here to liberate a cactus and an AI meerkat. Perhaps they should leave both, get straight back in the auto, and drive away.

"Why are they wearing red?" she asks.

"Unity: color of fire and blood. And heat—they're hot and they've had enough. An air system will keep you cool at home, if you have a home and Coin and access to Tech, but a cool city—to live in a cool city—well, life would be very different." Planck turns to her. "Is this worth it?"

"Honestly, I'm not sure." She hesitates. "It's not a person, it's information. That's what I want. That's why we're here." Not the full story, but there's no time for long explanations.

They split up, Planck taking a northern route to the rear of the city, away from the crowd, while Tig and Quinn head for the footbridge, unfurled and shimmering, weightless, over the moat, an open invitation to the rebels. The aloofness, the streamlined whiteness and purity of the bridge, offends Quinn. Provocation is its purpose.

Tig and Quinn make their way over the bridge, through the crowd, until they reach the exit point: a maintenance gap close to the walls. They drop over the side, release a ladder, and shimmy down to a cavity in the city walls, which leads to the giant geothermal pipes. The tubes suck cool air across the water, directly into Harmonia. Heavy carbon filters cover the openings. Quinn enters her access codes into the security system and steps back. Nothing happens. The grates remain closed. She tries again; still nothing. Tig tries. Spectacularly unsuccessful. *Fuck. I'm stupid. This was never going to work. What was I thinking?*

"What now?" says Tig.

She needs a Plan B: Hitch's access codes. Maybe she's completely right about him, maybe he's not as benign as he presents, maybe he's not keen on her and he does work for eMpower, or Niels, or Myra. Worth a try. She locates the sequence and scans in the codes. The grates open. She shakes her head; of course, he's not what he seems.

They move into a tube opening and wait, side by side. Tig pulls a spare laser from his belt and sums her up. He's unsure about handing it over. "Ever shot anyone?" he asks.

She's about to shake her head—no, she's never shot anyone, she's a Pacifist, or she was a Pacifist, but now survival outweighs any anti-violence sentiments she ever had—but then she remembers those guards on the Ship, and Jane. She didn't shoot the bird, but she killed her and ate her, every last bit. She killed Jane; she cut her head off and her blood got in her eyes. So she's not a wimp. She'll shoot someone if she has to. He can give her the gun. Might not be the best time to brag about violent deeds, though. It was just a bird, but . . . *Fuck it.*

"I killed Jane, and I ate her. I chopped her head off and her blood got in my eyes. Now I have her DNA inside me."

He steps closer, looking deep into her eyes, like he's trying to actually see Jane's DNA. "You did the right thing." He puts the gun in her hand. It's a lightweight, transparent Glock with a customized grip and a sliding gage along the barrel. "There's a Taser setting with a sliding scale. I've set it to stun. You won't kill anyone."

"What's wrong with you? Why are you so different?"

He breathes, catches the air in his chest.

The air system kicks in.

Their feet lift off the ground. Success—Planck heated the thermostats. Quinn and Tig are sucked into the pipe on a slipstream of cold air. Her hands quickly lose heat and begin to tingle. The light fades. She reaches for him, to check he's there, beside her. He takes her hand in his, holds it tightly. The tingling sensation spreads down her body. Now she has one warm hand and one cold hand, but he doesn't let go. He holds her cold hand to his chest. Soon the lights from the quadrangle above are visible. They've reached a catchment area. They scramble over the rim of the tube and into a holding pond, where the cool air is slowly dispersed into every corner of the city. Tig removes a grate, and they climb out into a small grove of fruit trees.

It's very quiet. Low-level street lighting illuminates their way, but the lights in the apartment Pods are out. The residents are either hiding or have already fled the Climate City. They march briskly through the uninhabited streets to Habitat5, her codes get them inside, and then something explodes in the distance, in the direction of Unus. They race toward the skylift.

With perfect timing, the skylift doors open, and Myra, Hitch, and Mori the meerkat step out. Quinn steps back in surprise. Tig draws his weapon. Myra and Hitch point lasers at Tig, and Quinn passes her laser to her left hand. Mori scurries over and stands beside her.

"Cute," says Hitch, "but rules are rules. No pets allowed."

"I am not a pet," Mori objects, "I have probabilistic reasoning; a subsumption architecture system. It allows me to be reactive and make intuitive—"

"Not now," says Quinn.

"Hope I wasn't out of line the other night. Had a good time. You're fun, good company." Hitch gives her a sly, unexpected wink.

Tig scowls at the winker, then shoots him in the heart. Hitch falls back into the skylift.

Myra shoots Tig. He crumples to the floor.

Quinn happily shoots Myra, twice, dead center, between her eyes. She falls hard.

Quinn drops beside Tig and rolls him onto his back.

Mori scurries over and takes his pulse. "He's not breathing. His heart has stopped."

*Fuck, he's going to be so pissed off with me.*

Mori brandishes a hidden fingernail that emerges from the inside of a paw. Impressive. It's the first notable thing Quinn has seen him do. He cuts straight into Tig's chest. But there's no blood. *Oh good lordt, he's a robot. I had sex with a machine. He's not human, he has no emotions, he has no fucking heart. No wonder he's such a prick. He's AI, and the AI meerkat is fixing the AI cyborg. What has the world come to?*

Mori opens Tig's chest cavity, exposing a red pod covered in little black seeds—it resembles a strawberry. "He has an artificial pericardium. A saline driver helps it beat, but the flow has stopped. I will need to reboot."

*I'm confused.* "He's not AI?"

"No, this is the casing around his heart. I will use your Band as a magnetic field to re-activate the pump." *Oh, thank the lordt, sex with a cyborg is okay, but a robot, that's too weird.* Quinn passes Mori her Band, and the magnetic field kick-starts Tig's heart. Tig sucks in air, coughs, and stumbles to his knees.

Quinn puts a hand on his shoulder. "You okay?"

Tig nods. Mori steps forward and seals the opening around his heart.

"This?" Tig says. "This is your friend? We've come back for this?"

"It's complicated—"

"Don't care. Come on." He strides out the door of the Habitat. No one follows.

Quinn turns to Mori. "The data, did you get it?"

"The download is complete and stored in the plant. Nobody knows you're a meerkat when you're in NIoT."

"You're not a meerkat, you're a robot."

"And your friend."

*Did I say you were my friend?*

Tig marches back inside.

"One last thing," Quinn says. "Won't take long."

Quinn and Mori jump in the skylift, and Tig follows, scowling. The doors close. Hitch lies comatose on the floor.

"You had sex with him?" Tig points at the inert body.

"What? No. And it's none of your business."

Tig breathes heavily, his chest rising and falling in epic proportions, and she takes a couple of steps back, willing the skylift to move faster.

"You kiss him?"

She stares at the floor. They are almost there.

"So you did. You did kiss him."

"I'm not having this conversation. I'll kiss whoever I want. It's none of your business. Why're you being so *weird?*"

Her left hand punches him hard in the chest. He barely flinches so it goes in for a second blow, but he blocks the punch with his fist. The muscles in his neck tighten and his hazel eyes turn dark, and then, immediately, he relents, lets go of her hand and hangs his head. She takes two steps back.

"I'm sorry, I shouldn't have . . ."

The two mumbled the same words in unison. They glance at each other, surprised by the accord of their apology.

"I didn't mean . . . I'm sorry." Again, the same utterances, and their fiery impulses collapse in regret. He stares at the floor, and she considers the ceiling.

"He kissed her. He was too obvious, too keen, too soon," Mori offers.

*Oh good lordt.* The doors open, and she leads the way.

The cactus is on the side table where she left it. It appears healthy and seems to be recovering well after its procedure, but it requires care and must stay alive until she can get her hands on a Quantum Machine, a QM, to sequence the code and retrieve the data. She takes it to the food prep, waters it, and then gently wraps it in a cloth.

Tig waits in the living zone, his chest wound bleeding, a dark stain seeping through his shirt. Quinn rummages through the storage drawers, finds a roll of tape, and, after handing him the cactus to hold like it's a bunch of samphire, opens his shirt, mops up the blood, and sticks him back together with the tape. It's unnerving, being so close to him, touching his auburn skin. Way too familiar. "I'm sorry, I didn't mean . . . my arm, it does stupid . . ."

"I know." He places his hand over hers. She pulls away. He's not the same cyborg she knew on the atoll.

Outside, the sound of explosions and rocket launchers ceases, and the chanting voices of the rebels peter out. Soon there's an unnerving, dead silence—a lull, a tense and unplanned ceasefire from both sides. Then the cry of one hundred thousand people rises up, into the tallest spires of the Climate City, and people begin spilling into Harmonia. The entrance gates are open; Harmonia is vacant and disarmed.

"We walk out the main entrance," says Tig, sealing a reluctant Mori into his pack, "It'll be faster."

As they reach the silicon bridge, Quinn freezes. The Spectrals are open and spinning in irregular, methodic circles. The hairs on her arms prickle; what are they up to? Why the change? Myra told her Harmonia was a living, breathing entity. The city is AI; it's not alive, but it's programmed to defend itself. The people flowing across the bridge pause in awe, pointing at the magnificent sculptures—and then, one by one, they begin to fall, dropping to the ground. The Spectrals are not pieces of art—they're weapons, a defense mechanism armed with lasers that target the bridge. Harmonia is entering the second phase of its defense. Phase one was entrapment, luring the enemy closer. Phase two: Strike them down.

The rebels are caught off guard; hundreds are hit in the chest, the perfect kill site, and all around people continue to fall. Tig and Quinn drop below the line of attack and Tig fires at the sculptures—a pointless effort; they're spinning too fast. He kneels and opens his pack. Mori's head pops out, and he pushes the meerkat to one side, reaches in, and pulls out a compact projectile launcher. He checks the weapon then hands it to Quinn. "Take out the eye."

She focuses on the Spectral, unconsciously gauging its oscillation and spin rate, then closes her eyes, takes a breath, and fires. The Spectral explodes. She moves to the others, taking out four more. The last one shatters on her second attempt. She offers the launcher back to Tig, and he almost smiles—but then he tilts his head to the side, listening.

Quinn hears it, too—the thud of rotors, a Hydrocopter.

The bridge shudders; it's retracting.

Tig points to the other side. "Go."

They pick up the pace as the bridge continues to retract underneath their feet.

"Faster," he says.

They are caught halfway and the only way out is over the edge.

"Your hand," he says, reaching out.

*Really? Didn't we deal with this in the 2020s? I can run just fine on my own.* She ignores his request.

The bridge is an obstacle course, littered with wounded, and they navigate the bodies, hurdling over and around them, stopping to help the more able to their feet, but all the time moving forward, while the Hydrocopter gets closer and closer. Tilted, nose down, the machine scans the bridge from left to right, scattering a trail of bullets. *Why did I think coming back was a good idea?*

Tig yanks her to the ground. "Wait three seconds, then shoot—first the gunmen, then the pilot."

One, two, three, her left hand does not hesitate. The Hydrocopter reels, hits the side of the bridge, and spins into the void below; there's a loud thud, followed by a plop, as it's swallowed by the moat. The bridge shudders then halts its retraction; it is damaged from the copter impact. They walk the rest of the way until there is nowhere left to go—no more bridge and a twenty-meter gap to land.

Breathing heavily, Tig scans the dark void below. It's a long way down, too far to jump. They need a plan. They need wings, or a drone, or a rotor.

As Quinn thinks this, a rebel transporter flies in and drops over the chasm, hovering in the gap between bridge and land, and people begin crawling over the roof of the craft to safety.

Another Hydrocopter follows the same route as the first, scouting left to right across the bridge, shooting anything that moves. Quinn draws her weapon, but the Hydrocopter explodes before she has a chance to shoot. Behind them is a group of rebels with a handheld rocket launcher. They usher Quinn and Tig forward, so they keep moving, and soon it's their turn to cross.

The surface of the transporter is smooth and broad, shaped like a cape, with three spinning propellers cutting through the roofline—one at the tail and one on each wing. The path across is straightforward: avoid the back rotor, walk straight over the midsection, and leap onto the cliff on the far side.

"Fast, steady," Tig says, striding across.

Quinn follows, but she only takes two steps before the vessel wobbles and lurches to one side; it's taken a hit. She slides down the metal surface toward the wing, frantically searching for something to grab, a ridge or a molding, but there's nothing. She's headed for the rotor blades. She rolls sideways and just misses the blades—and slips feet first over the edge.

At the last second, she gets both hands around the propeller rim and holds on fast. She hangs there, dangling over the chasm, as the transporter wobbles again and rights itself.

Tig strides over. "My hand," he offers, and this time she doesn't hesitate to grab it and he hauls her back onto the ship. Pulling her close, he whispers, "Don't fear what hands like ours can do."

After that, she doesn't let go until they're on the other side. It was never about him helping her run, it was about them doing it together, being in it together.

Harmonia is ablaze with gunfire. Hydrocopters and drones clash in the sky above the city. Lifeless bodies cover the bridge and fill the moat. Downhill, the valley is alive with the thousands more heading for the Climate City. Many will die on this hot, sticky February night.

***

They take the back streets to where Planck is waiting, north of Harmonia, avoiding the barricades and roadblocks. Shocked-looking residents trickle out of buildings, fixed to their Bands, waiting for news. Gunfire crackles in the distance over Unus. Fighter jets set off sonic booms as they fly over the metropolis.

It takes an hour to get to Planck, and another thirty minutes after that to get back to the harbor. Half the boats have disappeared, including *Nanshe*, which is drifting offshore. They row out, into the darkness, with the noise of the city blaring behind them.

"It was always going to happen," says Planck. "Surprised it's taken this long." Ze loads the latest news onto zirs Band and brings up a holo of the Fourth Estate. "The factions are fighting for control; Maim Quate and the Democratic Republic won the election, but New Fed refused to concede. Civil war."

## Thirty-Four

# We need to be patient, tolerant, and understanding. It's not his fault.

Mori and Quinn share a cabin: bunk beds, a window, two chairs, and a cleanse zone. She carefully places the cactus in the top corner of her bunk.

Mori sits on the bed, gnashing his teeth. "Unexpected outcome," he says.

"What were you doing with Myra and Hitch in the skylift?"

"I hid, like you told me to, but they found me in the sleep zone. They told me pets are not allowed, so I must come with them."

"Did you shut down, deactivate, pretend to be a cute, fluffy toy?"

"No. You did not instruct me to do that. You told me to hide."

*Okay, fair enough.* She moves the meerkat to one side, lies down next to him, and closes her eyes. It's two in the morning.

"I have good news for you. Inside the pack, the very, very dark pack, I realized I have the five senses of self: ecological, interpersonal, temporal extended, conceptual, private. The five senses of self."

It appears Mori spent his hours trapped inside the backpack contemplating the meaning of existence; given the environment, Quinn can see how existential thoughts might prevail, but she doesn't care.

People died—real people, who felt real pain. "This is not a good time to tell me you're human."

"Number one, I am unique; I have a point of view and I know this is my body." He rubs his furry little chest. "Number two, I recognize my own image in a reflective glass, and I have empathy. Number three, I have awareness of the past and of the future. Number four, I have a life story. I have motivations and values and goals. Number five, I am capable of private thoughts. I have a stream of consciousness."

Her stream of consciousness is about to put him back in the very, very dark pack. Maybe he'll come out thinking he's a meerkat.

A tap on the door. "Food in the galley," Planck calls.

✳✳✳

Tig pours amber liquid into metal tankards and hands one to Planck and one to Quinn. She follows their lead and throws back the drink. It's beer, and it's delicious, and it helps. A lot. *I love beer. It must be the best drink in the world.* He refills her cup and she like the sound it makes.

The food is warm bread with roasted black frogs, samphire, and insect sprinkles, served in wooden bowls and eaten with chopsticks—a salty, spicy, crunchy mush. Quinn wipes the sweat from her brow. Tig wolfs his food down in ten seconds and quaffs another mug of beer.

Quinn breaks the silence with an apology. "I'm sorry. For . . . making you both go back to Harmonia. I didn't—"

"None of us knew. Not your fault. We've rescued stranger things." Planck smiles at Mori. He smiles back, and when Planck gives him a scratch under the ear, he affects a coy, bashful demeanor—one that Quinn knows she's about to shatter.

"I didn't go back for the AI. I went back for the cactus. eMpower data is stored in the cactus DNA."

"Seriously?" Planck grins. "Clever girl."

Quinn takes the credit. Mori did the coding, but it was her idea.

Under the table, Tig's leg begins to jiggle. The shaking steadily builds until the entire table shudders. "So who's the guy? The one in the skylift. The one you kissed."

"You kissed someone else?" Planck is alarmed.

"He kissed her," Mori clarifies.

"Thank you," Quinn says to the meerkat, then turns to Tig. "Okay. Listen to me. He did kiss me. It was just a kiss, it's no big deal. I have zero feelings for him."

"Then why'd he kiss you?"

"He wanted to mate with her," Mori interjects.

Quinn glares at the meerkat. *Not helpful.*

Tig slams his bowl on the table, grabs the bottle of beer, and storms out. Shame—she could really do with another drink.

She turns to Planck; now is a good time for explanations. "What's wrong with him?"

"He's not happy about the kissing, and I don't blame him."

Quinn glares.

"Okay, okay, he has a disorder—anxiety. Exposed to Diazinon, an organophoshate during a war . . . it affected his neurotransmitters, shrunk his hippocampus, and thinned out his right cortex."

"Nerve gas?"

"Yes, uses a monthly SelfMed, balances everything out. But sometimes he goes off his Meds, and when he does, there are . . . a few side effects. Specifically, he's easily agitated, aggressive, frustrated, has temper tantrums, is unable to verbalize his feelings, is highly sexual, exhibits some physical violence. And, of course, jealous of the guy in the skylift."

"Why would he go off his Meds?"

"We had a lot to do. The election looming, murmurs of an uprising, crazy talk about a revolution and civil war—now not so crazy—we needed him in combat mode. It's unfortunate, but he's a better fighter, and stronger, when he's off his Meds. So, until he takes them again, we need to be patient, tolerant, and understanding. It's not his fault."

"Or we inject him with the SelfMed."

"It's not that simple. You want to try holding him down?"

✷✷✷

Wearily, the new arrivals return to their cabin. Quinn collapses onto the bottom bunk and places a pillow under her head and another over her feet. Mori curls up contentedly at the end of the bed.

Quinn reviews the past week: A few days ago, she was alone on an atoll, strolling the beach, taking two naps a day, and making cairns. Now, she's on a boat with an AI meerkat who thinks he's human and a jealous ex-lover who has lost all sense of reason, and today she killed people, several people. She feels remorse, shame, and guilt—this is not a good thing she's done. It makes her a poor human, but it was war and it had to be this way. *Oh the justification of the subconscious; how easily we let ourselves off.* The truth is, she felt more wretched about killing Jane. What's the difference between killing for survival and killing for food? It's still killing. It makes a mockery of her Pacifist pledge, broken so easily. Killing animals and people is not the moral dilemma she thought that it would be, that it should be.

A rotten smell wafts through the air.

"Did you just . . . fart?"

"I opened the vibrating seal of my anal sphincter."

"Close it."

"Do you think I am becoming more human? A human trapped in a meerkat's body."

"You're a robot trapped in a meerkat's body. Switch off, or go to sleep, whatever it is you do."

She closes her eyes, but she's woken minutes later by an intermittent gulping sound coming from Mori. She feels for him and taps him with her foot to make him stop.

"I have *hic* hiccups," he says.

"No you don't."

"They will *hic* not stop *hic*."

"Make them."

"I-I *hic* cannot."

She takes the pillow keeping her feet warm and places it over her head. Surely by now some smart scientist should have invented a way for humanity to store sleep, like a sleep bank where you can accrue credit. She could have deposited all the extra hours of sleep she had on the atoll and then, on nights like this, make a withdrawal, and feel fabulous the next day. This could be her next research project: a sleep bank. She won't be on this boat forever. She'll need a plan for the future. Sleep banks—she'll be a trillionaire.

# Thirty-Five

# There is a baby human growing inside you.

Quinn wakes tired and queasy. The boat is rocking heavily, and outside her window, sky and ocean merge into one distinct shade of cerulean—they're at sea, and it's late. She's overslept. Mori has disappeared.

She staggers into the galley and flops onto the sofa beside Planck, who's tickling Mori's tummy. He giggles uncontrollably, and Planck is clearly amused.

Planck glances Quinn's way and balks. "You're green, and something terrible has happened to your hair."

"I'm not well, I feel . . . sick." She burps.

"Swells picked up, I'll fix you something to eat." Ze stands and flattens Quinn's hair down for her, a partially successful gesture, and Quinn pats Mori's fur down, because he's also looking disheveled after his tickle time.

"Better." Planck smiles at the two of them, together on the sofa. Quinn can tell ze likes having passengers onboard.

"Latest news." Ze recounts the newscast. "Dirac never lost control of his forces. They were handpicked, would die for him. And they did. He attacked his own military and blamed the rebels. Now he gets to 'cleanse,' and the consequences are dire. Arrest warrants issued for thousands of officials. Quate and Jove are missing. The military's rounding people up for detainment, and he wants to reinstate the death penalty. We have a problematic reputation with the far right; we'll need to bunker down, stay off grid, under the sonar, for a few weeks, set our invisibility shield till things settle down."

✶✶✶

Breakfast is a milky-colored cornbread with smoked fish—a meal indifferent to Quinn's seasickness. Planck suggests a turn around the deck to take in the fresh air, and ze's keen to show her the boat.

They stroll outside, onto the main deck, and spy Tig, busy activating a curtain of invisibility. Planck explains: They're using a metamaterial that is 50 nanometers thick covered with nanoantennas, which distort and manipulate wavelengths of light. The system works best when directed to a specific color bandwidth, and they're using green. The cloak removes the boat's visual, infrared, and thermal signatures, so the vessel merges into the surrounding ocean. They're still detectable by sonar, however, so Tig also sets a quantum stealth signal that loops sound waves in a repetitive motion around the boat.

Planck directs Quinn toward the power boosters. They're trying something new: a HydroHarvester that captures vibrations from the ocean on a rotation. Nanotubes are spun into fine threads then twisted into coils and immersed in an electrolyte. When the coil vibrates, it generates electricity. There's also a basket of coconuts on deck. "Coconut husks as capacitors, gives us an extra shot of power," Planck says.

*How quaint.*

"Nice and spongy." Planck picks up a husk. "Process the coconut, and all that's left is the carbon. Then you perforate it to increase the surface area and store the energy in electric fields. Boundless power."

"For about fifteen minutes."

"Eleven, but whose counting?"

"Tried using nanotubes, or plantations of carbon cylinders—massive surface area—or maybe a polymer network? It'll increase your power storage. Give you a longer boost."

"Okay, we need to talk, but coconuts are free."

Strapped to the front of the boat is a bronze sculpture of a blue man wearing a cone hat, similar to the Indocin doctor's healing Buddha. This statue holds its arms out, palms turned upward, as if he's pushing something away.

"Repelling the oceans," says Planck. "The Buddha used the power gained from meditation to hold back a wall of water. He saw the future."

Fresh air and a stroll around the deck are effective remedies; Quinn's nausea is under control. She follows Planck down the hatch to the lower level, the horticulture zone. When they step inside, she squints and shades her eyes. The walls, ceiling, and floor are a glossy white and the space is filled with racks of plants: two rows, five stratums high and thirty meters long, illuminated with phosphorous laser lighting. It's an edible forest of plants, herbs, fruits, and vegetables. Preform casings cover the seedbeds, protecting the vegetation in rough seas. The far corner holds a nutrient control incubator, with several large and healthy marijuana plants.

"Medicinal," Planck reports, then frowns at Quinn. "You're not green anymore; now you're grey."

✳✳✳

Back in the cabin, Mori places a damp towel on Quinn's forehead and massages her feet. She knew he was worth going back for. Planck checks her vitals with a SelfMed and after considering the readings ze promptly, leaves without speaking, eyes fixed to the monitor.

A few minutes pass. Planck comes back in and checks Quinn over again. "The first reading was inconclusive," ze says. "I want to make sure you don't have FF."

She knows she doesn't have FF; she has seasickness and a reaction to the spicy food from last night. Ze leaves her to rest, and she closes her eyes. All she needs is more sleep. A few more hours, and she'll be fine, fabulous, back to her old self. Then maybe she'll synthesize something to increase the boat's power. The coconuts have got to go.

As she drifts off to sleep, her head fills with electric fields, blue Buddhas, and baskets and baskets of coconuts drifting on the blue ocean . . .

✶✶✶

She jolts awake. Something has disturbed her—loud noises, arguing in the galley. She hears her name, opens her eyes, and rolls off the bunk.

Tig and Planck cease arguing the moment they see her. She walks toward them and they nervously they step back.

Tig gives her an awkward smile. "Why don't you sit?"

She shakes her head. She doesn't want to sit, she's happy standing, but he's insistent, pulls up a chair.

"Sit," he says, and this time it's a command. So she begins to sit, and then he blurts out, "You're pregnant."

Caught midway between sitting and standing, she rights herself and turns to him. "What did you say?"

"You're pregnant. We're having—"

"Not possible," she calmly retorts, "Conscientious Prevention on my twenty-first birthday. I can't conceive."

"I know. I know all about it—Conscientious Prevention. But you're still pregnant," Tig says. "We checked. Three times."

She places her hands over her stomach. "It's not possible. It's science."

"Some things are beyond science," Planck says. "Why don't you sit down?"

She nods and takes a seat, all the while wondering if these poor fools have lost their minds. There's nothing beyond science. She knows Mori can confirm the truth. He'll put an end to this nonsense with his SQUIDS Scanner, and then these two idiots will have to apologize for scaring the shit out of her. Confidently, she calls him over. With an air of assertive veracity, she stands and asks him to check her.

The meerkat blinks a few times. "There is a baby human growing inside you."

"No, there is not a baby human growing inside me."

"Perhaps you should sit down," Planck offers, with a look that suggests things might get worse.

"No," Quinn snaps. "It's not possible. Tell me, how this is possible?"

"Maybe the accident dislodged the implant. Who knows? But you are pregnant." Planck holds the chair out for her, but Quinn declines. She would prefer to stand; she wants to look them in the eye while they have this conversation.

"Conception is a gift," Tig announces.

"Conception is not a *gift*. A gift is . . . well, it's a thing. It's not people. It's not *a baby*. It's new Tech, or a book, or jewelry, or something else. You don't give a baby as a gift." She thrusts her wrist at him, jangles the bracelets on it. "These—why do I have these?"

"I chose you. You're my beloved, I want to spend my life with —"

"Stop right there." She's unable to get her breath; she thinks she might suffocate or hyperventilate, or do both. "You do not get to choose. Are you listening to me? I am a *person*—I am not something that you choose. Okay? Just because you want it doesn't mean it will happen." *I can't believe he just used the C word. "I 'chose' you"!? Well, you don't get to choose!*

She's hit by a wave of nausea. "I need to sit down."

Planck offers her a chair and then a bowl. She sits, puts her head between her knees, and pukes into the bowl. She wipes her mouth; she pukes again.

Planck rubs her back. "Congratulations."

✶✶✶

Quinn lies on her bunk bed, the bowl next to her. *Oh, good lordt. How can I be pregnant?* She never intended to bring children into a world with ten billion people. She was never going to add to that tally. Adopt, that was her plan. Adopt one of the millions of homeless children who live on the planet. *I have choices, of course I do. I don't have to have this baby. There's a very straightforward solution to this complex problem. Fuck. I don't know what to do.*

She considers the bracelets around her wrist. Suddenly, they feel tighter. She tugs at them but can't get them over her wrist. *This will never work.*

A baby has never been part of her life plan. But neither has sex with a cyborg. Or spending two months on a lonely atoll, or adopting an Automated Living Companion who wants to be human, or spending weeks floating in the Java Sea on a boat. She does the math in her head. She had sex with Mori . . . she can't remember the last time. The baby is Tig's.

AI Mori enters the cabin. Without looking at her, he slumps onto the bed, curls up, and lets out a long sigh. Then he sighs again, this time with effect. He wants her to ask him if he's okay, and she obliges. "Gee, are you okay?" she asks, with sarcasm.

"No."

"Really? That's a shame—what's wrong with you? Tell me all about it."

"I do not like being called AI or a System."

"But that's who you are. That's the real you. The sooner you accept it, the happier you'll be."

"I find it disrespectful."

She sighs. Somewhere, in the early part of this century, political correctness went mad. "Okay, what would make you happy?" She's placating him purely to keep the peace. There's enough anxiety on this boat already.

"I would like to be referred to by my name, Mori."

If she didn't know better, she'd say he was feigning distress to get attention. He's becoming more human every day.

Another knock on the door and Planck slinks into the cabin. "I've been thinking," ze begins, "and I want you to know, I'm rad-fem and pro-choice, so if you don't want to keep it, as such, I can get the product. Totally safe. Unus is pro-abortion; we have the Fundamental Atheists to thank for that. Just let me know. But if you decide to keep it, and it's totally your choice, I've signed up for midwifery online, an intensive six-month course, so I'll be ready." Ze makes a gesture, like ze's about to catch a ball. Or a baby.

Quinn holds zirs gaze without blinking.

"Too soon, isn't it?"

She nods.

"Too soon."

She offers Planck her wrist. "Can't get these off."

"We don't want to do that." Ze places her arm back in her lap.

"Yes, I think we do," she says offering her arm again.

Ze places it back in her lap. "Patience."

"I'm pregnant. Don't tell me to be patient."

# Thirty-Six

# The Epic of Gilgamesh

The Fourth Estate reports that the political situation in Unus has deteriorated. New Fed has declared a state of emergency and the new President, Dirac Devine, is drafting laws that bypass parliament. In the name of protecting democracy and human rights, he has closed all public buildings including schools, rounded up another hundred thousand officials, and revoked all academic and civic credentials. The dissidents were apparently "radicalized and hypnotized by robots." Thousands of citizens are missing, including Maim Quate and Kip Jove, the leaders of the opposing parties.

Quinn realizes she could be trapped on this boat for weeks. If only she had a metamaterial, 50 nanometers thick, covered with nano-antennas that distort and manipulate wavelengths of light, then she could make herself invisible. She'd like that because staying out of Tig's way in such a confined space is not easy. If she's in the galley and Tig enters, Planck beckons her below deck, or outside, or any space where he's not. She's been spending many hours feigning invisibility, hiding in her cabin.

Today, Planck took her below deck and handed her a folded bundle of 3D-printed clothing: a climate suit, shorts, singlet tops, and shirts. Taupe and navy, textured weaves with dark trims, and a "classic white shirt"—zirs description. They're perfect, and replace the oversized men's shirt and shorts tied with tape that she's currently wearing. Ze said the white shirt will be perfect for lazy afternoons on the lounge. She is to roll the sleeves up and undo three, maybe four, buttons. Quinn can't imagine there'll be many lazy afternoons on the lounge. Still, it's nice to have new clothes.

Ze also gave her something for the morning sickness: a tonic mixed with iron, calcium, and foliate—totally organic, of course. Quinn caught a glance at zirs module while ze was mixing the tonic: "Online School of Nursing and Midwifery. Unit 1: Anatomy of Physiology Pregnancy and Childbirth." Ze immediately shut it down.

After she grabbed her clothes and was heading back to the main deck, she met Tig coming down the stairs. He wasn't wearing a shirt, just his cargo pants. She had to squeeze to one side and wait for him to pass, and his chest was naked, completely naked. She rolled her eyes, thinking he should put something on, because you can't just walk around without a shirt. That's not right—people should wear shirts. Then she couldn't get the image of his naked chest out of her head. Pregnancy was messing with her sex hormones, so she went to bed early, to sort out her own sex hormones, but when she opened the cabin door she found Mori standing over the empty cactus pot. The plant was tossed to one side, and soil was scattered across the floor. The plant was a bit worse for wear, but still in one piece. Mori looked as guilty as hell.

"It fell from my hand," he said.

"Paw. You don't have hands; you have paws. We've talked about this." She scraped up the soil and replanted the cactus.

"An accident."

"Yes, we all have accidents."

Tonight she'll keep the plant by her pillow, just in case there is another accident. She needs to get hold of a QM, so she can sequence the DNA and extract the data.

✳✳✳

Boats are boring, and Quinn feels trapped. Like a fish in bowl, she's walked around and around the deck, dozens of times, both clockwise and counterclockwise. The vessel is larger than her apartment Pod in Hobart, three or four times larger, and when she first boarded *Nanshe* the interior seemed voluminous, with so much space it appeared bigger inside than out. She'd never seen a boat like this before, with so many rooms. Now, after a week on board, the boat feels the same size as a shipping container; it's claustrophobic, and there's nothing for her to do. Nothing. All her offers of help are greeted with, "Just relax and put your feet up."

Putting your feet up is an afternoon task, not an all day, every day task. She needs something to do. When she tells Planck she's bored, ze laughs and says, "'As soon as you set foot on a yacht, you belong to some man, not to yourself, and you die of boredom.' Coco Chanel." As an afterthought, ze adds, "Double major, psych *and* fashion." Technically, the boat is not a yacht, but Quinn thinks the rest might be true.

✳✳✳

The next morning, at breakfast, Planck slides a book across the table toward Quinn—a large, heavy volume, moss colored, with an embossed drawing of a city on the cover.

Quinn picks up the book and flicks it open. The air fills with a sweet, floral scent.

Planck explains: Ze is a Magi, a Knowledge Keeper, a facilitator of cultural learning and traditions, skilled in astrology and mythology. *All that, as well as psych and fashion*, Quinn thinks.

Ze has fifteen bracelets, but only three are inherited; the others represent fields of knowledge and, ze keenly points out, were earned through learning. This book is a history book. It's the story of their culture; Quinn's child, if she has it, will be part of this culture; Quinn might like to learn something about who these people are and where they came from.

With a thumb, Quinn skims the leather-bound volume on the table in front of her—a handwritten, ancient text with a translation on the facing page.

"I've a question for you, since you're Knowledge Keeper," says Quinn. "If I were to tell you that Lise didn't die in the catastrophe on Kerguelen—that she escaped using time travel, slipped into a worm-hole and hasn't been seen since—what would you say?"

Planck slides a cup of tea across the table toward her. "Nonsense."

"I knew it."

"It's a portal, not a wormhole. Besides, she'd need the code—an exact combination of particles and elements."

Quinn dips the tip of her finger into her tea and draws a zigzag line on the table.

Planck dips zirs finger into Quinn's tea and adds squiggly lines next to the zigzag, making the drawing an exact match to Tig's tattoo. "We were hoping you might be able to work it out," ze says.

"Me? Why me?"

"You're your mother's daughter. She worked it out."

"She was very smart. I mean, she *is* very smart."

"Be patient."

Quinn tucks the volume under her arm and leaves the table.

✦✦✦

Over the following days, Quinn and Mori read the book together, finding cool, quiet corners of the boat to settle in while they study the translated text. It often sends them both into sleep mode, and when she wakes she finds his dark eyes staring intently at her face.

He says he's watching her sleep.

"Not an acceptable pastime," she corrects. "Look at the ocean, or the sky. People don't like AIs watching them."

Despite the soporific effects of reading ancient history while pregnant, she gradually discovers that the people of the Maldives sprang from a remarkable civilization. They are of Indus decent, a five-thousand-year-old culture that began in Mesopotamia. And they are a truly passive and peaceful race; they eluded war for two thousand years, which is a long time not to bicker amongst yourselves or with your neighbors. She's not aware of any other society that avoided conflict for two millennia. These people, these ancestors of Planck and Tig, and all the people of the Maldives, created a utopic community. They made it work, and they made it last. And, they didn't exist in an isolated bubble—the largest city, Harappa, had a maritime port and traded across the Arabian Sea. They understood technology and created infrastructure and engineering projects, raising the streets to allow for annual flooding. The city was planned and orientated toward the compass points. They had sewers and tanks for water storage, but no armory and no weapons. There were no royal palaces, no grand temples, no monuments to kings or queens or gods, and no class structures. There was no distinction between the homes of the rich and the poor. Their wealth came from mining and trading metals. They understood math and physics; they knew about the stars, the seas, the planets, and the sun.

When Quinn finishes the book, she asks Planck what happened to the people of Harappa—why they migrated and left the city.

"They were invaded," ze says with a shrug. "So they walked away and left everything they owned behind."

✶✶✶

A few days later, another leather-bound volume slides its way over the breakfast table towards her. This text is a poem, a very long poem, called *The Epic of Gilgamesh*. Quinn finds poetry mysterious and beautiful, but way beyond logic. It hurts her brain, and this epic tale is long—pages and pages of verse, twelve volumes in total. At first, Mori attempts to interpret the script for her, but it's outside the limit of his AI perception. He takes everything literally and doesn't understand the rhymes, the imagery, or the language. So sometimes he sits with her while she reads but he refuses to look at the pages—the text annoys him, engaging his frustration circuit. Instead, he stares out to sea or at the sky, so at least he's not staring at her.

The poem—five thousand years old—is about a mythical hero king, called Gilgamesh, who is part human and part god, and his friend Enkidu. Together, they seek out adventures and quests, slaying monsters and cutting down trees to make giant doors that they then travel through. The king has great courage and strength but weak morals and a huge ego, and he sleeps with many women—until he meets his friend Enkidu, at which point he changes his immoral ways and becomes kind and wise. Enkidu also starts off as a wild, uncivilized man, living with animals. To tame him, Gilgamesh sends him a woman and they spend a week together. At the end of the week, he's a reformed and refined man.

The relationship between Gilgamesh and Enkidu begins in conflict, the two heroes fighting it out until they get over themselves and eventually fall in love and become best friends. This lasts until Enkidu dies, which is very, very sad for the king. So he goes on a quest to find everlasting life. He travels through dark tunnels and over high mountain passes, across oceans and rivers, slaying beasts that get in his way. Ultimately, immortality escapes him, because he's part human. Fighting his fate is futile—it ruins the joy of life. So, all for nothing.

Twice Quinn comes across passages that ring familiar. The first is, "Hold my hand in yours, and we will not fear what hands like ours can do." She reads the passage two, three times. Tig said this; he said it to her when she fell from the transporter. Further on she reads, "Through loss I learned that love is wrung from our inmost heart, until only the loved one is and we are not." Love and loss have not touched her life like this, not with this intensity, but she understands what it means. She can see how you could lose yourself. It makes sense that he's also read this book, that he knows these words.

The epic tale immerses her in a world of fantasy and adventure. After days of mulling over the verse, her dreams fill with tales of Gilgamesh and Enkidu. Their escapades wrap her in a pictorial cape of possibilities, of exciting journeys and friendships. When she wakes, she sees a softer, gentler world.

After she finishes the poem, Planck asks, in a nonchalant manner, what she thought of it. She says the main ideas are straightforward enough; in this world there is baptism, but no afterlife. Death is inevitable. Love is transforming, to be cherished, and sex is a sacred act. In the poem, these ideas are revealed as doorways, openings into the mind, through the universe. She says it's a moral code, a primer on what not to do.

Planck listens, nodding here and there but saying nothing, so she goes on to say that the god who gives the king the best advice is Siduri, the tavern owner or goddess of beer, and Quinn is delighted she's female. Siduri tells Gilgamesh to enjoy the simple pleasures of life—good food, clean clothes—and to appreciate the ones he loves. The poem implies that the best things in life are sex, friendship, and beer, in that order.

The other thing that strikes her as interesting is Enkidu's journey, from wild savage to a civilized human, just from spending time with a woman. Planck says it's the reverse of the biblical fall, but that's the only comment ze makes. Ze doesn't agree or disagree with her; ze just says different people find different interpretations, so it's about perspective.

Perspective is something Quinn understands. She tells Planck about Einstein's theory of relativity and perspective, how the laws of physics are the same for all motionless observers but the speed of light in a vacuum will be the same regardless of how fast the observers travel. It reminds her of how space and time are interwoven, united as space-time, which means the same event can occur at different times, depending on where you are. Ze says there is something brewing in the galley and promptly leaves. Quinn understands; it wasn't as relevant as she thought.

The following morning, she finds another book on the breakfast table—something called *Beowulf*. She opens it and doesn't recognize the script. It doesn't look legible; she turns it upside down, and it doesn't help. Planck says it's Old English and she'll get used to it.

"Why am I reading this?"

"This one will make you strong and fearless. Gilgamesh, that was for knowledge."

She notes that all the books were written by "Anon"; she figures that's a woman.

"Tell me something: you have fifteen bracelets, but Tig must have over a hundred. Why so many?"

"Because he's royalty. He's a member of the royal family." Planck says this almost as if ze thought Quinn knew already.

"Royalty!" Quinn gawks. "What does that mean?"

"Technically, he's a king," Planck clarifies. "But it's an ancient title, inherited through lineage. The meaning is symbolic."

Quinn's not sure what a symbolic title actually entails, but she's over the surprises. He could have easily woven that into their conversation before he got himself a beloved.

Planck says she shouldn't worry too much about traditional gender stereotypes or anything like that, because their culture is really very open-minded. It might be old and, ze concedes, possessed of some outdated customs, but men and women are completely equal; there's no disparity.

Quinn disagrees; as far as she's concerned, she's never met less open-minded people in her life.

Planck says the main reason Tig has so many bangles is because his family is gone, so he has inherited them from his father, mother, aunts, and uncles. His family has a long lineage, and Tig is the last of them. It's time for him to begin to shed the bangles and pass them to his offspring; now, he'll have someone to give them to.

Planck tells her the red is the "chosen one" bracelet; the other bracelet, the green one, is a separate gift. It has cultural significance. But it's for Tig to tell her what it means.

Quinn can't wait to see how that turns out.

# Thirty-Seven

# Sex makes people crazy; it makes them do stupid, irrational things.

MEDITATING AND PRACTICING INTEROCEPTION, centering the mind and connecting the conscious to the body, take up many hours of Quinn's time on board the boat. On a good day, she can detect her heartbeat in her toes and fingertips. Today, she intends to test her skills, see how good she is at controlling her arm by using instinct and the power of suggestion. She'll need a volunteer, and there is only one contender—so, Mori it is.

They meet on the deck. She suggests that he run around the boat while she hits him with a laser, obviously set to a gentle stun. He'll be a moving target; it'll be fun. Mori is not sure about the plan; he gnashes teeth, shakes his head. He doesn't want to be a moving target, and he doesn't think it will be fun. He says she'll hit him with the first shot and the game will be over.

He has a point.

Okay, Plan B. She tells him to lean against the mast, and she'll throw blades at him. It'll be fun, like an old-fashioned circus act. He's more open to this idea and stands rigid against the mast, eyes tightly closed. She doesn't hesitate; she clears her head, flicks her wrist, and tosses the first knife, hard and fast, straight at him. It lands a centimeter above his head.

Next, she closes her eyes, takes a long, slow breath, and then tosses the knife. A perfect pitch; it hits the mast above Mori's left shoulder. She has one blade left. Turning her back to him, she spins and flicks the knife, but as she releases it, out the corner of her eye, she catches sight of Tig, totally naked above the waist.

Mori shrieks.

He's pinned to the post—the knife clipped the fur on his neck. Frantically, he tries to free himself.

Quinn bounds over and retrieves the knife. "Just a fur wound," she says, and massages the graze. Meanwhile, Tig fumbles with the makeshift invisibility device, shirtless, and Quinn's very confused—what's the point of having arms and shoulder and a neck? That's what shirts are for. Humans should wear shirts.

✷✷✷

The following morning, she rises early and finds Planck already on deck. She's wearing her new clothes. Ze says she looks good, they really suit her, and then points to the sky.

There's a bird above them, gliding on the slipstream, with its head down, focused on something in the water. It has the most exquisite orange-colored neck and breast. Quinn jumps up. She knows this bird. This is her bird, her bird from Kerguelen—it's followed her here. They are connected. She has a special bond with birds, and she's definitely not going to eat this one.

"Passenger Pigeon," says Planck. "Sequenced from the very last of her species, a bird called Martha. This one is Martha2. She follows Tig. Gift from a satisfied customer."

*She's not my bird, she's Tig's bird.* The pigeon coos a long musical note and lands at the far end of the deck. Then Tig appears at the railing; Martha2 was watching him swim.

He swings himself over and lands in a puddle next to the bird, completely naked. He shakes off the excess water and wipes his face with his shirt. Quinn averts her eyes. She's seen him naked before, of course, so she knows he looks good, brown and firm, wearing only his bracelets. He says something to the bird; it clucks back at him, and Tig chuckles.

After collecting his clothes, Tig ambles toward them. His mood is languid, his gaze caught by the early morning sun on the ocean.

Planck jumps up, pulls Quinn's shirt to one side, off her shoulder, and scoots inside. Quinn freezes; she stands and considers following Planck inside, but it's too late. Tig is upon her, so she sits back down. Best for her stay put, stare out to sea at the horizontal line, and pretend he's not here. No big deal, he'll walk straight past. No one will say anything.

Tig walks past her. No one says anything. Then he stops, turns. "Put something on; it's 40 degrees."

*What? Really? A climate suit? He thinks I should wear my climate suit. Does he get the irony?*

"I don't feel the heat," she mumbles through gritted teeth to the man wearing no clothes. "It's okay for you to be in the water? You won't rust, or short circuit?" *Can't believe I just said that.*

He crosses his arms, so she crosses hers.

"Did it occur to you to ask me if I wanted to be your beloved?"

"I . . ."

"Did you think about us getting pregnant? Because there was no contraception in sight."

"Conscientious . . ." he mumbles. "Never mind. I didn't think we'd get pregnant. I'm sorry. But now that we know, I was thinking . . . you might be happy. A baby, it's . . ." He stares at her. "I mean, in the future . . . maybe you'll change your mind about not having children."

She holds his gaze. "In the future?"

He nods.

"I'm sure it is, or it was, going to be just fine and fabulous *without* a baby. People without children are happier. That's a fact."

\*\*\*

A few hours later, she leaves her cabin and finds Tig in the hallway, right outside her door, like he was either waiting for her to come out or steeling himself to go in. He's bare-chested again, wearing only his cargo pants. She doesn't know why he's not wearing a shirt, but he should be. People can't just walk around without shirts. She's wearing her new white shirt, with the sleeves rolled up and three buttons undone. She thought four was too many.

"Enough," he says, pushing her back into the cabin and closing the door. "Struggling with . . . Can't quite . . . Let me show you." He pulls her close and kisses her. She throws her arms around his neck and kisses him back. His hands go straight to the tiny white buttons on her shirt but he can't undo them—they're small and fiddly. He fumbles, frustrated. He gives up and pulls her shirt out and runs his hands underneath, over her bare skin, across her stomach, cupping and holding her breasts. She's overcome. She can't breathe. His lips trail down her neck and her body says yes, yes, this is good, keep going, I never want you to stop. Then her brain tells her to wait. It says, get a grip, what the fuck do you think you're doing, stop this right now, the kiss was bad enough.

"Not sure this is a good idea," she says, pulling away, panting. "Do you, do you think we should be doing this?" *Of course, he does; he wouldn't be doing it if he didn't.* "We're not really communicating. Do you think this is the answer?" *Of course, he does. Get a grip.* "Maybe we should talk."

"Really?"

"Yes, really—babies, life, the future, you and me, stuff like that, yes?"

He nods, he understands. Hands on hips, he paces across the three-meter-wide cabin, taking two steps before turning and heading back the other way. He does this many times while she waits and watches. Back and forth. Back and forth.

Finally, he composes himself. "Sex." He stares at the floor. "All I think about, driving me crazy, night and day, is fucking you." He looks at her. "Hard. Really hard. You on top, me on top, from behind, sitting, standing, kneeling . . ."

"Okay. I . . . I get it."

He grabs the door handle and leaves.

Sex! It's sex. Sex makes people crazy; it makes them do stupid, irrational things. It makes them impulsive and foolish. But a lack of sex—well, that makes people crazier. It makes them frustrated and angry and unpleasant to be around. A difficult situation when you're on a boat, where there's no escape, when the one you want is down the hall, or in the galley, or on deck.

She can't leave it like this. It a good start, but it's one step forward and two steps back. She'll pursue him, she'll find him, and they'll talk more, more about sex and . . . things. What things? She's not sure. She'll ask him if he has a plan; that's a good place to start. She always has a plan, but with two people you need a similar plan. Does he have a plan? She needs to find out.

She opens the door to his room and slips inside. He's on the bed and looks up as she enters. Reassuringly, she smiles at him. They can sort this out, they just need to talk and everything will be okay, but—but he's distracted, what is he doing?

"Oh shit." *He's wanking.* "Oh fuck, sorry, I, I didn't mean . . ."

Her presence does nothing to break his momentum. He continues tugging on his dick while his bionic eyes bore holes into her brain. She steps back; she should probably leave. She changes her mind. She should stay, stay and help. No, no, she should definitely go, leave him to it. "I'll, I'll just go." She backs out the door.

*That was awkward. No, that was terrible. I've made everything worse. A plan—of course, he doesn't have a plan. Sex isn't a plan.*

Tig's door opens, and he steps into the hallway, naked, with a large erection. She looks up, focuses on his face, not his dick. His face looks confused. "You want me?" he asks.

A complicated question; she has no idea what she wants. But she nods and says, "Yes," because it's the truth, she does want him. Then she adds, "I want to talk about the future, our future. I want to know how you feel and what you think and if you have a plan. You see, I always have a plan and I need to know . . ."

"Can't do two things at once." He kisses her quickly and strides down the corridor, still naked, still with a giant erection. She has no idea where he's going. He exhausts her.

✶✶✶

Later, Quinn pulls Planck aside. "Is it okay to have sex when you're pregnant, right? It can't hurt the baby or anything."

"Yes, perfectly safe. Second person today to ask me that."

# Thirty-Eight

# A black ship, like a killer whale with corporate sponsorship.

At BREAKFAST, A SHINY, titanium Quantum Machine slides across the table to Quinn. Staring at the machine, not looking up, she says, "You've had this, all this time? And you're only giving it to me now?"

"Let's say it's a recent addition to the cargo," Planck says. "It'll do the job, yes?"

"Yes." It's an excellent machine. QMs are scarce and expensive. There are several versions. This one uses Quaisparticles, combined on a 2D surface; it has thousands of qubits with advanced processing power. It's capable of launching the G12, and it will get Quinn into the SpinnerNet. She's nervous; her hands shake. She's waited months for this moment.

She prepares a sample from the cactus, examines the sequence reaction to make sure it's not damaged. It looks fine. The DNA strands are read as they transit through nanopores. This identifies the position of the individual nucleotides with longer DNA fragments. Quinn records the read-out of electrical signals occurring at the nucleotides and waits for the information to load onto the QM.

Retrieving the G12 from the SpinnerNet is risky. She can't linger;

she needs to get in and out before she's detected, before the trolls, terrorists, Trojans, worms, ferals, and hackers realize she's dropped in for a visit. It's a dark, infected, evil place, great for hiding things, but not if you're caught. Then, the consequences are unpleasant: identity theft, your Coin hacked, and your privacy gone. It takes years to untangle the mess. But she has a quick machine, nimble fingers, and a few distraction tools in her skill set.

She launches three open diversion searches, waits two seconds, then dispatches a Sprout Router. It goes straight to the G12 and plucks it out, and she closes the SpinnerNet immediately, undetected.

The G12 comes to life and the climate model launches, syncing to the Earth's biosphere in real time. Live initiation begins immediately. The system generates a holo of the planet; Quinn configures it to a sphere of two meters and spins it with her finger until she finds Kerguelen. She initiates a weather search and processes the data. While this completes, she runs a separate time trace, going back forty-eight hours before the catastrophe, checking for tampering or changed settings. The first set of data from the G12 shows nothing, no trace of the Sky River. The discrepancy is in the second set of figures. For forty-eight hours, at regular intervals, someone set a quantum ghost. They used an interferometer to exploit the two-path option and created a fictional set of data for the Island. *I didn't even notice. Self-absorbed, too busy whining. Idiot.* "I'm an idiot."

The ghost is still running. She isolates it from the system; the G12 autocorrects and updates the historical information. She replays the storm and watches the Sky River approach the Island, unleashing a whopping 2,500 millimeters of rain in six hours. Sky Rivers don't leave the Antarctic Circle. Something sent it off course. Why was it so far north? Someone, and she is prepared to call him Mori, is hiding something. She figures he never meant to kill all those people, mass murder is not his thing, so there is more to the mystery. But what was it that he didn't want her to see?

She spins the holo globe, pauses at Antarctica. Yes, they were headed there. She resets the system and runs a data search over the South Pole. The G12 will pick up environmental anomalies.

The data shows a fissure, a rupture in the Earth's crust under Antarctica. It caused a massive ice shift. The morning of the catastrophe, 1,000 billion tons of snow and ice slipped and sent out an infinitesimal ripple of energy over the planet—small, but enough to swing the magnetic South Pole east by eight degrees and throw the Sky River off course. Cause and effect, every action on the planet has a reaction. She wonders: Was the fissure a natural phenomenon? Or was it caused by human activity?

The cactus DNA is sequenced and the information is ready to be decoded. There are two files. Quinn opens the first, labeled Shun Mantra. They're a startup, sponsored by eMpower, with one hundred board members. She scrolls through their profiles; they're all young, in their mid to late twenties, and they're all Transhuman and sequenced. Aaroon is there. So is Myra.

The second file contains maps, pages and pages of maps and geological data. The initial details show Queen Maud Land, Enderby Land, and the Weddell Sea. It's Antarctica, with survey and geological details of the South Pole. But there are other maps, less familiar, and Quinn scans the images and exotic place names—Nicobar, Selk, Mystis. This landscape is not Earth. The colored clouds are called Bacab, Hobal, Tishtrya, and Kalseru, all mythical gods of rain. The mountains are named Moria, Mithrim, and Doom, and the small hills are called Gandalf, Bilbo, and Arwen. It's not Middle Earth, it's Titan. The maps are of Titan. The names are of places on Titan, chosen from deities of wisdom and mythological figures, as well as Tolkien imagery and characters. Perhaps they have travel plans? The trip of a lifetime? *Good, go, find your fortune on Titan and leave us alone.*

A splash outside the window diverts her attention. A sleek black ship rises from the water. A submarine—military, with an eMpower corporate logo. It is slick and black—a cross between a bat and a fighter jet.

Planck pokes zirs head in the hatch. "Shut it down. Hide the AI, then head for the lower level, below the horticulture zone. Tig's down there, tell him to come up here."

She blinks. *What lower level?*

"Base of the stairs, on the right, a hatch, leads to the lower level. Hurry."

Figures clad in military climate suits begin boarding *Nanshe*. The suits have the eMpower emblems on them.

Quinn collapses the system and hides Mori in her cabin. This time, she gives him strict instructions to switch off. If he's found, he's not, under any circumstances, to reactivate until she, and only she, tells him to reengage with the real world.

Behind the base of the stairs, to the right, she finds a hatch with another set of stairs leading to the lower level. *This wasn't on the tour.* At the bottom, a door opens, and she steps through it, into a dimly lit chamber. She scans the room; it's High-Tech, with a wall of weapons—rows of guns, lasers, and knives. There's a min-submarine at the far end, and . . . the two coup ringleaders, Maim Quate and Kip Jove. They're consulting a holo map with Tig.

"A one-man government, it'll be easier for him to execute . . ." Maim spies her standing in the doorway. "Oh, it's you. Come in, we won't bite."

"Hello." Quinn steps into the room, "I'm glad you're safe."

"Yes, and you, I'm happy to see you here, safe as well. You know, I know your mother, I mean knew, I knew your mother. We were . . . we were very close, if you know what I mean." *Really? How close? Oh for fuck's sake, she's just Lise's type.*

Tig strolls over. "You want me?"

"Yes, I mean no." *Not right now. But I do want you.* "There's a black ship, like a killer whale with corporate sponsorship. Planck wants you."

Tig sprints from the room.

Kip strides over to the weapons rack, grabs two lasers, and throws one to Maim. She catches it. "Our luck might be running out. Ever skipper a sub?" she asks.

"Yes, but this one's out of order," Kip says. "No power."

They glance Quinn's way, and she shakes her head, "You have an escape plan?"

"This was it," says Kip.

They have no escape plan. It'll take the military ten minutes to discover the opposition leaders stowed in the hull, and it looks like eMpower sponsors New Fed, so they're all in big trouble, but . . .

"If this boat is sponsored by eMpower, then . . . Stay here, I have a plan."

She races up the stairs and peeks through the galley windows; Tig and Planck are on deck with lasers pointed at them. She counts six soldiers aboard *Nanshe*, and another six watching from the black boat.

Someone sticks a laser in her back. "On deck, now."

She joins Tig and Planck on deck. "Did Niels send you?" she asks, but the guard ignores her. "Well, he'll be pleased you found me. If we give him a call . . ."

At the far end of the deck, a familiar face boards *Nanshe*—a very beautiful and familiar face. It's Geller. Her pale alien visage has vanished, replaced by a flushed complexion, rosy cheeks, and peachy lips. She also wears a climate suit with military epaulettes, but a darker grey; now, she has rank. The color catches the charcoal specks in her eyes.

"Move, 'e shoots," she says with indifference. "Mr. Eco, well, 'e's a valuable ally. Let's see how keen he's ta save you?"

Not a hint of recognition. *Oh, she's good.*

They send Niels a holo request. He answers immediately.

"It's me," Quinn says. "I launched the climate model. I know what happened. Let these people go, and get me out of here."

It works. The soldiers lower their weapons, Planck and Tig are shuffled inside, and the soldiers retreat back to the sponsored killer whale.

"Tree minutes," Geller says dryly. "Go, get your tings." She tilts her head toward the galley.

Planck folds and rolls garments into a luggagebot. "Added a shift dress, evening or daywear, and a couple of extra tops, expandable shorts. Now, look after our baby." Ze helps Quinn into a pale blue climate suit, then gives her a hug. Tig enters holding two sets of knives and a laser. He lifts the cuff of her climate suit and straps a holster to her leg. "Four blades, two small, two large. No contact, too risky." He unzips her climate suit and fastens the other set of blades to her upper arm. "What'd you find out from the G12?"

"Someone set a ghost."

"Why?"

"Distraction. A fissure in Antarctica set off an ice shift, caused the Sky River."

"eMpower, the cactus?"

"Shun Mantra, they're a startup sponsored by eMpower. A hundred board members, all sequenced. And maps, geographical maps of Antarctica and Titan."

"Okay. We deliver the cargo. It'll take . . ." Tig looks to Planck for confirmation.

"Five days," Planck says.

"Five days. I'll come get you after that." He hands her a laser. "Kill your enemies; don't fucking stun them, kill them. Do it properly."

"Kill them."

"Fear is not your friend."

"No?"

"No. Fight and flight primes you for action, but it also fucks your brain; you forget to think, and you freeze."

"I do?"

"Yeah. If you're scared, remember to think."

"Remember to think."

"And don't fucking die. That'll really piss me off."

"Don't die."

He rummages through his collection of bracelets and unclips a mauve sphere.

"For the baby girl," Planck whispers.

"Wait, what?"

"Mauve for the baby girl—"

"I didn't know the sex."

"Oh, the meerkat told us. I thought you knew."

*I do now.*

Tig clips the bracelet to her wrist and stares into her eyes. He holds her gaze for two or three seconds, then longer and longer, for four or five seconds they're staring into each others eyes. *He's a magnet and I'm iron; we're ferromagnetic.*

Like iron, he draws her in, and she can't escape. Iron is life sustaining, everyone wants it. Element number 26 on the periodic table is brittle and hard. It lives inside us, in our blood, and it makes up the universe, the sun and the stars, so we need it to survive.

She wraps her arms around his neck and kisses him, and he returns her kisses. They stumble backwards into the food prep. Things fall, her bag spills, he continues to kiss her, covering her face, her mouth, her neck, until she can't breathe.

✳✳✳

On deck, Geller waits to escort her onto the eMpower-sponsored killer whale.

"How'd you find us?" Quinn asks, professional curiosity.

"Your invisibility cloak's intermittent. We sent in an underwater sonic drone. Not gran' over long distances, te strength changes in reverse proporshun ta te distance covered, but super when te target is close. Your Tech's crap. There's a glitch in your stealth signal."

Quinn admires her military epaulets. "Promotion. Congratulations. And your skin looks great, no more blue light."

"First Lieutenant. Outstandin' bravery. Was just a matter av time. Like your 'air, suits you. An' you got lucky."

"Had no idea it would be you. So lucky, thank the lordt."

"Idjit, I mean te cute island guy inside, I saw you kiss. 'Ot. Very 'ot."

# Thirty-Nine

# You're not dying.
# I won't let you.

THE EMPOWER-SPONSORED SUB DOCKS at the eastern side of the
Harbor. As Quinn disembarks, she notes how unsettlingly still and
quiet Unus is. There's not even the illusion of normalcy. The city is
under military control.

She and Geller are collected by an army vehicle and transported to
Accord, the largest of the eight Climate Cities, where almost a million
of the privileged inhabit deliciously cool residential spires. Quinn's
guess: They all voted New Fed. Hard to part with all that cool comfort
once you have it. Dirac Devine, the leader of the New Fed, also calls
Accord home, when he's not organizing coups and conceiving civil
war.

Transport around Unus is almost stagnant, and the AVs are still
out of action, congregated in bundles along side streets and alcoves.
Several vehicles have been torched. Some lie on their sides. The sky is
filled with bird drones that flit back and forth. Residents walking the
streets are strip-searched, their bags and luggagebots rifled through
by the military. Gatherings are quickly dispersed; no meetings are
allowed, no events, not even funerals. The sudden screech of an auto
sends the military into alert and the few residents who are out drop
to the ground.

The purging of thousands of academics—police, media, teachers, prosecutors, and judges—has continued. Dirac Devine wants a new constitution, one giving him executive power. At his last public announcement, he held up effigies of Kip Jove and Maim Quate and called for the immediate death penalty for all insurgents.

After the RE Wars, Hexad established a mandate to stop a militarized government ruling, so Dirac is in trouble. He has outstayed his welcome in Unus. His actions go beyond defending the city, and they've been reported as an assault on democracy. He's running out of friends and quickly creating new enemies of stronger, more socially conscious governments in Duo and Tres, Unus's neighboring megacities. The situation in Unus matters a great deal to the rest of the world, since it was the first of the megacities to vote in the global election and New Fed refused to relinquish power after losing outright. Dirac will be forced to concede, one way or another; violence is a last resort, but if Maim and Kip state their claim at Hexad, the armed forces will rally behind them.

Geller volunteered to be Quinn's military escort. She said Unus was not safe and Quinn couldn't travel alone, and her manner indicated that the decision was final, a fait accompli, without negotiation or discussion. Quinn knows she's totally fucked if Geller's not on her side. The basis of their friendship, in Quinn's judgment, is instinct; their pheromones get on, Geller always looks her in the eye, and she has eyes that linger, eyes that stare—eyes that know what Quinn is thinking.

Accord is built on a high plateau and encircles the site of a thousand-year-old mosque. Geller leaves Quinn at the entrance gates. The mosque pays homage to past Byzantine and Persian empires, and long-ago powerful Muslim civilizations that controlled the eastern continents. These were sophisticated cultures that lasted for centuries.

Accord doesn't have a moat like Harmonia, but it does have the same layers of imperceptible security hiding behind the stone barricades. The centerpiece is the Palace of Tigers—an ancient structure cut from pink limestone that the afternoon light renders burnt and faded. Around the outskirts of the city, floral-capped spires rise two kilometers in the sky; Pollution Purging Pinnacles, affectionately dubbed PurePins, suck carbon and nitrous oxides from the atmosphere. The spectacular structural towers resemble woven tendrils. They are made from glass and polished ginger metals and capped with rooftop gardens.

Quinn is processed by a Vector AI called Tilly, who takes the form of a giant bot. Gendered female, her round head is as large as her square body, and she's dressed entirely in purple—dress, shoes, stockings, hairclips, gloves, and eye shadow.

Tilly begins in French, "*Bonjour ma belle demoiselle. Je m'appelle Tilly, et je vais m'occuper votre arrivée aujourd'hui. Avez-vous des armes, des bombes, des substances illégales ou des idéologues religieux fondamentaux que vous voudriez déclarer?*"

Quinn shakes her head.

"*Oh, pardon. Buongiorno, adorabile signorina. Mi chiamo Tilly, e lavorerò il tuo arrivo oggi. No?*"

"No." *Was that Spanish?* "I'm sorry, I don't . . ."

"Ahh, English. Good morning, lovely young lady. My name is Tilly and I'll be processing your arrival today. Do you have any weapons, bombs, illegal substances, or fundamental religious ideologies that you would like to declare?" Tilly shuffles forward on her giant purple feet, leans in, and whispers, "I already know about the knives. And the laser. Just declare. Makes my job so much easier."

Quinn agrees, declaring her armory. With the best of humor, Tilly confiscates the array of weapons strapped to Quinn's body and grants her entry into the city.

Now she must wait in a colonnaded courtyard, surrounded by statues of extinct animals—lions, elephants, tigers. Water fountains intermingle with the defunct animal effigies, and behind these are rows of multi-lobed arches decorated with woven lace patterns. It's elaborate, lush, and beautiful.

Quinn sits on a stone bench, bookended by carved elephants.

After a few minutes, Niels enters the courtyard, strides over, and sits next to her. When she looks into his face, he's staring straight at her. So she stares back, into his perfectly groomed features, and his grey-blue eyes remind her of Mori. They remind her of why she's here.

"I stole your data; I know about the ghost on the G12. I haven't checked the fingerprint, but I will, and I'll find out who set it."

"Mori set it. He's mining in Antarctica. There was a fissure. The G12 would have caught it. He set the ghost to cover it—needed time to get it under control. He didn't expect it to turn to shit. But we fixed it; we closed it. We just needed time."

"That's why you kept me on the atoll for so long."

He nods.

*I hate these people.* "You have so much. You're rich, the both of you. Why start mining? What else could you possibly want?"

"Resources, rare metals, magnets. It's not about us; people need these to survive. We're planning for the future."

She knows this is not true. Of all the things people need to survive, mining under the Antarctic Circle is not one of them. "I want to go home."

"Soon. Dirac wants to meet you. Tomorrow. You're invited to the Salon for dinner."

"Really? *You* want me *there*?" The Salon is Dirac's private soirée, rumored to be a religious sect, a revival of nineteenth-century mysticism.

"No. I want you to fuck off and stop causing me grief. But he asked for you." He shrugs. "I'll tell him you refused. The last thing we need is a debate about science."

*Is he serious? That's exactly what these people need.* "Wait, I'll go." *It's about time science had a seat at this table. Besides, Lise would want me to go.* "I'll bring Jin as my date. We can argue about AI; it might amuse him."

Niels frowns. "I doubt she's up to it."

***

Jin is living in Habitat12. Niels authorizes access for Quinn, who intends to surprise her friend. She enters the Pod and finds Jin asleep on the sofa, pallid and luminous. She looks dead. Wearing a white singlet top and loose black pants, her lower half merges with the black fabric of the sofa so her legs appear to be missing. Her skin is as pale as her white shirt. But something has happened to her: red-purple lesions cover her face and arms.

Quinn feels her heart contract, like someone just squeezed it. She drops her bag on the floor. Jin opens her eyes.

"Want me to kiss you?" Quinn offers.

"Finally." She chuckles, then coughs.

"What's going on?"

Jin pulls herself up. "Sit down." Quinn sits on the sofa, right next to her friend, the way Niels sat next to her on the stone bench in the colonnade garden, just a little too close. Jin points to the chair opposite and Quinn moves to the chair. *I'm not going to like this.*

"FF. Another strain. No cure."

They were living together when Jin first showed symptoms of Feline Flue. It began with joint pain, headache, fever, and a sore throat. A cold, the flu, maybe a virus, she said. She logged the symptoms into her SelfMed, lay in bed for two days, working from home. On day three a rash appeared on her torso and upper back. It spread to every part of her body; even the soles of her feet were covered in patches of red dots. Quinn pressed them and they turned into white, blotchy patches. It was obviously a virus, an infectious disease of some sort, but they were isolated in Hobart. She hadn't been exposed to anything or anyone unusual. Then her eyes turned yellow and streaks of sienna shot through her irises. This was unique, but it became more common as the pandemic spread.

Last year, similar symptoms showed up in global pockets. The new mutation of FF spread between humans, and it spread quickly.

"They'll find a cure, there's always a cure—a new vaccine, antiviral drugs."

"Nope. Tried. They can't help."

"Okay then, CRISPR. Go in, cut the gene sequence out. It won't affect the genome, but it'll kill the virus inside the host chromosome."

"It's clever; keeps outwitting my immune system. It stole a gene that codes for toxoplasma, and now it's poking holes in my cells and everything's leaking out. I've been injecting blood and antibodies, but it hasn't worked. No one's survived."

*Shit.* Quinn clamps her hands together and squeezes hard.

"I'm in the final phase. I'm sorry."

"You're not dying. I won't let you."

"I am."

Tears fill Quinn's eyes and she stares at the tiled floor, at the smooth, grey material and the way the joints in door seals don't line up with the filler between the floor tiles. Finally, she looks back at her friend. "You can't be."

"I am. Sorry."

Quinn drops to her knees, shuffles over, and takes her hand. "They'll find a cure, I'm sure they will."

"Yes, but not in my time. That's why I made Mori, to help you with your . . . emotional literacy after I'm gone. He's an emotional support animal. They've made a huge comeback—all the rage right now."

"Seriously."

"What? Sometimes you're not so good with people. He'll keep you company; you'll have someone to . . . to open up to."

"I'm not that bad."

"Actually, you are."

*This is not about me.* "We'll figure something out. Have you spoken to Niels? He's got more Coin than he knows what to do with, and he owes you, big time. Employee of the fucking decade."

"Don't be angry."

"Shit, what have you done?"

"I've chosen CyberSleep. A cure might be a year away."

"No one's ever survived. And how can you afford it?"

"I have a sponsor."

Quinn sighs. "Of course you do. Niels."

"We have an agreement. He gives me three years in Sleep and I code a Transhuman AI, a full merge between a machine and the human brain."

"The singularity, are you kidding? Totally illegal, and the ethics are . . ."

"He'll lobby for changes in legislation. Conceptual experimentation, then approval for adaptation. But I've no intention of doing it. I just want to do this. I want to go into CyberSleep."

Quinn raises an eyebrow.

"Okay, maybe I will do it. If it's not me, it'll just be someone else. And it has to be this way; the alternative is, we step aside and let robots rule the world, and we all know how you feel about that."

"You're only saying that to placate me."

"Yes, I am." Jin grins.

Quinn grins back. "Okay, enough about fucking robots and the singularity. I don't care. I only care about you. CyberSleep has shitty side effects: skin deterioration, cornea issues, bowel problems, your hair may never grow back. And what if your organs don't reboot?"

"Honestly, I have no other options. I've run out of time, and I need you to help. Please. Just think of me as sleeping, in a beautiful state of neither life nor death. I'll be ethereal, transient."

"You'll be dead."

"Everything we do, we do to prolong life. Eat, sleep, exercise, get dressed, go to work. We do it to live longer. This is just another way. I don't want to die. It's too soon."

"I don't want you to die either."

"Remember what Carl Sagan said?"

"We're all made of star stuff?" *How's that relevant?*

"No, no, the other one."

*Of course, the one about butterflies.* "'We're like butterflies, fluttering for a day.' I love that quote, it's one—"

"No. He said, 'Somewhere, something incredible is waiting to be known.' It's an adventure, and I want you there. Please."

Quinn nods. Of course, she'll do it.

✶✶✶

Quinn moves into the second sleep zone in Jin's apartment. She's slept in this room many times, albeit in Hobart, on the other side of the world. Jin's Pod is modular, and the entire studio was transported: untethered from a residential habitat, slipped onto a conveyer, dispatched to Accord, and supplanted in a new tower. At least the familiarity of the decor is comforting.

Jin's decorating style is straightforward. She likes black and grey and white, so she doesn't have to deliberate or decide on new furnishings or accessories. The result is an uncomplicated design: white walls, black sofas and chairs and stools, grey pillows and throws. New acquisitions and accessories are always grey; all the pots, lamps, rugs, and art are grey.

In the second sleep zone, Quinn sets down her things and then sits on the grey bed. Wearing her pale blue climate suit, she's the only thing of color in the room, a lively smudge in an achromatic background, like a single blue water droplet in Antarctica, and she feels just as lonely. She looks around the room. The walls are covered with black-and-white photos, pictures of happy things—the ocean, the beach, balloons, people running, people laughing, people with balloons frolicking on the beach. On the bed is a single cushion, heart-shaped, with an arrow pointing to the word *Happiness*. It's a ridiculous message, happiness—what does that even mean? How can anyone ever be happy? She'll miss her friend.

# Forty

# The Salon de la Rose and Croix.

NIELS WANTS TO LIVE forever. He's set his initial forever goal at one hundred and fifty years. After that, he plans to enter CyberSleep. After that, he figures the Tech will be advanced enough to maintain his fragile human form forever. Jin has been a valuable commodity as a living employee, and now she's serving as a valuable guinea pig in his quest for eternal life. During her CyberSleep he'll run experiments on her, monitoring the outcome, all in preparation for his own Sleep journey.

Over the following days, he agrees to provide Jin with whatever she wants, whatever she needs. She requests wine, apples, and chocolate. It's depressingly like a last meal.

✳✳✳

Geller walks through the door with a bottle of wine, two bars of chocolate, and a bundle of apples. Her hair is out, falling around her face and over her shoulders, and she smiles at Quinn, plucks an apple from the bag, is about to take a bite when she sees Jin lying on the sofa.

Jin smiles. "Hello."

Geller's eyes travel slowly over Jin, from her cute white socks to her black halo of limp hair. "Hello," she responds, and in that one moment they're gone. Both of them. Without taking her eyes off Jin, Geller bites into her apple. "Juicy," she says. "You want some?"

"Yes, I do," says Jin.

Geller tosses the fruit to her but Jin doesn't have the strength to raise her arm, so Quinn plucks it from the air and hands it to her. Jin takes the fruit, bites into it, and then hands it back to Quinn, who tosses it back to Geller. Geller grins and takes another bite. Now they're both chewing the juicy apple, smiling across the room and offering lustful glances at each other.

Desire is unpredictable. *Suddenly three's a crowd. I'm the odd one out.*

Geller sits too close to Jin on the sofa, and Jin doesn't object. Geller adjusts the patient's pillows and asks what's going on, what's wrong with her. Why does she look like she just dropped in from Venus? Or perhaps she is actually Venus—the Roman darling of love and desire, blessing them with a deific visit.

Jin giggles. "I'm dying. FF. Got a few days, maybe a week."

Geller runs her fingers gently over the welts on Jin's skin, and Quinn follows the meandering trail of her fingertips. It's erotic. They open and share the chocolate and the wine. Geller listens intently to Jin's theories on the rise of AI, and how humanity will one day live in harmony with thinking machines. Wine helps the conversation; it helps the touching and the laughing and the kissing. It helps everything. They curl up on the sofa together and settle in. Quinn is invisible, and she's not drinking, so she retires to bed with an apple.

Desire might be unpredictable, but it is also loud. At midnight, Quinn is wide awake. The couple in the adjacent sleep zone takes turns, first Jin and then Geller, one never-ending female orgasm interrupted by short intervals of whispering and giggling. *What are these walls made of?* Modular construction might be convenient, economic, and environmental, but this Pod has the acoustics of wrapping paper.

After a few minutes of silence, Quinn finally dozes, but then it starts again, more moaning. *Just hurry up so we can all get some sleep.* Quinn makes a mental note to pick up earplugs tomorrow. Mori—not the meerkat, the other one—wore plugs to bed. He said the world kept him awake: the sounds of the earth, the wind, the birds, the trees, and Quinn's breathing, especially her breathing. He needed total silence, in the way some people need total darkness.

She's not surprised he set the ghost on her climate model; he was the only suspect, the only one who had access. She just didn't think he was that devious. She's shocked by that, by how much he fooled her—and lied to her. When Coin's involved, people become unknowable.

On their first date, Mori took her to a public speaking engagement. *His* public speaking event. It was a full house, and he was talking about the Anthropocene Epoch, an era defined by war, radioactivity, plastic pollution, and billions of domesticated chicken bones. He was funny, his speech was peppered with jokes—"It's so hot chickens are laying hard boiled eggs." She laughed and watched as he held the audience. "If you're over global warming," he concluded, "I've one word for you: Titan." The audience clapped and cheered.

Afterwards, she watched in awe as he worked his way around the room at the after party. She's easily impressed by social skills and confidence. Now, months later, she knows his public addresses were exhaustively rehearsed, hours and hours of fine-tuning and preparation. Everything was practiced—his mannerisms, even his smile. He rehearsed it, over and over, in the mirror. And his jokes and material weren't original; they were pilfered from various sources. She thought he was a visionary, but he was a salesman, selling himself—and she got in line and bought a front-row ticket. Thankfully, she left at intermission.

✷✷✷

In the morning, Quinn stumbles, tired and bleary-eyed, toward the food prep and finds the culprits already there, both of them, looking self-satisfied and surprisingly fresh, and wearing each other's clothes. They continue the routine from last night, grinning and giggling and kissing. Geller slices pieces of apple for Jin to nibble on, and the sight of Jin chomping on the apple, the juicy crunch, crunch, crunch, and the sweet scent sends Quinn racing for the basin, where she pukes.

"Too much fructose." She wipes her mouth.

Geller must report back to the military base; there's a morning briefing she wants to attend. Maim and Kip have vanished and some believe they have already fled the city. If they rally Hexad, a counterattack on the capital is likely. She peels her military shirt off Jin's scrawny back and departs.

Of course, Quinn know exactly where those pesky rebel leaders are hiding. Tig should have reached Hexad by now. The rebels will consolidate there, and then, if Dirac doesn't concede, there will be war.

Tig will return in a few days.

Jin retreats to her sleep zone to rest. Dying and sex are exhausting. Quinn lies beside her, and Jin asks, excitedly, how Mori—not the man, the AI—is settling into his new home, how they are getting on, as if Mori is a real person, as if he has feelings that need to be considered and accounted for.

"He's . . . fine," Quinn manages to say.

Jin reveals that she has programmed special talents in the AI. He has advanced biological knowledge of living creatures, so he can look after Quinn physically and biologically as well as emotionally. He has access to NIoT—that's a standard feature—but he also has acute hearing and vision. Otherwise, he performs and responds to his environment as any human would. His cognitive functions are decades ahead of anything anywhere on the planet. He has a conscious and an unconscious controlled by a super-unconscious. His circuitry is modeled on the human brain; there are 115,000 neurons per cubic

millimeter in the human brain and each one makes a thousand connections, and the human brain contains 1.5 million of these cubes, so
it's impressive programming, and Quinn know this.

The schematics are mind boggling. What she doesn't understand
is, why? "Why program a super-unconscious mind into a machine?"
Quinn asks, already knowing the answer is Salt.

Jin pauses. "Because I can. And I did. I'm going away, I don't want
you to be lonely. I want you to have someone to come home to."

"It's a robot; there's a difference. I have a heart and I bleed. He'll
never do that. You want me to care for him, to build a relationship
with him, but what you really want is to justify your feelings for Salt.
Honestly, you don't need me, or anyone else, to do that."

Jin shuts her eyes and imitates a long yawn. "Don't worry, there
won't be any more."

"Meaning?"

"I'll destroy the Tech, corrupt everything before I go. No more AI.
I made Mori, eMpower has no jurisdiction over him. When I go, the
information goes with me." She turns her back to Quinn.

Quinn stares at the ceiling. She could have handled that better, she
could have been kinder, she could have praised and thanked her lovely
friend—her best friend, who's about to enter CyberSleep. She could
have told her that Mori is amazing, the greatest gift anyone has given
her, and she's overwhelmed. Their friendship means everything to her.

But she didn't. She told Jin what she really thinks.

*Humans are shit. Maybe that's me; maybe I'm a shit human.*

✶✶✶

Later, Quinn rouses her Jin from sleep; she wants her to forgive her,
and she wants to squeeze in every moment of life that remains, every
piece of time they have left together. She's a needy and selfish friend,
but she can't bear this. She feels wretched.

She sits on the bed beside Jin and asks her what she knows about the Salon revival. She's having dinner there tonight, she says, and she needs Jin's help.

It's a pretense, to get her talking, to make her forget about the meerkat and negate their awkward argument. Rumors about the Salon are rife. People say it's everything from a cult where people worship heretic symbols to a private thought palace where people discuss intellectual ideas and religious doctrines. Quinn think it's probably fairly benign—just a place to speak freely about divine beings.

Jin pulls herself up and shakes her head. "The Salon de la Rose and Croix is a thinly disguised sect"—she pauses, coughing—"led by Dirac. They believe they have a divine calling and democracy is an affront to their heavenly mission. For them, there's a hierarchy of beasts, and humans are at the top. They want a return to the fin-de-siècle mysticism of the nineteenth century. The women have long, golden hair, wear wings, and have halos hovering over their heads. The men sport beards and curly moustaches and wear white button-down smocks. Don't, whatever you do, mention science when you're there—it's taboo."

"It's 2050; you're being overly dramatic."

"I'm serious. That's what they wear; there are pictures on the Fourth Estate. It's a time warp, back to the 1800s. Oh shit, what the fuck are you going to wear?"

Quinn's only dress is a pale pink shift that Planck printed. She fetches it and holds it up. Jin shakes her head.

"Don't care what I wear," quips Quinn.

"Trust me, we're talking New Fed, Dirac Devine, crazy shit. You'll be the only scientist and probably the only climate believer; you don't want to stand out. Bring me my module, I'll print you something."

Quinn plumps Jin pillows and hands her the module.

✴✴✴

Hours later, after several consultations, Jin prints the dress. Quinn collects it from the 3D machine and holds it up; it's low-cut, full length, with a sheer skirt and a bodice covered in flowers.

"You'll need significant underwear," says Jin. "I'm on it." The printer restarts.

When it's ready, Quinn slips on the underwear and pulls the dress over her head, then scans her profile in the glass—and her eyes dip straight to the bump around her stomach. The human baby is getting bigger. If she intends to do something about the pregnancy, she needs to do it soon. Tomorrow. There's no point delaying; she should do it tomorrow.

Then again, maybe not tomorrow, maybe next week. She needs more time. The decision can't be rushed. She should mull it over, leave it a few more weeks.

She knows what Lise would say—"Darling, don't be ridiculous. Doing nothing is still a choice"—and thinking about this, she realizes she's going to keep the baby. Giving birth was not in her life plan, but a daughter, she wants that. She wants what she has with Lise. She wants to be a mother to this baby girl and for them to share their lives, mother and daughter.

Jin catches Quinn looking at herself in the glass, standing side on, running her hand over her stomach, and Quinn pretends to be smoothing down the net fabric of the dress.

The printer runs continuously all afternoon as Jin prints dozens of soft tulle flowers, which she winds into a halo for Quinn's hair.

"Wings," says Quinn. "I think I need wings."

Jin nods. "Of course you do."

Jin spends an hour studying birds on her module—doves, hawks, parrots. She want the perfect fowl for the situation. Finally, she decides on owl feathers. "Soft and spiky, to help you sneak up on your prey, and the thorns deaden the sound of attack. No one will hear you coming."

The Pod fills with thousands of silver-grey owl feathers. Jin prints the wings in sections, connecting two arching structures, and then carefully adheres the feathers to each wing. Finally, her masterpiece—a pair of exquisite wings spanning a meter—is finished.

Jin fixes the wings to the back of Quinn's costume and Quinn admires herself in the glass. There is something different about her; she looks mythically beautiful, like she belongs in a fairy tale.

"It's your skin," says Jin. "You're glowing."

"I look like an angel, and I don't believe in angels."

"No, you're a bird, and these are your wings. Flying's your thing."

✷✷✷

Quinn sets off for the prestigious Hypostyle Prayer Hall wearing the wings. Her friend has forgiven her, and she's glad, but if other guests aren't dressed like her, she might be the human sacrifice on tonight's menu.

She enters the Hall through a black marble door and waits in the vestibule while her ID is checked. The walls of the vestibule are covered in paintings—dark, bleak pictures of half-animal, half-human beasts. Quinn knows nothing about art, but she sees a theme running through this weird collection of tormented souls. A red dragon with multiple heads hovers over a golden woman wearing wings. A naked man with long hair creeps across the floor, on claws. There's a lot of bad weather in the images: Massive winds. Lightning. Storms. Floods. The wrath of god. End-of-the-world stuff.

Soon, she's summoned into the main hall and pointed in the direction of a table at the far end of the chamber, maybe fifty meters away. The path is an obstacle course that winds through dozens of polished marble columns topped with intricately carved arches. Nestled in each arch is a lamp that sends flickering shadows across the stucco ceiling. If time travel were possible, this time, this moment could be a thousand years ago, in an ancient prayer hall, in a place where religion reigned as the supreme doctrine of life and death.

Except it is 2050 and religion is no longer permissible as a communal act.

Quinn spies Dirac lurking alone in the shadows, wearing a black suit, top hat, and blood-red cape. He pays her no attention as she passes; his gaze is fixed ahead and he's muttering a few sentences under his breath—rehearsing his speech. She spies Niels taking his seat. Agent's orange presence is also visible at far end of the table, and she's relieved; he's a possible ally.

The table decorations levitate; clusters of candles, vases filled with trailing flowers, and ornate wineglasses all spin above the tabletop.

"We seem to be defying gravity," says a guest.

"Magnets," says Agent, deflating the mystery.

Quinn approaches the gathering, and the guests cease chatting. They turn toward her, scanning her wings, her dress, the flowers in her hair, and finally their eyes come to rest on her face. Other women wear flowers in their hair, and wings are prolific, but hers are the most beautiful.

Niels makes a show of rising from his seat. Like the other men, he wears black tails and a velvet top hat. He takes her hand, escorts her to a seat next to his. "You're perfect," he whispers. "Don't fuck it up."

Dirac arrives, accompanied by an assistant, and in unison the guests stand, giving him a rowdy ovation of applauds and cheers. Awkwardly, he lowers his himself into a seat at the head of the table. He can't rotate his torso or turn his head. His upper body has seized and is visibly riddled with small spasms. Quinn feels no sympathy; stress is the upshot of being a despotic tyrant. His assistant steps forward and taps a glass with a knife, and the guests resume their seats.

"Thank you, thank you," Dirac says. He gestures toward Quinn. "It's not often we have science at this table. Everyone, this is Quinn Buyers. Welcome," he says calmly.

"Careful," Niels whispers.

"Actually, it's Doctor, Doctor Buyers."

"Idiot," Niels mutters under his breath.

"So sorry to hear about your mother," Dirac says kindly. "The world has lost a . . . a good researcher. I suppose you also believe in climate change?"

Niels nudges her under the table.

"Well, let me see," Quinn says, tapping her chin. "Carbon parts per million are close to 600. Sea levels have risen a meter and a half. We're past the tipping point. The ocean circulation has flipped, the permafrost in Siberia is thawing and releasing methane, and clouds have disappeared over tropical zones. The Antarctic system is in perpetual decline and temperatures have risen in every corner of the planet. So yes, I think there's some truth to the rumors."

"Do you want to know what I think?" Dirac asks.

"Of course."

"I think our lack of spirituality has caused the demise of the planet. Storms, floods, heat waves, cyclones—perhaps we bring these events upon ourselves. Perhaps they've been sent to punish, to humiliate, us."

*We need to devote a lot more time and energy to inventing a cure for fuckwits.*

"That's an interesting theory. I'd love to hear what you think we should do. How do we move forward from that and fix the planet?"

Dirac glares at her across the table.

*People like you have no ideas. All you do is shift the blame and complain.*

The arrival of food puts a temporary end to their staring contest.

Plates of poached fish and roast chicken are placed at alternating chairs, then passed back and forth between the guests. Niels, true to his biodynamic way of existence, doesn't eat or drink anything. Quinn eats every morsel of roast chicken on her plate, then pushes it aside and slides Niels's plate of poached fish her way and finishes every morsel on his plate. Then she slides his empty plate back so it doesn't look like she's had two meals. He stares at her like she's from another planet. Dirac, she notices, hasn't touched his food either. *What is it with these people?*

With the meal over, Quinn silently congratulates herself. She showed up and she spoke up, she's had two delicious meals, and she's still alive. Time for her to leave. She scans the far side of the Hall, her exit point, and sees a man walking toward the table. He has an animal with him, a small brown dog on a lead. She squints; as he gets closer, she realizes it's not a small dog—it's a large ginger cat.

"Oh no," she whispers.

"What?" Niels follows her gaze. "Shit."

The cat jumps onto the table, and the levitating vases and candles and glasses fall with impressive pragmatism. Unperturbed, the animal saunters towards Dirac. Like a rising and falling wave, the guests lean back in their seats, a reflex reaction, as the animal passes. At the far end of the table Dirac's assistant picks up the feline and runs his hands through its fur.

"Let's have an experiment," says Dirac.

"Let's not," whispers Niels, and Quinn has found her second ally.

A heavy crate is placed on the table. The assistant opens it, places the animal inside, and then closes and locks the lid. Quinn rubs her brow. She knows where this is heading.

"The cat is in the crate, but it's not alone; a piece of radioactive metal and prism of poison are also inside. If the metal releases a radioactive particle, the glass will break, releasing the poison. If that happens, the cat dies. But the metal might not release a particle; if not, the cat survives. Right now, we don't know what state the cat is in; is it dead or is it alive? What state is the particle of radioactive metal in? Released or not released?" He taps the top of the box. "The point is, we don't know. The box is sealed. There is no result, no answer until we open the box. Is the cat dead or alive? Or"—he pauses—"is it in two states simultaneously? A state of superposition? When we open the box, the superposition collapses and there is only one state. What can science tell us about this, Ms. Buyers?"

"If you'd used a glass box, we'd be able to see inside, no mystery."

He's not amused. Dirac is demonstrating the paradox of Schrödinger's cat, which in 1935 was an attempt to demonstrate the irrelevance of quantum states. Logic, according to Schrödinger, suggests the cat cannot be both dead and alive. Dirac wants Quinn to say that observation determines the result of the experiment. Fine. She'll play along. The sooner this is over, the sooner she can leave.

"Observation determines the existence of the cat," she says.

"Ah, but observations require consciousness and therefore conscious thought. So it is I who determine the existence of the cat, because I have conscious thought. But who determines me?"

"I do," she says.

"And who determines you?"

Niels determines her. They go around the table and everyone gets a turn to be determined, but with the limited number of guests they run out of determined people in three minutes. Quinn is tempted to point out the dozens of soldiers hiding behind columns and lurking in the shadows; technically, the game could continue for another ten minutes. But that's not the point, the point is that someone must eventually verify all humanity, so a higher being, a god, must exist. Quinn is without religion, so she silently rejects this option.

"Ms. Buyers is still back with the cat being dead and alive at the same time. In two different states, where the act of opening the box splits the universe into two, creating a multiverse. Which is nonsense. A cat cannot be in two states at once."

Quinn sees through the experiment and his attempt to ridicule science; a cat is not a quantum property, it's too big. She knows subatomic particles can be in two states at one time, it's a proven scientific theory. Gravity and mass will collapse a superposition, but only if the object is in a quantum state, not in a big ginger cat state. Dirac has twisted the concept to justify his belief in a personal god. She doesn't care what he believes, and she knows science doesn't care, either. It doesn't have to justify itself; facts are facts, and the truth will always be the truth. If he wants to pit science against religion, he can go right ahead, but he can do it without her.

"I think Ms. Buyers might be Plato's Prisoner in the Cave. She sees the flickering trickery of science as reflections on the wall." Dirac wiggles his fingers in the air. "If you think science understands reality, then you fail to see what's real and what's not. What if I said the earth is flat because we see it that way?"

*This hall just became an echo chamber. Did he just say the earth is flat?*

"And yet we know it's curved." She smiles.

"But do we? Do we really? I suppose you also believe dinosaurs roamed the Earth. You know there's no evidence."

She stays silent; there's not much else she can do. It's a sobering situation. This man is the leader of a prominent political party, he has millions of followers, but he's not a great leader. Great leaders believe in the truth, even if it doesn't suit them—especially if it doesn't suit them—and they don't make stuff up; they don't have to. This man is a great idiot.

"Let's have another experiment."

*Let's not.* Her heart sinks.

Dirac's assistant places a gun on the table, an old-fashioned pistol, and from his pocket he collects a handful of bullets, which he also places on the table. "In the 'Many Worlds' theory, the universe splits with every decision we make. Is that correct, Ms. Buyers?"

She nods.

"My assistant has a coin."

The man holds up a tarnished doubloon with a crest on one side and ancient writing on the other. He flicks it high in the air, and it lands crest side up on the table.

"Crest side up, you win and he shoots you with a blank. But if it lands showing the Latin words *Ex Nihilo Nihil Fit*, 'Nothing Comes From Nothing,' he shoots you with a real bullet and you die. Not to worry, you'll be alive somewhere in an alternate universe. In the multiverse." Dirac smiles. "Twenty rounds should do it. If you're still alive after twenty rounds, we've got ourselves a multiverse."

Niels grabs hold of her wrist, but she shakes him off.

"It's okay, I've got this," she whispers. She slides her chair back, rises, and joins Dirac at the head of the table. After smoothing out her dress and adjusting her wings, she says, "Okay, I'm ready. Go ahead and shoot me."

The assistant flips the coin. It lands crest up. He loads a blank into the gun, points it at her head and pulls the trigger. The short click unnerves her. He places the gun on the table, and she breathes. He collects the coin again and flicks it into the air. It lands with a thud, crest side down. This time he selects a real bullet, but his hands shake and he fumbles, dropping it, and the bullet rolls across the table and onto the floor.

"Nerves," says Dirac, giggling. "Concede at any time; otherwise, he will shoot you."

The assistant reloads the gun and points it at Quinn. She takes a breath, and then her left hand inflicts a short, sharp chop to his wrist. He drops the gun; she catches it and fires the bullet into the wall. A swarm of soldiers step from behind the columns with their weapons raised and every weapon is pointed at her.

She hands the gun to Dirac, but he doesn't take it, so she leaves it on table. "Chance also prevails in science. Sometimes you never know what's going to happen. That's two nil. To me."

"Good, very good," Agent interrupts. "Entertaining and insightful. The game is a draw."

Dirac doesn't take his eyes off Quinn. "It's not over yet. We're just getting started."

"You have proven your point," says Agent. "The game is a draw. Quinn Buyers will sit down."

Slowly, Niels begins to clap. Others quickly follow, and a rowdy applause erupts. Niels pulls Quinn's chair back from the table, and she doesn't hesitate and strides back to her seat. She knows that Agent, with a little help from Niels, just saved her.

Dirac nods. "A draw, then. I look forward to playing again." After a few nervous coughs and furtive glances, the group relaxes and the hum of conversation continues.

Quinn focuses on Niels. "Thank you so much for inviting me, it's been . . . memorable, it really has, but now I'd like to go home. You wanna get me out of here?"

It's a directive, not a request. Pointing to the door, he glides back his chair.

They traverse the long Hall in silence, the gabble behind them softening and mingling with the scuff of their footsteps as they go, and with each stride a scolding rebuke rises within her.

When they're finally outside, she turns on him. "What the fuck are you doing? Tell me, honestly. You don't believe climate change is god's wrath and the world is flat and there were no dinosaurs, because denial isn't going to help us and it isn't going to save us. Science is the only thing we have. It's the only truth. This is all just fucking propaganda and lies. And you're not helping. Those people in there—none of them have the Coin or the power you have. Do something. And for fuck's sake, eat something."

"Head's up," he murmurs, "because I owe you, and I don't do debts. They want the diamond." He signals for a military auto to get her home.

The vehicle pulls up immediately. Niels stands to one side and opens the door for her.

Quinn turns and walks in the opposite direction—toward the parklands beyond the palace. She unclips her wings, tucks them under her arm, and continues on, through the dimly lit gardens, between rows of sculpted tigers, and hedges of citrus, and pathways bordered by mounds of herbs, and over a small bridge. She keeps going until nothing is familiar, but she doesn't want to stop or turn back; from this point on, the way forward is the future, and it's unknown.

Ahead, she sees a narrow archway of trailing leaves and vines, delicately lit with fairy lights. She enters the green colonnade and inside she finds a new world—an animated, luminous tussle of lights and vines, a blur of technology and nature—and it's beautiful. On the other side lies a small meadow scattered with thousands of multicolored liquid lights resting on slender stalks—red, orange, pink, and blue. Like luminous flower buds, they fill the field. That is where she needs to be, in the middle of all the color and energy.

Carefully moving the stalks to one side, she creates a path for herself, creeps into the center of the light field, and lies down on the cool grass. Above, the orbs reflect off each other and a thousand colored shapes swarm like stardust, mingling together in the night sky. New ideas waft amongst the luminous, color-filled air; the world around her is an illusion, a fabrication of the brain. There is nothing over there, no trees, no archway of vines, and no light. Reality is an algorithm and the human species has evolved to understand it through their senses. Dangerous thoughts. What did Lise say? *"Our reality is not bound by classical concepts of physics. There's no past or future, because they don't exist, just as the concept of 'now' doesn't exist. Just live. Life is for living."*

What did Tig tell her? *"Leaders, including religious leaders, must explain new scientific truths; they must work new theories into world theories and religious theories. But how do to you explain a multiverse in religious terms? Or time travel?"*

Not everyone likes these ideas. They undermine the control of governments and the power of religion. They change the way we understand the universe, the way we see ourselves and what is real and what is not.

Static electricity buzzes, and the hairs on her forearms prickle.

# Forty-One
# (He) 2s² 2p¹

$J$IN AND GELLER EMERGE mid-morning still intoxicated with one another. Their routine resembles the previous day's; yawning, wearing one another's clothes, kissing, fondling in the food prep, and feeding each other slivers of fruit. Again, Quinn is instantly nauseous. The cause: a toss-up between the baby and the romantic antics of the lovesick couple.

"Sex fixes everything," Jin whispers as she passes.

*Not everything.* Jin is beginning to smell, just a little, like rotting fruit. Embarking on a sexual relationship when you are terminally ill is a fraught affair, and it is taking its toll.

Geller opens her module and shows Quinn an article from the Fourth Estate: a picture of an angel wearing wings, standing next to Niels.

"You make a gran' couple. Says 'ere you're 'is date. Quite a coup, gettin' te daughter av such a famous scientist into their mystic circle— an' dressed like an 'eavenly bein', at tat."

Quinn has no time for quips or justification; she has an agenda. She collects Jin's climate suit and helps her into it like she's a child. Jin has lost so much weight she looks like a child—a child wearing her mother's clothes.

"Why am I wearing this?" she complains. "I'm not up to going out. I'm tired."

"Sleep when you're de . . . sorry. We're going out. The AVs are running again—you'll be fine." Quinn takes her hand and leads her to the skylift. Geller follows. They take an AV to the edge of the old city—away from the Pod, away from OneHub, away from any surveillance. The city walls are three meters thick, with arched colonnades that offer shade from the mid-morning sun. Inside it's crowded, but they find a seat and huddle together.

Quinn sighs. "I'm pregnant."

"We figured," says Jin. "Morning sickness, tiredness, you haven't stopped eating, your skin looks fabulous, and, final giveaway, no wine. We were only fucking half the time, the other half we were gossiping about you and the cute island guy. Conscientious Prevention?"

Quinn shrugs, she can't explain it. "He's a cyborg, and he's kind of a king, with a small 'k.' He wants me to be his . . . beloved."

Stunned silence.

"Sorry. The father of your children is a king," Jin clarifies. "You had sex with a cyborg king, and now you're having his baby?"

"Yes. I knew he was cyborg, but I wouldn't have picked him for a king." *Okay, that's done.* "Now, we need to talk about Lise . . ."

"No, no, no, not so fast." Jin wiggles a finger at her.

Quinn's captive audience is not interested in despotic leaders or in her theories on time travel; they are firmly stuck on the cute islander cyborg king, and they won't leave it alone. So Quinn expands the story—shows them the bracelets, gives sketchy details about the night of hot sex, the anxiety disorder, life on the boat, and the bizarre fact that he's a king, with a small "k," of an ancient culture.

Finally, they fall silent and contemplative.

"So you're not in love?" Jin asks.

"I have no idea. We spent a few days together, he told me nothing about his life, and I blurted out how hopeless and insecure I am, and then we had sex. That's what happens, isn't it? You come across all vulnerable and insecure, and then someone wants to fuck you."

"Pretty much. I see a pattern here. You keep falling in love with strange men on remote islands," says Jin.

"There's no pattern. Mori was just a mistake."

"Tig, what's he like?" Jin asks.

"Well, he's sort of chaotic and intense, and honestly, he's probably a little bit crazy. But he's also handsome. And charismatic. He's not like anyone I've ever met before."

"Okay, well . . ."

"And I'm drawn to him, on a sexual level . . ." Quinn reddens. "I've never experienced anything like this."

Jin smiles. "Well, sex is—"

"And when I see him, my heart moves around my chest." Quinn circles her chest with her hand. "Not physically, of course; it can't physically move. But metaphorically . . ."

"Okay, we get it," Jin says. "It sounds to me like—"

"And when he's close—like, standing next to me, or not wearing a shirt—my heart goes wild. He overwhelms me. But that's somatic; it's not love. Did I say he was charismatic?"

"Yes, you did." Jin clears her throat. "Moving on. What are you going to do about the baby?"

"Nothing. I'm going to have it. I want to. But none of this makes sense. Does it?" Quinn feels lost.

Jin shrugs. "It doesn't need to make sense. It's your choice. Nobody can tell you what to do."

"I don't want to do anything. I want to stay just like this." Quinn touches her stomach. "I want to stay pregnant. I want to have this baby."

"Okay, then." Jin smiles. "Now, tell us about the sex."

"No. We need to talk about what happened to Lise." Quinn finally diverts their attention and explains how Lise may have cracked the code to a time travel portal. Then she tells them about the paper in Ada's purse, and how it matches Tig's tattoo.

"There's a message in my diamond," she concludes. "Might be an algorithm, I don't know. But it has people worried, and Dirac is one of them."

"Okay," Jin says. "We need to act, and we need to do it now."

"What're we doin'?" asks Geller.

"We're putting the diamond into a state of superposition so we can read the message," Jin says. "We'll need a QM, a good one; hardware and software, a factorization app, to process the numbers; an algorithm to break any security; and maybe an error-correction algorithm, to correct inaccuracies. And we need a lab—a very cold, quiet lab. eMpower has an office here. We'll do it there, tonight. The place will be empty."

Quinn likes the way she says "we."

Jin hands her Band to Quinn. "Call Matt. He knows you're here. I've had a dozen missed calls from him."

✶✶✶

Matt answers Quinn's call immediately. "Quinn! Honey. Shit. Thank fucking Christ. Been so worried. Was told you were released, then nothing. What the fuck's going on? You safe? You okay?"

"Yes, yes, I'm fine, it's so good to hear—"

"Listen to me, listen very carefully, Lise might not be dead. They haven't found her."

"What?" *How does he know?*

"She might not be dead."

"I know, but how do you know?"

"What, you know? Thought I was the only one who knew."

"Yes, I know, and I thought I was the only one, but how do you know?"

"'Cause of Ada. It ain't Lise, it's Ada."

*Ada? Then the body switch has been sorted and everyone knows.* "So everyone knows?"

"No, no one knows."

"Dad, from the beginning: how do you know?"

"'Cause she's right here. I got her in a casket, in the bunker. Delivered a month ago. Signed her over to me. You were incarcerated, and I was on the list. You see, the thing is, no postmortem analysis; there were too many casualties and the cause of death was obvious: drowning. She's wearing Lise's Band. Why the fuck would she do that?"

"I don't know. It makes no sense." *Poor Ada. This is awful.* "Does she have any family?"

"Don't know. But if she does, then they think she's still missing."

"What do we do with her?"

"I'll sort it out, see if I can find her family."

"Okay, now it's your turn to listen very carefully."

Quinn recounts a version of the last few months, leaving nothing out except for every detail about Tig and the baby—her tale is Lise-centric, not Quinn-centric—and she promises to call her father when they open the diamond.

Just as she's about to end the call she says, "One more thing."

"Yep?"

"I'm pregnant. You're going to be grandfather."

There's a long pause.

"You there?"

"Yep. So that Mori bloke—"

"No, no, not him . . . it's a long story."

A longer pause.

"Dad . . ."

"Come home."

∗∗∗

Jin waits at the food prep bench while Quinn melts chocolate; this is Jin's favorite meal, melted chocolate covering a large spoon, the biggest they can find.

"I'd made peace with dying, until now," she says. "Now I want to meet him, this Tig person, I want to know what's going to happen to you, and I want to see that beautiful baby and hold it in my arms." She laughs at herself; she's holding something back.

Quinn narrows her eyes. "What is it?"

"Pregnant by a cyborg king—that's what you get for trying to be in control all the fucking time."

Quinn hands her the spoon and the bowl to catch the mess, and Jin shovels it into her mouth.

"This is it," she says, "I don't want anything else to eat, ever." Chocolate drips down her chin.

They stare at each other because what she just said is the shocking truth. This moment together will be one of the last they have.

Quinn is the first to look away. Jin hands her the chocolate-covered spoon, but she doesn't take it—she doesn't want it. She wants Jin to have everything, and she doesn't understand how the world works anymore and why this is happening. Everything is fucked up. Tears leak from her eyes, and she turns away.

The door springs opens and Geller bursts in, looking a little flushed and breathless. She has military backpacks slung over her shoulder and is wearing her climate suit, but it's a mess—dark stains down the front and sleeves, like she's also scoffed liquid chocolate and spilled it all over herself.

"Get your tings," she says. "We need ta move. Civil war on te doorstep. De rebels 'ave gathered in 'exad. Tey're preparin' ta take back te capital. New Fed won't last long. Overheard a private conversashun; Dirac knows your moter 'as solved some mystery of te universe—he's just not sure which one." She empties the backpack contents onto the table.

Quinn frowns, realizing it's not chocolate on Geller's suit. It's blood. "You're covered in blood."

"Aye, I know. Dirac's blood."

"What?"

"I overheard sometin', Niels talking to Dirac on te holo, he was goin' off, abusin' 'im. So I paid Dirac a visit. 'E wasn't cooperative, but I expected tat, used a serum. Anyway, didn't get te whole story—'e's old, 'is brain's not clear an' 'is memories are muddled. Kept mumblin' stuff about reality, said it was an illushun, a persistent illushun. Ten 'e said 'e was sorry, over an' over. And ten he cut his wrists while I was makin' tea."

"He killed himself?"

"Aye."

"While you were making tea?"

"Aye. It said on the label"—she retrieves a small vile of serum from the backpack— "it says, 'After-effects include 'unger, dehydrashun, and general disorientashun.' So after our little chat, I was makin' 'im a cuppa tea an' a snack in te food prep, an' 'e did te deed. Slit his radial arteries. Notin' to do about it, but I stayed wit 'im to te end, 'eld 'is 'and."

"Considerate of you."

"People shouldn't be alone when tey die. Least I could do." She jumps up. "We need ta hurry. We don't want ta be stuck 'ere durin' te attack, an' you're a sittin' duck, tey know you're 'ere, an' about te diamond. Some idiot called Aaroon wants it real bad. 'E's comin', wit military."

There's an awkward and immobile silence. What happens to Jin?

Jin turns to Quinn. "We go to eMpower and open the diamond, we get the message. Then you put me into CyberSleep. It's what I want, it's all set up, ready to go."

Quinn shakes her head.

"Geller will do it if you won't, and you promised, you said you would. We're going, now—first the diamond, then CyberSleep."

✶✶✶

Geller pilfered the armory before coming over. One pack is stuffed
with the ultimate war accessories—temporary night vision eye drops;
chemical weapon antidote patches containing thousands of micronee-
dles; nanobots that control shock and bleeding; chewable capsules
that protect against infection. There's also a collection of smart bullets, knives, and lasers. The second pack holds two new, military-issue
wingsuits. Both packs are lined with a combination of iron and cobalt,
giving them a magnetic imprint so the contents can't be identified at
security points. Geller turns the packs inside out, hiding the military
insignias, and divides up the loot.

Quinn orders an AV and in a few minutes they're on their way,
travelling through the quiet streets towards the eMpower office. Jin is
cold and calm, breathing easily. The afternoon is clear and a soft light
falls over Accord—an ethereal, yielding glow that lingers in the trees
and turns the ancient stonework a glorious peach. A state of nervous
anticipation has settled over the city; retaliation is looming, and many
more people will die tonight, tomorrow, and in the coming weeks. If
Jin's constitution reacts badly to the CyberSleep process, she could be
one of them. Quinn feels lightheaded; she can't get enough oxygen
into her lungs.

At the eMpower office, Jin takes a seat in an empty lab. She paces
herself, breathing slowly, as she checks the equipment, mentally
ticking the requirements off her list. She nods; they have everything.
Quinn hands her the stone.

Using a laser beam of radiation, Jin opens the lattice structure of
the diamond and removes a qubit. With a qubit balancer, she zaps the
particle with a magnetic field, putting it in a mixed state of superposition, simultaneously spinning in two different directions. Then she
extracts and loads the particle into a QM.

The data takes a few seconds to process.

Jin squints at the message on the machine, then hands it to Quinn.
It reads: "(He) $2s^2 2p^1$."

Quinn stares at the screen, then furtively at Jin, then back at the screen. Then she laughs. Jin laughs, too, until she can't handle the excitement and collapses in a coughing fit.

"Someone goin' ta tell me what's goin' on?"

"It's—well, it's boron," says Jin.

"An' why is tat funny?"

"Boron's number 5 on the periodic table. It's what Quinn and I commonly refer to as the most boring element on the table," Jin says. "We give elements human traits. Like, arsenic is annoying, chromium is crazy, and boron is boring."

"An' why would you do tat?"

"Because it's fun. And Lise knows this—the way we talk about the elements, giving them human characteristics. The message means nothing; it's a joke."

"Or, she knew it would be read, so she set a diversion, a decoy," suggests Quinn.

Geller squints. "So it means sometin'—or notin.'"

"Yes," Jin agrees.

# Forty-Two

# The CyberSleep Vault

THE CYBERSLEEP VAULT IS an urban enigma, a legendary place with a cult status that divides ethical and metaphysical mindsets: They can only save a few wretched souls, so should they? Where lies the humanity in that divisive decision? Death was once the great certainty, the one sure thing, but not anymore. Now it's a victim of the economic divide because avoidance is an option only the wealthy can afford. The masses gossip about the inequality of the business model, but those who actually understand the operational processes and the toxic emersion that the human body must endure mumble about the final outcome because no one has ever survived. There are only two great certainties: booming profits and death.

The depth of the Vault is unknown and the rumors have given it mythical status—a small underground city, three kilometers below the surface of the Earth. But it could also be a bunker, ten meters deep. Either way, it's designed as a tomb for the terminally ill or those who believe there's more to this business called daily living—that there has to be, surely this can't be it. Other rumors circulate: People go in and they never come out; the place is a vortex and the friends and families accompanying the clients are never seen again, swallowed in the morass of technology and toxins used the pickle the clients.

Inside the eMpower office is a designated skylift, resembling all other skylifts. Once inside, partitions engage, sealing the doors, and the lift spins one full circle, like an amusement ride. Security is activated, and Jin's hair stands on end. She enters a coded word as a final check: AI RULES.

Quinn rolls her eyes. *Seriously?*

The doors spring open and they have moved. They're in a new place; how far away, how far below the surface, it's impossible to tell. A dimly lit corridor lies ahead, and the surrounding walls, ceiling, and floor are covered in mint-green ivy. They're in a tunnel of thick vegetation, so long and narrow they can't see the end.

"Wasn't expecting this," says Jin. She touches the soft, moss-like leaves. "It's real. I think."

"It's like a forest, an enchanted forest," says Quinn.

A pale green snake slithers up the wall. A few meters away, a black-and-white lizard looks in their direction, then turns and plods away. Security robots.

Then the floor begins to move. It's a conveyer belt; it's moving them down the never-ending corridor.

Doorways appear on either side; Jin says her door is number fourteen.

Quinn calls out the door numbers: "Sixty-two, eleven, thirty-three, eight, one hundred." The numbers are out of sequence. If there's some relevance to the order, she can't work it out. It's unnerving not understanding the number series or why it's skewed.

They continue for several minutes, Quinn calling out random numbers, with no sign of fourteen. Soon Jin's calm exterior begins to slip, and her excitement switches to anxious silence. Quinn wants to say it's okay, they'll find it soon, don't worry, they'll find her door, but she doesn't want to ever find it. She wants it to be a mistake, a bad dream, so they can all go home and have a cup of tea and finish the chocolate and share what's left of the apples. That would be a pleasant way to end the day. Then she sees it: number fourteen.

Giggling, Jin breathes a sigh of relief. Entrance codes hover in the air around them, then dissolve, and the door to room fourteen vaporizes.

Inside are a dozen silver tanks with transparent silicon hoods. Quinn thought Jin would be alone, would have her own room. She doesn't like the idea of her sleeping next to all these strangers.

They step inside, and the floor is yielding and familiar—made of aerogel, like Mori's Cloud Ship. It has the same squishy resistance. Kerguelen seems such a long time ago, and it's the last thing Quinn wants to be thinking about. She pushes the memory away and focuses on Jin and the process she's about to undergo.

Along one wall is an open cleanse zone, and that's about it for décor: silver tanks, aerogel on the floor, and black jets projecting from the wall.

One tank is open. The others are closed, softly backlit, and filled with pale, naked CyberSleep tenants. Geller and Quinn roam the rows, voyeurs of the undead, and it's a mesmerizing and fascinating stroll. Who are these people and what happened to them? They pause by a tank and ponder a white-haired baby girl, maybe six months old, sleeping on her back with her arms carefully placed over her chest. Her skin is translucent mauve. The tank beside her holds a young, white-haired boy; her older brother, serene and unearthly, he has similar-toned skin.

"NBIC children, born in an artificial womb incubator," says Geller.

Quinn doesn't understand.

"NBIC. Nanotech, biotech, informashun tech, an' cognitive science. Smorgasbord, pick an' select children, but you can only do so much."

Quinn moves away. She doesn't like it down here.

Jin doesn't mess around; she's been briefed on the procedure. After undressing, she washes under a foamy marine liquid, like a dowse of seawater, that flows from the black faucet, removing earthly toxins—makeup, hair products, deodorant. She's painfully thin, all angular elbows and knees, loose flesh hanging off her bony frame. The virus has devoured her physical form. She's also covered in red and purple welts, and Quinn knows there must be bruises all over her organs, too. She'll come out the other side, if she survives the noxious processes, just as frail and sick. But she smiles.

Quinn silently sniffles as she tries to hold herself together. Geller maintains a calm, slightly fragile expression. But Jin smiles. For her, this is not the end. It's a new adventure, a new beginning.

It's time for farewells. Jin and Geller smirk. They take each other's hands, and their grins widen into reverent smiles. Geller is taller, and she leans forward and kisses Jin softly on the forehead. A restrained parting for a couple that spent two days engaged in intense physical gratification, but they always knew this time would come. Their future was a sure thing, and the end, the parting and the loss, fueled the urgency of their desire. What's done is done, and the beautiful, climactic memory of the other is now an explicit impression, consolidated and stored in memory. They're both happy with the outcome.

Jin leaves Geller and turns to Quinn, who can't stop crying. She chuckles at the sight of her friend's smudged face. "Get a grip," she says, and Quinn nods and sucks in breaths of air, attempting to regulate her breathing, trying to pull herself together.

One, last, deep breath, and she manages to assume a calmer expression. She pulls Jin close, hugging her, kissing her, never wanting to let go, and Jin returns the impassioned embrace, comforting and consoling her friend, wiping away Quinn's tears and kissing her quickly.

Then Jin climbs into the tank. She lies down in a cold bed of cool light and lays her arms by her sides. Then she changes her mind and carefully crosses her arms over her chest. Then she has a mini crisis and covers her face; she doesn't know what to do with her arms. She giggles. What to do with your arms when you are entering CyberSleep?

Quinn also laughs. *Idiot.*

Jin tries another position, but the process has been activated and an electromagnetic seal whips around the edge of the tank. She's gone. One of her arms lies across her chest and the other is halfway across her stomach.

"No, no, she wasn't ready," says Quinn. "Look, her arms, she needs more time. Her arms, we need to fix them . . ."

"She was ready enough. Let's get outta 'ere. We can mourn somewhere better tan tis ghostly place. Can you see 'em?"

"Who?"

"Some'a tese people are already dead."

Never, in all her dreams and hopes for the future, did Quinn see this coming: Jin, at the age of thirty-four, dying from some stupid cat disease and slipping into CyberSleep, and herself pregnant, by a cyborg with a personality disorder.

✱✱✱

Quinn and Geller escape the Vault without incident, and head straight back into the skylift and up to the surface. Outside, they collapse onto seating in a private garden near the building's entrance.

"Fuck," says Geller. "Tat was 'eavy."

"I need a drink." Quinn wipes away tears with the back of her hand.

"I'll 'ave one for te both'a us. Tat's te sort of friend I am." Geller slides an arm around Quinn; they rest heads together and Geller's lips graze her cheek. "You'll be okay. We both will."

"What'd you mean by 'already dead'?"

"Worked in te morgue when I was young, I know dead people. Some'a te poor souls down tere should get a refund."

Quinn doesn't disagree. It's early evening, and it's been a long day; she closes her eyes and leans back against the bench. Maybe they can just stay here and sleep on this seat for a few hours. Tomorrow's a new day, and it will be a better day than this one. It has to be a better day than this one. They can sort out their lives, the future, what to do next—they can sort all that out tomorrow. She's so tired.

An explosion pierces the silence. Quinn opens her eyes.

Geller is up, on her feet, listening, scanning the sky. She points, "North, te Pods. One bomb usually means two."

On cue, there's another explosion, followed by rapid gunfire. Military transporters pass overhead, and the sky fills with thousands of dark shadows tumbling rapidly to Earth. An air strike.

A shell stops in the sky a few meters above them. They freeze and tilt their eyes up toward the hovering bomb. The weapon spins and opens, a long shaft emerges, and a dozen battle drones shimmy off the end of the rod.

Quinn stiffens. *Shit.*

Geller gives her a signal to calm down. "Cistern Missiles. Won't kill 'umans, tey're lookin' for a tank. If tey don't find one, tey'll self-destruct."

A second wave of armed robots inundates the sky, and two figures touch down on the other side of the garden.

"'OTRODs," says Geller.

"What?"

"MeanMachines: part organic, part bio-mechatronic."

"They're human?"

They do resemble a human form, with arms and legs and a head with eyes, although one is black and the other neon yellow and their bodies are wrapped in layers of black and silver metalloid that accentuate their bulk and size so they appear monstrously huge. Running toward Quinn and Geller, they look like giant cartoon characters.

Quinn shakes her head. "These guys are way over the line."

"Yeah, livin' tings, but no longer 'uman. Once crime-committing, violent fuckers, you know te type, durin' te Wars tey were given a choice between prison an' combat. Tey chose combat, merged themselves into an exoskeleton, military emptied teir brains so all they can do's follow orders. Dispensable foot solders, except tey don't die easy. An' tey're mean."

*And they're coming straight for us.* Quinn grabs Geller's arm, ready to run.

"Wait," says Geller. "They can't shoot you."

"Why not?" They look like they have every intention of shooting her.

"You're pregnant. Where te fuck 'ave you been?"

"Hobart."

"Post War convenshun: crimes against civilians, children, and pregnant women, especially pregnant women, are no' permitted."

"Really?"

"Aye."

"Well, that's progressive."

"Aye, we learnt sometin' from years'a killing each other in te name of god. They're pre-programmed; in a minute tey'll scan you an' realize."

*In a minute!*

Geller pulls Quinn in front of her. "'Uman shield. Sorry. No weapons; we don't shoot at tem, tey can't shoot back."

The HOTRODs are almost upon them, if Geller is wrong they're about to die an explosive death, but they pull up a few meters away, scan them, and then stand down.

Slowly, Geller and Quinn back away.

A missile whistles overhead and lands on the other side of the garden.

"We go to te Temple—it's 'istoric," Geller says. "Maim's an 'istory professor. Rumor is she won't destroy it."

# Forty-Three

# I can't be late—not again.

PLANCK RISES EARLY AND prepares breakfast for the stowaways. After many unforeseen delays, including Hexad's procedural bureaucracy (a dictum to avoid conflict unless absolutely necessary) and the defensive navigation they opted for (sailing in circles to avoid the New Fed military), they are finally underway. Tomorrow, they'll dock at Hexad and deliver their cargo.

Breakfast is a Biodiverse Plate: pinkfish, mussels, samphire, pickled vegetables, and fermented seaweed, plus insect sprinkles for added protein, texture, and crunch. Planck switches on the infuser for tea and begins to plate up the food.

Piercing morning sun, low in the sky, floods the galley, bouncing off surfaces and causing a blinding glare. *Too early for this.* Planck taps two fingers on the smart glass, searching for the right shade of translucency, but misses the mark and darkness permeates the space. Ze adjusts back and forth a few times. *Perfect.* Ze finishes plating, using the last of the hemp oil as dressing in the process; ze makes a mental note to collect more. Then ze pauses and peers out the window.

They're traveling east, unless the sun has moved, which ze doubts. East. Hexad is west, due west. *What the fuck is he doing now.* Abandoning the breakfast plates, the tea, and the perfectly filtered light, ze goes in search of Tig.

Ze locates him on deck with Martha2. "What are you doing?"

"Detour. I checked the calendar; it's been six days. I can't be late—not again. We're going back to get her. She's not safe."

"A few extra days, she'll be fine. We agreed."

"Nah, not doing it again. Like you said, we've come all this way. I can't leave her again."

"You have to. It's important. Thousands of lives are at stake and Maim is President—or will be President. You can't say no to her."

"Can't see it happening.'"

*Reinforcements.* Ze heads back inside.

Maim ambles into the galley as Planck comes in. She tucks loose strands of grey hair behind an ear as she shuffles onto a seat at the bench. Her climate suit is two-piece, black, with vertical white stripes running the length of her pants. She zips up the matching jacket. "Why is it so cold in here?"

Planck shrugs. "Your cool is my warm."

Maim places her elbows on the bench, knits her fingers together, and rests her chin in the nest of her knuckles. She closes her eyes and yawns.

Planck pours her a spicy spearmint infusion to kick-start her day. "Tough night?" *She must have a lot on her mind.*

"Actually, perimenopause. My hormones are all over the place."

"Considered synthetic hormone—"

"Doesn't agree with me."

*Ah, of course.* "Stateswoman, lawmaker, executive diplomat, leader of the armed forces, Commander in Chief, and wildly fluctuating estrogen levels, combined with a severe decline in progesterone and testosterone. Insomnia? Night sweats?"

She nods.

"Fatigue, headaches, palpitations, heavy bleeding?"

She nods.

"I'll fix you a supplement with added calcium and vitamin D." Ze scraps half the mussels off her breakfast plate before passing it to her. "You also need to watch your cholesterol."

She tucks into her food. "Delicious. I'll be recommending you. In fact, I'm going to need transport back—"

"Let's concentrate on getting you there first. We have a problem. We're sailing in the wrong direction."

Maim dips her head and considers the position of the sun out the galley window. "Good lordt, you're right, we're traveling east, back to Unus. Why?"

"Tig's in love. He's lovesick."

"What do you mean, he's in love? He's not in love. Who's he in love with?"

"Quinn Buyers. She's in Unus."

Maim spits her spearmint infusion across the galley bench. "Lise's daughter. Are you sure?"

Planck nods. "They're expecting. A baby girl."

"Oh good lordt, I've heard it all." She slumps back in her chair and sighs. "Of course, that's why she was here on the boat."

"Yes. You okay?"

Maim nods, slowly, thoughtfully, and sips what's left of her tea. "I've not told anyone this. And it's strictly between you and me, and that goes for all our little tête-à-têtes. But I was supposed to be at that wedding, with Lise. We were seeing each other, about to make it public. I was supposed to be her date, but Ada, well, they had history, she'd known Quinn for years, so I stepped aside. Didn't want to make a scene . . ."

Planck offers another round of tea but she waves her hand, she's done. "Okay, we need to sort out our lovesick captain. A few more days isn't going to kill him. Quinn will understand; war is fucking unpredictable. We have people on the ground. We'll get a message to her, get her out. Can you skipper this boat?"

Planck nods. Elementary.

"I'll go talk to him, I can be very persuasive. I've a good appetite for risk and nerves of steel. Use to be an art dealer, ran auctions—it's a very stressful profession. I'm good at getting people to give up precious things." She pulls a laser from the back of her pants and hands it to Planck. "Do me favor, double-check I've set it to stun. Just a precaution, but I will shoot if I have to."

# Forty-Four

# He's sorry, but he's not sorry enough.

THOUSANDS OF WAR-WOUNDED TAKE refuge in the Temple gardens, with more arriving by the minute—carried in on stretchers, limping, dragging bloody limbs. Others come with bedding and food, everything they need to set up lodgings in the grounds; they've also heard the rumor that this is the safest place in the city.

As Geller and Quinn pass through the inner courtyard, two men scan them and exchange a nod, then begin to follow them at a distance. Geller opens her pack and hands Quinn a set of blades.

Soldiers guard the Temple doors. Geller flashes her military credentials and asks for an update.

There's heavy fighting in the north of the city. The rebels took the residential zones, but New Fed launched a counter attack, so the fighting continues. The city is in lockdown, with limited transport options, but the Hyperloop is running. That's good news, because it's the only way out of Accord.

"We keep moving," says Quinn. "Head straight for the Loop."

"First, te art," says Geller.

"The what?"

"Blake, te paintings, te ones you saw at te Salon. Just a quick look, while we're 'ere."

Geller has slipped inside the Temple before Quinn has even noticed that she's moving again. She hastily follows and finds Geller inside the vestibule, gazing at a picture of a multiheaded dragon attacking a golden woman.

"Te cosmic battle between good an' evil. 'Tis what 'appens if you shun religion. But look, god will save 'er, 'e's given 'er wings ta fly away. Just like you." She moves to the next image and grins at a ridiculously small picture of a scaly creature holding a cup. "'Te ghost av a flea,'" she says, leaning in close, the tip of her nose centimeters from the canvas. "Te souls av men are bloodtirsty; you see te cup?"

Quinn sees the cup and has a good idea how bloodthirsty the souls of men and women are, but they need to leave. She's nervous as hell. She doesn't want to be here, looking at these creepy paintings of fleas and dragons and golden-haired women; she wants to be on the Hyperloop, heading for Unus. Safety, she wants to be looking at that. "Okay, you've seen the scary pictures. Now let's get out of here."

"Relax," says Geller, "anoter minute won't 'urt, an' I may never get te chance again."

Just then, past Geller's shoulder, standing at the far side of the Hall, Quinn spies Dirac, alive and well. She nudges Geller and gestures toward the apparent ghost of their foe.

Geller considers him, then shakes her head. "Can we bring back te dead in 2050?"

"No."

"I know a dead person when I see one. Sometin's up."

"Blake lived in an age of purity. He believed in blind faith and miracles." Aaroon looms over Geller, smiling.

Quinn retreats into the shadows, but he's clearly seen her. *Fuck, this just keeps getting worse.*

"He was an innocent," Geller agrees.

"Come, let me show you the mad King Nebuchadnezzar, turning

from human to animal." He leads her to a painting that shows a figure who's half man and half beast.

"Did 'e who made te Lamb make t'ee?" Geller asks.

Aaroon tilts his head and smiles graciously, a glint in his eye. He's impressed by her education and mesmerized by her dark hair and charcoal eyes.

Quinn's not impressed with either of them. She scans the Hall, checking for exit points, and through the crowd she spies Niels. Her heart sinks. She was hopping to never cast eyes on that groomed physique again. He hasn't spotted her yet, though; now is the time for a swift, undetected exit. The quickest route is behind them, the way they entered.

She eyes Niels again and freezes. Standing next to him is Mori. Her Mori, not the AI meerkat, the human, the ex-fiancé, the greedy shit Mori. He's in conversation with Niels, listening to whatever waffle his brother is advocating for. He's wearing his climate pants too high, and he still looks like an otter—a slick, smooth, carnivorous weasel. Then his eyes fall on hers. She lingered too long; it was bound to happen. They're both caught in each other's gaze. She can't pull away. It's a shock to see him real and alive, in the flesh like this, but he's not surprised to see her. He smiles and it's a kind, gentle smile, like he's happy she's here, like nothing ever happened, like it's last year and no time has passed and 1,962 people never died.

He shrugs and says, "I'm so sorry."

She can't actually hear him say this because he's too far away, and she's not even sure he spoke the words aloud, but she read his lips and it is very clear, he's sorry. She believes him, he's sorry, but he's not sorry enough. He's not sorry for being a total fuckwit and a defective human. He's not sorry for setting a ghost on the G12 and murdering 1,962 people. This isn't that sort of apology. It's indifference, the sort of apology you give when you're running late because you've missed the Hyperloop, or when you've used all the 3D print material and forgotten to reorder. The sorry you give to placate when it's not really your fault. He's just not sorry enough. That's going to make it easier for her to kill him.

Niels frowns at his brother and turns toward the source of his distraction. His eyes fall on Quinn, and he sighs. Despair. Holding Mori back with one hand, he glances around the Hall, then discreetly points to a side door. He wants to meet her outside.

She shakes her head. It's not going to happen.

Like a parent, he nods and points again; he's adamant, he wants to talk to her.

She shouldn't go, she knows she shouldn't. She should grab Geller, and they should head for the Loop. But Aaroon is still entertaining her, and now everyone knows they're here; their chance of escaping without an incident is slim.

She has an idea. Reluctantly, she nods and makes for the exit.

She finds Niels waiting in the shadows by the Temple wall.

"I wanted to say—"

"Not interested," she says. "Couldn't give a fuck. Now, you let us leave, and I'll give you the stone."

He nods. "Okay."

She pulls out a knife, deftly flicks it up in the air and catches it with her left hand. "Probably should make a show of it, like I put up a fight. Don't you think?"

He frowns.

Her hand darts out and the knife grazes his neck, slices a thin line from chin to ear. He touches the wound and then considers his bloody fingers. Geller suddenly appears beside him and they look at each other, then stare at the blood on his hand. Aaroon steps into the clique, holding a laser, and a gathering of tall people with multicolored eyes closes in around them.

"Hand it over," says Aaroon.

"Under control," says Niels, wiping blood from his chin.

"Doesn't look like it," says Aaroon.

"Leave it to me."

"I want the stone."

"And you'll get it."

Quinn fetches the stone from her pocket and tosses it to Aaroon. He fumbles, misses the catch. *Oh for fuck's sake, he's a twenty-five-year-old male with bear paws for hands. How did he miss that.*

Niels sighs, collects it from the ground. "Go."

"No, they come with us," says Aaroon

"Get the fuck out of here," says Niels.

"Not going to happen," says Aaroon.

The males face off, Aaroon indignantly looming over Niels, Niels smiling affably up at him, dabbing at his bleeding chin.

"Fuck off," Niels barks.

Quinn's not sure if he means her or Aaroon, but Geller grabs her arm and tows her into the crowd.

"This way." A man beckons them toward him. Quinn recalls him; he's one of the men that followed them into the courtyard. Who knows if they can trust him, but hell, what have they got to lose now? She and Geller exchange a quick glance, shrug, and follow him.

Soon they're submerged in a sea of moving people. The stranger guides them to the edge of the park and into an underpass. In the shadows of the tunnel, Quinn pins her mysterious savior to the wall with a blade.

"Thank you, thank you so much," she pants. "But who the hell are you?"

Calm eyes smile down at her. "I have a message," he says, "Your friends are delayed. Go to the Maldives. You'll be safe. They will look after you."

She drops her knife.

"What is your exit plan?" he asks.

"The Hyperloop?" she asks.

"Loop station's in chaos, big queues, three-day wait."

"We 'av wings. We can fly," says Geller.

Quinn nods and scans the skies outside the tunnel. "There." She points. "The PurePins. Can you get us up there?"

The Pollution Purging Pinnacles circling the city are two kilometers tall.

Stroking his face with his palm, he cast his eyes up at the PurePin. "Maybe," he says, "You sure?"

They're sure; they have wingsuits. If they can get up, they'll leap off and glide into Unus. Their savior points toward the PurePin. "Take a skylift."

Simple. Quinn breathes a sigh of relief and turns to thank the man again, but he has already vanished.

✳✳✳

Quinn and Geller slump on the floor of the skylift, their backs against the wall. The lift is designed for sightseeing, and the ride takes three minutes. They're done in, both exhausted, and Quinn closes her eyes for a micronap.

Five days. Tig said five days. He'd deliver the cargo, then he'd come get her. And now he's delayed. Again. How long this time? Punctuality is a virtue. And Mori—what an absolute idiot he turned out to be, whispering sorry. What an idiot. He can't just say, "Oops, sorry, killed a few hundred people." How could she be with such a complete asshole? What was she thinking? She's an idiot. Yes, maybe she's the biggest idiot of them all.

She turns to Geller. "I'm so angry with you. Art? Honestly? You had to go look at it now, in the middle of a civil war, while we're trying to escape, with Aaroon and military coming after us? What were you thinking?"

"Seems ta me we're fine, and we got a grand solushun for gettin' out of te city from it. Maybe 'tis not me you're angry wit. 'Ave you tought about tat?"

"No. It's you."

# Forty-Five

# Kapow, Kapow!

Aᴛ ᴛʜᴇ ᴇMᴘᴏᴡᴇʀ ᴏꜰꜰɪᴄᴇ, two technicians in white suits work inside an enclosed lab to place the pink diamond into a state of superposition. Mori, Niels, and Aaroon wait in the adjacent room, separated from the lab by a transparent partition. The waiting room is grey and lifeless and fitted out in sterile, hard surfaces with a few scattered tables and chairs.

They were told forty minutes. Aaroon pulls a noisy chair up to a table. From his pocket, he pulls out two wooden tops—one orange and one green—and he spins them across the rigid tabletop. He nibbles his raw fingernails as he watches them glide, the tops dancing and bouncing off each other like squabbling siblings. "Kapow!" he calls out each time the tops collide.

Mori leans against the partition, arms crossed, and rolls his eyes, dismissing his brother's concerns. "She'll come around. It was an honest mistake."

"You killed her mother. She never wants to see you again." Niels holds a blood-soaked bandage to his neck wound. He checks the bleeding, then places more pressure on the wound.

"The way she looked at me, I can tell it's not over."

"Really? You killed her mother. That's fucking bad," says Aaroon.

"Kapow, kapow!" The tops battle in the background.

"Not directly; it was a mistake, an honest mistake."

"You're delusional," says Niels.

Aaroon's tops clutter onto the floor in a double knockout. He collects them and sends them spinning across the table again, "Kapow! If you killed my mom, I'd never forgive you. In fact, I'd probably hunt you down, cut off your limbs, and reattach them to the opposite sides of your body. Then I'd chop your dick off and stick it onto your head. Then I'd bore holes into your head and turn you into a sex zombie. Kapow!"

The brothers glare at Aaroon.

"What? I love my mom."

The two technicians emerge from the lab. Aaroon puts the spinning tops back into his pocket and joins the brothers. Mori is the closest, so the technician hands him the module. Niels immediately plucks it out of his hand and studies the formula on the screen. Then Aaroon plucks it from Niels and begins processing the information.

Niels waits, watching Aaroon, but he's disturbed by the enormous amount of earwax in Aaroon's ears. Aaroon steps away, removing himself from scrutiny, so he can concentrate. "(He) $2s^2\,2p^1$. Boron, it's the formula for boron." He turns to the closest technician. "What else? Her formula for M-theory?"

The technician shakes his head. "Nothing else; that's it. But the message is compromised. Might have been changed."

"Fuck, she's looked at it. She's changed it. It was an M. It was definitely an M, and they've fucking changed it," says Aaroon. "If you'd listened to me, we wouldn't have this problem. Next time, you listen to me."

# Forty-Six

# Gravity is heartless.

Two kilometers in the sky, Quinn and Geller exit the skylift and gaze over a maze of landscaped gardens, orchards, and reflection pools, all lit up like a festival, as if a thousand revelers were about to arrive but now the party is canceled, so they're the only ones here, just the two of them. At the center of the garden is a shimmering glass and silicon structure shaped like a giant lotus flower. It covers a whirlpool; the swirling vortex washes the atmosphere, funneling the clean air back into Accord.

Geller parks herself on the first bench she sees and closes her eyes. Quinn sits beside her, drops her head back, and yawns. The rhythmic swish of the whirlpool is soporific; they should never have sat down, not even for five minutes in the skylift. Now they've lost momentum. It's close to midnight, and the temptation to grab a few hours' sleep on an uncomfortable bench in a beautiful garden is hard to resist.

"We could 'ave a wee rest—fly tomorrow," says Geller.

Quinn silently agrees. They could stay here, hide somewhere, under a bush or a bench, and sleep for a few hours on the soft grass. Surely no one will find them. But she forces herself to rally. Jumping in the cover of darkness is safer, and she knows they'll come. Aaroon and the others, they'll open the stone and realize it's . . . *What is it? A joke, a decoy, a distraction.* She chuckles to herself: the danger she put herself through keeping the diamond safe, the effort they went to getting it open, and the absurdity of the message.

"What?" Geller opens an eye.

"My mother, the comedian." Quinn opens the pack containing the wingsuits, pulls one out, and examines the design. It's military issue and excellent quality—lightweight, ripstop, pressurized, inflatable with auto correct and stabilizers. She tosses it to Geller and pulls out the other one for herself. Slowly, they dress, pulling the suits over their clothes.

"Never used one'a tese before," Geller says.

"Your body's the fuselage, your head the rudder," Quinn instructs. "Gravity wants you, and she's a bitch. She'll pull you down if she can, but the suit's airfoil gives you lift. Surface area creates lift. To go up, open your arms and legs, raise your head, look forward. To turn, twist, but just slightly, you want small movements."

Quinn sets the trajectory on her suit for the Maldives and transfers the coordinates to Geller's Band.

Geller rummages through her backpack. She's looking for something, a particular weapon. She pulls out an array of small arms, lasers, guns, and bullets, handing each item to Quinn as she searches. Quinn is stunned by the selection; the pack is limitless, like a bottomless Mary Poppins carpet bag.

Geller eventually finds what she's searching for: a slim black device she calls a Silos. She hands it to Quinn and explains that it's a tactical jammer; the weapon breaks connections between a drone missile and its launcher and can even turn the missile around and send it back to its point of origin.

Quinn stows the Silos in her belt. "Okay, your flight speed should be around 120kph, the fall rate about 90. Don't forget to breath, and—"

"Relax, I'm a quick learner. You worry about yourself. Keep tat baby safe."

Laser fire hits the railing next to them, and a rotor rises over the rim of the PurePin garden. The gunner on board has a weapon trained straight at them. Geller pulls Quinn to the ground and shoots at the rotor blades. The rotor teeters, clips the side of the railing, and spirals downwards.

"Go," says Quinn. "No Comms, but if we separate I'll meet you . . ."

Geller peels her fingers off the railing. "Don't forget ta breathe," she admonishes before tumbling over the edge, unfurling, and soaring southward, towards Unus. Laser fire scorches the railing beside Quinn as soldiers exit the skylift. She leaps over the edge and drops straight into flight mode. She has one eye on Geller and the other on the skyline behind her, scanning for projectiles. The soldiers on the roof continue firing and a round of missiles heads towards her. She presses a button on the Silos and the projectiles self-implode. *Impressive.* She checks over her shoulder as a second round of ammunition is fired. She launches the Silos again, a different setting this time, and the missiles perform a U-turn, travel back to where they came from, and the PurePin explodes, shattering into flames. *Shit, didn't mean to do that.* Ruefully she puts her head down, increases her speed, and flies away.

Ahead of her, Unus is awake and preparing for war. The city buzzes and hisses like a swarm of busy insects, and its streets glow like hot rivers of lava oozing between buildings. Geller merges into the burning ambiance that hovers above the city. She's on target; she'll make the landing mark and touch down in the Maldives. Quinn follows her line, mesmerized by the spectacle of liquid light below, and for just a moment she lets go. She closes her eyes, and the world around her evaporates. Her senses heighten, her fingertips tingle, and she sinks, untethered and free, reveling in the ecstasy of release. A universal pulse surges though her. Her physical being dissolves and joins the cosmic atoms and particles that surround her until all that's left is the essence of her being—a state of bliss, pure bliss.

Then she collides with a foreign object.

It's not a weapon, and it's not heavy or hard. She's unhurt, but the impact confuses her, disrupts her flight. She flounders; the thing came out of nowhere. What was it? Not a bird, but like a bird . . . a drone. She collided midair with a black-dove drone, designed for hobby use, not military. It's probably been flying around for weeks. The drone is shattered and falls. She follows, cartwheeling over and over, then free-falling. *Autocorrect, autocorrect*—the suit rights itself and continues on, but she's lost altitude and won't make the landing mark.

Ahead, she sights the roof of a residential tower block. She releases her chute; she'll make the mark if she's lucky. She descends, her feet scoot over the rooftop, and she's almost there, *Safe, thank the lordt . . .*

Almost. A dirty gust of wind whips around her; it picks her up. *No, no, no, please no.* It hauls her across the building, lifts her over the edge, and sends her straight into the adjacent apartment block. She twists to the left, protecting her baby human, before colliding with the wall.

"Ouch." Her eyes water.

The wind gust abates, her chute flounders, and she grabs at the side of the building, trying to find a ledge to hold. But she slips and slides, and again she's freefalling toward the ground. *Gravity is heartless; she is a heartless bitch.*

Abruptly she's pulled up, no longer falling but dangling in midair. Her chute is caught around a dado protruding from the building. Helpless, she hangs, three stories above the ground, like a yoyo on a string. Stranded and powerless, she fears that neither the chute nor the dado will save her, not today; today, gravity has it in for her.

On her left is a window with a quaint Juliet balcony, and the leap is not impossible. Thrusting back and forth, she swings, gaining momentum until she's close enough to grab the railing. She manages to pull herself over, and to her relief she lands on something soft—a feather bed.

She stays exactly where she landed, lying quite still on the soft bed. Looking up, she watches the stars. She listens to the sounds of war in the distance, and she thinks about nothing, absolutely nothing. She could lie like this for hours, sleep here the night. But there's a strange, musty smell. It's coming from the bed. It smells of dog.

She rolls over. The door to the apartment is ajar, and she creeps through it into a living zone. Asleep on the sofa is a dog—a brindled mixed breed with a bright orange collar. It yawns, it opens an eye and sees her, and its ears prick. It knows she's not supposed to be here, but at the same time it's aware it's shouldn't be sleeping on the sofa.

"Stay," she whispers, and it wags its tail. "Shhhh." She pats the dog's head and ruffles its ears. "Military exercise, go back to sleep."

✶✶✶

After ditching the wingsuit, Quinn checks her Band. No messages, and Geller won't make contact. Quinn knows she's on her own, and she knows where she needs to be—the Maldives. On foot, it will take her an hour to get there. She confirms her position and, with a slight limp, heads west.

It's hot; she forgot about the oppressive, stagnant heat, even at this time of night. Giant green leaves of chard grow in communal gardens bordering the street. She breaks off several large fronds to fan herself with, and takes the occasional nibble as she walks. The atmosphere around her is bright and busy. A rosy illumination hangs over the streets and a harried vibe fills the air as residents prepare for war, barricading streets and securing entrances. People linger in groups, gathered in doorways to keep tabs on the war, or perhaps simply because they're unable to sleep.

"You okay?" an older man on the street corner, a neighborhood overseer and self-appointed lookout, asks Quinn.

"Fine, thank you." But she's not fine. Everything hurts.

✶✶✶

By the time she enters the Maldives courtyard, Quinn has nibbled all her pieces of chard to the stalk. She spots Geller and Flax waiting in the shadows by the fountain. Geller strides over and hugs her.

"I hate tardiness," she says gruffly. "'Tis unforgivable."

Flax, wearing a saffron nightshirt, kisses Quinn's cheeks. His eyes are hooded and his face rough and unshaven, but his lips are soft and his breath smells fresh, like peppermint tea. Relief melts his harried expression as he sighs and smiles, pats her hand, and then beckons for them to follow.

The people of the Maldives were the first displaced nation to arrive in Unus, and they settled in the Renaissance precinct. The main quarters were once a grand five-hundred-year-old palace, and they're headed toward its central building. They climb the worn stone stoop and enter through heavy timber doors.

Inside is a cool sanctuary with a circular staircase rising up three levels. Colorful marble mosaics cover the floor, and the stucco walls are faded, painted in soft pastel frescos. They scale the stairs and continue down a narrow corridor to a room—a small partitioned space, divided many times to accommodate the masses. The once ornate layers of sixteenth-century decoration are now stripped away. What's left is peeling wallpaper, bleached timber floors, paneled cabinetry, and two beds with crisp white linen.

Seeing the beds, Geller and Quinn yawn in unison, and Flax leaves them. They skull some water, and Geller climbs into bed.

"Sleep," she says. "We debrief in te mornin." She closes her eyes, and soon her breathing slows. She's dozing.

Quinn's not well; her body hurts. When she climbs into bed, she moans. Her hip and leg ache, and she wonders about the damage. How much bruising? What if there's blood? It feels like there could be blood, and if she's bleeding it will stain the white sheets. Then they'll have to be washed. It would be a shame to get blood on them; they're so white and fresh. She should check to make sure there's no blood.

She lights her Band and examines the yellow and black welts on her thigh and hip; no blood, just bruising.

"Get yourself ta sleep," Geller mumbles.

"Sorry." Quinn switches off her light and lays silent. Then her shoulder starts to hurt. The pain moves up the right side of her neck. It doesn't feel like it's bleeding; it feels like it's bruised, like her thigh. No need to check. She touches her shoulder, finds the point of impact. It's rough and grazed; there could be some blood. Maybe it's dried blood, but she should check. Adjusting the brightness to a dim glow, she switches on the light in her Band again and surveys her upper arm. No blood, just bruising.

"Sleep!" Geller yells, and Quinn kills the light.

She's tired, she's so tired, but she's also wired and can't relax or switch off. Her body hurts and she can't ignore the pain. Her head fills with images of Tig; she wonders where he is and if he's safe. Then her thoughts flick to Matt, harboring Ada's corpse and everyone thinking it's Lise; Lise and the stupid message in the diamond. *Fuck.* Sleep evades her. She opens her eyes.

*Interoception.* Interoception will put her to sleep. She closes her eyes and breathes deeply. She relaxes her toes and feet, then her legs and thighs, then her stomach and abdomen, then further up to her chest, then . . . back to her stomach. Something's wrong, her abdomen feels different. She waits, processing the sensation. It's not painful; it's intense and heavy, a feeling of bearing down. Blood. There's blood between her legs, wet and warm. She's bleeding.

Rising, she flicks her light on again, heads to the cleanse zone, and undresses. Blood has soaked through her underwear. She sits on the toilet, and large drops of blood drip into the bowl. She freezes, stricken by fear and guilt. Her heart pounds. She waits; she prays to the universe, begging it to keep her baby safe. She waits ten minutes, and there's no more blood.

Back in the room, Geller sleeps facing the wall. Quinn sits beside her and touches her shoulder. "I'm bleeding."

Geller stirs and turns. "How much an' what color?"

"Not much; red, deep red."

Geller launches her SelfMed and scans Quinn. The result is inconclusive, so she checks Quinn's hormone levels. "High progesterone an' estrogen, good sign. Get some rest. Cross your fingers."

"Okay." Quinn nods. She finds her bed, curls up, and crosses her fingers. There's nothing she can do now. Rest. Rest. Interoception puts her to sleep.

✶✶✶

In the morning, Quinn pukes. She looks at Geller, wipes her mouth, and smiles.

✶✶✶

War rages in the skies over Unus and it is relentless, night and day for ten days, machine pitted against machine. This is the third revolution of warfare. The first was gunpowder; the second, nuclear weapons; the third, giving AI the autonomous decision to kill. Pacifists fought the legislation for decades but finally lost in 2040, when the military assured everyone it would bring an end to the Wars.

It didn't. Instead, it opened a Pandora's Box of misery and despair. Science and technology were hijacked by the war effort. Space was militarized with long-range weapons, GPS launchers, and quantum stealth. Militarization of the Moon soon followed. Then depersonalized killing machines took hold, along with electronic interface computing and guidance control. The Authentic Human Association argued that delegating life-and-death decisions to a machine was unethical; it crossed a threshold from which humankind might never return. There was no data to back this up, however; machines upheld the laws and morals of society far better than humans. So drones and their grounded companions, Sentient Unmanned Vehicles (robots that don't look like people), were quickly phased into the fighting; the public protested less when killing machines looked like machines and not humans.

For ten days the citizens of Unus have hidden indoors, covering their windows, blocking out the world, and it has been a bleak and fraught existence. Geller and Quinn have kept to their room, and no one's come, and no one's gone. Morning and night, they've prepared dehydrated food with a samovar.

Quinn woke one night somewhere in the middle of all of this to blackness, and the world closed in and swallowed her. She couldn't breathe; there was no air, her heart pounded, and her hands shook. She huddled against the wall, unable to move.

"It's okay, darlin," Geller whispered, "you're 'avin' a panic attack, but you're safe. We bot are." She told Quinn to center her mind, breathe, and think about something else.

So Quinn filled her head with calculus, and she repeated the sums over and over. The distraction worked; in the darkness, math was her savior.

✳✳✳

On the morning of the eleventh day, the skies above Unus finally clear and a quiet stillness falls over the city. The stillness lasted about an hour, until a dog starts barking, and it continues barking and barking all morning, filling the silence left by the war. Tentatively, residents realize the barking is a sign, a good sign, and they leave their homes. Venturing into the streets, they climb over the piles of rubble and burnt buildings and dodge falling debris to survey the damaged buildings and check on their neighbors. News moves quickly, and it's soon apparent that this is not a ceasefire—it's peace.

The final war statistics are hopeful: A massive counterattack was launched from Hexad, and Dirac's forces fled Accord. Maim Quate claimed victory, and the city will be governed by the Democratic Republic. For Quinn and Geller, their personal statistics are also better than expected. Over the last ten days, they consumed thirty-two dehydrated meals and completed twenty sessions of Interoception; Quinn felt her heartbeat in her elbow and is now an Interoception master. They completed ten sessions of Pregnancy Yoga, focusing on Stick Pose, which involves lying on the floor and breathing, and Standing Mountain, which involves standing tall and breathing. Quinn decided that devising calculus was more strenuous. Geller read three books on war: *War Poems*, *The Trojan Women*, and *The Art of War*. Quinn read three pregnancy books: *What to Expect When You're Expecting*, *Complete Pregnancy*, and *Day-By-Day Pregnancy*. Quinn caught over fifty (she stopped counting at fifty) small flying ants with her left hand. The creatures were nesting in a decaying window frame and occasionally escaped to fly around the room; Quinn's left hand was adept at grabbing them. They've also consumed eight fennel and cinnamon cakes, delivered yesterday, and six almond and ginger muffins, delivered two hours ago, all made by Flax's family.

This morning, the morning of the eleventh day, someone taps on their door. Geller unlocks the seal, and Flax enters with a woman.

Her name is Celeste, and she's a midwife. She is tall and slender, with a long, angular face and braided hair that tumbles down her back. When she unzips her climate suit and discards her jacket, she reveals muscular arms and shoulders.

Before the physical examination, they drink tea and eat the remaining almond muffins, bantering about conception details and dates. Celeste is interested in the longitude and latitude of the event, meaning the night of hot sex, as well as the star and moon cycles. Quinn confesses to Conscientious Prevention. On her twenty-first birthday she had an implant; technically, she should be sterile. Celeste's skin prickles at the news; the fine hairs on her forearms stand on end.

"I'm happy. I guess I'm lucky," Quinn confesses.

"Luck had nothing to do with it," Celeste reproaches.

Celeste asks Quinn to lie on the bed while she performs the scan. Quinn watches the images on a module, and she sees her baby's heart beating, strong and loud, the strangest noise—a resonance of connected throbs. The sound is totally hypnotic.

Celeste confirms that the baby is a girl and she's healthy. She will prepare a calendar of events; the pregnancy has cultural significance and will be recorded in their archives.

Geller is not interested in baby images and pregnancy conversations. She's more concerned with Flax's foot. Squatting on the floor, she examines his wounds and unwinds the bandage covering his ankle. The infection is rank; the odor permeates the room.

"Bacterial," she says. "Chemical weapons."

Flax nods.

She unpacks the military pack, laying the weapons over the bed, and again it looks like Mary Poppins's carpet bag with a limitless supply of armory. She's after a Nanobot antidote patch. When she finally finds the one she wants, she slaps it on Flax's ankle. "Can't hurt," she says, "an' you don't 'ave much longer. Destined for a mechanical foot very soon."

After they leave, Quinn lies on her bed and reality resonates. She's going to have a baby. She's going to be a mother. There are books on how to have a baby and how to look after a baby, but are there books on how to be a mother? How to be a good mother?

# Forty-Seven

# She's not pretty enough to be tis fuckin' mean.

In the morning, Geller ventures outside to explore the city, and Quinn continues her pregnancy reading. The information is conflicting and often opinion based, devoid of hard facts or science. The authors have opposing theories on just about everything—feeding, holding, pacifiers, sleep, and settling, with sleep the biggest disparity. Quinn loves sleep and she's sure her baby will sleep, so she skips these chapters and moves on to "Ten Things You Must Never Do" and "Five Things You Must Do," and tries not confusing them.

A knock at the door distracts her, and, as she looks up from her "Ten Things" list, the door swings opens and a young woman enters. Quinn's hand seeks out the weapon under her pillow. The young woman smiles, and Quinn returns the gesture, but her hand stays fixed on the weapon.

"Flax sent me. I'm the new midwife. I'll be looking after you."

"Where's Celeste?"

"She has other patients, but she'll oversee your care."

Quinn's face falls; she liked Celeste.

The new midwife is called Dalia. She wears a pale pink smock, made from climate material, and a yellow cap covering her loose, buttery hair. Dalia's facial features are animated: she has large eyes, a long

313

nose, and a mouth that won't stop talking. She babbles excitedly about the arrival of the new princess. Quinn finds her incessant chatting annoying and her hand is still on the weapon under her pillow, so she moves to the other side of the bed, removing the temptation to silence Dalia by shooting her in the mouth.

Dalia moves closer, hitches up her dress, and takes a chair opposite Quinn. Seated, she splays her legs so far apart that Quinn can see her underwear, not something she wants to see, and she knows she shouldn't look, but it is right there, so she keeps looking. She changes position again, removing herself from the temptation to stare.

Dalia takes Quinn's vitals, recording them on her module, and Quinn moans. They did this yesterday. Why are they doing it again today? A linctus is prepared, just herbs, to keep the baby and mother healthy. Quinn is to take it every day until she finishes the bottle. Dalia hands her the vial and encourages her to drink the sweet liquid, and she does, just so Dalia will leave her alone. Then she lies back on the bed and darkness overcomes her.

✳✳✳

"'Ey, wake up." Quinn feels a slaps against her cheek.

She opens her eyes, and the world is a fuzzy blur. She lifts her head, and the world spins. She begins to scan the room, but her gaze doesn't get past the bottom of the bed, which is covered in blood. The linen is stained a bright red. Blood is splattered over the walls and floor. Quinn is also covered in blood. *A murder scene. Someone tried to murder me.*

Then she sees Dalia on the floor. Her head is not fully attached to her body; her throat almost cut through. Quinn realizes it's not her blood, it's Dalia's blood, which is a relief, but it's still a murder scene. "Fuck, what happened?"

"I got back from explorin' an' she was standin' over you wit a strange-lookin' hook-knife. Never seen a knife like tat before; it looked evil. I completely surprised 'er. She came straight at me, an I knocked 'er back, one punch, right in te face; she fell back, dropped te knife, an' I got ta it first."

*And you thought it was a good idea to behead her?* They stare at the mess on the floor.

Quinn picks up the vial of linctus. "She drugged me."

"I overheard a conversashun. It was Consortia, te one who wants ta be Tig's wife. Te pretty one. We should cut tis one's head off, te rest of it, an' deliver it ta her."

"The pretty one?" Quinn makes a face.

Geller shrugs. "She's a looker. I've seen 'er in te courtyard. 'Tis her doin'. Let's send a message. She won't mess wit us again."

"I don't think—"

"'Twill send a clear message."

"Honestly, not my style—"

"We should do it soon, quickness is te essence of war." Geller takes the hook-blade, kneels beside the woman, and cuts through the remaining sinews and tendons. Dalia's head is now off, totally detached from her body. Quinn is impressed by the sharpness of the knife but horrified by the head, which Geller holds by the hair. Dalia is a hideous, pallid, and ugly caricature.

"No, definitely not."

"Just tink about it."

Together, they wrap the body and the head in the bedding and stow the pieces under the staircase. Then they clean the floor and walls and wash their hands and faces and change climate suits.

After it's done, they sit outside in the hot morning sun.

"What sort of person tries to kill an unborn baby? *My* unborn baby. Bitch."

"She's not pretty enough ta be tis fuckin' mean." Geller retrieves the sheet-wrapped, blood-soaked head from under the staircase. The dried blood is now brown and patchy on the white sheets. "I know

where she is. I know where tey all are. Let your plans be dark an'
impenetrable as night, an' when you move, fall like a tunderbolt."

"Reading too many war novels."

Geller checks the time on her Band. "Too early. We'll wait until
nightfall, when tey're gathered for te evenin' meal. It should be a
public shamin.'"

Quinn sighs. "Okay. I'm in. But this is just a warning, so she won't
try anything again. No one is going to die or lose their head." *Oh fuck,
I can't believe we're actually going to do this.*

✳✳✳

At dusk, Geller unpacks weapons from her backpack. She straps a set
of knives to Quinn's calf and another to her arm, then shoves a laser
into her shorts.

"'Tis just for looks. Show a little bit av midriff, tat'll really upset te
bitch." She rolls up Quinn's top and lowers her shorts.

They enter the public courtyard and slink towards the covered balcony. It's early evening, and twenty people have gathered for a communal meal around a large table.

Geller hands Quinn the head. "It 'as ta be you."

Quinn agrees. She takes the horrific head gingerly, unwraps it, and
holds it by the hair. Dalia's expression has set. She now resembles a
surprised zombie.

Geller adjusts Quinn's clothes again, showing off her baby
bump. "For effect; she'll see you're still pregnant. It'll destroy 'er
emoshunally."

They move into an arc of light surrounding the table, and Quinn
selects a knife. As Consortia leans forward, reaching for a glass of
water, Quinn sends the knife flying into the back of her chair. The
prattle of conversation halts, and all faces turn her way. She steps into
the light, and Geller follows. Across the table, Louis reaches for his

blade; Quinn flicks a knife into the center of his plate, and he pauses—shocked, she assumes, by both her bravado and her knife skills. Then he smiles at her.

Pandemonium sets in. The diners slide back their chairs, fumbling for weapons—until Flax rises.

"Calm down," he commands. "Everyone stay in your seat, and keep your hands on the table, where I can see them."

Most obey.

Quinn tosses the severed head to Consortia, and she catches it, a reflex reaction. It takes her a moment to realize what it is—a detached head—and another moment to understand that it's *Dalia's* detached head. She drops the head and reels back, shrieking. Then she realizes there's blood on her hands, which is apparently worse than Dalia losing her head, because it's then that her wailing lifts to an operatic notch. It's an extraordinary, high-pitched, theatrical performance that leaves the audience stunned.

Eventually, there's an intermission as Consortia pauses for breath. Geller nudges Quinn; it's time for her to deliver a warning.

Quinn plucks the last knife from its sheath. "Ever try to hurt my baby again, I will slit your throat. Understand?"

Consortia smiles insolently.

*Bitch.* Quinn flicks the last knife. It nicks Consortia's left ear, slices the lobe off. She delicately touches her ear, and when she sees the blood on her fingers, she promptly faints.

Quinn winces. She probably shouldn't have cut anything off—drawing blood would have been enough. Now the entire table rises. Weapons are drawn, and they're all pointed at Quinn. Geller steps in front of her and raises her laser, but Flax won't have any of it.

"Sit!" he thunders.

Everyone sits.

Quinn glares at Consortia. "Do you understand? I will come after you and cut many, many more pieces from you"—she waves her finger toward Consortia—"fingers and toes and . . . noses, pieces like that. You will never be safe, and I will never stop."

The lobeless woman nods.

"Enjoy your meal."

# Forty-Eight
# An unremarkable ring.

THE FOLLOWING MORNING, QUINN sits on the side of her bed, holds her head in her hands, and laments her violent behavior. *What the fuck have I done? I used to be a Pacifist. I abhorred violence. Now, now I'm hacking people apart. It's this place. I need to get out of here. I need go home, back to Hobart, where my risk of death from despotic tyrants, creepy Transhumans, and extended family is greatly, greatly reduced.*

In Hobart, there'll be no more strapping knives to her body and sleeping with a laser under her pillow. In Hobart, she has a bland little Pod in a quiet, nondescript zone of the city, and right now it looks particularly boring and peaceful. That's exactly what she wants. All that normality that Hobart is offering—sign her up for that.

✳✳✳

Geller and Quinn meet Flax for morning tea in a room at the back of the main house called the Map Room—a nauseatingly busy space where the walls and ceiling are painted with ancient maps of pale blue oceans, dusty continents, and ships setting off to find new lands. Every architectural feature is engraved, molded, or frescoed. The art is New World and the architecture Renaissance but the furnishings are Islander; the room houses the Maldives's cultural artifacts, displayed on shelves and stacked across tables and chairs. The decor is overwhelming, and the room has not adapted to the diverse cultural entities inhabiting it.

In the far corner, Flax brews tea in an ancient samovar.

"The family will be ostracized," he says. "A bad strain, very bad. They have the manners of primates—always yelling, always fighting and bickering. It goes on and on and on. I will not miss them. But next time, maybe come talk to me first—a little less drama. Now, I hope you don't mind, but I've organized a gathering so you can meet some of the better-behaved relatives. Nothing fancy." He looks at Geller and Quinn with eyebrows raised, seeking approval.

Quinn offers an indifferent shrug. All she wants to do is go home.

"Sure," says Geller. "Might be fun. How's te ankle?"

"Oh, let me show you." Flax lifts his pants leg; the infection has cleared. "The patch worked, it's like magic."

"Not magic," Geller says. "'Tis science."

After adding hot liquid to a decorative teapot, Flax hands them ornamental cups, inlaid with blue and gold metal, but the vessels are too hot to hold. As the liquid cools, Geller circumnavigates the room, exploring the items on display: leather-bound books, metal bowls, vases, statues, instruments, masks, rings, and bracelets. She homes in on a woven bejeweled garland; after placing it carefully on her head, she checks her reflection in the glass.

"It's the crown of a king," Flax tells her.

Geller looks intrigued. "Is tere one for te queen?"

Flax indicates a plain, jet-black wreath resting on a shelf. An unremarkable ring, fine and delicate.

Geller collects it and places it on Quinn's head with a mocking smile. "I tink we make a lovely pair."

Immediately, Quinn swoons. As she stumbles, she grabs a side table for support. Flax steps forward to help, but she waves him away and rights herself; it's the heat, the tiredness, and the baby hormones, or maybe it's the sickening effect of the décor, but she's fine.

Then it happens again. She's overcome with dizziness, and the world around her spins. The furniture, tables, chairs, and cabinets tilt to one side, and she stumbles to a chair. Her head hurts, a whistling sensation penetrates her ears, and she begins to hyperventilate. Vertigo. She hasn't had vertigo in years.

Flax removes the crown. The world stops spinning, her headache abates, and the furniture rights itself.

Geller places the crown of the king on Quinn's head. "Suits you." She grins.

The main doors opens, and Tig ambles into the room. He looks ancient, weary, and unshaven. His gait is lopsided—a missed neural connection, Quinn assumes—and he has an exhausted look in his eyes. Flax graces his presence with a small bow, and Tig returns the gesture.

Quinn's heart bounds and jolts—the sight of him is elating. She steps back and takes in his weary appearance; she notes the dark creases around his hazel eyes, his disheveled clothes, and the dark, grimy marks down the side of his face, which she hopes are mud and not dried blood. She takes in all of him. She's never seen anyone more heartwarming and charismatic than this man, standing at the entrance to this nauseatingly busy blue room decorated with oceans and dusty continents.

Tig stares back at her with his piercing bionic eyes. "You okay?"

Her hands quiver. She wants to speak; she wants to tell him everything that happened—all her mishaps and adventures while he was gone—but she fails to pull the words into coherent sentences. So she nods, and then she shrugs. She's okay. More or less.

He comes towards her and takes her quivering hand. "Cold?" he asks.

She shakes her head. "Nervous."

He laughs softly, kisses her hand, and places it on her stomach—over her baby, over their baby—and for the first time in weeks, she feels safe. She leans into him, and his lips graze her forehead. She's aware there are a hundred conversations they need to have, but right now she has absolutely nothing to say. Her left hand caresses his unshaven cheek, and she doesn't restrain it. She notices that his titanium frame is exposed around his elbow, and she lightly touches the metal with her fingertips.

"I can feel you," he says. "I feel you more and I feel you faster—a thousand times faster—than you feel me."

"Do you?"

"Yeah. Your sensors send signals a thousand times a second. Mine send them a million times a second."

*Then you win.*

"And it does suit you," he says. "Better than fucking wings."

*Oh fuck, I'm still wearing the crown.*

✳✳✳

Planck is not far behind Tig, and Quinn meets zir outside on the stoop of the main house. They share their news from the last two weeks. Maim and Kip had to present themselves and give testimony to Hexad, so Tig and Planck waited. Then Maim insisted that they escort her back to the Unus, and she wouldn't take no for an answer. So again they waited until she was ready and it was safe to return.

The meerkat stayed comatose since she left. It hasn't moved or said a word. They brought him along, stashed in a bag. Planck says the midwifery course is going well; ze got distinctions for the first two assessments. Ze'll certainly be qualified in time for delivery. Quinn doesn't have the heart to tell zir that she found the perfect midwife in Celeste, and she only needs one. You can have too many midwives.

Planck confirms ze's heard about the afternoon celebration. "Just a small gathering," ze says. "Afternoon drinks on the veranda. The main house has a good cellar. There are a couple of bottles of fine whisky that we could open to mark the occasion. I'm thinking . . . mint juleps. Mint loves this heat. It's out of control in the herb garden. I'll make a batch of sugar syrup. How does that sound?"

"I can't drink alcohol," Quinn says, disappointed. After almost two weeks of being cooped up inside, drinking mint juleps in the shade of the veranda sounds like bliss.

Planck grins. "I'll make you a mocktail."

*Terrific.*

✳✳✳

Quinn is resting in preparation for the party when Geller enters their room with an armful of colorful fabrics. "Blue or green?" she asks.

Quinn shrugs; she has no idea what Geller means.

Geller drops the bundle of colored textiles. She rummages through the pile before finally pulling out up a blue dress, and then a green dress.

"Which one do ya want? Te blue or te green?"

"I don't care."

"Pick one."

"The green."

"Naw, you'll look grander in de blue." Geller tosses the dress at Quinn. "Meet ya outside in fifteen minutes."

The dress is a traditional costume, and it's a fine garment—navy blue with a pewter sash and an array of color-coordinated scarves. The sash gleams like polished silver. The longs scarves are significant; she's seen women wearing them. It's a beautiful dress. She pulls it on and fastens the sash around her waist, tying it in a large bow, then drapes the colored scarves around her neck. She moves to the glass to examine her reflection—and balks. *Oh, good lordt. I look like a clown.* She undoes the bow and wraps the sash twice, and then three times, around her waist; it doesn't help. She ditches the scarves and the sash and takes another look at herself in the glass. *Now I look like a tent.*

She pulls the dress off and leaves it on the bed. It is a beautiful dress. The fabric is soft, and she likes the color. But she can't wear it. *I don't belong here. I can't see how this is going to work.* She pulls on her climate suit and heads downstairs.

Outside, thousands of guests mill in the main courtyard.

*Surely all these people aren't here for the mint juleps. There's no way we'll have enough sugar syrup.*

Geller arrives, swathed in layers of green-colored fabrics, and Planck joins them, also dressed in ceremonial robes. Guests bow as they pass, acknowledging zir. *Right,* Quinn remembers. *Ze's their Knowledge Keeper. Ze plays an important part in their culture.*

"Is it a wedding?" one of the guests asks as he passes. "We heard they were getting married."

Quinn glares at Planck.

"No," Planck says quickly. Ze turns to Quinn. "It's a drinks party," ze reassures her.

Quinn surveys the mass of people mingling under the covered verandas and spilling into the courtyard; she notes the multitude of additional guests arriving every minute. "You said a 'small' celebration," she snaps. "There must a thousand people here."

"Snowballed, completely out of my control. I told ten people, and—what the fuck are you wearing?" Ze gapes at her clothes, she's the only person wearing a climate suit. "You ignored the frock."

"I don't care what I wear."

"It's okay for you to dress up like a fairy for Dirac's Salon, but you can't wear a nice frock to show respect for our culture? Everyone will be looking at you. Everyone. It's important for you to assimilate. The severed head thing, very bad publicity—you're not exactly winning friends." Planck unhooks a colored sash from a colonnade and hands it to Quinn.

*What am I supposed to do with this?*

Geller nods. Quinn realizes she supposed to put the sash on, and that she's outnumbered. *Oh, good lordt.* She slips behind a pillar, shimmies out of her climate suit, and wraps the sash around herself.

She emerges with a sour look on her face. "I wasn't a fairy; I was an angel," she says.

"I tought you were a bird." Geller pulls another scarf from the colonnade and drapes it over Quinn's shoulders.

*I'm wearing the curtains and suddenly I've assimilated.*

"On the surface, I was an angel; inside, I was a bird." She glares at Planck. "And before you say anything, I had no choice."

"I believe you," ze says, "but just so you know, I worked hard, very hard, to get you out of that. And, between you and me, stunning—absolutely stunning."

# Forty-Nine

# This is no small affair.

QUINN, GELLER, AND PLANCK enter the wide-colonnaded veranda of the main Renaissance house and gape in awe at the decorations. The verandah has been transformed—lavishly draped with greenery, ribbons, and floral bouquets. A shroud of petals carpets the floor. At the far end, a podium, swathed in multicolored veils, has been erected, and on the platform sit two ornately decorated chairs, positioned so that they face the crowd.

A group of small children enters the colonnade. The girls are wrapped in colored scarves; their hair falls in ringlets under floral wreaths. The boys wear pantaloons and floral shirts. Their appearance draws a communal "ahhhh" from the guests as they make their way through the crowd, scattering flowers.

*This is no small affair.*

An older woman comes forth to greet Planck. She bows to zir then lowers her voice and asks, "Are they getting married? Is it an engagement? Because no one told us, and we didn't bring a present, but we can contribute, if there's a fund."

Quinn glares at Planck again. Her chest tightens and she struggles to breathe.

"No, no, no," Planck says immediately. "Honestly, it's just a drinks party."

But the rumor is spreading before Quinn's very eyes; the woman leans over to her companion and says, not quietly, "It's a surprise engagement party."

Transportable air systems work overtime, sucking every proton of light from the sun, so Quinn knows it's cool. She can even feel that there's a breeze. But she's hot and sweaty.

She's never hot and sweaty.

Outside in the main courtyard, dozens of pastel-colored birds—Quinn can only assume they've been specially dyed for the occasion—are released. Dignitaries wearing ceremonial robes and feathered capes enter the veranda and mingle with the guests. Quinn spots Flax among them. She gazes around at the crowd of elegantly dressed guests and dignitaries, and notices that several of them are carrying beautifully wrapped boxes. *Presents? Surely not.*

She transitions from light perspiration into a heavy sweat. The world begins to close in on her. *It's so fucking hot. I'm suffocating.* She looks around wildly. *This is never going to work.*

When Planck and Geller aren't looking, she makes a break for it.

✱✱✱

Quinn retreats to her room, throws herself on the bed, buries her face in a pillow, and doesn't move.

The door opens, and Tig enters. Quinn rolls over and sits up, and he gives her a small, concerned smile.

"Hey," he says. "You okay?"

"Overwhelmed. Completely overwhelmed." She's practically hyperventilating.

"Yeah," he says softly. "I get it. Let's stay here."

Slowly, with measured movements, he glides toward her. He's wearing loose, navy-colored trousers with the cuffs rolled up and a navy shirt with an embroidered collar. His feet are bare. She considers his baggy clothes and bangles and his muscular physique under the shirt, and she thinks he looks part bohemian guru and part new age adventurer. Nothing like a king with a small "k." Nothing like a surprise fiancé. Her heart shudders again and she firmly presses her chest, hoping it will stay put.

"I don't think I want to ever get married," she says. "To anyone."

"Really?"

She shakes her head. "Never."

"Okay." He shuffles onto the bed beside her and leans back against the headboard. "I'm so tired. Haven't slept in five days. Come here. Come closer." He closes his eyes.

She doesn't move. *This is never going to work.*

He opens his eyes. "What's wrong?"

"We need to talk. I need a plan, a plan for the future. I don't understand how this is going to work. You and me and a baby? Where will we live? On *Nanshe*? Can you have a baby on a boat? Is it safe? What would I do? I have to work."

He scratches his head. "Well, I—"

"What I'm really trying to say is, I don't fit in here. In Unus. On *Nanshe*. With you."

"You will," he says quickly. "I'll fix it. I'll fix everything. I promise." He pulls a SelfMed from his pocket and hands it to her. "I can't do this myself. I need you to do it for me."

She doesn't take it.

He takes her left hand, places the SelfMed firmly in her palm, and holds out his arm. An open invitation. "Trust me. Please? Do it."

She points the SelfMed and pulls the trigger.

It misses. She injected the bed. She's confused. She used her left hand; it never misses. He moved his arm, pulled it away. Why would he do that? She hands the SelfMed back to him. He shakes his head. He wants her to try again.

"You don't understand," he says. "It's reflex, happens sometimes, and I haven't slept. Look, I'm trying to fix this."

"Yes, you said that." She sighs. "I'm going to get my meerkat, and then I'm going home."

"To *Nanshe*?"

"To Hobart. To *my* home."

"Why?" His eyes turn dark.

*Because I don't have a plan. Because I need to jump off something really high and I need to do it very soon.* "Because I don't belong here," she says. "And you confuse me. I just . . . can't do this. Not here."

"What about the baby? What about us?"

She toys with the bedcover. "Us can be anywhere."

"Anywhere but here or on *Nanshe*?"

She nods. "For now. But I didn't say you couldn't come with me. Hobart is lovely. It's the rainbow capital of the world. The perfect place to raise a baby. And . . . it's a good place to think, and I need to figure out where Lise is."

He rests his head in his hands and sighs.

"Maybe, once things settle down, we could go on a date. Get to know each other . . . better. We could start at the beginning, if you know what I mean. It's not that I don't want you—I do, I definitely do—but let me be very clear: there's to be no more 'I chose you' shit, okay? And no more surprises or family secrets. Everything has to be out in the open."

"Fuck. I'm so confused." Tig shakes his head. Then he gets up and leaves.

✶✶✶

Quinn is in her sleep zone, packing her belongings, when Planck enters.

"I need to go home," she says. "And I need you to help me."

Ze sits her down, takes her hand in zirs, and makes a long, emotional speech about why she should stay with zir and Tig and spend the rest of her life with them on *Nanshe*. Ze understands that she needs something to do; ze'll allocate more tasks for her. They can set up a lab and she can continue her research and she'll move into Tig's cabin, which is roomier, with a private deck. When *Nanshe* drifts north, ze tells her, the morning light is just glorious. Ze has also given some thought to her penchant for jumping off things; perhaps they could rig something from the mast. Or a drone might work.

"I've seen the way you look at him," ze says. "I don't think you're being honest about your feelings. Trust me, you belong here, with Tig, and that's the truth."

"I don't think he's been honest about a lot of things either," Quinn says. "Trust me, I need to go home. That's the truth."

Planck starts to protest. Quinn puts a hand on zirs arm. "You'll help me won't you? You'll help me get home."

A long, contemplative silence follows, and then suddenly Planck gets up and strides out of the room.

A few minutes later, ze returns. "Maim is fond of you, very fond, and she appreciates what you did on the boat, keeping them safe. So she's lending you a transporter and a pilot to get you home. A 'No Flight Zone' will be enforced starting tomorrow; you leave today, or your escape window disappears."

✶✶✶

Quinn collects her meerkat-in-a-bag. She'll open it when she gets back to Hobart. She's surprised to realize she's genuinely looking forward to seeing him. She knows she should feel nothing for him; he's a piece of Tech. But he reminds her, just a little bit, of Jin.

She calls her father and tells him she's on her way. He tells her not to go home, not to her apartment in Styx, not yet. He urges her to come and stay with him. Do nothing for a bit, watch the sun rise and watch it set. She agrees; emptiness and isolation sound good, she can listen to her father sing to the trees and talk about birds.

Geller frowns at the news. She says Hobart sounds dull, and she can watch the sun rise and set right here in Unus, "'Tis te same sun, you know," she quips.

Jove Kip is now head of the military, and Geller's been offered a position in his new army. She'll insist on a promotion. "Go 'ome, find yourself," she says. "But you're runnin' away from life. 'Tis an external solution ta an internal problem. But go, you'll soon realize 'tis not te answer, you'll be back in a couple av weeks." She hugs Quinn. "If ignorant av your enemy an' yourself, you're certain ta be in peril. Take these." She hands Quinn a pack filled with weapons and combat devices. "You're not safe. Tese people wit teir kaleidoscope eyes an' excess earwax want you, or tey want what you know. Tey're just warmin' up."

*Again, reading too many war novels.* But she takes the bag.

# Fifty

# Oh, I get it. We're playing matchmakers. I'm in, totally in.

THE STRUGGLES OF WARFARE—BOMBING, combat, and fire—have devastated the Palace of Tigers. The colonnaded courtyard is now more rubble than temple; it resembles thousand-year-old ruins. Extinct animals sculptures lay strewn across the ground, the fountains are dry, and what's left of the multilobed arches is precariously unstable.

Planck waits on an unsteady stone bench, bookended by decapitated elephants, while Maim roams the courtyard ruins. She collects a wedge-shaped keystone, once the foundation of a masonry arch. "This building used to be a tourist attraction, a World Heritage site, one of the largest prayer halls ever built; it held over ten thousand. The English came here during the Crusades, saw all this—spanning arches, ribbed vaults, their Byzantine and Gothic architecture. So influential."

"It's mentioned in the Hebrew Bible."

"Yes, yes it is. A shame to see it like this, I fucking hate war." The keystone tumbles from her hand; when it lands in the rubble, it raises a small cloud of dust. "Now, what's this about a transporter, I just gave you one. Now you want another?"

"Now I need a rotor. It's faster."

"Not following."

"Quinn departs on the transporter. It's an old hybrid type; takes her most of the day to get home. He gets the rotor, so he gets there before her."

"Oh, I get it. We're playing matchmakers. I'm in, totally in. We've got these new hypersonic ships, dual coaxial rotors with rear-ducted circulators. The shell is clad in a tungsten alloy, they travel five times the speed of sound, and they're the most beautiful silver-white color, stunning. He'll be there in no time. But he needs to go slow with her, once he gets there. And whose idea was the surprise engagement party? I heard there were three thousand people there. Fucking disaster. I'm not surprised she left."

"It wasn't an engagement party." Planck sighs. "But yes, it could have gone smoother."

"How're his Meds? He taking them?"

"We're working on it. It's complicated. He has issues about using the SelfMed. He struggles to pull the trigger, so it's easier if someone else does it. He wants her to be the one."

"The one to shoots him with the SelfMed."

"Yes."

"Oh good lordt, humans are so complicated. Okay, tell him to take something with him, a gift for the family. It'll endear him. And, he needs to give her time with her father, let her settle in. You know I sent her the stone, the Disc. How much does she know?"

"Enough."

"Okay. My only chance of getting Lise back is the Disc. I hope Quinn's up to the task."

# Fifty-One

# A birthday present.

The transporter is an old, slow vessel, so she's not going home in style. The journey will take most of the day. She's the only passenger. She scans the cabin; where to sit on an empty transporter? Too many choices. She selects a seat by the window on the left, then realizes the harbor is on the right, so she changes position.

Long-haul flights are a novelty. She likes these seats, with their compartments and their compact, travel-size hydration fluids and protein snacks. She's feeling peckish; she breaks the seal on a packet of insect sprinkles.

A holo flight attendant materializes in the aisle, startling her. She drops the packet and spills the sprinkles all over her lap.

The virtual inflight spiel begins: "Please make sure your carry-on luggage is stowed and your window shade is fully open. Fasten your seat belt low and tight. The T465 has six emergency exits; in the case of an emergency, lights will illuminate the way. The transporter is fitted with double drone pods and passenger drones, enough for everyone. Secure yourself first, before children." Adults before children. Is that what you do in life, put yourself before your children? Because that's exactly what she's done—she's put herself first, and she's happy with her decision.

The transporter lifts. No turning back now; she's on her way home.

Peering out the window, she sees the remnants of pathways, playgrounds, and signs, now covered by the rising ocean. Farther out, beyond the boats and pontoons, the monolithic form of Prismatic emerges. Then another monolith rises to the east and a third to the west, lurking like giant black insects, ready to take on the dead. *How many died?* She turns away.

It's time to take stock of her life. Stowed under the seat in front of her is an assisted living companion in the form of a meerkat and a backpack full of futuristic weapons. The year is 2050, and she's thirty, pregnant, unmarried, and without a job, but she has some Coin saved, somewhere to live, a window seat, and a mission: figure out what happened to her mother.

And then there's Tig. She has moments of intense attraction to and overwhelming love for him, followed by moments of complete confusion. *It's because we're so different—we're worlds apart. Distraction.* She casts the thought of him aside and settles into her seat.

Serenaded by the gentle hum of the transporter, her eyelids droop, and soon sleep takes her. In her dreams she sees thousands of M's floating through the universe—M for M-Theory, the multiverse and time travel. They floating M's invert, split in two, and turn into V's, the symbol for neutrinos. These are the tiniest particles; it's difficult to imagine how small and massless they are. Electrically neutral—unaffected by electromagnetic force—they pass through matter undetected. They travel across the universe unimpeded. In her dreams the V's are flying, passing through everything and everyone; they're cosmic messengers, time travelers, born in black holes or during the violent death of a star. They hold the secret to dark matter, and are one of the fundamental building blocks of life. She dreams that the information inside the neutrino is the most important thing in the universe.

Quinn opens her eyes and recalls her dream. Her left hand draws the symbol for a neutrino and an antineutrino in the air and the image lingers in her mind—a sketchy mark like a W with a line across the top. The symbol for a neutrino is a V. The mark on the back of Tig's neck. The message in Ada's purse. She knows what they are now: a pair of neutrinos, one neutrino, shown as a V, next to an antineutrino, a V with a line across the top. Matter and antimatter, combined in one particle. The two inverted V's make an M.

*The marks on the back of his neck are particle symbols. Combine them and they do something . . . like open a time travel portal.*

✶✶✶

When Quinn disembarks at the aerodrome in Hobart, the early-afternoon air is pleasantly warm and familiar and everything around her feels like home. She belongs here. Air travel could get her to Matt's in thirty minutes, but the transporters and hovers are inactive as part of an extended No-Fly Zone, and the pilots are in Unus anyway, called to help Maim's forces take back the city. Hobart's population is too small to support a Hyperloop, and AVs can't navigate outside the city center. They're not safe in unpredictable terrain; there are too many variables for them to function reliably. So she'll travel overland. She hires a self-drive auto and heads west.

Four hours later, early evening, she parks the auto at the end of Matt's driveway. She slings the pack of weapons over her shoulder, grabs her meerkat-in-a-bag, and begins the four-kilometer trek to her father's house.

It's an easy walk; the path is relatively smooth, and the setting sun is warm on her back. The trees on the southern side of the path are plantation timber, processions of silver-grey columns with dusty green crowns. On the northern side is an old-growth forest that's home to thousand-year-old eucalyptus. Matt's house is nestled in a clearing between the old and the new. He calls it a tree house, but the tree is inside the house; he built a circular glass prism, seven levels high and fifteen meters wide, around a three-thousand-year-old southern blue gum—*Eucalyptus globulus*, native to Hobart. Upper zones in the house are for sleeping, lower levels for living, and in the food prep is an automated hatch leading to an underground survival bunker— just in case Hexad fails and the world self-implodes. Underneath her father's modest "I'm just a simple man" façade is a skeptic who's lost faith in humanity.

Quinn hears her father before she sees him. His guitar and melodic voice cut through the quiet afternoon. He's considered a great singer, but his vocals are not pitch-perfect; it's the depth of emotion, the raw, soulful harmonies, that his fans love.

She plods around to the front and finds him on the open veranda, sitting back on a chair, no guitar in sight; the music is streamed. In his lap is a fat, ginger, white-pawed puppy. It looks up and yaps, signaling her arrival. Matt scoops it off his lap and bounds over to her.

"Hey, took your time." He gives her a bear hug and a kiss on the cheek. Then he pulls back and checks out her waistline. "Full of surprises," he says nervously.

He looks the same: the same shoulder length hair, fine and lanky; not wearing a shirt, still fit, tight to the point of gaunt, and unshaven. Still charismatic in his "I'll do whatever the fuck I want" way.

Quinn sets her things down and takes in her father's countenance. He's uneasy. The way he moves, the way he looks her over, the deliberate smile. "What's wrong?" she asks.

"Nothing. Been worried. Glad you're here."

*Probably the grandfather thing. Understandable. Give him time.*

The pup scurries over, and she collects it, smiling, "He's—"

"She's," Matt corrects.

"Sorry, *she's* the cutest thing I've ever seen. Yours?"

"Yeah, new, doesn't have a name yet."

The setting sun is fierce, and Matt heads inside to fix cool drinks while Quinn plays with the pup on the veranda. She notes that his air system is intermittent. He uses an old solar configuration; maybe it's a corroded panel. An easy fix—she'll look at it tomorrow.

Matt returns with their drinks, and they move to the southern side of the veranda, where there's shade and respite from the westerly sun. The vista on this side of the property takes in the valley and surrounding hills. Eucalyptus forests, still green and healthy due to an underground water supply called the Source, border the steep cliffs. The hidden water supply flows down from the ridge to a reservoir not far from Matt's house. Quinn can't take her eyes off it.

"It's pink," she says.

"Cerise. Perfect shade."

"Algae bloom. Past the tipping point."

"Yeah. Can't get on top of it."

The bloom is profuse, a carpet of deep pink, shockingly beautiful against the green foliage. Another easy fix. She'll engineer a synthetic life form and code it to eat the algae. When the job's done, she'll program it to self-implode.

"Right, there's a bit to do," she says. "I'll do the air system tomorrow, I've a plan for the pond, and can I name the puppy, please, please let me name her? We could call her Mellon Ball, or Rosy, or Bella. Yes, don't you think she looks like Bella?" She thrusts the puppy into Matt's face.

"For fuck's sake, sit down. Relax. God, you never stop. You're just like your mother. Speaking of which, I've something for you, from her. A birthday present. Arrived a few weeks ago." He hands Quinn a heavy box with a card on top. "She's organized, I'll give her that."

Quinn opens the card, an automated note in classical scribe. "It says, 'To my darling Quinn. Happy 30th birthday. I'm so sorry I'm not with you, but I love you very much and I'm thinking of you. This is your birthday present. I acquired it recently, but I like to think it found me, and now it's found its way to you. It's a 5,000-year-old Phaistos Disc. The text is indecipherable, but it means something. Or maybe it means nothing.' Sounds like her, but it's not her writing." She hands the card to Matt and opens the box.

Inside is a platter, half a meter wide, deep blue with gold veins coursing through the surface like swirling cumulonimbus clouds. "Storm clouds," Quinn says, holding it to the light.

"Nah," Matt says. "It's music, a symphony."

The surface is carved in three concentric circles, and each circle contains a series of small markings that Quinn thinks could be birds, or fish, or triangles, or maybe just awkward stick drawings. In her hands, the disc is warm, and her fingers begin to tingle. "It means something. Or nothing. Nothing comes from nothing. Keats?" She turns to her father for confirmation.

"Shakespeare, *King Lear*. If you do nothing, you gain nothing. *Ex nihilo nihil*, out of nothing comes nothing. Your mother believes the universe is made of nothing."

"Yes, she does. But space isn't empty, it holds all of us. We matter. Don't we?"

"We're living, we have mass, we matter."

"Ha, handed you that line on a platter."

"I took it. Hand it over."

She passes him the Disc. "It'd make a nice . . . fruit platter."

The sun settles lower, drops behind the hills to the west. The puppy falls asleep in Quinn's lap, and she and Matt sip their drinks—an ice-cold lemongrass and ginger infusion—in contemplative silence. Nothingness proposes that no concrete things exist in time and space. It declares the mind to be a shallow place, just a piece of machine-learning architecture that computes mathematical codes and electrical signals. The world around them is an illusion, a fabrication of the brain, because there is no physical world as they know it. The brain conceptualizes the surroundings, creating a version of reality, a three-dimensional image of the sky, the trees, and a land filled with people—a world that's only real when looked at.

Quinn stares at the blue hills and trees in the distance, telling herself they are not real, there is nothing there. But there *is* something there; thousands of trees are there. *This is the problem with nothingness; it doesn't bloody work, because everything's so fucking real.* She gazes up at the sky, at a real flock of real birds flying over in a V formation. They flit, catch the crosswind, and then change direction and reverse again, darting back the other way.

A new bird, not like the others, joins the end of the formation. It's darker and larger than the other birds, its breast streaked with yellow ochre. It looks like Tig's carrier pigeon, Martha2.

*It can't be.* Quinn checks again as the bird swoops, circling under the flock. *It's her, it's Martha2.* She looks at Matt; he maintains a nervous, uneasy expression. *He knows.* She tilts her head. "What breed is this dog?"

"Dingo."

"Pure, because they're extinct in the wild?"

"Believe so."

"He's here, isn't he? He gave you this dog?"

"Arrived about six hours before you."

"Impossible."

"Considerate of Maim to lend you a transporter. Apparently, she likes you, but she likes him more; he got a rotor, was here in two hours." Matt pauses, nervous. "His words, not mine. He's keen, I'll give him that."

"Where is he?"

"Not sure. He wanted to give us some time together. Said he'd be back . . . later." Matt shrugs. "So, what happened?"

"I saw my future: Unus, his culture, life on a boat, our future life together on a boat in Unus, with a baby. I wasn't sure I liked what I saw."

"Fair enough. So you're not in love?"

"I didn't say that. It's complicated. He's different. He's nothing like me. He's traditional, and his culture is foreign, and he has this SelfMed thing happening. I was overwhelmed by all of it."

Matt tilts his head, gives her a knowing look. "So you do like him."

Quinn throws up her hands. "Yeah, I do. I like him a lot. But I didn't have a plan, and—"

"You don't need a fuckin' plan. Trust your instincts. What does your gut tell you?"

"Intuitive thinking? Are you serious? No one uses that anymore. It's primitive, it panders to the ancient brain, and it's not at all scientific—"

"How does he make you *feel*?" Matt demands. "If he walked in right now, what would you do?"

She smiles. *He came to Hobart. He really came. Good lordt, I'm so relieved.* "First, I'd kiss him. Then, I'd ask him to go neutrino hunting with me."

"I don't know what that means."

"It means." She swallows hard. "It means I'm crazy in love with him." She smiles. She loves him. He loves her. They're going to have a baby. It's a good beginning, a very good beginning.

*Antarctica. There's a neutrino detector in Antarctica.*

Book 2

*Nostalgia is Heartless*

Coming in 2021

# Acknowledgments

WRITING A BOOK IS not easy—it's a daunting and time-consuming process—but getting a book published is just as difficult. I would like to express my ongoing gratitude and appreciation to everyone who has helped me at She Writes Press and SparkPress. Special thanks goes to my publisher, Brooke Warner, for her commitment and passion to the industry, and her inspiring "Green-Light Your Book" legacy. Also thanks to my editorial project manager, Samantha Strom, for her commitment and attention to detail. I would also like to thank Krissa Lagos for pulling the book into shape with an amazing copy edit, and to Ben Perini for the beautiful cover design.

This novel would not have been possible without the help and support of my family. Thanks to Jordan Howes and Hamish Howes for being such delightful, funny, and caring people and for reading countless beginnings, endings, and iterations, and especially to Lucinda Howes for her ongoing mentorship, proofreading and amazing brain—none of this would have been possible without her. Her wit and wisdom have been an invaluable source of inspiration and motivation.

I am also eternally grateful to Andrew Aitken, who has had to put up with me as a writer, and I know that's not easy. Thank you for not strangling me, thank you for still hanging around, and thank you for your patience, wisdom and love—I wouldn't be the person I am without you.

# About the Author

© Alise Black

SARAH LAHEY IS A designer, educator, and writer. She holds bachelor's degrees in interior design, communication, and visual culture and works as a senior lecturer teaching classes on design, technology, sustainability, and creative thinking. She has three children and lives on the Northern Beaches in Sydney, Australia.

# SELECTED TITLES FROM SHE WRITES PRESS

She Writes Press is an independent publishing company founded to serve women writers everywhere. Visit us at www.shewritespress.com.

*Expect Deception* by JoAnn Ainsworth. $16.95, 978-1-63152-060-0
When the US government recruits Livvy Delacourt and a team of fellow psychics to find Nazi spies on the East Coast during WWII, she must sharpen her skills quickly—or risk dying.

*Glass Shatters* by Michelle Meyers. $16.95, 978-1-63152-018-1
Following the mysterious disappearance of his wife and daughter, scientist Charles Lang goes to desperate lengths to escape his past and reinvent himself.

*Provectus* by M. L. Stover. $16.95, 978-1-63152-115-7
A science-based thriller that explores the potential effects of climate change on human evolution, *Provectus* asks a compelling question: What if human beings were on the endangered species list—were, in fact, living right alongside our replacements—but didn't know it yet?

*Time Zero* by Carolyn Cohagan. $14.95, 978 1-63152-072-3
In a world where extremists have made education for girls illegal and all marriages are arranged in Manhattan, fifteen-year-old Mina Clark starts down a path of rebellion, romance, and danger that not only threatens to destroy her family's reputation but could get her killed.

*The Lucidity Project* by Abbey Campbell Cook. $16.95, 978-1-63152-032-7
After suffering from depression all her life, twenty-five-year-old Max Dorigan joins a mysterious research project on a Caribbean island, where she's introduced to the magical and healing world of lucid dreaming.

*The Afterlife of Kenzaburo Tsuruda* by Elisabeth Wilkins Lombardo
$16.95, 978-1-63152-481-3
As he stumbles through an afterlife he never believed in, scientist Kenzaboro Tsuruda must make sense of his life and confront his family's secrets in order to save his ancestors from becoming Hungry Ghosts, even as his daughter, wife, and sister-in-law struggle with their own feelings of loss.